Hilliard's university

Ottawa

Oct 16-17/04

FREEDOM AND DEATH

FREEDOM
AND
DEATH

A Novel by

F
KAZ
Nikos Kazantzakis 18204

BRUNO CASSIRER · OXFORD

English Translation by Jonathan Griffin

First English Edition 1956
Reprint 1966

Printed in England by
LOWE & BRYDONE (PRINTERS) LTD, LONDON
for
BRUNO CASSIRER, OXFORD

Distributors:
FABER & FABER, 24 RUSSELL SQUARE
LONDON W.C.1

I

CAPTAIN MICHALES gnashed his teeth. He usually did so when wrath took charge of him. He thrust his right fang forward and let it flash through his black moustache. "Captain Wildboar" was his apt nickname in Megalokastro. With his sudden rages, his deep, dark, round eyes, his short, stubborn neck and that jutting fang, the heavy, broad-boned man was really like a wild boar, rearing for the spring.

He crumpled up a letter in his fist and stuffed it into his wide corduroy belt. He had been a long time spelling it out and convulsively seeking for its meaning. . . . He won't come (he understood) this Easter either, and so his ill and dying mother and his poor sister won't see him, because, so he says, he's still studying. . . . What the Devil is he studying? Will he always go on studying? He doesn't say that he hasn't the face to come back to Crete, because he's married a Jewess and not a countrywoman of ours. That's what that favourite son of yours has come to, brother Kosta! If only you were living! If only you were there to lift him by the ankles and hang him up head downwards from the beam like a sack of seed!

He stood up. A fine giant of a fellow. The crown of his head nearly touched the ceiling of his shop. The black, tasselled band which bound his hair behind had fallen loose on his back, and Captain Michales grabbed at it and pulled it tighter round his thick-boned skull. Then he made for the door, to get some air.

Charitos the apprentice, a wild shoot of a brown-haired village lad with frightened, blinking eyes and protruding ears, crouched behind a coil of ship's rope. His glance swept over the sails, planks, pots of paint and tar, heavy chains, iron anchors—all sorts of ship's gear and tools. But in his fear he saw nothing but the Chief, now standing on the threshold, filling the whole of the doorway and staring out towards the harbour. He was his uncle, but he called him Chief and trembled before him.

7

"As if I hadn't enough vexation already this evening," Captain Michales muttered. "What does the dog expect of me, sending word to me that I must go over to that miserable house of his this evening. And now, on top of it, the vexation with my nephew! His mother would have me write to him, and I did write to him. But he doesn't even show up!"

He gazed leftwards at the harbour—at the steamers, the sailing-ships and the sea. Sounds came from up on the mole: dealers, sailors, boatmen and porters were swarming between oil- and wine-casks and piles of rubbish, shouting, cursing, loading and unloading. They were hurrying to be done with it by the time the sun went down and the fortress gate shut. The sea poised sultrily, and the harbour stank of rotting oranges, turnips, wine and oil. Two or three middle-aged Maltese women sprinkled with spray stood on the walls and chattered hoarsely. They were waving to a broad-beamed Maltese steamer, which was coming in with a cargo of bottles.

The sun sank in a red sky: the last day of March was ending. A sharp northerly breeze sighed, Megalokastro shivered, the shopkeepers chafed their hands, stamped their feet and drank herb infusions—some even drank rum—to get warm. Up above, the peaks of Strúmbulas were covered with snow, and further off Psilorítis[1] rose, dark blue. Frozen masses of snow glimmered in white streaks from deep hollows protected from the wind. But the sky shone crystalline, steel-coloured.

Captain Michales raised his glance to the massive Kule, a strong, thickly built tower on the right of the harbour entrance, with the winged marble lion of Venice on its front. Megalokastro was entirely surrounded with walls and fierce, battlemented towers, which had been founded by its Christian masters in the hey-day of ancient Venice and had been slaked with Venetian, Turkish and Greek blood. Here and there remains of earlier taste were still left, as for instance the stone lions of Venice, carrying the gospel in their claws, and the Turkish axes which had been carved on the fortifications on that bloody autumn day when the Turks had trampled down Megalokastro after long years of hopeless

[1] Mount Ida (translator's note).

blockade. And everywhere, now, among the tumbled blocks there luxuriated an undergrowth of fig-trees, stinging-nettles and caper bushes.

Captain Michales lowered his gaze and fixed his eyes on the base of the Kule Tower. The veins of his temples swelled, and he sighed. There, in that dungeon, against which the waves beat, was the accursed prison where generations of Christian warriors had gasped out their lives, chained hand and foot. "Truly the bodies of Cretans, strong though they are, do not come up to the strength of their souls. I accuse God," he thought, "for having not given us Cretans bodies of steel, with which to hold out for the hundred, two hundred, three hundred years until we have set Crete free; then if we liked we might turn to dust and ashes."

Then his anger rose again, and he thought of his nephew living abroad as a "Frank".

"He's studying, he says. . . . What the Devil is he studying? He'll come back like his Uncle Tityros the schoolmaster! A seedy creature with glasses and a hollow rump. A good pig, but dammit! with worm. Puh!"

He spat in a large arc, and hesitated a moment longer before going to the small spice shop kept by Demetrós.

"You *have* come down in the world, bold race of Mad Micháles the Turk-gobbler!" he said to himself, and his fear-inspiring grandfather "Mad Micháles" rose up in flesh and blood to his inward eye. How could he die, who had so many children and grandchildren? Far and wide the old people still remembered him, the way he used to gaze along the coast of Crete, shading his eyes with his paw. He was looking to see if the Muscovite ships were coming out of the sea and sky. He tilted his fez awry, sauntered up and down the walls of Megalokastro, bowed before that accursed Kyle and sang in the Turks' faces: "The Muscovites are coming!" His hair and his beard were long, his boots high and hitched to his belt and never—it was said—did he take them off. He wore, too, a long black shirt, for enslaved Crete wore mourning, and every Sunday after Mass he used to swagger along with *his* grandfather's bow over his shoulder and a quiver full of arrows as well.

"Those were men, still," snarled Captain Michales, frowning, "those were giants, not worms like us! So were their womenfolk —yes, even wilder. Ah! time, time! Mankind's going downhill, going to the devil!"

A curtain rose within him and revealed, after his grandfather, a skeleton with loamy nails—his grandmother. When she grew to a ripe age, she left the rough-walled house and her heap of children, grandchildren and great-grandchildren, to bury herself in a deep cave up above her native village, at the foot of Psilorítis. For twenty years she stayed in that hole. One of her granddaughters, who had married a man of that village, brought her every morning a lump of barley bread and some olives and a small bottle of wine (there was water enough in the cave), and at Easter two red eggs in remembrance of Christ the Lord. And every morning the old woman appeared, crouched at the cave's entrance, plaster-white like a ghost, with her long hair and nails and her rags, gazed at the rising sun and flourished her thin arms at it for a long time, either in blessing or as a curse. Then she dived back into the maw of the mountain. Twenty solitary years. But one morning they did not see her come out. They understood. They called the village priest, climbed up there with burning torches and found her, a crooked trestle of bones in a little, bathlike hollow, with her arms crossed and her head gripped between her knees.

Captain Michales shook his head, took his eyes from the prison and let the dead sink down again within him.

In the little shop over the way sat sleepy, swollen-eyed Demetrós on a narrow sofa. He held an ass-hair fly-whisk and moved it languidly from side to side, to keep the flies from the little bags of cloves, nutmeg, mastic and cinnamon and the little glasses of laurel and myrtle oil. Yellow-headed, cucumber-nosed, perpetually morose. Now a scratch, now a yawn, now a blink of the sleep-heavy eyes. Still he had not dropped off to sleep, and it seemed to him as if, from over the way, Captain Michales swung round and looked this way. So he raised the fly-whisk to give him good-evening. But that vigorous neighbour turned his head in the other direction, and Demetrós sank back into his doze.

Captain Michales shoved his hand into his broad, twisted belt, found the crumpled letter, pulled it out and tore it into a thousand pieces.

"As if *one* schoolmaster wasn't enough to make our family look silly! Now we've got this one! And whose son? Yours, Brother Kosta—and it was you who grabbed up a torch and set fire to the magazine and blew Arkadi Monastery—Saints, crucifixes, monks and all, Christians and Turks—sky-high!"

Vendúsos, the well-known lyre-player, came hurrying along to the harbour, wrapped in a woollen jacket. He had ordered a cask of wine from Kissamos for his tavern and wanted now to collect it. But when he saw from a distance that Captain Michales' headband was pulled down to his eyebrows, he understood and sheered off.

"The dragon's in another of his rages, this evening," he muttered. "I'd rather go a different way."

The sun now sank over Strúmbulas cliffs, the streets fell into shadow, the white minarets became rose-coloured, and in the harbour dealers, carpenters, dockers, boatmen and the ships' dogs sought relief from their day's work. They still made a din and a barking, but the world turned mild. Captain Michales pulled a tobacco pouch from his belt and rolled himself a cigarette. His anger passed away in smoke. He stroked his raven-black chin, and that fine white fang of his came again into sight.

"My son must live, my Thrasáki," he muttered. "He'll wash our face clean again. He'll set a torch to his Uncle Tityros. And he'll set a torch, too, to that nine-times-wise nephew of mine, who isn't ashamed of mixing our blood with the moneylenders. He'll take up the standard of our clan!"

And suddenly life seemed to him good, and God just. Captain Michales had now no accusation against Him.

A Turk, a bald-headed old man in rags and clogs, drew near, trembling, raised quivering eyes and looked at Captain Michales, who looked down at him and shook his head.

"What do you want, Ali Aga?" he asked roughly.

It was his neighbour. He could not bear the disgusting fellow. That slimy snail, half man, half woman, neither man nor woman, sat in the afternoons with the Greek women of his neighbourhood and took part in women's gossip.

"Sir," the old man murmured, "I was sent by Nuri Bey. 'Greetings,' he says, 'and will you give him the pleasure,' he says, 'of coming this evening to his konak?' "

"All right, I've had the message already through his servant—the black one. You can go."

"He says it's very urgent."

"Go, I tell you."

It annoyed him to hear the womanish eunuch voice. Ali Aga bit his tongue, turned with a shiver to the wall, and made off.

"What have I to do in Turks' houses? What does the dog want with me? Why doesn't he come himself? I shan't go!"

He wheeled round. "Charitos," he called, "go in and saddle my mare!"

He had suddenly thought of taking a ride on his mare, to work off grandfather, grandmother, nephew and Nuri Bey—a ride on his mare, and he'd be rid of the lot!

Just as he raised his arm to take down the key and lock up, a fresh, joyous neigh rang out from the street. Captain Michales knew that horse's voice and turned: black and shining, sleek and slim, the noble, frothing beast came forward, stepping proudly. A plump, barefooted Turkish lad held it firmly by the rein and was leading it at a walk and unsaddled through the streets of Megalokastro to calm it. It has certainly come some distance at the gallop, for there was still foam showing at its mouth, on its chest, and under the shoulders. But its strength was unimpaired, and snorting it tossed its foam-flecked neck and dripping mane. Every now and then it pranced, stamped hard with its slender forelegs on the paving, and neighed.

"Look, children, here comes Nuri Bey's horse!" shouted somebody outside the barber's shop kept by Paraskevás, the man from Syra.[1] Five or six unshaved men and one man covered with lather rushed to the door. With open mouths and craning necks they stood there and gazed at it.

"By my soul," shouted a lanky youth with a sparse goat's-beard,

[1] An island in the Aegean, not far from Athens (translator's note).

"by my soul, if someone asked me: 'Which would you rather, Nuri Bey's horse or his hanum[1]?'—I'd choose the horse."

"You've got as much sense as my paint-brush," laughed Janaros the master painter, whom they also called Pitchfork because he had a bushy, bristling moustache. "You silly idiot, Hanum Eminé is beautiful, twenty years old and wild. Choose her, you poor thing, and give your thighs a bit of fun!"

"I like the horse, I tell you," answered the goat-beard. "I don't go in for dirt."

"Not the horse, my good countryman, and not the Hanum," Signor Paraskevás ventured to break in, in his high voice. He too had rushed out, scissors in hand, "Neither the horse, nor the hanum! They're all more trouble than they're worth!"

The goat-beard wheeled round: "Hey, you tit-bit from Syra," he said, "the whole of life is trouble, only death brings repose. I mean well towards you—don't talk like that to Cretans. We might misunderstand you and bury you alive. . . ."

The poor man from Syra shuddered. The friendly, decent chap could himself no longer understand how he had got to Crete, to shave these wild beasts here. Every time a Cretan from the mountains came over the threshold of his shop, the man from Syra would jump up and examine him with dread. Where was one to begin on him? For months he had not shaved or washed, for years not had his hair cut. He would arrange the towel, grasp the scissors and bustle around the chair, on which the Cretan sat admiring his grotesque face in the glass: he looked to him like a wether, that monster did, or like Saint Mamas, the enormous herdsman, whom Signor Paraskevás had once seen in a holy picture, altogether overgrown as he was with the rankest beard, whiskers and locks, ten barbers could not have made a job of him.

Signor Paraskevás' scissors suddenly grew small. Where was he to set work with them in this undergrowth of hog's bristles? Then he would sigh, make up his mind at last and begin in God's name with the lathering.

"Alive?" he now asked, and drew back in alarm. "Why, my good friend, would you bury me alive?"

[1] Wife (translator's note).

"Because do you know what we call people who talk like you? Dead!"

The man from Syra swallowed, pretended he had heard nothing, and went in.

At that moment Stefanés, the aged captain of the *Dardana*, which the Turks had sunk in the '78 rising, came hobbling by. A shell from the Turkish ship that had holed her had smashed his knee. And since then all he had been good for had been to thump the dry land with his stick and to limp about the harbour quarter. He had two sticks: one, straight as a dart, he used when things were going well in Crete; and the other, a crooked staff, when things went crooked and the air reeked of powder. To-day he had got the crooked staff, as he came by. He listened to what was being said, and stood still.

"Don't quarrel, young fellows," he said; "that's easy to decide."

"Tell us, Captain Stefanés, which you'd choose for yourself."

"You idiots, Nuri's horse to ride, and Eminé Hanum to make sit behind on the crupper—like Saint George!"

"Me too, me too, me too, Captain Stefanés!" bawled the Cretans, shaven and unshaven. "May God hear what you say!"

Captain Michales had raised his eyes: the horse was now close to him, graceful yet fiery, like a black swan with its neck arched high. It turned towards him and its eyes gleamed as if it recognised Captain Michales. It checked for a moment, and neighed. Captain Michales took a step towards the beast. He could not restrain himself—he took a second. He was near it now: his hand itched to touch it, to feel the heat of its body, to brim itself with foam. The Turkish boy saw him and stood still.

Captain Michales' hand strayed over the broad moist chest, with its necklace of light blue stones clasped by an ivory crescent. It eagerly stroked the neck, the nostrils, the head, patted the damp mane, travelled longlingly over the back and crupper, went down and along the steaming belly and was still not satisfied. That hand seemed as if it wanted to engulf the whole horse.

And the proud, graceful animal bowed its neck and itself took an insatiable pleasure in the man's caresses. It turned its huge plum-dark eye and with a snort sucked its hot breath in over the man's hair. And suddenly it decided to play. It snapped at Captain Michales' black head-band, lifted it high and waved it in the air without letting it go. The horse's eye coquetted with the black beard in front of it. And the man himself felt his heart go soft. Never had he looked at a human being with such delicate delight. He began to whisper words of endearment, and the horse lowered its neck as though it listened, and rubbed gently against the man's shoulders. Unexpectedly, Captain Michales raised his hand, caught the head-band from the horse's lips and wound it, sprinkled with foam as it was, around his hair. Then he turned and signed to the Turkish boy that he could go on.

"I shall go there," muttered Captain Michales, still following the horse with his eyes as it now approached the main gate, "I shall go there."

He had suddenly made up his mind, and now returned to shut the shop and to set out on his way to the konak of Nuri Bey.

But Captain Stefanés, who had observed him as he stroked the horse with so much feeling, stood before him, leaning on his crooked staff, and wished him good evening. He had no fear of man-haters. He was himself a real man, a sturdy seadog. In each of the risings of 1854, 1866 and 1878, he had run the Turkish blockade in his *Dardana* countless times and landed food and munitions for the Christians in remote natural harbours. And when they shelled him and sank his ship, his blood had flowed from his smashed knee. But he had swum into Saint Pelagia's Bay, holding in his teeth, above the waves, the letters which the Athenian Committee had sent to the famous Captain Kórax, leader of the Mesara region. Since then indeed he had come down in the world, he limped, had grown poor, let his clothes go into rags, went on wearing those captain's boots of his that had been patched again and again, did his daily round of the harbour and admired, though with burning heart, the foreign ships. It did him good to smell tar and to hear the voices and greetings and the noise of anchors upon the hard, deep bottom. The body was weak, the pockets empty, but the soul stood upright in that breast of his and gazed out over the sea like the Gorgon figure-head.

And so he leaned on his crooked staff, stood firm in front of Captain Michales, and spoke:

"Hey, Captain Michales, did your ear catch the talk down at the barber's? If you had to choose, they were saying, between Nuri's horse and Eminé Hanum, which would you choose?"

"I don't care for shameless chatter," said Captain Michales, and went over to his shop without so much as looking round at the ship's master.

But the obstinate sailor did not give up. He behaved as if he had not heard, and overhauled the other.

"Nuri has brought her from Constantinople, and she's a Circassian, they say, with beauty for five, and wild—a real man-eater. My neighbours the Hags hear from her woman, the dark Christian she brought with her, what goes on behind the cage doors at the Bey's. And they spread it about. Bless their little tongues. . . ."

"Captain Stefanés," repeated Captain Michales with irritation. "I tell you I don't care for shameless chatter."

But the tough seaman stood his ground. No, he would not have his mouth shut. He had shown no fear in face of the powerful Turkish Armada, and was he to show fear in face of this man? He shall hear it all, whether he likes or not.

"Nuri Bey," he held forth, "is your blood brother, Captain Michales; don't you forget it. And so it's right that you should know what goes on in his house. The Bey, that terrible wild beast, sits—so they say—tied to her feet, and gazes into her eyes. And she presses her lighted cigarettes against his neck and giggles. And sometimes, they say, her thoughts stray back to her own country. . . . To the tents, to the smell of dung and milk, and the neighing of horses—and then it takes hold of her, and she smashes the porcelain cups, empties the scent bottles on the floor, and whips her black woman. . . ."

Captain Michales, growling like a dangerous sheep-dog, held the key out in front of him and shoved the old sea-wolf aside from the doorway so as to be able to shut the shop. But the sailor could not now hold his tongue. It would have been better not to engage in any conversation with such a wild beast, but now he was well and truly involved. . . . So hoist sails, whatever comes of it! He therefore made haste to finish his story:

"The hanum is jealous—so they say—of Nuri's horse. The evening before last, when the Bey tried to embrace her, she pushed him away. 'First you must do me a favour,' she said. 'Anything you wish, mistress of my heart, everything is yours.' 'Bring your horse into the yard. Light lamps, so that I can see, and slaughter it in my presence.' The Bey sighed, bent his head and ran out of the room. He shut himself up in his own room. And all night long he could be heard pacing up and down and bellowing. I'm telling you so that you may know. He's sent for you, to come to his house. He needs you. Don't deny it. Ali Aga told me. So it's as well you should know how the loving couple are at logger-heads."

Stefanés rubbed his calloused hands, glad that it was over and that he had finished his say without being overcome by fear.

"Yes, Captain Michales, that's how it is. Well, if it's lies, the Hags had better look out!"

Captain Michales gave a jerk, the door banged and he locked it. He stuck the key in his belt. He turned to the castaway captain:

"You seafolk," he said contemptuously, "have no respect for women!"

And he went off.

"You dry-land captains," Stefanés retorted peevishly, "know all about that! Always paddling in horse-dung!" Shouting this, he hobbled quickly round the corner, as if fear had suddenly got hold of him.

Captain Michales pulled the black head-band over his forehead, so that the tassels covered his eyes. He wanted to see no one and be seen by no one. Breathing heavily he stumped through the Turkish quarter.

The sun had gone down, trumpets rang out, the guards picked up the keys and double-locked the four city gates. Till sunrise no one might stick his nose outside Megalokastro, or come in. Turks and Christians remained fenced in together all night.

Darkness broadened out and spread its shield over the alleys. Women no longer appeared in the streets, the lamps were lit in the houses, the tables laid. Respectable men hurried home to dinner, the more gay lingered in the taverns for another drink or two. Megalokastro, as dusk hid it, felt hungry and addressed itself to the evening meal.

That was the hour when the triplet sisters, known as the Hags, would be standing behind their door, close against one another. They had bored three holes in the door, high up, and pressed their faces to them. They studied the passers-by and commented on each one's ugliness or good looks. All three old maids had snow-white hair, eye-brows and eye-lashes and red rabbits' eyes from birth. They never went out all day. It was said that they could not see well in sunlight, and longed for evening when they could stand at the three little holes and gape at the passing world. Nasty, poison tongues. Through the peep-holes not a fly escaped them. Their house lay at the corner of a shopping street, at the point where the Turkish quarter left off and the Christian houses began. They saw everyone and gave everyone his nickname, from which in a life-time he could not shake free. It was they who had called Captain Michales "the wild boar". They had christened his brother, the schoolmaster, "Tityros". For once, when his father brought back a big cheese from the village, his learned son had asked him, in classical Greek: τὶ τυρὸς εἶναι ἀφτὸς, πάτερ; ("What sort of cheese is that, father?") The Hags had heard, and he became Tityros.

All through the day they cooked, sewed and swept in the half-dark. They had nothing else to worry about. They had no men-folk or children to look after, and God had created for them an excellent brother, a man of gold, Mr. Aristoteles the chemist. The poor man, though unmarried, worked from morning till night making up powders and ointments; sallow, patient, with feet swollen from long standing and with bad breath, he carried the loaded market basket morning and evening for his sisters. When he was still young a pretty maiden with a dowry and of good family had been found for him. Mr. Aristoteles would make an ideal son-in-law. His pharmacy was in the heart of Megalokastro, on the main square, full of bottles and phials, scents and soaps, and every evening teachers and doctors gathered there to take to pieces and put together the major world problems. And melancholy, shrivelled Mr. Aristoteles listened, said nothing, merely looked at them with his small, blue, tired eyes and wagged his plucked head, as though to say to each one: you are right, you are right. But his one thought was that his life on this planet was going to rack and ruin. He had wanted to marry—not because he cared about women. God forbid! No, he merely wanted to beget a son who would take over the pharmacy. But where was he to put his sisters? They must marry first—that was the custom. . . . The years went by, his hair became white, his teeth became loose, his back became bent, and Mr. Aristoteles' firm red cheeks sagged and shrivelled. Mr. Aristoteles had grown old. His life was drained away. He took to mastic. Not the kind you drink, but the kind you chew. And so the grinder of ointments chewed and chewed all day, and when evening came listened to teachers and doctors debating about free will and the immortality of the soul, and whether the stars are inhabited. And he himself wagged his bald head and said to himself, again and again: even if I do get married now, I can't have a son now, I can't have a son now, I can't have a son now. . . . He held the pestle upright on the table, chewed his mastic, and ground his medicaments in the mortar till a late hour, deep in care.

To-day the Hags were early at their posts. It was cool. Their hair was untidy, their hands and spindly legs had gone to sleep, but they kept manfully on their feet and waited. They stuck their ruby eyes to the peep-holes and kept them firmly aimed at Nuri Bey's green, arched doorway.

"Keep your eyes fixed on that," said Aglaja, the middle one, "something is cooking there. Think what the Moorish woman told us yesterday!"

"The Bey came in from his village this evening in a rage— I saw him. He banged into the door and sent it flying open, and immediately afterwards I heard shouts and cries. I'm sure he beat the servants again."

"Who else is there for him to beat? The horse? Eminé? No fleas on him," laighed Phrosyne.

But just as the Three Graces were whispering, the street seemed

B

to them suddenly to grow dark. They drew back and looked at each other.

"Captain Michales!" they muttered, and pressed their eyes again to the peep-holes.

Breathing hard, but light of foot, the sturdy man with the raven-dark, curly beard went slowly by, and the tassels of his head-band were over his eye-brows. He was keeping close to the wall, and his hand rested on his broad belt, firmly grasping a knife with a black hilt.

He brushed against the door through which he was being observed, wheeled round for a moment as though he felt the six eyes upon him, and the white of his eyes flashed in the twilight. The three sisters trembled and held their breath, but the heavy man went slowly on and stopped opposite the big doorway. He took a quick glance round: solitude, not a soul about. Then in one spring he crossed the narrow alley, pushed Nuri Bey's door open, and went in.

The triplets yelled. . . . "Kyrie eleison," said Aglaja, and crossed herself. "Did you see the way he went in? Like a robber."

"What's Captain Wildboar after with the Bey? The bean has a maggot in it. I bet he wants to sell him the horse. . . ."

"Or Eminé. . . ." And the three Graces—Aglaja, Thalia and Phrosyne, began giggling again.

Captain Michales, who had stepped over the threshold with his right foot, glanced every way. He stared at the negro who awaited him behind the door. An old, worn-out slave whom Nuri Bey had inherited from his father, this negro lolled like a mangy dog behind the street door every day till midnight. Captain Michales touched him on the shoulder with his finger tip, and the old man sank back and let him pass. He walked slowly forwards between huge pots filled with roses. There must be, somewhere, a lemon-tree in blossom, for the air had a scent of lemon-blossom. The freshly-watered earth smelt of dung. In the depth of the garden, where the old residence glimmered in the twilight, a partridge in a cage was still cackling. Light came through the high wooden lattice. Feminine laughter could be heard.

Captain Michales breathed in the Turkish air against his will, with bent head.

"What am I after, here?" he thought. "Turks' stink!"

He stood still and gazed around. There was still time: no one had seen him, except the negro. He could still go away again; Charitos had by now saddled the mare; he would ride, race up and down the big square to quiet himself down. But he was ashamed. "They'll say I'm afraid," he muttered. "Forward, Captain Michales!"

With swift strides he went on. There was the central door. It stood open. A large, burning lamp with green and red glass hung in the door-space. Under it stood Nuri Bey, all red and green. He had heard the outer door, he recognised the step. He came forward to welcome his guest.

A stately, rather stout man with expansive gestures. From his round face there looked out a dark pair of almond eyes, and the light from the lamp called out a steely glitter from them. His thick moustache was thickly smeared with black pomade. This Bey had a serene Oriental handsomeness: he was like the moon-faced lion which Turkish women of the past used to embroider upon costly Persian stuffs. He wore long blue woollen stockings, but his belt was blood-red and the turban that enclosed his hair was snow-white. His shoulders were perfumed with musk, and he smelt like a wild beast in heat in the spring.

He took a step forward and stretched out his short-fingered hand.

"Don't be angry with me, Captain Michales," he said, "for bringing you to my house. But it was necessary. You'll see for yourself."

Captain Michales growled and, without a word, followed the Bey to the men's quarters. For a short moment he remained on the threshold, as though in angry thought. He cast a stolen glance backwards. Nobody. The big lamp in front of the divan was lit. There was a fire of coals burning in a large bronze brazier. In the hot atmosphere it gave out a smell of burnt lemon-peel. On a round table in one corner there stood a long-necked porcelain jug full of raki, two glasses and some sweetmeats.

They sat down close to each other on a small settee. Captain Michales was near the closed window which gave on to the garden. Nuri Bey took from his belt his dark, iron tobacco-box with a mother-of-pearl crescent in the middle. He opened it and held it out to his friend.

Captain Michales rolled a cigarette, and Nuri Bey did the same. They smoked. For some time they remained without speaking. The Bey cleared his throat. He did not know how to put the matter, to prevent his guest from taking it amiss and losing his temper. He knew that he was not the man to let a fly run up and down his sabre. And what he had to say to him this evening was difficult.

"Shall we have a raki, Captain Michales? It's a nice mature one. It's made from lemons. I ordered it for you."

"What have you to say to me, Nuri Bey?" asked Captain Michales, and held his hand over both glasses. He did not want to drink.

The Bey coughed and crushed his cigarette into the cinders in the brazier. As he bent his face over the burning coals, it glowed copper-red.

"If I have to speak out," he said, "don't take it in bad part, Captain Michales."

He waited a little, for the dark Greek to say something and rouse his temper. But Michales kept silent. The Bey stood up, went to the door, opened his shirt at the neck, and sat down again. Suddenly the slippers he was wearing were too tight. He kicked them off and placed his naked soles on the ground. This refreshed him.

He turned to his dumb companion. His mind was now made up. He raised his hand to twirl his moustache, but let it fall again. Careful! The irascible Captain might take that too in bad part.

"Your brother Manúsakas," he said, and sighed, "your brother Manúsakas, Captain Michales, scoffs at Turkey. The day before yesterday, March 25th, he was drunk again, hoisted an ass on to his back and took it into the mosque to pray. I came in from the village and found all my people beside themselves. Your people were armed, there was serious trouble brewing. I'm telling you this, Captain Michales, so that you may not make a fuss later. It was my duty to tell you, and yours to listen. Do as God directs you."

"Pour out the drinks," said Captain Michales.

The Bey filled the glasses, the world smelt of lemons.

"To your good health, Nuri Bey."

"And to yours," answered Nuri Bey quietly, looking him in the eyes.

They clinked glasses. Captain Michales stood up and brushed the tassels of his head-band back.

"Is that what you wanted to say to me, Nuri Bey?" he asked. "Is that why you sent for me?"

"If you are god-fearing," said the Bey, and caught him lightly by the belt, "don't go. This is a spark, but it can cause a fire in which our village would burn up. Order your brother not to put our government to shame. We're of the same village, the same soil. Sit down and let's set this right."

"My brother is older than me, sixteen years older," said Captain Michales, "He has children and grandchildren and years of discretion. He's strong enough for seven. What he wants to do he does. No words of mine are any good."

"You're the captain of the village. People listen to your words."

"Words are dear, Nuri Bey. They don't easily get past my teeth."

The Bey bit his lips, but his heart hardened. He examined Captain Michales, who had already got up and was looking at the door, ready to go out. "This *giaour* comes of a savage, upstanding stock," he thought, "and my race has some old scores against him. Was not Kostaros—may pitch defile his corpse!—his brother, who slew my father against a rock? I was still a mere child, I possessed myself in patience till I should be ripe to take blood for blood. But I had no luck. The accursed man got himself killed at Arkadi—he was blown sky-high. And his son was still a sapling, it would have been shameful to kill him. I waited for him to grow up. But as he was just growing a moustache, he escaped me. He went, so they say, to the Franks, to study. . . . When will he come back? My father's blood cries out!"

He stood up. He placed himself in front of the door. Within

him rage rose and sank. He did not know where to begin. Captain Michales' tangled beard of prickles flashed in the soft glow from the lamp. He had taken an oath, it was said, not to cut it off till Crete should be free. Nuri Bey's eyes sparkled with scorn. Let him wait for that, the *giaour*, if it doesn't bore him. Let his beard flow down to his knees, to the ground, let it lay hold of the earth and strike roots there, but Crete—no, it won't see freedom! For twenty-five years we got ourselves killed in front of the Venetian walls of Megalokastro before it fell into our claws. We're not letting it go—it's not letting us go, it's become part of our flesh.

He groaned. He thought of his father, he thought of the Musulmans who had met their death in the trenches round Megalokastro. Between him and Captain Michales a stream of blood rolled.

"Let the bellows rest, Nuri Bey!" said Captain Michales, raising a hand to push him out of the way and get to the door. "It's no good puffing and blowing—what you want can't be done."

Nuri Bey was a strong man. He restrained his rage.

"Don't go, Captain Michales," he said, softening his voice, "don't go like this with wild thoughts, as though we had had a quarrel. If it seems to you hard, I take back what I said. I have said nothing, you have heard nothing. Are we not friends? I sent for you that we might have a drink and taste a dainty morsel. It's a partridge from our village—I've just brought it in. I thought we would eat it together and remember old times, Captain Michales. When we were young. When we used to play together, in the good old days, in our village."

"I'm not eating, it's a fast-day for us," he answered.

Full of regret, Nuri Bey took him by both hands. "If I'd known," he said, "by Mohammed, I'd have got you some black caviare."

He filled the glasses. "Your health, Captain Michales," he said, raising his glass. "I'm glad you've consented to come to my house and drink a raki with me. There, may my blood be spilt like this if I wish you any harm."

So saying he sprinkled a couple of drops of lemon raki on the floor.

Captain Michales yielded, and sat down again on the settee near the window.

"I too wish you no harm, Nuri Bey, but it's a matter of honour to weigh our words."

With those words, he emptied his glass.

They fell silent again. The Bey felt hot: he got up and opened the window.

A small fountain outside in the garden made a cool and friendly splashing. The scent of the roses and lemon-trees came in. Laughter was again to be heard from the women's quarters.

The two men remained in silence. Nuri Bey exerted himself to find a way of starting the conversation afresh. And Captain Michales listened to the water and the laughter, breathed in the fragrance of the garden—and again his heart began beating hard. Is that Crete? Laughter and scent, and you drinking raki with the Turks? So he brooded. Suddenly he shut the window.

"Don't be angry, Captain Michales. I opened it without asking you," said the worried Bey, and filled the glasses again.

Captain Michales came back and stared at the Turk. They were born in the same village, the one a Bey, to be all rich acres. And the other a *raia*—an underdog. His father, Captain Sifakas, owned the stone house. At that time he had not the permission to ride a horse. He sat on his little ass, and whenever he saw the enemy of Christians, Hani Ali, father of this same Nuri, old Sifakas had to jump down, to let the great man pass. But one afternoon Captain Sifakas was in a bad mood and did not dismount. So Hani Ali raised his whip, and the defiant head streamed with blood. The old man said nothing, he held his heart in and waited. A Christian is no Albanian, he thought, he's a right-thinking Christian. The day will come when he'll pay me back my due. Hardly a year had gone by when the 1866 rising broke out. His eldest son, Kostaros, ran into the bloody Hani Ali one night outside Megalokastro and slaughtered him like a lamb, on a rock in the Cave of Pendevis. But now just look at his son: he had come and taken up his throne in Megalokastro, in this huge residence, with the valuables and the fountains and the wooden lattices. And he ate and drank and kissed, and rode on his horse every fine afternoon through the

Greek quarter as far as the Three Vaults, striking the sparks from
the roadway.

He took out his tobacco-box and rolled a cigarette. His nostrils
filled with smoke. Did he hate this Turkish fellow here beside
him, or was he fond of him? Was he disgusted by him? He had
often asked himself the question, and could come to no conclusion.
And when by chance the two of them met in the narrow alleys of
Megalokastro or on horseback outside, Captain Michales would
look at the clear, lovable face of Nuri Bey and his heart would
rejoice, and he did not know what to think. Should he kill him or
no—ought he to embrace him as an old friend, well-met?

As small children they had played together on their village
threshing-floor, run races for bets, wrestled, thrown each other,
laughed, fought, made it up. And one afternoon, when they were
grown men already, they had met, both of them on horseback, on
this side of Nuri Bey's estate, an hour from Megalokastro, quite
close to the Cave of Pendevis. For a while they had ridden side by
side in silence. Both were sullen, for in those days again Turks
and Christians had been killed, Crete was again catching fire, the
raias were again raising their heads.

They rode without a word. The famous Venetian walls came
in sight, blood-red from the glow of the setting sun.

"This dog," thought Captain Michales, "—I can't bear the
sight of him any longer, the way he rides for fun through the
Greek quarter and bewitches the women."

"I can't bear the *giaour* any longer," thought Nuri Bey. "Every
time he's drunk he comes out from his house on horseback and
insults the Turks. Last year he caught me by the hips, lifted me up
like a sack and tossed me on to the roof of his shop. People came
thronging, placed a ladder for me to get down, and laughed
at me."

Nuri Bey's cheeks burned. Angrily he turned to Captain
Michales and said:

"Hey, Captain Michales, either I must finish you off, or you
me. There's no room for both of us in Megalokastro."

"Choose the weapons, friend Nuri Bey! Shall I dismount, so
that we can start?"

Nuri Bey did not answer. His glance had rested on the Greek at his side, and his eyes were filled with that heroic figure. "What a man!" he thought, "what pride and what courage! He never says a superfluous word, he never boasts. He doesn't quarrel with those beneath him. He knows no fraud. He has no respect even for death. Happy the man who has such an enemy."

At length he opened his mouth:

"Not so fast, Captain Michales. It would be a pity. . . . I take back what I said. Yes, by my faith, neither my Mohammed nor your Christ wants that. You're a good *palikare*,[1] I think, and so am I. We ought to mingle our blood, but in a different way."

"In a different way?"

"Become blood brothers."

Captain Michales spurred his mare and rode on. His heart swelled, it rose to his throat. For a while all he could hear was the brood throbbing in his jugular vein. At length it subsided and his brain cleared. A strange agitation had taken possession of him. Perhaps it was pleasure, at the thought of mingling blood with this young Bey, brought up amid the scent of musk, of no longer being obliged to kill him, of banishing the temptation which, every time he saw him, thrust the knife into his fist.

The man was splendid, even if he was a Turk. The pride of Magalokastro, and nothing false about him. He was kindly, generous, noble, a man through and through. Curse him!

He tugged at the reins. The mare pulled up short. Nuri Bey spurred his horse and drew level with him.

"All right," said Captain Michales, without looking at him.

They rode back without a word to the Bey's estate. They came into the courtyard. A labourer ran up, took the horses and led them to the stable. The Bey clapped his hands, and an old daily servant appeared and bowed.

"Kill a cock, the big one with all the feathers," the Bey ordered. "Get out some of the old wine. Yes, and get two beds ready—spread the silk sheets on them. We're eating and sleeping here to-night. Go and shut the gates."

[1] Young warrior (translator's note).

They were left alone. They knelt down, close together and facing, under the hollow olive-tree which, still heavy with blossom, stood in full glory in the middle of the courtyard. The sun had gone down; the evening star shone large and bright between the olive leaves.

Nuri Bey rose, went out and fetched from the well-head the bronze cup which hung there for travellers to drink from and bless the name of the builder of the well—Hani Ali. Then he sat down cross-legged on the ground.

"In the names of Mohammed and of Christ," he said, and pulled the knife out of his belt. Captain Michales rolled the right sleeve of his jacket up high. The muscular arm showed sunburnt and firm. Nuri Bey bent forward and with the knife's tip slit a powerful vein which stood out from the flesh. Dark, hot blood gushed out, and Nuri Bey pushed the cup underneath. He let a finger's breadth flow in. Then he undid his white head-band and tied it tight round the cut arm.

"Your turn, Captain Michales," he said.

"In the names of Christ and Mohammed," said Captain Michales, and pulled out his knife. He slit the Bey's stout white arm, and its rich blood flowed into the cup. Then Captain Michales took off his black head-band and tied it tight round the Bey's arm.

They placed the cup between them and began slowly mixing the blood with their knives—without a word.

Evening was now well advanced; smoke rose from the manor chimney—the labourers were at their meal in their quarters. The two men wiped their knives in their hair and hid them once more in their belts.

Nuri seized the cup and raised it high. His voice rang deep and solemn, right for an oath:

"I drink to your health, Captain Michales, my blood brother! I swear—yes, by Mohammed, that I will never harm you; not with word and not with deed, whether in war or in good times. Honour for honour, manhood for manhood, loyalty for loyalty! I have more than enough Greeks, you have more than enough Turks—take your vengeance among them!"

So he spoke, and pressed the cup to his lips. He began drinking the mingled blood slowly, drop by drop. He drank half of it. He wiped his lips and offered the cup to Captain Michales.

And he took it in both palms:

"I drink to your health, Nuri Bey, my blood brother! I swear— yes, by Christ, I will never harm you, not with word, not with deed, whether in war or in the good times. Honour for honour, manhood for manhood, loyalty for loyalty! I have more than enough Turks, you have more than enough Greeks—take your vengeance among them!"

And he drank the blood to the bottom without a pause.

Now Captain Michales opened the window and threw his cigarette out. It fell like a small red star into a pot of roses and was extinguished in the freshly sprinkled manure. He stood up. His face darkened. The Bey shrank back. He too stood up.

"I've not forgotten. That's why one of us is still alive."

Like a flash of lightning that evening on the estate under the olive-tree darted through his mind. The glad drinking bout with the old wine. The deep sleep in the silk sheets. . . .

He took the bottle, filled his glass and drank. He filled it again and drank again. He sat down.

"Haven't you a dwarf in your house?" he asked. "A *karagios?*[1] Call him and let him dance for us or play the drum or sing. If not, I shall explode."

Nuri was glad. The rage was taking a good course, it would dip into raki and be smothered there. It must be conjured away!

His heart longed to do something big, something unheard-of for his blood brother, something that would surpass friendship and love, that this gloomy, pitiless man might be a little tamed, a little cheered. He racked his brains, ransacked his house from top to bottom, to find something for his blood brother. Old gold pieces out of the chest, silvered weapons off the walls, stuffs of fine wool and silk, casks from the cellar—what should he give him? And suddenly his mind rose up to those wooden lattices; he hit upon his costliest treasure, and laughed. Nuri turned to his guest:

"This evening I am going to do something to gladden you,"

[1] A jester (translator's note).

he said, "something no Turk has ever done for anyone except his brother."

Captain Michales looked at him, but said nothing. He filled his raki glass again.

Nuri stood up and went to the low door leading to the women's quarters.

"Maria!" he called.

An old Moorish woman came hurrying down the stairs. She was broken, toothless, arid as bean-straw, and had a little golden cross hung round her neck.

"Tell your mistress she should get her mandoline and come here."

Amazed, terrified, the Moorish woman raised her blinking eyes and stared at him.

"Go!" he shouted, and pushed her out.

Captain Michales took away the glass he had already set to his lips, and turned to Nuri:

"What's this mean?" he snapped.

"To gladden you, blood brother. I trust you."

"There's nothing gladdening here. Only shame for you as a man, shame for your wife too, having to show herself before a stranger, shame also for me, raising my eyes to look on her."

Nuri stammered: "I trust you." He was already sorry, but was ashamed to go back on his decision.

He stood up, placed a cushion of down upon a small sofa in the corner and another against the wall, for the Hanum to have something soft to lean against. Captain Michales also rose and turned the lamp lower, so that it cast a gentle half-light over the room. He took from his belt a small rosary of black ebony, and began to play with it nervously, staring at the floor.

Feminine voices rang out upstairs, with sounds of rapid footsteps, doors opening and shutting, a tap running, water being poured away, then silence for a while.

Captain Michales looked up. "The bitch won't come," he thought. "She's wild, a Circassian, she's refusing. So much the better. Far better. What evil spirit is keeping me here? I'm going!"

At the moment when he decided to get up, the staircase creaked. One stair after another gave out its sound. A gay tinkling of little necklaces and pendants was audible. Nuri Bey ran forward, opened the low door and in greeting put his hand to his chest, lips and forehead.

"Welcome, Eminé Hanum," he said tenderly, "welcome, welcome."

In the doorway, in the half-light, there gleamed a young woman, whose face was moon-round like Nuri's. It suggested the plumpness and whiteness of her body. Huge, slanting eyes, painted cheeks, lips, eyebrows and lashes. Her nails and hands were stained red with cinnamon. She was holding a small, glittering mandoline like a child in her arms.

She advanced an elegant little foot in its tiny red slipper, craned her neck, saw the shadow of the man near the window, gave a display of terror and a sharp cry.

"You needn't be ashamed, mistress of my heart," said Nuri, catching her under the arm. "It's my blood brother. How often have I spoken well of him to you! Captain Michales. The hearts of both of us are heavy this evening. Come, do us the pleasure of playing the mandoline to us and singing us a song of your country to cheer us. That's why we asked you, mistress of my heart, to come downstairs."

Captain Michales listened, with his eyes fastened on the ground. He clenched the rosary in his fist as though he would break it. He had heard much of the beauty of this Circassian girl, of her wildness, and her singing which sometimes, during the feast of Bairam, pierced through the thick wooden lattices and disturbed the neighbourhood. Then Turkish and Christian gallants would creep in the darkness to the street corners, to listen to her. All sighed like young calves, and Nuri would keep her well away from the lattices. He would clasp Eminé's bosom with his hands and feel proud, as though he were clasping the whole world.

Captain Michales caught the heavy smell of musk, which spread abroad as the hanum stepped forwards to the corner where the Bey had prepared her place. She came past him; her eyes flashed and she looked at him. At that same second Captain Michales also raised his eyes. The two glances met. And broke away at once, both of them wild.

The hanum sat down on the cushions and crossed her feet.

"What darkness," she giggled. She wanted to be seen.

Nuri Bey stood up again and screwed the lamp-wick higher. Light flooded the room, and the Circassian's cheeks, hands and delicately arched, red-coloured soles shone out.

Captain Michales looked at her stealthily. But immediately he lowered his eyes, and two beads of his rosary cracked in his fist.

"Good evening, Captain Michales," said the Turkish girl, and her nostrils trembled.

The voice came from the man's throat hoarsely:

"Good evening, Eminé Hanum, excuse me."

The hanum laughed. Far away in her own country the women worked with unveiled faces beside the men and rode their horses astride. There a man enjoyed a woman and a woman a man till they had had enough. But as a small child she had been taken away, and her father had sold her to an old Pasha in Constantinople; later this Cretan bey had come and stolen her, and Eminé had never managed to live with men and have enough of the atmosphere of men. And so her nostrils shuddered like those of a hungry animal every time she met a man.

All day long she crouched behind the wooden lattice and watched young lads go by, Turks and Christians, and her bosom hurt her. And when she went out walking, thickly swathed in her silken veils and with her nurse, the old Moorish woman, gliding behind her, she liked to go past the coffee-houses, which were full of men, or down to the harbour with its robust porters and boatmen, or out through the fortress gates, where shaggy, unwashed, sweating peasants came in. Then the Circassian would draw deep breaths, she could not have enough of the stench of men.

"By God's love," she had said one day, turning to her old nurse, "by God's love, Maria, if they didn't stink, I wouldn't go running all over the place to see them."

"Whom, my child?"

"Men. How did you manage, when you were young?"

"I believed in Christ, my child," said the old Moorish woman, and sighed.

She looked at Captain Michales in silence. After all, how often and with what pride had the Bey spoken of this man, who now sat before her? What had she not heard of his heroic deeds, his drunkenness and wildness? Also that he would never say or listen to a word about women! And there he was now before her—her husband himself had brought him.

"Eminé, mistress of my heart," said Nuri Bey, "sing us a Circassian song for our pleasure, to make us forget the cares of the world. We are two men here, have pity on us."

The hanum giggled. She laid the mandoline on her lap, struck a couple of loud chords and threw back her head.

"What are you going to sing us, wife?" asked the Bey happily.

"You'll see," she answered.

The notes of the mandoline became faster; she swayed in the half-light like some wild beast, and drew a deep breath. And suddenly there shot from her jutting throat a fountain out of the bowels of the earth—the woman's voice. The house shook and Captain Michales' temples were pierced. What an uproar there was, what ecstasy in his fists, his throat, his loins! The mountains laughed, the plains turned scarlet with Turkish soldiers: over them stormed Captain Michales on Nuri's charger, behind him thousands of Cretans in black head-bands, before him no one. The villages shouted, the minarets snapped like felled cypresses, the blood rose as high as his horse's belly. . . .

Captain Michales clutched his temples. The Circassian's throat fell silent. Suddenly the world stood firm again. Crete was again there, and Megalokastro, and the Bey's *konak*. The Bey too gazed at Eminé and sighed and drank. . . . The soul had forgotten its flight and gone back to prison.

For a while no one spoke. At last Eminé stirred, stroking the mandoline on her knees.

"That was an old Circassian song," she said. "The men sing it when they ride out to war."

Nuri got up. His knees were trembling slightly. He walked over to his wife and raised his glass:

"Your health, Eminé," he said. "Three things' I was told by our muezzin, three things Mohammed loved (God's mercy be upon him!): sweet odours, women and song. You, my Eminé, bring us all three. May you live a thousand years—a thousand, two thousand!"

He emptied the glass at one gulp, smacked his lips and turned to Captain Michales:

"Drink, blood-brother! You too, drink to her health," he said, and filled his glass for him.

But Captain Michales thrust two fingers into the over-filled glass and pressed them apart, hard. The glass broke in two, and the raki spilled over the table.

"Enough," he growled heavily, and his eyes grew troubled.

Eminé gave a cry. She leapt up from the sofa and stared at Captain Michales with tears in her eyes. Never had she seen such strength in a man's hand. She turned to her husband challengingly:

"Can you do that, too, Nuri Bey?" she asked breathlessly. "Can you do that? Can you do that?"

Nuri turned pale. He gathered all his strength into his right hand, stretched it out and was about to insert two fingers into the other glass, to split it. But he broke out in a cold sweat, and drew back. He felt put to shame in front of his wife, and cast a dark look at Captain Michales. Once again he's made a fool of me, he thought. I won't stand it any longer.

He seized Eminé by the arm and shook her like a madman.

"Go up to your room!" he shouted.

"Can you do that too?" she repeated, and her cheeks were burning. "Can you do it too? Can you do it too?"

"Go up to your room!" the Bey ordered for the second time. He grasped the mandoline and smashed it into a thousand pieces against the wall.

The Circassian gave a dry, contemptuous laugh:

"Yes, that you can do—smash a mandoline. Yes, *that* you can do, Nuri!"

She slid from the sofa and grazed past Captain Michales. Her dress brushed the back of his hand. Once more the air was stifling with musk. Captain Michales felt his hand burning.

Smiling mockingly, she described a circle round Nuri—once—twice—gave him a playful push and laughed. And suddenly she ran to the stairs and vanished.

The two men were left standing opposite each other in the middle of the room. The Bey rolled his moustache, and his chest rose and fell violently. Captain Michales bit his dry lips sulkily and watched him. Both laid their hands on the hilts of their knives, which stuck out from their belts.

At last Nuri half opened venomous lips:

"Captain Michales," he hissed, "go!"

"Nuri Bey," he answered, "I'm going when it suits me. Take the unbroken glass and give me a drink."

The Bey clutched the hilt of his knife and glanced quickly at the lamp. He had the idea of putting it out and leaving them in the dark, to wrestle until one of them was dead. Yet his heart was undecided.

"Take the unbroken glass and give me a drink," Captain Michales repeated quietly. "Otherwise I'm not going."

Nuri turned towards the table and advanced one foot. It was heavy as lead. Bathed in sweat, he reached the table. He filled the glass too full. His hand was shaking, the raki spurted over the partridge.

"Drink," he said, and pointed to the glass.

"Hand it to me," said Captain Michales.

The Bey groaned. He seized the glass and pressed it into Captain Michales' fist.

And he raised it, gravely and sombrely, saying:

"To your health, Nuri Bey. I'm going to d⌐
and tell my brother not to scoff at Tur⌐

With those words he moister⌐
black head-band round his he⌐

The lamp threw a shaft of ⌐
quite dark garden, and Captain ⌐
out of the street door, without ⌐

Darkness reigned. Megalokastr⌐
It yawned, shivered, shuttered firs⌐

crossed itself and went to bed. A few belated people still moved in the streets, a few pairs of lovers embraced under the shuttered windows. Here and there subdued talk could be heard from lighted cellars. Night workers.

The Hags had become frozen in their effort to keep up the watch behind their door. Captain Michales was taking his time about returning. The darkness, too, had become impenetrable, and their brother, monosyllabic and morose as usual, came home. So they laid the table and exchanged a few words. What the meals would be tomorrow, how there was no more coal, no oil for the salad, no oil for the lamp. How Aristoteles must pull himself together. They talked, served the meal, cleared it away, prepared their nightly camomile tea for the digestion, donned their night-dresses which reached to the ground, and crossed themselves; but their thoughts were on the green door.

Captain Michales went home by the longest way round. He felt he could not contain himself within four walls this evening. His heart was swelling, overflowing, There was not enough room for it in his body or in his house. Suddenly even Megalokastro was too small for him. He strode on. Houses, alleys, human beings stifled him. He went with long strides, and with his teeth clenched—like a hunted wild beast. He came to the main street. It was empty. Spaced-out petroleum lamps threw pale red glimmering shafts upon the pavement. He passed through the Bazaar. A Turkish cook-house was still open, a coffee-house, two or three taverns. Someone called him. It seemed to be the voice of Captain Polyxigis. He quickened his stride and made off. He came past the Pacha's door, past the Venetian marble fountain with the lions. He raised his eyes and saw the Tall Plane-tree—accursed ʀee! He moved nearer. Nobody was coming. He crossed himself. "God bless your remains," he muttered. "Till we meet again , my fathers!"

 this magnificent plane-tree, for generations and genera- Pachas had hanged the Christians who had dared to eads; and winter and summer on its strongest bough e rope with the noose ready.

ristian, one night I'll rise up, take an axe and cut

you down. Curse you!" he muttered, and gazed furiously at the old plane-tree, as though it were a Turk.

He resumed his way and plunged into a long, dark allay. He came out by the Three Vaults. Not a soul! He unbuttoned his shirt—it was stifling him. He breathed deeply and looked around him. There, to the north, gleamed and bellowed the sea. About him in the air the dark-blue mountains were visible—Iuchtas, Selena, Psiltorítis. Above, in the sky, the stars flared. Like a wild horse he went in circles, ran back and forth. He reached the moat which girdles Megalokastro. Up above, on an isolated hill, some mud-huts lay apart. That was Meskinia, the lepers' village. By the sea there was another, lower hill, called "Seven Axes". From it, two hundred years ago, the Turks had stormed out and occupied Megalokastro. And seven of their axes were still embedded in the ground. Ahead, out to sea, far off and vaulted like a turtle, appeared the uninhabited island of Dia.

Behind him he heard women's voices and a soft rustling of silk. There emerged an aged Turk with a stoop, holding a huge, flaring lantern. Tittering and chattering, two Turkish ladies followed him, with black veils and open parasols. The night reeked of musk.

Captain Michales growled:

"All the devils are on my track." He turned his eyes away towards the sea, so as not to see the hanums. "All the devils—but they shan't succeed!"

Now he longed to get home. But he wished to see no one. They would hear his stride a long way away, he would cough. They would understand that and hide. That would be all right. Once he had kicked open his door, he would be quite alone. No wife, no children, no dogs: quite alone!

And then he would make his decision.

Bent under the lamp, his wife Katerina and his daughter Renió sat and waited. Behind them, at the window end of the long narrow divan which went the whole length of the wall, was the place where Captain Michales, and nobody else, sat. And when he was absent, a weighty shade sat there, and neither the wife nor the daughter dared go near it. They felt as if they touched his body, and shrank back with a shudder.

The mother was knitting a stocking. The lamplight fell obliquely upon thick, brown, straight hair, proud eyebrows and firm cheeks; it revealed a bitter mouth and a broad, obstinate chin. This woman had a strange charm—charm and strength and independence. As a girl she had been a real defiant captain's daughter. Since no son had been granted to her father, Captain Thrasybulos Ruvas, Katerina had enjoyed a son's masculine freedom and favour. But with her marriage she fell into the claws of a lion. In the first years she showed defiance and put up a resistance. But in time she bowed her head. He was Captain Michales. Who could fight him? Strength and independence slackened. She grew softer.

She knitted, knitted and thought. Her whole life was flowing past her like water. . . . Sometimes she looked up. High up around the four walls were ranged, in wide dark frames, all the heroes of 1821—wild beasts, iron-beards. In the middle, in front of one of the warriors, burned a small silver lamp. . . .

Katerina silently shook her head. Her whole life, in her father's house and in her husband's house, had been lived under arms. When she was still unmarried, during the 1866 rising, she too had put on a cartridge-belt, taken a musket and fought, to keep the Turks from trampling on her village. Even as a child she had cut up old books, which the monks had brought from the monasteries, and had made cartridge-cases out of them, with other girls. Katerina knew the smell of powder well, and loved it. Captain Michales was good, a real man, and she loved him. And yet a life like hers was hard on the woman, and somewhere inside her she was unhappy.

She left off her knitting and raised her eyes again. Above the divan hung a huge old lithograph: Samson, bound and being insulted by the Philistines. The unbowed young hero was to be seen in the middle, trussed hand and foot with nets, thongs and chains, and behind him a rabble of youths, tugging at him, hitting him and mocking him. And up above in the tower Delila was leaning out of a little latticed window—a malevolent, full-bosomed, scornfully grinning woman.

Katerina's glance slid from picture to picture, as though she saw them all for the first time, and she sighed. Then without a word she bent over the stocking again.

Her daughter, a plump, blooming thing of fifteen with her father's thick, bushy eyebrows and her mother's broad obstinate chin looked up from her knitting. She stroked the savage, lanky cat which lay in a ball at her feet.

"Why are you sighing, Mother?" she asked. "What are you thinking about?"

"What should I think about?" answered the mother. "My life. And you, you poor thing, who've fallen into the claws of a wild beast. I'm thinking, too, of the baby—I've lulled him to sleep again, so he shan't cry and rouse the evil spirits again in your father. Thrasáki is the only person he's well disposed to—because he's like him."

She looked at the coverlet and listened. "He's gone off to sleep," she said, "bless his heart!" And after a moment: "His father all over, the image of him! Have you seen the way he gets angry? The way he puckers his eyebrows? The way he hits his friends? The wild way he has of looking at women?"

Renió said nothing. She was afraid of her father, but she loved him and was proud of him. What he did seemed to her right, and if she had been a man she would have done the same. She too would have wanted to see only her son—the girls could just creep away as soon as they heard the door open and him coming. From the day when she had completed her twelfth year and her bosom was becoming full, her father had forbidden her to come into his sight. For three years he had not seen her. She always stayed in the kitchen or concealed herself upstairs in her little room, as long as he was in the house. The girl could scent his footsteps far off, and hid at once. The cat, too, scented him, and she too made off, even sooner, with her tail between her legs. It had to be so. Her father was right. Renió could not unravel the "why?" But she was sure her father was right.

Her mother too felt the same, but she was not reconciled to it. Her husband was the same as her father, and would do the same. How many years Captain Ruvas, her father, had let pass without

seeing her! She was already twenty, and still unmarried, when one
night the Turkish soldiers fell upon the old captain in his home.
He killed as many as he could, but there were too many. They
took him prisoner, brought him out to the yard, and were given
the order to hand him over to the Pacha in Megalokastro. And
so Katerina came out with her mother and saw him. His clothes
were all torn, there was blood all over him. He raised his hand:
"Farewell," he called to them, "and don't be sad, you women.
Bake the funeral cakes for me in the proper way. I'm dying for
freedom, don't cry! Look after yourself, Katerina! And bear a
man child—then you'll have a Thrasos, one like me!"

He was taken to Megalokastro and placed in front of the
Pacha's door, under the tall plane-tree. Then came a Turkish
barber, took his knife and beheaded him. Mustapha Pasha had a
tobacco-box made for himself out of the skull.

All this went through Katerina's head now, and she knitted
her stocking and sighed. She got on well with Captain Michales,
she had nothing to complain of. He was a palikare, honourable
and honoured, a serious man. He did not run after other women,
or play cards; he was not niggardly. He got drunk only twice a
year, to calm himself down. He was a man: no harm in that.
Others did worse, he merely got drunk. And yet, this year, life
was really too hard. The girl whom she had borne this time last
year—Captain Michales refused to look at her eyes.

"I won't see it, I won't hear it!" he shouted at her each morning,
as he opened the door to go to his shop. "Where the Devil did
she get those blue eyes?"

No one of his stock had blue eyes. And this infant had. Where
the Devil had she got them? As though some black sheep had
strayed into his house, as though his blood was defiled. Captain
Michales could not endure the thought.

The unfortunate mother swallowed her tears and said nothing.
What should she say to him? She possessed herself in patience,
knelt down in front of the great ikon of her house—the Archangel
Michael with the golden wings, the flaming sword and a new-born
soul which he held curled up in his hand like a trembling infant.
. . . She fell on her knees before him and implored him—was he not

the protector of her house?—to speak with her husband, to stride in upon his dream in the night and to chide him, that his heart might become a trifle gentler. . . .

The Captain stayed in his shop all day, she sent him his meal by the apprentice Charitos. And the mother let the baby shriek and cry and rocked it on her knees. But towards evening she gave it something to make it sleep, that it might not wake till next morning.

From the other room they heard little Thrasos, dreaming and crying out in his sleep. The mother laughed:

"Bless him, he takes no rest, even asleep!" she said. "He's always dreaming that he's out hunting and at the kill, or in command of soldiers and slaughtering Turks. . . . When he's grown up, he'll do what he now dreams. Like his father, like his grandfather. Ah, the woes of Crete have no end. . . ."

They sat silent. Renió looked out of the window into the night. A north wind was still moaning, one of the shutters was creaking. If you stopped before any remote house you would hear a young woman singing her little son a lullaby. Renió shut her eyes, listened, and her bosom trembled.

"He's late this evening," she said after a moment, to change the path of her thoughts.

"Nuri sent for him, they say. What does that dog want with him?"

Renió laughed.

"Father will lift him up again by his red belt and pitch him on to the roof!"

The mother shook her head:

"But then Nuri will lay hold of ten Christians to get his revenge. The woes of Crete have no end, I tell you."

"As long as Father's alive, I'm not afraid."

"I said the same about my father, but one night. . . ."

She stopped. Gossip—that was the name of the cat—jumped up on to Renió's lap and pricked its ears. The two women also listened. Renió hastily cleared away the twine, the needles, the scissors. The cat had already vanished into the kitchen.

"He's coming," said the girl. And now a dry cough was heard

outside the door. "There he is!" said the mother, and stood up.

"I'll go and warm up the supper," she said. "He'd prefer to come in and see no one. That's why he coughed."

The street door rattled. Captain Michales opened it, stepped over the threshold and pushed the bolt to. He crossed the yard, went in and looked round: no one. He unwound his head-band and pulled off his jacket—it was soaked with sweat. He sat down in his place at the corner of the settee, near the window giving on the garden. He took his handkerchief out of his belt and wiped the sweat from his forehead, neck and chest. He opened the window to get some air.

He heard the two women in the kitchen lighting the fire to warm his supper. For a moment he thought he heard the boy, and his blood at once warmed. He pricked up his ears and listened. Silence. He pulled out his tobacco-box and rolled a cigarette. He took the tinder-box and lit it. But his mouth was bitter, full of poison. He threw the cigarette out of the window.

His wife came in with the supper-dish. Captain Michales said, without raising his head: "I'm not hungry. Take the dish away!"

His wife said nothing. She took the dish away again and was gone.

A heavy silence weighed on the house. Captain Michales got up, pulled his jacket on again, wound the black head-band twice round his head and went to the door. He pondered his decision, remaining for a while standing. He cast a quick glance round him. The warriors of 1821 glimmered all around the walls with their weapons, their cartridge-belts and pistols. Their moustaches were twirled into needles, their hair fell to their shoulders. . . .

For a while Captain Michales forgot his own thoughts. He gazed at them and greeted each one. He was not very sure of their faces, of where they had fought, which manly deeds they had carried out, and from which region they came—Rumelia, the Morea, the Islands, or Crete. One thing only he knew for certain: that all these men had fought against the Turks, and that was enough for him. All the rest was schoolmaster's stuff.

He went out into the yard. The well, the vine-branches overhead, the flower-pots round about, all constricted him. He approached the small stable adjoining the yard. The white mare gleamed in the half-dark. She pricked up her ears, turned her head saw her master and whinnied with pleasure. Captain Michales went up to her. With wide-open hands he stroked her neck, belly and crupper. . . . A warm, cherished creature, always ready whenever he ordered. Proud and obedient. Never did she disturb his mood—she was with him always, like his own flesh, until death.

He stepped back from the mare's warm body and groped for his boots. He pulled them on over his knees, over his thighs, up to his loins, and his chest braced itself for the spring with strength from within.

He vaulted into the saddle.

"Charitos," he called.

His wife came out. "He's asleep," she said.

"Wake him up!"

Once more he rolled a cigarette, and waited without moving. He smoked, and no longer felt any poison in his mouth. He blew thick smoke through his nose, and waited tranquilly.

Charitos came out, rubbing sleepy eyes. Shaggy hair, long neck, bare feet—like a wild twelve-year-old goat. He was his nephew, son of his brother, Fanúrios the shepherd. He had come from his village, sent by his father, he said, to learn his letters. But Captain Michales thought book-learning stupid. "Do you want me to make you into a starving nobleman? Or a schoolmaster? Can't you see the misery of your uncle, the schoolmaster Tityros, whose life's made a burden by the school louts? You'll ruin your eyes, you poor youngster, wear glasses and get yourself laughed at. Stay in the shop and you'll grow big and your brain will get solid. Then I'll give you an advance, and you can set up a shop of your own and become a man." He said the same to Fanúrios. "Do as you please," he answered. "The flesh is yours, the bones are mine. Lick him into shape, make a man of him."

Captain Michales caught him by the nape and shook him:

"Go to the trough," he told him, "wash yourself and wake up. Then come and let me give you your orders."

Charitos went out to the yard, drew water from the well,

washed himself and with his nails combed out his unruly hair. He went back to his uncle.

"I'm awake," he said.

Captain Michales clapped him on the shoulder: "Go to the five houses you know," he commanded, "and knock on the doors till they open. Take a stone, and knock till they open. Understand?"

"I understand."

"Vendúsos's, Furógatos's, Kajabés's, Bertódulos's and the Téké[1] where Efendína lives."

"Efendína Horsedung?"

"And tell them: Greetings from my uncle, Captain Michales, and tomorrow, he says, is Saturday. On Sunday good and early will they please come to his house. Understand?"

"I understand."

"Go."

He called his wife:

"Kill three hens, and cook them. Clear the cellar, set out the big table, the benches and the glasses."

His wife wanted to speak and say to him: "It's the time of the fourteen fast-days, have you no fear of God?" But he held up his hand. His wife said nothing, went in, sighed.

"We're having another feast, curse my luck!" she said to Renió, who was standing at the sink, washing up. "We're to kill three hens, he says, and clear the cellar."

The stairs were heard creaking. Captain Michales was going up to bed.

"What's come over him? The six months aren't up," said Renió, but her heart leapt with pleasure. She liked it when the house was in confusion, when the dainties passed to and fro, when the men sat in the lower room and drank.

"Her heart has swelled up too soon," muttered the mother, "the evil spirit has woken up in her again."

She crossed herself: "I am a sinner, O God," she said, "I'm saying things I shouldn't, but I can't bear it any longer. He tramples on the great fast-times now. He no longer fears God!"

Her thoughts turned rebelliously to the Archangel Michael up

[1] A Moslem religious house (translator's note).

there in the ikon. How often have I confessed repentance before him, she reflected, how many prayers have I addressed to him? How often have I filled his lamp with oil, and lit candles to him? All in vain. Even HE is now on his side!

"Ah! If only I were a man!" she muttered. "By my soul's salvation, I'd do the same. I too would have five or six friends and, when my heart was smouldering, I'd invite them to the cellar, make them drunk, let them sing, play the lyre and dance, and so be lightened. That's what it is to be a man!"

II

HEAVY night, full of sultry spring air, lay over Megalokastro. Shortly before midnight the crisp breeze from the north had dropped, and now a warm, damp wind took its place, making the trees belly. It came from Arabia, crossed the Lybian Sea, swept the Plain of Mesara from Tybaki and Good Harbour to Saint Barbara, left behind it the famous vineyards of Archani, leapt over the fortress walls and, through the chinks of doors and windows, fell upon the women like a man and upon the men like a woman, not allowing them to sleep. Malignant April came to Crete like a thief in the night.

Even the Pacha of Megalokastro, a hard-bitten elder, started out of sleep, feeling hot and lascivious, and clapped his hands. Suleiman, his Arabian, appeared. "Open the window, Suleiman, or I shall faint. . . . What's the matter with me? What sort of a wind is this, Suleiman?"

"It comes from Arabia, Pacha Effendi, and it's hot. But it means no harm, have no fear. We Cretans call it Cucumber Wind, because it ripens the cucumbers."

"Cucumber wind, well I never! Go and call the slave—Fatmua —she's to be ready if I need her. And bring me a jug of water from the basin and a fan, to give me some cool air. . . . This Crete may yet be the death of me!"

Even the Metropolitan of Megalokastro, a god-fearing octogenarian with a wavy, snowy beard, was all on fire, threw off the bedclothes, got up and leaned against the window of the Bishop's Palace, to get some air. Profound stillness! The houses were slumbering in deep darkness. The old lemon-tree stood blossoming in the square before the church, and the world smelt sweet all around. Above, in the vault of Heaven, numberless lamps were burning before God's throne. With awe the Metropolitan lost himself in the starry sky, for a moment his heavy stately body hung high up in the night air, surrounded by God's deep stillness:

then he fell back to earth and found himself once more leaning on the window-sill. The Metropolitan crossed himself, the warm spring wind was banished, and now the old man felt his whole body cool and light. He went back to his bed, to sink sinless into God's enbrace.

Captain Michales tugged at the sheet and sat up angrily in bed. It must be after midnight. He grabbed at the jug which stood near him, pressed it to his lips and took two or three deep gulps, to wake up, to drive away the shameless dream which had been weighing on him all night. But it kept clinging to him like a woman and would not let him go. "Damn sleep!" he growled, "damnation take it. It opens the door to evil spirits, and in they come."

He sprang up, went downstairs barefoot and out into the yard, drew water from the well and plunged his head into the bucket to extinguish the blaze. But the sweet saliva remained in his mouth and the folly upon his eyelids. He went back and sat down again on his bed. He opened the window near it: pitch dark. He listened. Megalokastro was sunk in sleep, its breathing could not be heard. A strange, hot wind, reeking of earth and water, sighed, and the leaves of the trellised vine by the stable rustled.

Captain Michales leaned with his back against the wall and began to smoke. He did not mean to yield to sleep again. It was a Turkish creature, a mad one, and he did not trust it. He smoked and gazed up at the ikon of the Archangel Michael, protector of his race: Heaven's Fury with his quiver on his back. On the right of the picture, hanging in a row, shone the silver pistols he had inherited from his father, on its left the crown of honour from his wedding, made of waxen lemon-blossom. From the next room, for a moment, he heard his wife Katerina sigh. Above, in the rafters, a mouse was nibbling, and all of a sudden the cat rushed soundlessly and stealthily up the stairs. Then profound stillness.

Captain Michales smoked. Neither the agitation nor the shame had fled from his brain. He waited, breathing heavily, with his gaze fixed on the window, for day to come.

At the other end of Megalokastro, near New Gate, Barba[1]

[1] Uncle (translator's note).

Jannis was going home bathed in sweat, with his sleeves rolled up
and a flaring oil lamp in his hand. He stumbled along the narrow
alleys and cursed his fate. People would never allow him the one
thing left to him after the death of his wife: his sleep. From early
morning he toiled along bringing drink to the inhabitants of
Megalokastro—in winter the sweet barley-water "salepi" to warm
them, in summer sherbet to cool them. Did he ever take a nap?
One of the neighbour women, or a relative, would be taken with
child: "Quick, my poor Barba Jannis, deliver her!" Barba Jannis
indeed acted also as midwife. He had learnt it from his regretted
father, who was a blacksmith and delivered people's mares and
she-asses. Barba Jannis had transferred his father's art from the
mares and she-asses to women. Yesterday evening he had delivered
poor Pelagia, his niece. It had not been easy. Three hours the
pangs had lasted, but he had brought the child forth: a lusty,
pitch-black boy.

And now, while he talked to himself as he went along and
cursed his fate, he caught the sound of a horse's hooves behind
him. But no horse like those we know, which eat barley, neigh
and make dung. Barba Jannis recognised it by its hoof beats, which
were soft, as though muffled in cotton, and by the holy scent of
incense which pervaded the air . . . Barba Jannis understood. This
was not the first time. He pressed close to the wall, crossed himself, and waited. The light, onward sweeping tramp drew near,
the fragrance grew stronger.

"Remember me, O Lord," he muttered, "Saint Menas, my
saint, good evening."

He opened his eyes joyfully. In the roadway there appeared,
glittering out of the darkness, on a gold-harnessed bay and in a
silver coat of mail, with his red lance at rest upon his shoulder,
the grey-haired hero and protector of Megalokastro, Saint Menas.
This evening, as usual, he was riding on his rounds. At midnight,
when the town lay lost in sleep, Saint Menas used to step silently
out of his ikon-shrine, and struck out over the walls and through
the Greek quarter. Where anyone had left a door open, he closed
it. Where a light showed in a window and a Christian lay sick, he
paused and prayed God for a cure. Men's eyes had not the strength

to recognise him. Only the dogs wagged their tails. Yet there
were two men in the town who did see him: Barba Jannis, and
Efendína Horsedung, the *hodza* who was weak in the head. As
soon as Saint Menas had finished his round in the grey of dawn,
he went back into his ikon-shrine, and no one would have suspected what secret things had happened in the night if Murzuflos the
lamplighter had not noticed, as he cleaned the church in the morning, sweat on Saint Menas's horse.

Barba Jannis watched the saint out of sight in the darkness,
and crossed himself.

"Tonight I've seen him again. Great is his grace, my affairs will
go well," he murmured, and pulled out from his jacket a round
grape tart, which he had been given as payment for his trouble
over Pelagia. He began to eat it contentedly. Then he reached his
hovel and put out the lantern.

Captain Michales smoked and paced up and down. His mind
droned like a beetle and flew over all that he had seên and suffered,
loved and abhorred in his life—his village, his father, his house,
human beings, Turks and Christians. He gathered the whole of
Crete together, from Grabusa to Toplu Monastery, from cliff to
cliff, insurrection to insurrection. But nowhere would his thoughts
pause: they kept running on and sliding back to a shameless red
mouth, and would not leave it.

Captain Michales wandered up and down in agitation and cast
wild glances at the Archangel Michael, as though he were asking
him to abandon his inactive existence in the picture-shrine and
restore order. Then he turned round and glared through the
window at the sky, now not so utterly dark: "It's getting light
now," he called out to it, "it's getting light, and I'll be able to
see where I'm going!"

He strode down to the yard, plunged his head again into the
bucket and calmed himself down a little. Then he crouched on the
threshold and waited.

Like a bull Captain Michales fought with himself, but Nuri
Bey too spent the whole night rushing up and down in the men's
quarters, going out into the garden to get some air, coming in
again, smoking one cigarette after another, drinking one raki after

another and bellowing. He raised his eyes to the wooden lattice.
The Circassian had bolted it and would not let him come near her.

"I don't want you," she shouted at him through the keyhole.
"You've disgraced yourself, you're no use to me."

She too was unable to shut her eyes. Half-naked, she went to
the window, and stretched out her arms ardently towards the
Greek quarter. She saw in the dark the eyebrows, beard and
strong hands of Captain Michales, and whinnied like a mare.

"The woman's right, she's right," murmured Nuri Bey, and
began to weep. "I shall go to the dogs, like Efendína. The *giaour*
will call me too, whenever he gives a feast, to play the *karagios*
for him."

In the morning the Moor found his master in a heap on the
threshold, dead drunk. His moustache, chest and jacket were
covered with vomit, raki and cigarette-ash.

At the moment when Nuri Bey was thinking of him, Efendína
was asleep on his back and smiling happily. He had received the
news late in the evening. There was to be another feast, eight days
long! He would eat pigs' flesh and sausage—they would go down
like butter. He would get wine as well, and forget his misery for
eight days—yes, and to hell with it! To hell, too, with holiness—
it too! He shut his eyes, stroked his small, fair beard and fell
asleep. And behold, just when Nuri Bey thought of him, Efendína
had a dream: the door opened, and a pig came in, well grown,
well nourished, with a fez on its head like a Turk, and with a
knife slung round its neck like a talisman. As soon as Efendína
looked at it, it stood up on its hind legs and greeted him, Turkish
fashion. Then it took the knife and stuck it into its thick neck. It
rolled to the ground, and Efendína bent over it: it was freshly
roasted, wrapped in lemon leaves, and smelt lovely. Efendína
gave a shout of joy and woke up with his mouth full of saliva.

While below, on earth, the poor human beings were catching
fire and seeking to put it out in torments and embraces, the vault
of Heaven was turning, the stars going their way, and suddenly
behind the peaks of Lasithi the Morning Star sprang forth and
clanged in the wind. The thickly-feathered cock in Captain

Michales's yard opened his round eyes, took in what was happening in the sky, beat with his wings, puffed out his chest and began to crow. Up above, in the rich farmer Krasojórgis's yard, the lewd Cyprian ass snuffed the air, smelt the dainty, dew-fresh grass, and the Cretan she-ass raised her tail bolt upright and began to bray.

Megalokastro awoke. From one end of the street to the other, from Idomenea's well to Tulupanas's bakery, a stretching and a stirring began afresh in Captain Michales's quarter. First of all, the wife of Mastrapas untied her husband, that holy man, from the bedposts, to which she tied him fast every evening out of jealousy, to prevent him from going secretly downstairs and finding the fat maid, Anesina, with her cow breasts, in the kitchen below. She bound him fast every evening and only loosened the bands a little if he woke her up to make water. But even then the cord remained round his ankles and his wife held him fast, lest the prisoner should contrive to slip away.

Captain Polyxigis had been back some time from his nocturnal adventure, very tired and reeking of musk. Mr. Demetrós yawned by the side of his wife Penelope, who was again in a bad mood, had thrown the bedclothes aside and was muttering: "Why am I twenty-five? Sometimes my body catches fire, and sometimes it goes out and makes me feel like a tortoise." At that moment, at grey of dawn, it had caught fire. She sat up fiercely, cast a sideways glance of hate at the yawning Demetrós, and went out.

The sky became pale, the song-birds had woken up under the eaves and up above, in Krasojórgis's house, the blackbird was singing in its cage.

"Krasojórgis's wife is lucky," muttered Penelope, and sighed. "Krasojórgis is a rich farmer, but he's still got his strength and vigour. And doesn't disappoint his wife."

She listened. A rattling and grunting came from the house further up. Fat Krasojórgis was lying on his back and snoring. His moustache reeked of wine and onions, his breath came heavy as from a cellar. By him his young wife Katinitsa was still asleep— Barba Jannis's daughter, a merry, well-fed, drink-loving creature. She was smiling and cooing. For she was dreaming that she was

c

engaged and had gone for a walk in a walled garden, holding her young man by the hand. He put his arm round her shoulders. And it was not Krasojórgis, the fat fellow, but a slim, spruce palikare with a fine waxed moustache, long raven hair and silver pistols in his belt; his breath smelt of cinnamon. He was the image of that picture which all visitors to Captain Michales's house admired. It had, written under it, "Athanasios Diakos", the name of a well-known hero of the fight for freedom. Well, he put his arm round her shoulders; sleep lay over her like a tendril heavy with dark clusters, and she walked along in bliss, smiling and cooing like a dove.

But as the Devil would have it, Krasojórgis heard her out of his sleep, gave a start and opened his eyes.

"Hey, wife!" he called out, "what's all this simpering and cooing in the early morning? Is it a bit of gingerbread you're munching? Give me some of it!"

But she turned her back on him angrily:

"Don't disturb me, let me alone," she said, "I'm sleepy!" And she closed her eyes and tried to find her dream young man again.

From Tulupanas's bakery rose cloud on cloud of the first, thick, pale blue smoke. The old baker, always gloomy and taciturn, was awake and beginning work all alone in his bakehouse, in order to forget his worries. But how could he forget? He had a dear and only son, a lad of twenty, fair-haired and handsome, whom he had always clothed and looked after devotedly. Suddenly, three years ago, the boy had begun to have swellings, his face had become covered with boils, his finger-tips had rotted, his nails fallen off. And now already his lips were beginning to fester. Father and mother were unwilling to take him to Meskinia, to the lepers' place. How could they part from their son, since they had no other? They kept him shut up in his room, that no man's eyes might see him. How then could old Tulupanas any longer sleep happily, and why should he open his mouth to speak? He bent down to the kneading, pushed the dough into the oven, pulled out the baked bread, made his round of the streets selling ring-loaves and spinach-pastries, wore himself out with work, to forget. But how could he forget? Every morning, when he went in to see his only son, he was forced to see how the rot progressed.

Old Tulupanas worked at the oven and sighed. As he looked up for a moment and saw a light still burning in the window up above, he shook his head and sighed: "Poor Frenchwoman!" he muttered, "you too are suffering, you too are suffering under your fate. . . . No, the hearts of men find no rest."

And in fact all night long the light had not been put out, the poor Frenchwoman had not closed an eye. She coughed, spat, groaned. Kasapákis, the doctor, had brought her back with him from Paris as his wife and transplanted her to this nest of Turks at the end of the world. At first she had sighed, later she had coughed, and now in the end she was spitting blood. And the doctor, it was said, would have none of her now, and was carrying on with his maid, a filly from Arkalochóri. "Where's the railway you said ran past our house?" the Frenchwoman had wailed during the first weeks. "That's what you said in Paris." And the fat doctor laughed. "In Megalokastro we call the donkeys our railway," he answered.

Captain Michales crouched, limp and silent, in the middle of his yard, and waited for the sky once more to decide to get light. When he heard his cock, he raised his eyes. The sky was changing to a bright glow. He sprang up, strode into his room, put on his clothes in haste, wound his wide sash tightly several times round his body, thrust the black-handled thing into it and took the little bottle of oil which hung before the icon's shrine. He filled the little lamp—it was already beginning to flicker, and gazed at the Archangel Michael, his Chief.

"I'm going," he said to him. "What we have to say to one another we've said. So I'm going. Watch over the house!"

He went down to the yard, opened the street door, saddled the mare, mounted and rode to the hospital. It was light. The soldiers took the keys and made ready to open the four fortress gates. The houses were still shut, but some hearths were smoking. Barba Jannis was already out and about, already crying up, at this early hour, his hot, thick barley-water liberally laced with pepper. Captain Michales spurred his mare on, rode quickly past the big plane-tree, eater of Christians, turned off to the market-place, reached the Three Vaults and stopped for a moment, looking round. The whole arc of mountains glowed rose-red: in front of him Angry Mountain, a naked precipice, behind him Psilorítis, the great lord, serene, with his snowy head. On his right that marble dragon standing on its head, Iuchtas. Over there, the sea shimmered pale blue, flecked here and there lightly with blue-green foam. The Maltese ships' boats, black with red sails, had already begun their work on the sea. The sun rose up out of the waves in glowing mist. The mare turned, saw the sun, her eyes sparkled, she threw back her neck and whinnied to greet it.

The trumpets pealed, the Turkish flag went up on the flagpole and, grinding, the iron fortress-gate opened. The peasants, who had been waiting outside since the first grey of dawn, all rushed in at once, treading on each other's feet. Their asses and mules were laden with wood and charcoal, with bottles of wine and oil, with baskets of vegetables and fruit, and with brass jars of honey. To get into the fortress they had to pass through the dark tunnel which traversed the whole thickness of the Venetian walls. Inside there, under the stone vaulting, voices and curses, neighing and tramping of beasts and men clashed their echoes. The whole dark, subterranean gullet clanged again with the din.

Captain Michales forced a way through the raving horde, came out among the fields and rode down to the coast. Megalokastro lay behind him, and he took the beach path towards Cruel Mountain and past the Red Hills. To his right the dark green land gave forth its fragrance, to his left the sea. The sun flew low and hung like a gold talisman on the breast of the town.

"In the name of Christ and of the Archangel Michael," muttered Captain Michales, turned to the East, and crossed himself.

Megalokastro had filled itself with sun. First the minarets seized upon it, then the light blue cupola of Saint Menas's and the roofs of the houses. Soon it went lower and hung there in the damp alleys. The young girls opened their windows to it, and in it came, and the old grey women went into the yards to warm themselves. They crossed themselves and praised the Lord that March, that month accursed of God, which plagues the aged with sudden cold, was over. Now their limbs would sun themselves. Welcome April, and Saint George.

Through all the fortress-gates the Cretan donkeys streamed in, quite early; nimble and always gay, they raised their tails and brayed at the inhabitants to announce the advent of spring.

Penelope went back into her yard; she yawned so wide that her bones creaked. Middle-aged, with breasts and haunches of double girth, she ate well and had a good digestion. She washed and scrubbed her husband Mr. Demetrós, fed and groomed him like a horse, and every evening tried hard to animate him. She had no children and loved cats, canaries and spring meadows. This morning early she had strange pins and needles in her back, and if she had had a tail like an animal, she would have raised it high and brayed, to announce the Spring to Katerina, to the wives of Krasojórgis and Mastrapas, to the doctor's wife and all the neighbours. Why were they still lying in bed? They ought to get up and let the sun touch them, to make them all bray together and roll in the fields! Spring has come! To-day her four walls could not contain her. She cooked quickly and sent out the little maid to knock at the door of Katerina, the Captain's wife, opposite and say: "Greetings from my mistress Penelope, Demetrós's wife, and if you would like, she says, we're taking our meal and going out to the fields to eat it there. Spring has come, she says." But how could the Captain's wife leave her house, since it must be cleared to let the five boon-companions tramp in, early next morning? She was preparing the hens as dainties for the feast— one to be boiled, another stuffed with sweet corn, the third roast on the spit.

"We can't. Tell your mistress we can't to-day, and please will she excuse us. But if she would like to step round here this afternoon with her sewing things, the neighbours are coming too, and so is Ali Agha to amuse us. Captain Michales will be absent all day to-day. She need have no fear."

Penelope frowned and sent the little maid to the other neighbours: to Mastrapas's wife, to Krasojórgis's wife, to Polyxigis's sister. But the first was expecting, so she said, Manóles, the pope, who was to exorcise the house; the second, so she said, had a headache and giddiness, and Polyxigis's sister was doing the baking betimes for supper: her feet had swollen and she could not move.

"Perish the lot of you! Addled idiots!" growled Penelope, enraged. "Don't you ever open your peep-holes to look out? Or would that make you feel naked? Come, Marulio, go to the doctor's wife, Massella: she can understand, even if she is French, what spring is. She'll come!" Marcelle, not Massella, was her name, but Penelope called her Massella. Penelope made fun of her because she talked broken Greek a⌐⌐ h⌐⌐d many big-town airs. "Parisia," according to her, was bigger than Megalokastro, and a great river flowed between its streets; also the women there went to the coffee-houses, talked boldly with the men and showed their feet up to the ankles. Those were fairy-tales, certainly, but the heretical Frenchwoman had a pretty way of telling them and you could see she believed them herself. "I've often noticed her eyes go dim. And what she has to put up with from that impudent husband of hers, with his airs and graces—for shame! To Hell with him! He has no shame, carrying on with a girl from Arkalochóri. . . . The poor woman must come out into the country. We'll go as far as Saint Irene of the Four Springs. That'll wear her out."

But the little maid came back with cast-down face: "She can't she says, she can't. She's coughed all night and had no sleep. Another day. And will you excuse her?"

Penelope swore. In her mind she ran through the whole neighbourhood. Should she—God forbid!—invite Kolyvas's wife? Her husband's a grave-digger, and she herself's a hypochondriac and sees ghosts. All the dead flutter past her pillow. Serves her right. Why does her husband strip them of their clothes and dress his wife and his own bag of bones in them?—and the dead are left naked in the damp of the earth and are angry and quite right too No, she wouldn't have Kolyvas's wife. Should she send again to Archondula, that bitter nut, to ask her to be so kind as to go out with Penelope the grocer's wife? Her father, so they said, had been a dragoman in Constantinople and played cards with the

Patriarch; now that he was dead, she received a bag of gold pounds
from the Patriarchate every year, and ate caviare by the spoonful!
No, other people's food was not good enough for her! The visits
of the Metropolitan and the Pacha were not good enough for
her! When she was still young, she found that one man reeked
and another stank, the conceited creature! Let her now stew in
her own juice, left sitting there on the trunk with her trousseau.
Serves her right! Serves her brother right too, the deaf-mute. Sins
of the fathers. . . . For once a Christian had been brought to Constantinople to be hanged, because he was supposed to have killed
a Turk. The dragoman—curses on his bones!—knew the truth:
the murderer was not the Christian but someone else, a Bey. But
would anything make that blackguard of a dragoman open his
mouth to speak? He was afraid and remained dumb. So his only
son too became dumb. No, you're not going out with Miss
Archondula, no, not even if she were willing.

Her mind swept away from the snob's grand house and wandered further. "Should I ask Vangelio? But she won't come either,
because she's in such a hurry. She's getting her trousseau ready
and is set on marrying Tityros, the schoolmaster, at Easter. . . .
Why the Devil has the unfortunate girl chosen *him*? That yellow
head, that half-helping with glasses? Did I hear it said she loves
him? But there's a curse on her, poor thing. Her brother, the
pretty ne'er-do-well with the gold watch, has frittered all her
money away on finery and debauchery."

After long searching up and down, Penelope came to a decision.
She climbed on to the trough, cut a bunch of leaves from the
trellis, went into the kitchen, wrapped the food in the vine-leaves,
filled a basket with some bread, some olives, a couple of oranges,
a small bottle of wine, a spirit-lamp, coffee, sugar, a knife and fork
and a cloth, and came out into the yard.

"Come with me, Marulio," she said to her little servant-girl.

She shut the street door and trotted down to the harbour.
Thick-set and broad-shouldered, she suggested, with her rocking
gait, certain fat-tailed sheep recently imported into Crete from
Asia Minor. The poor woman was embarrassed, for she could
feel how her bottom wagged. But what could she do about it?

Even those dumplings are God's work, she said, and felt consoled. "Luckily for me my legs aren't swollen like Miss Chrysánthe's, Polyxigis's sister. I can still get about, God be thanked, and I order that pig of mine about. I manage him, he doesn't manage me. I'm a match for ten girls, ten lads can't put me down, I'm rightly called the Strong Woman."

After much pitching and tossing she crossed Broad Street. It was swarming with porters, artisans, farmers. What a shouting and squabbling! What great coarse asses' throats these Kastrians have, thought Penelope, pursing her lips. For she was from Rethymno and proud of it. Kanea for weapons, Rethymno for books, Megalokastro for mugs. Every evening, scarcely were they done with their work when they were all lolling in the taverns and swilling away, chewing dried fish and gobbets off the spit, and reeking of wine, ouzo and meat. The Rethymniots, on the contrary, with their slow, dignified gait, deep bows and lordly ceremony! Only her Demetrós was different from all the rest of Megalokastro, but he, bless him, was half a corpse! Why couldn't she bring him to life at night? "All my efforts in vain. . . . Yes, if he were only from Rethymno. . . ."

She sighed. She went on and was now near the harbour. "He will be sitting there as usual, flapping his fly-whisk," she thought. "Yes, he can do that all right."

But Demetrós had got tired of flapping his fly-whisk some time ago and was now immersed in a large volume in which he recorded in two kinds of ink—red for the meat, blue for the rest—the food he consumed each day. He was deep in study, reading the dishes and savouring them till his mouth filled with spittle. . . . He had got as far as the last few days, and was spelling them out slowly, relishingly, as though chewing: The Year 1889, March 20th: Fresh broad beans with artichokes and green onions. Lots of oil. Well blended. March 21st: Baked cucumbers with garlic. Burnt by that wretched Tulupanas."

A little girl came into the entrance of the shop:

"Mr. Demetrós, sir, Christofákas's wife has sent me. You're to give me six ounces of Chios mastic for cooking."

"I see what you want, my child, I see. But it's there, high up!"

And he drawled the words out as long as he could, to show that the mastic was somewhere on the peak of the world.

The girl departed, and Mr. Demetrós plunged again into his studies. "March 25th, the Annunciation: Boiled cod with lemon, cod with parsley, roast cod with garlic, cucumber salad. Very tasty."

But now he had had enough of his studies too. He took up the fly-whisk again and sighed: "I, the son of the famous Captain Leanbottom, what have I come to? My grandfather owned a warship and set the Turkish frigates on fire. My father owned a gun and killed Turks. And I've got a fly-whisk and kill flies. Curse this face of mine!" he muttered, and slapped his good-natured face with his open hand. And as his warrior father came into his mind, the shop became too small for him. He stretched out his arms and touched the walls to right and left. Like a Samson he wanted to burst the walls, so as to make the world wide, so that he, Mr. Demetrós Leanbottom, should not feel confined.

Just as the moment when he was vowing to himself to burst the walls asunder, the shop darkened. On the threshold towered Penelope, tall and round and fat and out of breath. As Mr. Demetrós saw her, his face grew troubled. "What the Devil does she want from me now? Isn't the night enough? Where does she get the energy, the shameless woman? Has someone put petroleum in her buttocks? Ah! The respectable women of Rethymno!"

"Welcome!" he said aloud, and hastily opened the book.

"Up you get, Demetrós," his wife called. "Up you get! We're going out into the country together! Don't moulder away, give those bones of yours a chance to warm up, bless you! Here you are, stuck in a swamp like a frog. Pull yourself together! I've brought our meal with me. Your favourite dish. . . ."

She bent down and whispered into his ear:

"Aubergines wrapped in vine-leaves, with lots of pepper. . . . You'll see how good they taste out in the country!"

Mr. Demetrós shuddered:

"I'm not coming," he shouted, "I'm not coming," and clung to his bench.

c*

"Come, Demetrós, poppet, come! As a favour, I promise not to scold you."

But he flapped hard with the fly-whisk, as if Penelope were a fly, a blue-bottle, and he wanted to chase her out of the shop.

"I'm not coming!" he shouted again, "I've got lots of work to do to-day, can't you see? I'm doing accounts. What I owe, what I'm owed, so as to see how we stand. Go alone, there's an angel."

"Let's be off, Marulio," said Penelope, taking her little maid by the scruff of the neck. "I'll take you as my neighbour and husband! Let's be off, we'll have our meal together out in the sun." And she turned her towering back on Mr. Demetrós and retired.

"Curse my fate," she muttered, striding along. "I ought to have taken a palikare for husband, a guzzler and swiller and wencher who'd have begotten a dozen children on me ere I was tame. And I should have lived in Rethymno, where the best people live, and not here with the Kastrians—the asses!"

She muttered to herself and moved on, raging. She was already hungry. She saw the sun getting higher, and her nostrils quivered —she could smell the fresh grass. She was still holding the diminutive Marulio by the scruff and pulling her powerfully along. The girl dragged along, gasping, with the loaded basket. She kept losing her trodden-down slippers; then she took them off and laid them on top of the vegetables. After that she trotted on, barefooted, beside her mistress.

By Saint Menas's church Penelope stopped. She crossed herself: "Dear Saint Menas," she murmured, "you know what I want, help me!"

Shrieks and laughter rang out. The alley filled with children. The bell had rung, and they were rushing to school. Penelope's heart leapt. She remained where she was, to admire the children. "Ah!" she said, "if only the lot were mine! And not all by Demetrós, God forgive me!"

In an instant her eyes went dim, and before her mind there passed the young men she had seen in the streets and in the villages and in dreams, "God forgive me," she said to herself, "but I think Barba Janins's wife, with her thousands of men, is right. How many men has she had children by! God alone knows—*and* by whom she had my neighbour Katinitsa, Krasojórgis's wife! And Barba Jannis did try to be hard of hearing, but a flea got into his ear all the same. He saw his horns, groped for them and felt them. But what was he to do? Once only, when he was ill, he called his wife. 'Ah, wife,' he said, 'in God's name, in Whom you believe, tell me the truth. Are all the children we've got mine?' But his wife said nothing. 'Tell me the truth, wife. You can see I'm dying. What are you afraid of?' 'And suppose you don't die?' the creature answered, 'suppose you don't die?' "

Penelope laughed as she remembered, and drew to one side to let the schoolchildren by. She looked at little Thrasos, the son of her neighbour the Captain's wife.

"Thrasáki, Thrasáki!" she called, and looked in the basket for an orange to give him.

But how could Thrasáki hear her? He had his arms round the shoulders of his two neighbours, on his right Manolios, Mastrapas's son, on his left Andrikos, Krasojórgis's son. They were running, chattering, laughing. They were never tired of going over, again and again, how yesterday they had strewn small shot about the threshold of the school door at the moment when Tityros had turned his back and was preparing to teach them the song they were to sing on next Sunday's outing: "Spring has come, the flowers are there again. . . ." They all began bawling, and Tityros too found it fun: he raised his birch and said: "Children, let's go out into the yard. The lot of us. And sing out there. Then the day after tomorrow, when we're outside the Three Vaults, we shan't disgrace ourselves. . . . Forward!"

He led the way, with his head in the air, but as he set foot stoutly on the threshold he slid and fell to the ground like a jar. And his glasses were smashed to bits.

"Didn't he break any bones as well?" asked Andrikos, worried lest they should be whole.

But Thrasáki reassured him: "He did, I tell you, he did. Didn't you hear the crack? That was his bones."

"And did you hear the way he yelled 'Oh!' " said Manolios, rubbing his hands contentedly. "He must have broken his hip— he couldn't get up. He yelled 'oh! oh!' and groped for his glasses."

"That means we're shot of the outing and can do what we planned. Agreed?"

"Agreed!" cried his two companions. A dog came by. They picked up stones and chased him away.

By the téké, next door to Saint Menas's, they heard a shrieking and a brawling. They stopped.

"Hamidé Mula is beating Efendína," said Thrasáki. "Let's wait. Might see some fun."

They stood on tiptoe, to see through the grille in the wall. The big weed-grown yard stretched before them, and in the middle was the Saint's tomb, decked with strips of coloured stuffs. Near the tomb the old barefooted mother, with her hair coming down and her nose standing out like a spear-point, was holding her son by the neck with one hand and in the other a forked stick. She threatened him:

"Have you no fear of God?" she screamed. "You'd go again to the house of those Greeks, where they stuff you with swine's flesh and make you drunk with wine and defile you. I'll lock you in, you damned blockhead, I'll beat you senseless. You shan't go!"

Efendína made a movement to escape from his mother's claws. He shrieked as though she were trying to murder him.

"You shan't go," she screamed, and shook him. "You shan't go! Have you forgotten the shame you bring on yourself every time you do go? When you're sober once more, you're sorry and you howl. Then you tear off your cap, and your scab shows. And you smear it with horsedung and run out on to the streets and bray like an ass. . . . And the Greeks pelt you with lemon-peel and give you a woman's name. They call you Efendína—Efendína Horsedung! Aren't you ashamed, in front of this Saint, your grandfather?"

So she abused him shrilly, and pointed at the tomb with its bright-coloured shreds.

"Day and night I think of him!" shouted Efendína, and he raised his hands high. "I swear it, day and night I think of him!"

"Then why do you defile yourself?"

"Don't you want me to become a saint? A saint, like my grandfather? How the Devil do you expect me to become a saint if I don't sin? If I don't fall into sin, shall I repent? Shall I weep? Cry to God? Show my scab to men? No! How then can I become a saint?"

Hamidé Mula stood with open mouth. Now she stared at her son, now at the tomb, and fell silent. Perhaps her idiot of a son was right. Perhaps it was true, what she had heard about the old man, the Saint, Efendína's grandfather. He had spent his whole life getting ripe for the halter and the stake, and only when he shrivelled up and could take no more wine, meat and women had he fallen into saintliness. He climbed up the minaret of Aja Katerina and would neither come down nor eat and drink. He wept, struck himself and cried to God. He bellowed for seven days and nights, and then he gave a mighty cry, so that the hair of the people of Megalokastro stood on end and the ravens flew up into the sky. God had pity on him and sent him food to prevent him dying. . . . Was that perhaps her son's way, too—to become a saint?

Hamidé Mula felt bewildered. She did not know whether to beat her darling or to squat down in the corner of their yard and sun herself, for she was shivering. She laid down the forked stick near the tomb and relaxed her nails from Efendína's neck. She raised her fist and shook it at him.

"There! Devil take you, do as you wish. Eat, drink, dance about. And then rub horsedung over your scab!"

So saying she flung herself, full of anxiety, back into the sunshine in the corner of the yard.

"A pity," said Andrikos, "she hasn't sliced him up."

"Just wait, my father will see to that tomorrow," said Thrasáki. He gave his friend a nudge. "Come," he said, "tomorrow at sundown the thing's going to be done. I'm inviting you. Bring your catapults too. I'm bringing a rope."

"I'll bring a stick," said Andrikos.

"I'll bring a stake," said Manolios.

"We're letting Nikola, Furogatos's son, come in as well. He's got strong hands."

"But what happens if her father sees us?" asked Manolios, and stood still.

"Pff. . . . What's it matter if he does see us," said Thrasáki contemptuously. "Is he able to beat anyone? He's not a Cretan, he's from Syra."

"But shall we be able to hold her up?" said Andrikos. "She weighs a ton. Suppose she shrieks?"

Thrasáki frowned. "Listen, Andrikos," he said, "these affairs need a stout heart. Haven't you got one? If not, get out, and I'll find someone else."

"Me?" said Andrikos, injured. "My heart's like a mountain."

"We shall see tomorrow," said Thrasáki, and ran faster. They were nearing the school. "Be quiet now," ordered Thrasáki. "Don't let a word out, or it'll be the worse for you! Tomorrow my father will be drunk, and I'm free. And you'll slope off. Say it's for the evening service. Then your mother'll give you a copper to light a candle. We'll buy roast peas with it."

"And take them home to her," suggested Manolios.

"Idiot, why should we take them home to her?" shouted Thrasáki. "We eat them."

Meanwhile Captain Michales was riding past Cruel Mountain. His head-band was down to his eyebrows. To his left foamed the sea, to his right was rock, iron-bearing rock, the wild, bare mountain. An accursed mountain. Passing it, a Christian makes the sign of the cross and abuses Turkey. For in whatever hole, whatever cranny of it you search, you find the bones of slaughtered Christians.

Captain Michales crossed himself. Among those cliffs, ten years ago, a brother of his, Christofés, had been killed with both his sons. Many days afterwards people had followed the ravens and found in a gully the three corpses, piled on one another. Their tongues were missing. For as they rode by, gaily in the evening, they had been singing the Moscow Song. That was the day of Thrasáki's christening, and the brothers and nephews were on their way home, drunk and pleased with life. They waved at the sea's horizon and called on the Muscovites to come. The Turks had laid wait for them, fell on them from an ambush, and cut out their tongues.

"Forsaken Crete!" Captain Michales muttered, and spurred his mare. "For how many generations have you cried out, unlucky land, and who has heard you? Even God needs a threat for His miracle. The mighty ones of the earth want a good threatening. Grasp your gun once more, you fool: that will be your Muscovite. There is no other!"

He sighed and rode, with troubled eyes, slowly away from the sea into the plain, and from the plain into the mountains. His nostrils dilated: the Cretan precipices were fragrant with thyme and sage.

"How beautiful Crete is," he murmured, "how beautiful! Ah! If only I were an eagle, to admire the whole of Crete from an airy height!"

And truly an eagle would see beauties to admire in Crete. The way its close-knit body rose and poised, sun-browned, the way its coasts gleamed, now with white sand, now with blood-red, sheer promontories. He must needs rejoice over the villages, the big farms, the monasteries, and the little churches glittering against the iron-dark rock or planted deep in the soil. And over her three tormented, Turk-oppressed towns with their Venetian walls and their turkified churches: Kanea, Rethymno and Megalo-kastro.

God too, higher than the eagle, must have the same view, if He had not forgotten Crete, generations and generations ago, and delivered her, soul and all, into the hands of the Turks.

No, without the soul. For the Cretans resisted, boiled with rage and refused to place their seal under God's seal. It was injustice! They raised their heads to Heaven and shouted "Injustice!" and bestirred themselves like good Christians to put right this intoler-able divine injustice. God too is a fighter, they reflected, He must be waging war somewhere else, on some other star, against other Turks. We will call Him, till He hears us.

There are peoples and human beings who call to God with prayers and tears or a disciplined, reasonable self-control—or even curse Him. The Cretans called to Him with guns. They stood before God's door and let off rifle shots to make Him hear. "Insurrection!" bellowed the Sultan, when he first heard the shooting, and in raving fury sent Pachas, soldiers and gangs. "Insolence!" cried the Franks, and let loose their warships against the tiny barks that fought, braving death, between Europe, Asia and Africa. "Be patient, be reasonable, don't drag me into bloodshed!" wailed Hellas, the beggar-mother, shuddering. "Freedom or death!" answered the Cretans, and made a din before God's door.

At first this happened only once in a generation, but later, after the great rising of 1821, the clamour grew hotter, indignation quickened its step. Crete's heart swallowed for a time its contempt, its sense of injustice, its suffering, until it swelled and at length overflowed. It burst out against the dreadful beast, whose claws held it prisoner. It consumed its own flesh, burned its villages, trampled down its olive-groves and vineyards, piled the corpses on its naked plains as high as God's threshold. And fell back, bleeding from a thousand wounds, into the beast's claws. It exploded in 1866, the time of Arkadi, rose again in 1878, and fell to earth again. It began afresh to swallow injustice and misery, and now, at the beginning of the year 1889, the heart of Crete was again near to overflowing. In the villages the Christians were making wry faces, clenching their fists and gazing northwards towards Greece and, further afield, towards Moscow. Their grandfathers were awake in them and making them itch. They could no longer endure staying in their homes, in their villages, at rest. They were losing their sleep. Every Sunday they would call for the schoolmaster, the pope or the lyre-player: he must tell them or sing them of the woes of Crete, to make their rage rise and come to a head. Always at the onset of spring, as the spring fields began to warm and surge, and the superfluous force of life stoked them up, the hearts of the Cretans grew wild. The Turks knew it and sent orders—and soldiers—to hold them in.

Captain Michales's heart swelled, it could bear the misery of Crete no longer. He drove the spurs into the mare's belly and rode past Cruel Mountain. He came to the red soil, then took the shore way. He felt hungry and dismounted at the widow's inn. The owner came—a gay, capable widow, rank and fat. She smelt cool, of onions and caroway seeds. Captain Michales looked past her:

he did not like coquettish women, waggers of buttocks. He stared
at the road before him and at the sea.

"Welcome, Captain Michales! We don't see you often!" said the
widow, and winked at him artfully. "If you're not fasting, I've
hare stewed with fresh onions and caroway seeds."

She bent down to get him a dismounting-stool, and the cleft
of her hospitable bosom was visible, downy and cool.

"You should eat meat, Captain Michales," she said, giving him
another wink. "You're on a journey, and it's no sin."

But Captain Michales was angry. He hated the woman and the
food and his own hunger.

"I won't have anything," he said, "I'm not hungry!" He leapt
on to the mare again and rode further.

He left the mountains and came out on to the plain. Peaceful,
gracious green; the hum of bees; the twittering of birds, come
trustingly back to their Cretan nests of the year before. To-day,
on the 1st April, Crete was sparkling—with joy, surely—under
the soft spring sunshine. . . . But Captain Michales saw nothing.
He hurried forward. Where was he going? Why had he started off
this morning at grey of dawn? Whom was he hunting? Who was
hunting him? A cloud covered his senses. The sunlit coast was
overcast, the path rolled onwards like a river, up there the Lasithi
mountains steamed and wavered like smoke. Two hefty peasants,
who passed him on their asses, raised their hands to their chests
and greeted him: "Long life to you, Captain Michales!" But he
made no reply to their gaze and greeting. His mind swept to
Nuri's konak, it slunk around it and surveyed the high walls like
a thief. He was calculating how and where he could spring over
them and get in. . . . But then his mind became troubled, and he
could not think what the next move was to be, once he had
jumped down and penetrated into the garden.

Sweat broke out on his brow: he thrust his hand into his sash
and fingered the knife-hilt.

"The dog's right," he muttered, "one or other of us is one too
many."

And as he gripped the knife and in spirit climbed over the high
wall, slid down into the garden among the pots of flowers where

the lamp with the red and green glass still burned, he heard above him, behind the wooden lattice, a laugh. At once the sweat poured in heavy drops from his brow, over his neck, and from his shoulders. A light burst upon him, and he realised: he was not breaking into that house to kill! A demon had got into him, a new, unsummoned one that had nothing in common with the demons of his stock. This one was scornful, shameless, fragrant with musk, and its face was—oh shame!—a woman's face.

"Aren't you ashamed, Captain Michales?" he groaned, "what have you come to?"

He saw his forefathers raising their tomb-stones to curse him. He shrank back and clenched his fist. "Hey, grandfathers, stay in your holes in the earth! I'm alive, I'm in command, don't shout!"

He wiped his brow with his head-band and pulled himself together again. The mountains stood firm once more, the coast glittered, under his feet the river straightened out and became a road again. Now once more he remembered why he had ridden out to the Hospital Gate and where he was bound for. He had given the Bey his word yesterday and must keep it. He meant to go and see his brother Manúsakas at Ai-Janni.

To this small village, wide with gardens, an hour from the large village, Petrokéfalo, where his family came from, fate had blown his brother Manúsakas like a grain of seed, some years ago. He had taken root there and flourished. Now, as an oak its branches and twigs, he had children and grandchildren sprouting all over the village and drew nourishment from the soil.

One unforgettable day—it was September 14th in the year 1866 —Manúsakas, sweeping along with his palikares in search of Turks, stormed into Ai-Janni and found there, in a peasant's house, a young woman with her hair down, keening. They had just slain her husband on the threshold. She was newly married and she was cursing God: He is unjust, He is no Christian, He loves the Turks. Manúsakas, who was forty and had lost his wife two years before, gazed at the young widow, and his heart was lost. He left his palikares to rest and feed in the yard, and himself went into the house, a powder-blackened, long-haired savage. When the

widow saw him, she was terrified. "Holy God!" she shrieked, and
hid her face in her lap.

But he did his best to look gentle and approached her:

"Weep, woman," he said, "weep yourself out and lighten your
heart. I too had a wife, and those dogs of Turks killed her. I too
yelled and shed tears and lightened my heart."

He squatted down close by her; he watched how she struck
herself and howled; he waited. He stared at her and his heart
shuddered with longing. Ah, if only he could seize her and clasp
her in his arms! So, with her neck bare, hot and convulsed as she
was with the keening—never had Manúsakas felt such a yearning
for a woman. He laid a hand warily and softly on her shoulder.

"That's enough," he said to her tenderly, "that's enough.
You'll destroy those eyes of yours, woman. Aren't you sorry for
them? Lovelier ones, by my soul, the world never brought forth.
And remember, I've been about the world—I, Captain Manúsakas, now kneeling before you. I won't boast to you, but you
can ask anywhere from Kissamos to Sitia, and they'll tell you
who I am."

He fell silent. He was afraid a word too many might escape
him and the widow be terrified again. But he could not bear it. He
drew still closer, a little, and bent over her and began to tell, in a
soft sing-song voice, of the things he had seen and suffered, how
many widows and orphans were left in the same anguish, how
many tears had been shed, from one end of Crete to the other—a
stream. These were the trials of Crete. And whoever was born a
Cretan had to know them and must not flinch.

Slowly the widow raised her head. She longed to hear of the
trials and sufferings of the world, and it consoled her. She wiped
her eyes, cleared her throat, and began in turn to tell how they
had killed her husband; and raising her hand she pointed at the
blood, which was still on the threshold. She meant never to wash
it off, she said, so as to have it before her eyes, think of it and
bewail it.

And he touched her gently, now on the shoulder, now on her
hair, now on her knee—very gently, and said to her:

"You're right, woman. I too did the same for my dear one.

They murdered her in my yard, as revenge, because she had a leader for her husband. The yard was full of blood, but the rain came and washed the blood away. The stones were again white."

He sighed and bent over the widow:

"The soul of man, too, is like stone, woman. Slowly, slowly, the blood will be washed away—all will be forgotten."

And as he saw that the woman grew angry at such words, he took his warm cloak, which reeked of powder, and placed it round her shoulders.

"It's turned cold," he said. "Don't catch cold."

And she looked, and felt ashamed as though a man had placed himself on top of her. She wanted to throw off the cloak, but she was afraid to hurt him. She bent forward and felt, at first with shuddering, but gradually with sweet agitation, a warm male smell arise from the woollen cloth and stealthily penetrate her body. From her shoulders to her back, her thighs, her flesh. . . . She thought of her husband, his first embraces, his arms, and how softly and supplicatingly they had insinuated into her body on the first night. . . . She grew warm under the cloak and found a little comfort. She felt the man's breath upon her, panting violently. A sweet sympathy overcame her. She turned to him.

"I can't get you anything to eat," she said, "and you must be hungry. You're straight from the fighting. But those dogs of Turks have robbed all my stores."

"I don't want anything to eat, woman," he answered. "God forbid! How should I eat and let you go hungry? Either you have courage, and we eat together, or by God, in Whom I believe, I die of hunger with you."

He dreaded lest too strong a word might have escaped him. He coughed and could not think how to put it right again.

"Don't be angry with me," he said, "for speaking to you so boldly. But what am I to say to you? How am I to say it? You won't believe me!"

He sighed again. He began to roll a cigarette, but gave it up. He was all bewildered and at a loss. The widow raised her long tear-wet eyelashes and gazed at him. She wanted to question him, but was afraid. She longed to hear what he would say, but was ashamed.

"It's shameful," Manúsakas began again, "but I can't hold out against it. I'm going to tell you the whole truth honestly: don't take it amiss, for God's sake! If I'm lying, may God hurry with His lightning and burn me up! As soon as I came in here and saw you weeping, a knife went through my heart, I'm telling you the truth, woman, I was undone—never in the world have I seen such beauty! I mean well. Don't be angry. Don't get up and run away. There, I'm not touching you. Listen, though, to what I've got to say: Your dear husband is dead, he's gone. My dear wife is dead, she's gone. Both of us are left alone in the world. Come and let me look after you."

The little widow cried out, reeled, and sank on her knees. Her teeth were chattering, she was trembling. Manúsakas rose and went to the door, to leave the woman alone for a moment and give her the chance to pull herself together. He saw his palikares stretched out in the yard; they had opened their sacks and were eating. Beyond the yard he saw the fertile fields, the fruit-laden olive-trees, and the windmills, turning and creaking peacefully. . . . "I'll strike root here," he muttered, his mind made up, "this soil is good and fruitful, and I like it. The widow, too, is good— sappy and fruitful: she'll bear strong children, I like her. I'll take root here! By the all-seeing sun above me, no, I'll not stir from here!"

When he went back to see how the young widow was, he found her with her bodice laced and her hair tidy. She had bitten her lips and licked them to make them red. And the warm cloak had not left her.

"Captain Manúsakas," she said, cunningly, rolling her eyes, "what you said was not proper, forgive my saying so. And if it's true, it's a great sin. The blood of my dear husband is still warm on the threshold. . . ."

Manúsakos sighed. He paced twice up and down.

"If only I had a bit of bread," he said at last, renouncing the conversation. "And a mouthful of wine! And if you wouldn't mind, woman—I can't do it myself—sewing on tight this button that's hanging loose on my waistcoat."

The widow said nothing. She was sorry for the man. She got up, found her needle, threaded it; and the man knelt down in front of her. She wiped her eyes, to see better. Then she began sewing the button on, tight. And while she sewed, she could feel the heart of Manúsakos beating hard and shudderingly within his waistcoat and the man's fiery breath upon her knees.

She was ashamed, sewed hurriedly and stood up. She opened the chest. That wasn't true, she said, the Turks hadn't stolen everything. She took out a woven table-cloth and spread it on a table. It was snow-white and lit up the house. And then she went and lit a fire and began cooking. . . . And now Manusakas lit a cigar and, taking a footstool, sat down by the threshold, like the man of the house. He looked out, but his ears were pricked towards the inside of the house. He heard the woman going up and down busily, poking the fire, cooking the food, coming out again, getting knives and forks and plates, and laying the table. . . . He heard, and his heart rejoiced. Never had he felt so comfortable, so hungry, so patient. He knew now, he was sure: this young powder-stained widow, now cooking for him and with whom in a moment he would sit down to a meal, would, after the prescribed period of ransom to the dead, share food and bed with him for life.

That was how Manúsakas won his Christiniá and struck root in her village. She held good and gave him children. She bore them to him twins by twins, and his yard became full. In due course he even had a grandson—his first grandson—and got drunk to celebrate. He hoisted his ass upon his shoulder and lugged it late in the evening into the mosque of the big village at prayer-time.

"He did right," muttered Captain Michales, "I would have done the same, the same and worse. But I've given my word, and I must keep it, even if he is older than me. I'm the head of the village."

Petrokéfalo showed in the distance, on the mountain-slope, and farther up the defile, surrounded by green, Ai-Jannis, Christiniá's village. He spurred the mare hard. She too recognised the village and whinnied and began galloping along the road.

Manúsakas's door stood open. Captain Michales ducked his head, rode in, and halted in the yard.

"Brother Manúsakas," he called. The whole family was sitting indoors, round the low table, eating. Manúsakas was leaning against the wall and had hung the whip near him. Opposite him, with her legs crossed under her, sat his wife, Christiniá, happy and grateful. She had got rather fatter, and her breasts sagged: she had suckled too many children. But her face still glowed like a rose in full bloom.

Manúsakas heard his brother's voice and sprang up. He came out into the yard.

"Welcome, brother," he said, stretching out his huge hand. "The table's laid, your sister-in-law loves you, get down."

"I'm in a hurry," said Captain Michales. "Shut the door. There's something I must say to you."

"Good news? Bad?"

"Depends how you take it. Shut the door, I tell you."

Manúsakas shut the house door, to keep his sons and daughters from hearing. He went over to his brother.

"Listen to what I'm saying, brother Manúsakas. If you can't carry your wine, don't drink any."

Manúsakas's face darkened.

"Why do you say that to me?"

"God didn't make the ass to ride men, but for men to ride. Understand?"

"I understand. Your blood-brother, Nuri Bey, has been upset by it and has sent you to do his dirty work. Has it upset you too on your own account, Captain Michales?"

"I wasn't upset. And don't throw my words in my face. You know what I feel. But it's no service to the Christian cause. The moment hasn't come yet for us to raise the banner."

But Manúsakas had become angry.

"When you get drunk and sing the Moscow Song, burst into the Turkish coffee-houses, insult Beys and send them sprawling on the pavement, do you think of the Christian cause? And do you now come to me in my own yard and play the schoolmaster?"

He bent down, picked up a stone, threw it to the ground violently, and gripped the reins of the mare.

"What have you to say, Michales? Am I right? Don't play the Saint Onufrios to me!"

Captain Michales was silent. What was he to say? Manúsakas was right. As soon as he himself got drunk, he gave no thought either to Crete or to Chrsitendom. To the Devil with sweet reasonableness! At those times he rode out on his mare, and the whole world seemed to him small and trifling, a nutshell, and he rode up and down and felt like trampling it under his mare's hooves. The Devil take it!

"You don't answer," said Manúsakas, looking hard at his brother, as he frowned and stared up at the mountain. "You don't answer. Now for what's worrying you—I can see what's going round inside you. Make up your mind, you're a palikare, aren't you? Make up your mind, I tell you. That is Crete's destiny. Let me too have my revenge, and the world can go to blazes! At their Feast of Bairam I'm going to take a mule over my shoulders and bring it into the mosque. There it can pray alongside the ass. They can kill me if they like."

"I don't care if they kill you, only if Crete is smashed."

"Idiot, it won't be smashed, have no fear. We men are smashed, but not Crete, the immortal. Wait a minute," he said, thoughtfully. "Brother," he went on, a moment later, "here's the truth I'm telling you. I'm stifling in this village, don't you understand? For a whole while I didn't understand it myself, but when I drink wine, my mind clears, and my heart overflows like yours. I can't go to Constantinople and kill the Sultan—so let me bring off my own strokes and prove myself a hero in my own small village, to work it off."

Captain Michales tugged at the rein and steered the mare towards the outer door.

"Weigh what I've said to you, brother Manúsakas," he said, "weigh it well, when you're alone. And do as God enlightens you. What's best for Crete. I've nothing else to say to you. Farewell!"

"Get down, I tell you, have something to eat, don't be in such a hurry. What demon's after you? Stay tonight in my house. It's big, thank God, there's room for you. And see your nephews and Christiniá. And my first grandson. I'm going to call him Leftéres,[1] so that he may see freedom."

"Greet them all from me. I'm in a hurry."

"And won't you just ride into the village and visit our old father?"

"I haven't time, I'm in a hurry, I tell you. Tomorrow morning early I've something to do. Health and happiness to you!"

"You're an obstinate, pig-headed fellow. What you get into your head you do, and the world can go hang. All the best!"

Captain Michales ducked over the mare, rode through the main door and galloped out on to the plain. He was happy. Manúsakas had spoken well, had stood up to him well and like a man. But for his horror of sentiment, Captain Michales would have flung his arms round him. Yes, you're right, Manúsakas. Act on what you believe, the Devil take it! Even if the water boils over!

He rode like lightning and came back to Megalokastro with his heart leaping. He had put his stock to the proof once more. And he had found it as he would wish.

Noon was already past, the sun was beginning to sink. When the women of the quarter learned that Captain Michales would be absent all day, they collected in his yard with their sewing things, their spindles and their vegetables to be peeled: Penelope, Chrysánthe, Polyxigis's sister, Krasojórgis's wife Katinitsa, and Mastrapas's wife, all in a Saturday evening good humour. The week was at an end. Tomorrow was leisure, good food and plenty of society. Praise be to God, Who created Sundays.

"Have you heard the sad news, Aretúsa my dear?" began Katinitsa in a sing-song voice. "Again last night there were shouts and screams in the neighbourhood, from Furógatos's house. Furógatos was being beaten by his wife again."

"Pity my Demetrós hasn't Furógatos's moustache," remarked

[1] The Free (translator's note).

Penelope. "Looking at it you feel deliciously afraid—he's twirled it so tight, and the wax he uses makes it stay so stiff."

"Why don't they change places, I wonder? He ought to give his wife his moustache and put on her dress," said Mastrapas's wife—the one who kept her husband tied by the ankles all night.

Miss Chrysánthe laughed:

"Last night, about midnight," she said, "he was yelling again, and brought all the neighbours to their feet with his yelling. My brother was passing by and heard him. In the morning he went to see him: 'Brother Furógatos', he said to him, 'why do you let your wife slash you to ribbons? You never raise a hand to lick her into shape. You're making all us men look fools. Aren't you ashamed of yourself?' And what do you think he answered? 'I am ashamed, Captain Polyxigis, I am ashamed, but I enj-j-joy it'."

The women shook with laughter, Renió got up and brought the food and drink: coffee, preserves and Sesame biscuits. And just as she was serving them, lo and behold, over the threshold came their neighbour Ali Aga with his stocking and knitting-needles and with the green bag given him by Renió slung round his shoulders. He was bald—without a single hair—and he shone from much washing. His shabby many-times-darned shirt was shiny, his little thin legs with their clogs were shiny.

Katerina greeted him politely:

"Welcome, Ali Aga," she said, "dear neighbour. Come and get a cup of coffee."

"I've just drunk some, thank you," answered Ali Aga, as he made a bow to each of the women. "And I've had a biscuit too, and some excellent cherry jam. Many thanks, all the same."

"Oh, what's it matter, Ali Aga? Might as well be hung for a sheep as a lamb. Drink another to keep us company," the women called out with one voice, for they knew his pride and his poverty. He was as poor as a church mouse and had had neither coffee nor biscuit nor jam—nothing. All his life he was hungry, and food was his one thought. He was always talking of good things to eat, and he dribbled as he talked. And the women seized at once on his favourite subject, for the fun of it.

"And what good things did you have to eat at lunch, Ali Aga," said Kate, starting the ball rolling and winking at the others. "You're such a connoisseur, God knows. I expect you had chicken's breast."

Ali Aga smiled contentedly. He smacked his lips and stuck the knitting-needles into his sash. Then the washed-out old man began greedily describing how tender to-day's chicken had been, with what he had seasoned it, what sauce he had devised and how nicely the oven had browned it. He talked and talked, smacked his lips, and sighed.

And the women, suppressing their laughter, plied him with questions and led him on.

"Won't you ever stop eating meat and sauces, Ali Aga? You'll ruin your health. Eat some vegetables, too, from time to time. Too much meat is bad for you, you know."

"I'll give you a plate of cabbage this evening, neighbour," said Mastrapas's wife. "You'll see how it helps your digestion. All that white bread you eat must be heavy on the stomach."

"And too much caviare, neighbour, does a man in." Penelope quickly chipped in. "I'll give you a dish of chopped olives. You'll see, they're bitter and they sharpen your appetite."

The proud old man, sadly unprosperous in a Greek neighbourhood, lived on such good-humoured charity. And thus the women whiled away their afternoon. Now that Ali Aga's evening meal had been taken care of, there began a long conversation about the signs of spring in the countryside, and about men—who were all libertines and, sighed Matrapas's wife, had no taste for any but unlawful flesh. And Katinitsa complained that her huaband ate too much and snored and prevented her from sleeping.

Múrzuflos, the stocky sacristan up there on the bell-tower of Saint Menas's, had for a long while been holding his hand to his ear and listening to Megalokastro humming like a hive of bees. Múrzuflos could distinguish the wild shouts of men crying their wares, the blows of the blacksmiths' hammers, the greyheaded beggars singing pitifully and knocking at the doors, dogs barking, horses neighing and the little bells of the kids coming in on Saturday evening to Megalokastro to be slaughtered.

And suddenly he felt scornful at hearing the voices and the tumult.

"Quiet! It's time for me to speak!" he growled, and gripped the bell-ropes of the three bells which hung above him. "Five and seventy years have I now been listening to you. I've had enough."

It was seldom that Múrzuflos opened his mouth to speak. What should he say? What he himself had not to say he uttered by means of his three bells. They were mouths, had tongues, shouted. Secretly, without confessing his secret to anyone, he had christened them and given them names: the middle one, the largest, was Saint Menas, the protector and lord of Megalokastro. On his right was Eleftería (Freedom), on his left Thánatos (Death). The voice of Ai-Menas always rang out deep and commanding. And immediately afterwards Eleftería spurted forth gaily and play-fully like cool water. Last, dragging heavily after, came Thánatos. These three voices came out of the entrails of that greyhaired church servant—out of the entrails of Crete. Fearlessly they announced, over Christian roofs, Turkish streets and the Pacha's palace, the longing for revenge and the yearning of the oppressed.

The soul of Múrzuflos with its three voices all of silver and bronze rang triumphantly out and encouraged Kastro, though enslaved by the Turks, to celebrate the four festivals of the year—Christmas, Easter, Saint Menas's day (November 11th) and, above all, Saint George's day, the name-day of the King of Greece. . . . Múrzuflos decked his imagination with laurels to welcome Saint George as he arrived in Crete, riding on a white steed, in a fusta-nella and white silk waistcoat, with a leather belt and silver pistols. He wore pointed shoes, too, with red tassels. Behind him on the horse sat a little girl, a King's daughter, Elefteria. She was the King's child from Athens. And every year, on April 23rd, Saint George landed at Megalokastro, and Múrzuflos, hanging on the three bells in the dance, was the first to see him as he came up from the harbour and to greet him by rapturously swinging Saint Menas, Freedom and Death.

But to-day Múrzuflos was depressed. For to-day, the 1st of April, seventy-five years had gone by—how, though, had they gone by?—since he was born. And he felt suddenly for the first time that he was growing old, and was afraid of dying without witnessing the liberation of Crete. Will someone else, then, ring the bells on that holy day? No, Múrzuflos's soul could not endure that. No, even if the Devil has got hold of me, on that day I shall run away out of the bottomless pit, hang on my bells and get started with the din!

A cold sweat bedewed his wrinkled, tight-skinned forehead. Will he come in time? His hands trembled, and he began with noisy gasps to ring the evening bell.

And down there in Captain Michales's yard, where they were chatting about men and women, and Ali Aga was opening his mouth to explain to the Greek women the words of Mohammed, the evening bell was heard. At once the women gathered their sewing together, broke off the work, crossed themselves and got up to go home. In every house, on Saturday evening, the fire was made up to warm the water for washing. The flushed, bare-footed girls scrubbed the doorsteps, scoured out the cobbled yards, watered the pots of flowers. And the old women took down the censers of the ikon-shrines and censed the house. Murmuring, with their eyes half-shut, they thought of the dead.

At the moment of the bell's first stroke, Manóles the Pope strode breathlessly into his house. From early morning he had been busy blessing the houses for the first of the month, visiting all the houses round. There, after drinking an ouzo, he had snatched up proffered dainties from the dish and stuffed them higgledy-piggledy into the depths of his pocket. Now he was bathed in sweat but in a good mood.

"Hey, wife," he called, clapping his hands.

Contented and well-nourished, toothless and dragging her log-like feet in worn-out slippers, the pope's wife trotted out from the kitchen. In her youth she had been beautiful, a great enchantress. A tiny olive-like wart on her chin had bewitched the pope at that time. Now the little olive had grown fleshy and hairy. But her eyes still sparkled with roguishness and zest for love. She observed her pope's bulging cassock.

"Welcome, old man," she said. "Shall I unpack you?"

In the middle of the yard the pope raised his hairy hands above his head.

"Unpack," he said. "Bring the dish."

The pope's wife brought a huge dish and began to empty the inexhaustible pockets, which sagged from the pope's hips about his legs.

The pope's wife worked and worked, piling on the dish the sweetmeats, sausages, rissoles, cucumbers, almonds, dates, nut-cakes, medlars, roast peas, cheese tarts. . . .

"Just listen to that damned Múrzuflos, he's deafening me. Hurry up, wife!"

The dish was full. "You're unpacked, old man," said the pope's wife, raising the dish greedily against her chest. "Now run along, for the good of your soul!"

Lightened of his burden, the pope stretched his legs and set out for the evening service.

Meanwhile Chrysánthe, Polyxigis's sister, had gone home, thrown her best shawl of Indian cloth over her stout, bowed shoulders and put two small votive offerings, a little bottle of wine and a little bottle of oil, into a basket. At the moment when Pope Manóles was passing by, with his cassock still stuffed, Chrysánthe stepped over her threshold and started with heavy steps for church. She too had been supple and slim in her youth, but now she was heavy, her eyes were troubled, and on her upper lip, chin and cheeks sprouted long ass's hairs.

"Ai-Menas be good to you, Miss Chrysánthe," said the pope in greeting, casting a greedy look at her basket.

But Miss Chrysánthe was gasping under her fat; her feet were swollen and heavy, her seventy-two joints too were clogged up, and her mind swept on ahead. "Ai-Menas," she said silently within herself, "you see how, every Saturday evening, I bring you your gifts, your wine and your oil. Do me, in your turn, the favour I've asked of you for so many years. Let me die before my brother. He's generous and, if he's still alive, he'll give me a fine funeral. He'll even have the grand lanterns carried before me."

The grand lanterns had been brought not long before from Constantinople, by the wardens of Saint Menas's church. They were magnificent, hung on chains, silvered, with glass of several colours and black silk cords. They were carried only at rich funerals. The unmarried, friendless Miss Chrysánthe, grown old in toil, had now no other demand to make of life than a funeral with the fine lanterns. When she was young she had prayed Saint Menas to send her a good husband: he was to be handsome and a hard-working family man. Later, after long hoping and hoping-against hope, she had asked the Saint to help her brother, Captain Polyxigis, in his business. Polyxigis, when there was no rising and he was unemployed, had opened a shop by the Kanea Gate and bought wine, oil, grapes, lemons and turnips from the peasants. And then he sold them again to the wholesalers—the whole-hoggers, as he called them—and filled his cash-box with Turkish pounds and gold Napoleons. "Help my brother's trade, Saint Menas, to go well. For the service I'm asking of you, you shall never lack gifts: candles, wine and oil—all that a saint needs. Let us also have plenty to eat. Plentiful, good food, you know, is as good as a husband and children: a great consolation for mortals. It's all very well for Ali Aga to say: 'I won't get stout and lay up fat for the worms'. . . . Ah! My poor Ali Aga, that servant of God, fasts because he's got nothing to eat."

She had sacrificed her whole life for that sturdy brother of hers. For him she washed, sewed, scrubbed, cooked and yearned. "What a vigorous man, what a real master he is! No one would think of calling him a good-for-nothing. Women are made for men—let him have his fun!" She was one with him, they had been born of the same flesh on the same day, and if she was growing into an old hen, that didn't matter at all—if only he stays young and slim! "Yes, I'm happy with him—poor me, I sit up for him at night and it gives me something to live for, even if I do sleep all alone." Every time he came home at grey of dawn from his gaddings, Miss Chrysánthe started gladly up out of her sleep, pulled off his boots for him, warmed water for him to wash in, and made him a cup of coffee, very bitter, to enliven him. And when she came near him, she sniffed secretly and longingly at his

moustache and hair for the heavy fragrance left there by the
women. So even poor Miss Chrysánthe enjoyed love in this
world.

But lately, now that she was really aging and her legs were
getting more and more badly swollen, she prayed Saint Menas for
only one thing as she brought him, every Saturday evening, her
present to put him in a favourable mood: to arrange, out of his
goodness, for her to die before her brother, that he might hire
for her the grand lanterns, lately arrived.

When, at the other end of Megalokastro, at the Kanea Gate,
her brother heard the evening bell, he made the sign of the Cross
on his silk waistcoat, without thinking and sketchily, in the midst
of playing the mandoline. Then he sprang up nimbly to shut his
shop.

He was a handsome man, well-built and thoughtless. A dandy,
always dressed like a youth of twenty, in woollen breeches, a
knitted silken waistcoat, a broad silk sash and cream gaiters as
worn by Turkish and Christian fops alike. The gaiters were slit
in the middle from top to bottom and laced with red laces, to
give full value to the smart masculine leg. Polyxigis put on his
big fez, on one side so that its tassel fell saucily over his left
shoulder, and set out on his way, striding from stone to stone,
to the good barber Paraskevás. Every Saturday he had himself
shaved.

On the way to the barber's shop he stopped frequently, to greet
friendly shopkeepers. Here and there, too, he cracked a joke, here
and there drank a raki, and went on his way with his fez still more
on one side and his step still lighter. He enjoyed feeling his body
so brimming with strength, and how all his internal organs were
going like clockwork. He enjoyed, too, having not a care in his
head. He had once read in a pamphlet something that had made
a great impression on him: Kanáres, the fighter for freedom, was
asked one day how he managed to perform so many heroic deeds.
And that fisherman and commander of munitions-ships answered:
"Children, I always tell myself: Konstantes, you've got to die
sometime." Since that day, Captain Polyxigis had worn his fez
on one side, and whether it was a war or a party that was in front

of him, he would mutter: "Polyxigis, you've got to die sometime," and he was always the first to step forward. He had also engaged workmen and had them build for him a roomy monument of stone and marble in the churchyard. It was an underground vault, set round with ledges and cushions, with a low table in the middle and a cupboard sunk in the wall, where full bottles and raki-glasses were always kept. For when he was in the mood Captain Polyxigis would fill a basket with dainties, take a few bold friends with him, and go with them to the monument. There they would set to, drinking seriously and discussing war, women and death.

So now Captain Polyxigis went along, and two red feathers adorned his temples. First, it was going to be a lovely evening: not a leaf was stirring, from the courtyards came the scent of April roses, the gutters were moist and the earth was fragrant. But this pleasure was not enough. Soon Signor Paraskevás would lather him, shave him and anoint his hair with good pomade, and then Polyxigis would emerge from the shop unrecognisable, like a lad of twenty. Then he would turn into the shadowy alleys, to have a look at his boon-companions and his wenches.

Captain Polyxigis signed: "Ah, if there is a God, let Him do a miracle! I want it now. I'm in my prime, now's when I want the miracle! A few years back I was a clown and understood nothing. How was I to understand what women and wine and war meant? A few years more and I shall have shot my bolt. How could I enjoy the world still with no teeth or digestion? I'll go and have a look at the women and talk like the fox about the grapes. . . . Saint George, I think, is the saint who understands me best. I always admire you in the ikons, the way you ride there and have a woman sitting behind you. Ai-George, my name-saint, my cousin, help me and have no fear. For I'm stirring my stumps already."

So saying, he pushed his fez over his forehead and turned into Broad Street.

Broad Street was one of the two chief arteries of Megalokastro. It ran from the Kanea Gate on the west as far as the Hospital Gate, where the large square the Three Vaults, and the Pacha's gardens were. There, under a group of dusty trees, stood a

D

wooden kiosk where, every Friday, a military band played. The
other chief artery ran from the New Gate down to the harbour.
At their crossing was the main square, the heart of the town. On
Broad Street were the cobblers' shops, glass and china shops, the
stores, the Greek coffee-houses and the groceries. Out of the
shops, which extended without a break, there came always a sound
of loud conversation: shopkeepers, assistants and apprentices
joking, chaffing each other, chattering and bursting out laughing.
And woe to him, if Efendína or any bow-legged, squinting or half-
witted creature came by! The cobblers would all bang at once on
their lasts, the apprentices would whistle, and where did they find
so many bits of lemon-peel and rotten tomatoes?

Every Saturday evening love was in the air. To-day, as usual,
Broad Street was bubbling. The bell for evening service had
brought it to tumult pitch. This week too was over, God be
thanked. Artisans' lads and shop assistants pulled off their aprons
and bent down to the gutters to wash their work away. They
washed and tidied themselves, twirled their moustaches and
brought out the chairs, to sit down. They ordered their coffee,
the way they liked it, and their nargile. Soon, too, on her way from
the main square, Racheni the Moorish woman would pass by: a
mountain of dark, glowing flesh with a necklace of thick glass
beads—the kind usually worn by horses—round her neck, and
with breasts that drooped right down to her belly. She had always
a friendly laugh and made eyes roguishly. Her teeth flashed, and
on her head there balanced a dish of Sesame cakes. And lo and
behold, from the direction of Idomeneas fountain came Tulupanas also, silent and sad as always, with a tray in each hand, the
one full of spinach pasties, the other of Sesame rings with cinnamon. It was no longer Broad Street. It was a great mansion house,
where the dainties were just being handed round.

For a moment Captain Polyxigis paused, and felt proud of the
Greek street: the full shops, the plenteous merchandise, not a
Turk in sight, the air pure. The Christians were laughing and
joking, the bell was ringing. "That is Paradise," thought Captain
Polyxigis," there's nothing missing, except the flag with the cross
on it. But that too will come, we Cretans will bring it about."

So he told himself and moved on. He gave greetings right and left and entered the barber's shop.

The shadows were broadening, the muezzin had now climbed the minaret to call the faithful to evening prayer. But before deciding to send his voice up to the sky, he paused for an instant, wound the green cloth round the white cap he wore, and glanced down and around at the world.

"Allah, Allah," he murmured, "try as he may, man will never be able wholly to fill the eyes Thou hast given him, when he looks upon the world."

He leaned out upon the lattice of the minaret and rejoiced over Megalokastro—how it spread below him, many-coloured and many-voiced, with its white minarets, with the copper domes of the Saints, with the flag of the Prophet, with the Pacha's gardens. Overcome with the sweet fullness, he sighed:

"Blessedness includes all, all, all! Women are there, and handsome palikares like Nuri. When I see him storm in on his charger, I become twenty again. . . . There are slender youths, too, white as little rolls of bread, who sing in the coffee-houses in the evening, and you feel giddy and don't know where you should go to praise God—to the mosque or to the coffee-houses. And even the stench here, by Mohammed, enchants me. When I go out to the Hopital Gate and take a deep breath and smell the dung cast out by our little Cretan donkeys, my heart becomes a garden and I believe it too is about to be manured. . . . And I wouldn't give this stench of Megalokastro for all the pachouli in the world. To others it's a stink, but it pleases me!"

So saying, he breathed deeply and put his hands over his ears. And suddenly out from the depths of his body his voice thundered, deep and pure, bearing all love and prayer in its impetus. What sweetness there was in it, and what might! And how far this voice of the muezzin surpassed all the bells of Múrzuflos! It climbed up towards the sun with outstretched beak, struck into the sky and called God. Then it fell suddenly upon Megalokastro like a lark. It had drunk its fill of God and was intoxicated.

At the moment when the muezzin was praising Nuri so lovingly, Nuri was returning moodily from his estate. He had gone there to wear himself out. But shame still clung to his face and neck and exposed chest, and burned him. His horse was puffing yellowish foam: it too had something wrong with it to-day—was weak at the knees and kept stumbling. The sea had a glow and foam and a swell, yet there had not been a breath of wind stirring. He crossed the River Jofyro. The first leaves were sprouting on the vines, the almond trees were already in blossom, the fig-trees were heavily fragrant.

"Nothing, nothing," groaned Nuri Bey, "nothing can console me. Curse the sea, the trees and the sun!"

Before him stood Captain Michales again, just as when he had stretched his two fingers in the glass: he heard the glass crack, and —Eminé fell on the Captain's neck.

"Shame on me!" he said aloud. "The earth ought to open and swallow me. Since you're no longer the best man in the land, what do you still want of life? Anathema upon it!"

He went over the whole of last night in his mind. What a turmoil it had been, what a drunken orgy—so much so that he had lain on his own threshold, dead drunk in muck! Then, he remembered, sleep had overcome him. And in it what a wild shrieking there had been, what a howling! Who had come into his sleep and called? When the Moor had come to him in the morning and washed him, the dream had turned to smoke and vanished. And yet a knife remained stuck in his heart.

To-day he had ridden through the Turkish cemetery, where the gravestones with the tortuous lettering and painted stone turbans stood upright like a marble people that had risen from the ground and was striving to get free, to wrench away from the monuments and come home to Megalokastro.

He tried to make out, up there in the corner away from the sea and between two cyprysses, the grave of his father. But as he found it, his temples began to throb. It seemed to him that the marble turban moved, leaned back, just as the blear-eyed Hani Ali had always done when wrath took hold of him. The world spun; he was giddy, and the horse stumbled. It blundered against a tomb, and the Bey seized its mane to prevent it from falling. He tugged hard at the reins, and the proud steed reared, trembling. This was the first day it had stumbled, the first day in so many years. A bad omen.

The Bey gave a cry. He wanted to dismount, to kneel down at his father's grave, but he was afraid of the dead. Like a flash of lightning it went through him. He remembered now, perfectly clearly, his last night's dream; his father had stood over his pillow, shaggy, dirty and barefooted—he who never deigned to touch the earth with his foot! He raised his long, blackened hand: "How many years already," he roared at him, "have I been wandering around your damned konak? Since 1866. Count them! Twenty-three years! I fondly believed my son, my only son, would think of me day and night and sharpen the knife to avenge my blood. . . . I glide about your miserable house, but all I hear is laughter and mandolines and song. And you abandon me, to wander in shame up and down the streets and fields! Why do we get sons? That they may avenge our blood. And you've not been ashamed to become blood-brother to the brother of my murderer! And you show him your wife without a veil! Damn you, you *giaour*!"

When Nuri heard the heavy curse, he had been overcome with anger. He had wanted to shout: "What, old man, are you trying to go on ordering me about, even from the grave?" But the words had stuck in his throat. He dug his heels into the horse. The sun had still not set. He returned by the Kanea Gate and stormed into the Greek quarter.

Captain Michales at the same moment came up to the Hospital Gate, at the other end of Megalokastro. He had ridden his mare hard. The sun was just sinking, it still shone upon the open fortress-gate. From afar he could see the lepers getting up. All day long they lay to right and left of the door in the dust and dung, stretching out their stumps of arms and begging. At sundown their day's work was ended: they stood up and moved off in line, one after the other, towards Meskinia, the lepers' village. They did not look at one another, but hurried forward. They did not utter a word. Their cheeks were eaten away, noses and ears were missing, many were blind, some seemed to be smiling because they had no lips and so always showed their teeth. All ran, as though the Last Judgement had begun and they had heard the Angel's trumpet, as though they were breaking out from Earth and had forgotten some part of their flesh in their haste.

Captain Michales turned his face away. He hated to see illness. "Only healthy people ought to live," he thought. "What use are these?"

He spurred his mare and came through the fortress-gate just as the military guard blew the trumpet for sunset and the Turkish flag was hauled down.

III

NIGHT, that night, lay heavy and dead upon the town. The air was sultry. Captain Michales slept badly. The damp weight was oppressive. Kastrians, men and women, opened their windows, went out into their yards and unbuttoned their nightshirts, to get some air. Several old women scented disaster and sat on their doorsteps, but dared not open their mouths for fear of betraying their thoughts. They were afraid the evil destiny of Megalokastro might overhear them and put into action what, they suspected, was not yet finally decided.

And so they whispered together and tried to keep small talk going—yet their speech kept returning to the secret, unavowed anxiety: "Do you remember the last time? Not a leaf was stirring. . . ." "Be quiet!" "And can't you hear a humming under your feet?" "Be quiet!"

And they bolted themselves up inside their souls again and waited for the relief of sunrise.

Veiled in copper-coloured shreds of cloud, a darkly wrathful sun came up behind the Lasithi mountains. The minarets caught fire, the sea flushed, Múrzuflos rang the trinity of bells. The Greek quarter awoke from its stupor, doors opened, and out stepped the householders, all washed clean, in their Sunday suits and shirts with collars. Husband, wife, behind them the mother-in-law and in front of them the children: the boys with a folded white handkerchief in their hand, the little girls with a slide in their hair.

They were on their way—the noble, grey-haired guardians of Megalokastro—to honour the mounted saint, Ai-Menas. They wanted, too, to hear to-day's sermon by the Metropolitan and to receive nourishment at his hands. To-day was Sunday, there was no business, the shops were shut, for one day the great trader, Satan, was asleep. So people were glad to accept the word of God —it cost nothing, one lost nothing by it. And tomorrow there would again be weights and measures and haggling, and each trying to eat up the other. Six days belonging to the Devil and one to God: light the lamps for both, then you'll be well in.

The church twinkled like the starry sky and smelt of candles and of incense; it was warm. There was a humming, as in a hive, of angels, saints and human beings. There was not room for all the Christians—many were standing in the narthex, others in the aisles. The stout Metropolitan stood by his throne with his gigantic body and snow-white beard, with the golden crozier and the kingly mitre, like some terrifying beast from Heaven, come down to this Earth to haul men home and scare them.

At the gate of the iconostasis, Pope Manóles had taken his place with solemn countenance, caparisoned in gold, and was intoning the Gospel for the day as Kajabés opened his door to proceed to church with his wife. Their wedding had been last Sunday, and, as custom required, the young couple must for eight days pray in their wedding garments to Saint Menas, protector of the country, and bring him a large cake made with cinnamon, mastic and sugar.

Their little house was near the harbour, just where the Jewish quarter began, in a welter of narrow, winding alleys plagued alike by sultry winds and cutting sea-air. Garufaliá took her husband by the arm and hung upon him. They walked slowly and proudly along and greeted with friendliness, both of them, the newly-wedded world. How the myrtle-decked streets shone and gave out sweet scent! How the cliffs smiled! How the world, beyond all hope, had advanced to the married state! Yes, some thorn-bushes in one of the garden hedges had brought forth white blossoms. . . . . Was this Megalokastro, enslaved by the Turks? Were these the alleys of the poor quarter and the odours of refuse? Was that the Cretan Sea, apt to be savage and far from tender to men? Garufaliá stealthily raised her sleepy eyes and gazed at her husband. "God, what is all this talk put out by the popes? Paradise is here, my good man. God, give me no other Paradise!"

They had now reached the market-place and were about to plunge into the street leading to the church. Kajabés turned and looked at his wife. His heart was joyful. Suddenly it seemed to him as if the world was no more, and in the chaos nothing was left except this living creature at his side, warm and perfumed, delightfully swathed in blouse and petticoats and skirts, with lots of buttons and laces . . . and her mouth fragrant in a sweet, warm, human way. . . . He had been put out, ever since the evening before last, when he had heard that he was bidden to Captain Michales's. He would have had just eight days with his wife. His blood grew hot. He stopped still in the market-place. What was the Kastrian Ai-Menas, with his local customs, to him, the wild man from Sfakia? And why should he waste his time in church, instead of going back home as quickly as possible? They're newly married, God forgive them. . . . He had only a little time left. Captain Michales, that ferocious beast, was certainly in his cellar already, waiting.

"Shall we not go home, wife, to our little house?" he asked, and his breathing stopped with longing.

The woman blushed scarlet, her eyelids grew heavy.

"As you decide, my little Jannis," she murmured, with her eyes shut.

They went back as though someone were after them. Quickly they crossed the market-place, passed the plane-tree and the Pacha's palace, entered the narrow alleys and reached the harbour. Kajabés opened the door with a kick, they went in, shut the bolts to and flung themselves on the bed.

Meanwhile Captain Michales, having gone down to the cellar at grey of dawn, was sitting there. On his right stood three casks of wine upon two stout boards, on his left two jugs, one of oil and the other of flour. Above his head were suspended in rows figs, pomegranates, quinces and canary-yellow winter melons with green veins. On the wall hung bundles of pot-herbs, sage and marjoram. The cellar smelt of wine and quinces. Soon the hot chickens, cuttlefish and sausages would overlay this smell.

He sat on a high stool and leaned his heavy head, bound tightly in its dark cloth, against the wall. His eyes stared at the low door opposite him, and saw nothing. He thought of nothing. He sat without moving. Only from time to time his claw of a hand pressed the edge of the table in front of him, and made the wood bend.

His mind was inert and heavy, but his heart was simmering.

D*

Life had turned out kind to him, he lacked nothing; he was a strong, healthy man, with a good wife and a family, and the world took him seriously. His son was like him—he too had no fear of death. As soon as he died his son would step into his footsteps. His son, too, had a birth-mark on his neck; thick, bushy eyebrows, also, like his, and eyes, like his, small and pitch-black. So what the Devil was the matter with his heart, to make it boil so? He could feel no pleasure, raise no smile, bring no joke or friendly word over his lips to relieve him. Always reserved, taciturn, fierce. One evening his wife's brother, kind-hearted Manolakis the tailor, had come to his house and had said something and laughed. Captain Michales had frowned, and poor Manolakis was as though paralysed, and soon got up and left. Then Captain Michales had turned to his son:

"He's got no shame," he had said contemptuously; "he laughs!"

When Crete is set free, he sometimes thought, my heart too will be free. When Crete is set free, I shall laugh. And yet, not long ago, he had had an extremely lifelike dream: because Crete was set free the bells were ringing, the streets were strewn with myrtle and laurel, a white warship had anchored in the harbour and the King's son from Athens sprang on to the mole, bowed down and kissed the soil of Crete; and on the mole he himself, Captain Michales, was standing, holding the keys of Megalokastro on a silver platter, to hand them to the King's son. Crete was set free, was set free—but his heart was not relieved.

"What the Devil's the matter with me," he growled, angrily. "What the Devil do I lack? I shall come a cropper yet!"

His blood came in waves, his brain seemed to grow too big, his eyes became bloodshot. Crete rose and fell within him—it was no longer an island, it was a wild beast gazing out to sea. It was the Gorgon, the sister of Alexander the Great, lamenting and slashing with her fish-tail and stirring up the sea. And as Captain Michales heard her lament, a shudder went through his brain and she again changed her aspect. Crete struck root in him like a plane-tree and began to feed on his vitals. From its branches there dangled greyhaired, barefooted forefathers; their heads looked bluish and they bit their tongues, and a powerful wind moaned.

And as Captain Michales stretched out his arms to pray to them, all vanished. His mind was empty. There remained only a lantern with red and green glass, and under it Nuri and the lemon raki and the cooked partridge. And suddenly a tittering. Two Circassian women.

Captain Michales leapt up, and struck the wall heavily with his fist, so that the house trembled. He raised his eyes to the low doorway and suddenly began to be angry and to curse, because his boon-companions were late.

At the moment when Captain Michales was striking the wall with his fist, the boon-companions were setting out from the four ends of Megalokastro. The first to get up, in the early morning, was Vendúsos the tavern-keeper: he crossed himself, stood in front of the ikon shrine with the ever-burning lamp, and prayed to his protectress, the holy virgin of the vineyard, to give him the strength to hold out. He was setting out for the great tournament: eight days it would last, from Sunday to Sunday, and eight nights, and if the Virgin did not help, they would be wasted. Some years ago he had commissioned the monk Nikodimos to make him a Virgin, not as the painters depict her, like a mother, but as he himself had seen her in a dream: a woman like the grape-pickers in August, mad for men, thick-lipped, with a white, Cretan headband round her head, and in her arms, instead of a child, a bunch of grapes. The monk had resisted at first. Nothing of the kind existed, he said, there was nothing of the kind in the scriptures, it would be a sin. She must hold Christ in her arms, not a bunch of grapes. But Vendúsos gave him a bottle of raki and several pounds of cod as payment, and the monk was pacified. He crossed himself, took up his brush and painted the Holy Mother of the Vine-tendril.

And now Vendúsos stood in his stockings, without shoes, before her and entreated her:

"My Lady of the Vineyard, who protectest taverns and tavern-keepers, I greet thee. I am going, I am going off to Captain Michales's cellar. Thou knowest what that will mean: I need thy help! As thou knowest, I gave money and cod and raki to have thee painted. Help me! Help me to hold out and not to get drunk

and not, this time, to be sick and make a mess of the walls. And
enlighten, O Maiden, that unruly beast of a Captain Michales, so
he lets us go quickly. Eight days and eight nights are a lot, Holy
Virgin, a lot, really they are!"

He washed and dressed, took down his lyre from before the
ikon shrine, went out into the yard and took leave of his wife
Marusio and his two daughters. He bade them come every two
days and see what was happening. He left them money to buy
their food for the whole week, and told his elder daughter, who
was good at writing, being a schoolteacher, to write down for
him on a piece of paper what he must say, and this he put in his
pocket. He looked round him at the whole house as though saying
farewell, crossed himself, and stepped over the threshold.

First he went by the tavern, pulled out the piece of paper, and
stuck it on the door so that people might see it: "The proprietor
is obliged to be absent for eight days on private business". This
calmed him a little, and he hurried off towards Captain Michales's
house. He was late. The dragon would make no remark, but would
frown, and that was enough.

As he passed the house of his elder brother, the wholesaler,
he quickened his pace. "He mustn't see me. He'll suspect where
I'm going, and I shall get another scolding. To hell with the old
ass!" He rubbed that cucumber nose of his, which drooped every
month a bit more and was already nearly touching his mouth.
"Ah! to hell with him!" he muttered again: "He'd like to give me
lessons, would he? But the day before yesterday I gave as good
as I got! I knew what was the matter with me, damn it, and was
pitching and edging along by the walls, when here comes our
fat father of a family and sticks his mug out of that damned fine
house of his. 'You ruined Manóles!' he says to me, 'Haven't you
done yet, always drinking and drinking?' Then I stood up straight
as a candle—close to the wall—and opened my little mouth: 'You
wholesaler!' I said, 'Haven't you done yet with not drinking and
not drinking and not drinking?' One or two people, who were
just passing, stopped and laughed, loudly. And the old ass—he
vanished, he vanished."

Talking to himself, Vendúsos went on his way. "It was God's

will, since I was born on Good Friday and my father was a pope, for me too to be made into a pope—even perhaps one day (the Devil has such a lot of legs) into a bishop. But how was I to be kept solidly at school, how was I to put my neck under the yoke? From a small child I was always playing the lyre, and the stones listened and danced. Wherever there were festivities and fun, there was I, and there I stayed, I was not to be torn away. That's why they called me Vendúsos the Keener. Gradually I got used to drinking freely and couldn't any longer live without the whiff of wine. So I started a tavern. And I ordered my own Holy Virgin, who suits me, and no one else in Christendom has one like her. When I call her she comes, and never minds running up and down for all sorts of odd things. She doesn't leave me in the lurch in the hour when I need her. She belongs to me only, and I'm not lending her to any silly idiot. Last year that blasphemer Captain Polyxigis wanted her from me, so as to order one like her for himself. But how could I give her to him? 'Would you give me your mare, Captain Polyxigis?' I asked him. 'No—so I won't give you my Virgin either.' "

At this point in his monologue, he suddenly ran into Furógatos and Bertódulos by Idomeneas's Fountain. They too were on their way, breathlessly, to the dragon's den. They were all in such a hurry that Vendúsos's lyre missed by a hair's breadth being smashed in the collision, and Bertódulos's hat being toppled on the ground.

"Hey, Vendúsos," cried Furógatos, "why are you running so hard into the lion's jaws? Stop! Let's roll a cigarette to give us courage."

They sat down on the marble steps of the fountain and pulled out their tobacco-boxes. Furógatos sat throned and towering in the middle; he had grown stout in his old age, and he had a giant's long legs. When they went out to dance, the soil of Crete rejoiced. If he had not had these legs, nobody would have bidden him good-day. For you do not bid good-day to a man who beats his wife. He had bushy eyebrows and a bristling moustache that stuck straight out, so that he really did look like a furious cat (Furógatos). He bent affectionately over his comrade Bertódulos and wrapped him in his cloak, which had been pulled off by the collision. He also arranged his small, stiff, decayed nobleman's hat for him firmly on his long grey hair.

Bertódulos was a blameless, friendly little old man with a thin, prim mouth, a jutting, freshly-shaved chin and two short side-whiskers reeking of pomade. He was the first man in Megalo-kastro, perhaps in the whole of Crete, to have feared neither God nor Man and shaved off his moustache. At first the Cretans had supposed that smooth skin natural and were not angry. But as they realised that he shaved, they became furious. That is not possible! He is destroying the order of things! He is mixing up women and men. Some threw stones and lemon-peel at him, others, more enlightened, ceased to greet him.

"Such freaks won't do for Cretans!" Barba Jannis shouted at him one day, twirling his moustache. "Here in Crete, Bertódulos, there are two kinds of human beings, not three; men, and women. We won't have men-women!"

And as, one Sunday, Bertódulos went past the Three Vaults, elegant, light-stepping and smiling, with his guitar, the drunken Furógatos caught hold of him and tried to pull his breeches off in front of everyone, to see, so he said, whether there was a Bertódulos inside them or a Bertódolina. But one or two sober people came between, and Furógatos burst into tears. He embraced Bertódulos, clasped him to him, caressed and kissed him. Bertó-dulos cried out: "You're cracking my ribs! Let me go!" and gave him a powerful kick. Since then the two had been inseparable friends.

It was his fate to be no Cretan. It was his fate to be from Zante, so he said, and to be a Count. He himself no longer remembered how he had got to Megalokastro, among the wild beasts, and there become a teacher of the guitar. And his name was not Bertódulos, but Count Mangiavino: only now, because he shivered all through winter and spring, wrapped himself in a thick green cloak or "berta", was shrivelled and bow-legged, said odd, comical things, and was easily frightened, the Kastrians called him Bertódulos. The name stuck.

But with each year the number of his pupils diminished. What should Kastrians do with a guitar? And those asses' voices of theirs were not suited to the love-songs of Zante. Poor Bertódulos went hungry. He would go to the coffee-houses and tell, with touching charm, of his life, of his sometime brilliance, of the distinguished ladies and the serenades and mandoline concerts in Zante. He would take his instrument upon his knee and hum some old melody. Then the owner of the coffee-house would feel ashamed and treat him to a cup of coffee and a biscuit, sometimes with Turkish delight or sugared orange-peel as well, and then the Count charmed his hunger away. Sometimes he even obtained permission to wrap the Turkish delight in a clean piece of paper and take it away with him. He was fond of his greyhaired landlady, a woman old as the hills, and was ashamed to revel in sweetmeats alone. He knew how much the poor thing loved Turkish delight, because you needed no teeth for that.

"He'll do for my cellar," thought Captain Michales one day, as he heard him recount truth and fable in Trialonis's coffee-house. That day he was speaking of Zante, the Flower of the East, which no Turkish foot had ever trodden; where, too, the poet of the Greek spring song had been born. Captain Michales called him over. "Listen, Mr. Bertódulos," he said, "you're a superior person. It's a disgrace to Megalokastro that it can't give you a living. So I'll pay you a monthly salary, and you shan't suffer. But you will come to my cellar, every time I send for you." "With pleasure, Sir," answered the Count, doffing his hat to the floor. "Thy slave, renowned Captain Michales."

Furógatos wrapped the little old man up like a baby. And he giggled gratefully, as if he were being tickled.

"Courage, my Bertódulos," said Vendúsos. "We're bound straight for a great storm, my poor friend. In that cellar Greek freedom will be born."

"Don't worry, Signor Vendúsos. For better, for worse, I've taken my precautions!" said he, proudly, and pulled out from his cloak a parcel he was carrying under his arm.

"What have you got there, Signor Bertódulos?" asked Vendúsos, fingering the parcel.

"A change of shirt," answered the clean little man, and blushed.

"Hey, that's enough," cried Furógatos, throwing his cigarette-end away. "We've had a breather. Now up, children! On into the labyrinth! With God's help, forward!"

All three linked arms, Bertódulos in the middle, and off they went to Captain Michales's door.

Middle-aged, with a solid, fair beard, with wild goggle-eyes round as eggs, and with his head swathed in the many windings of a broad, white Turkish turban, which he had also earmarked as his winding-sheet and now regularly wrapped around his head, so as to be always ready to enter Paradise in it: such was Efendína. Years ago he had been to Mecca, and ever since those holy, agonising days his brain had reeled with their heat, thirst, dirt and god-filled delirium, his mind had been filled with flames and terror. He had returned to Megalokastro and played the *hodza* in a téké where one of his forbears had become a saint. For a time several Turkish children came, and he taught them to read and write. Sometimes he hit them, sometimes they hit him, until one day young Braima, Nuri's nephew, broke his head for him, and the school came to an end.

The téké was near the church of Ai-Menas: an oblong, flat yard overgrown with cabbages. At the far end were three small dilapidated vaults and in the middle of the courtyard the saint's tomb: the wooden coffin with an upright marble slab topped by a green turban. The gold lettering had been worn away by rain and sun. Round about the tomb stood large and small benches, where the faithful took their places each Friday, gazed at the saint and talked, smoking nargiles the while and drinking coffee, which the exorcist, Hamidé Mula, Efendína's mother, prepared for them. The turban was hollow inside. The faithful threw small coins into it, to secure the saint's help for their affairs in this world and the next. They did not ask for such a variety of things as the Christians: good food, good women and good courage, in this world as in the other, were enough. So they threw into the turban presents for the saintly intercessor.

Each morning at sunrise Efendína sat down in the courtyard with his legs crossed, and placed on his knees a huge Koran. He swayed forwards and backwards until he was giddy, and then began intoning and howling. If it was cold, he would spring up, stretch out his arms, wag his head as low as his shoulders, dance like a dervish, whistle, spit, and stamp with his feet to get warm. Every noon, when his hunger became acute, he ran madly from one end of the yard to the other, puffed like bellows, and dripped with sweat, with nothing on but his turban and his sack-cloth pants. The neighbours would come by and watch him through the latticed window which gave on the street; some would laugh at him, others were sorry for him and called out: "In God's name, Efendína, what's the matter with you?" "I've flames inside me, neighbour," he would answer, without pausing.

Whenever he gave the slip to his old mother and got out into the open, the Greek children threw stones at him. Then he would run quickly on, and would try to jump across from one gutter to the other. But he could not. The street appeared to him like a river; he wanted to plunge in, but dared not. He drew back trembling, unable to swim.

Captain Michales invited Efendína each time he had a drinking-bout in preparation: for he liked to include a Turkish abortion. And Efendína received the news with fear and eagerness. He counted the months that passed before Charitos came again to the téké and piped stealthily into his ear: "Greetings from my uncle Captain Michales, and will you, he says, please come to his cellar."

All the year long he yearned for pork, white bread, sausage and wine. But the Prophet would not let him drink wine or eat pork. Nor would he let him look into the eyes of a woman. If ever this did happen, a trembling came over him, and one day, when an impudent young thing teased him and pretended to be in love with him, he fell to the ground and foamed at the mouth. One pleasure only remained to him in life, a sinful but very precious pleasure: Captain Michales's invitation, every six months, to drink wine, to eat pork and fill up that poor frame of his for the next six months. "By my faith, Captain Michales, threaten me," he used to say to him, "hold a knife to my throat! Shout at me: 'Guzzle pig's flesh, swill wine, or I'll kill you!' Force me, Captain Michales, so I shan't be sinning." And so he used to eat and drink and utter every

blasphemy he had kept bottled up during the last six months, because the Prophet forbade him to relieve himself by saying them.
Also he used to betray what he knew about "his neighbour"—for
so he called Saint Menas. Only a wall divided them, and he could
hear him every night ride forth from his church. Then Efendína
was frightened, buried his head in his pillow, and in the morning
stole the oil from his grandfather's lamp and with it secretly filled
the lamp of the Christian Saint Menas.

Twice eight—sixteen days in the year Efendína drank and
blasphemed in Captain Michales's cellar like a real man. Then his
brain worked like clockwork, he carried no flame about in him
and could jump across from pavement to pavement without fear.
But the good days passed like a flash, and sainthood and martyrdom began again.

All last night he had been unable to sleep for joy. He had got
up in the dark, slipped barefoot out into the courtyard, opened
the door softly so that his mother might not hear, and darted out.
He had kept close to the wall of Ai-Menas's, passed the Greek
school and reached the mosque of Saint Catherine. There he
stopped. A cold sweat dripped from him. Now he must cross to
the other pavement, to take the turning towards Captain Michales's
house. He put one foot forward, but at once drew it back and
began to tremble. That was not a street in front of him, but deep
water whirling boulders and baulks along in its course and raging
between the two pavements.

Efendína leaned against the wall, wiped the sweat away and
gazed up and down the street. "Will nobody come by, will nobody
come by—Turk or Christian, or even a Jew—and have pity
on me?"

Efendína waited, breathless. Over there, on the other footpath,
the wine, the pork, the sausages. Courage, my heart, jump over!

Again he took a run, but as he bent forward and saw the street
he shrank back and once more clung to the wall.

Above him the minaret of Saint Catherine began to gleam
brightly. Sunlight was already falling on the steps, and over there
Tulupanas's oven was giving out a smell. From Ai-Menas's there
sounded sweet, sustained intonings.

"Will no Christian on his way to church pass this way and have mercy on me? Will nobody come by? Is the world deserted? What desert is this? I am lost!"

Suddenly he shuddered and cried: "Hey, Christians, help!"

The door opposite opened: a high, ornate door with a heavy, bronze knocker. Mr. Charílaos Liondarákis, the avaricious money-changer, came out—a dwarf with enormous buttocks, a wild beard and short hairy fingers. He had shoes with triple soles, a short coffee-coloured overcoat and a walking-stick with a silver handle in the form of a lion's head. Mr. Charílaos Liondarákis belonged to an important Venetian family which had become Greek. His ancestors had had a lion on their banner and carved in relief on their palace.

He was on his way to church. He stared at Efendína and began laughing scornfully. He liked to see half-wits, lepers, blind men, beggars, unfortunates. It consoled him for his own appearance.

"Efendína," he shouted across, "courage, you poor idiot! Jump!"

"Have you no faith in God, Mr. Charílaos?" the poor man cried. "By the day that's above us, come nearer! Give me your hand, help me to get across! I want to go to Captain Michales's, and I can't!"

A girl with full lips and a dark little face came out of the door. Mr. Charílaos was in the habit of making love to her and climbing on a footstool into her bed. One night she had given him a piece of advice: "Swallow a fresh egg, sir, every morning on a empty stomach! Swallow that, and God help you!" So the little gnome swallowed an egg to make him strong.

"Sir, you've forgotten your egg! The hen's just laid it," said the experienced baggage, and pressed the egg into his hand.

Mr. Charílaos Liondarákis took out his pocket-knife, made a hole in the eggshell at one end, made a hole at the other, put back his short, obese neck, and swallowed.

"Help me, Mr. Charílaos, if you believe in God!" shrieked Efendína afresh.

The little gnome laughed:

"You'll go eating pig's flesh again, my poor fellow, and defiling yourself!" he said, playing with his stick.

"Even if the Devil gets me, I'm going! Poor me, it's the only pleasure I've got in this world. You'll be rewarded; stretch out that stick of yours, Mr. Charílaos, so that I can catch hold."

God had pity on Efendína, for at the corner there appeared an old bald man in clogs. He came from the public garden, for he had his bag full of wild turnips. Efendína stretched out his arms:

"Dear Ali Aga," he called, "dear Ali Aga, you're a good man, a believing Musulman! A lot of water lies in front of me, a lot of fire! Help me through it!"

Without saying a word, the kind-hearted old man took Efendína by the hand and led him slowly and carefully to the other pavement. He turned to him, to say something, but thought better of it—what should he say? He pushed the bag under his arm and made off. What should he say to him? he thought. Allah is merciful, merciful and mighty. He can turn pork into lamb in your mouth, and wine into water. He does what He wills. Eat and drink, Efendína. And trust in God.

When Efendína arrived panting at Captain Michales's house, all the guests had already descended into the lion's den. Charitos was running to and fro between kitchen and cellar, fetching the dainties. Efendína's nostrils quivered eagerly, he heard glasses clinking down below in the earth, and a smell of sausages hung in the air. Efendína leaned against the doorpost in order not to faint. In that moment he caught, within him, the voice of the Prophet: "Efendína Horsedung" (that was how the Prophet addressed him), "will you sell your soul for a morsel of pork? Think of Mecca, of the voice, the desert, the camels, the incense, the black stone on which I mounted for my ascension. . . . Think of your ancestor, who for so many days and nights, up on the minaret, without bread, without water, ever fasting, called mankind to prayer. And you should see him now: he sits in the midst of a cave of pilaff; before him flows a river of milk and cream; and on each knee he holds a boy worth seven maidens, and he often changes boys. . . . You are from a saint's family, do not forget! Efendína Horsedung, in this hour you are going to Hell. But the door is still open. Flee!"

Poor Efendína heard the voice of Mohammed with trembling

and glanced now at the street door, now at the little door to the cellar, through which the sausage fragrance came. And as his understanding wavered, Katerina came out into the yard and saw him.

"Is that you, Efendína?" she said, "Go down quickly or there'll be trouble."

"Is the food already down there, Mrs. Katerina?"

"It is. Hurry up."

"It's God's will," muttered Efendína. "God has sent me Mrs. Katerina. I mustn't resist: that would be a great sin. Am I to contend with God? Allah, Allah, I beseech Thee for one grace: let me commit all sins, let me too—poor me—enjoy this world above, and then, half an hour before my death, give me time for repentance! Is half an hour not enough? It is enough. I beseech Thee!"

He gave a leap forward, pushed open the little door and went down.

On a high stool opposite the door, weighty, frowning, in a cloud of cigarette smoke, sat Captain Michales. His whip hung from a nail above his head. To right and left on two long benches were the four guests: on one side Vendúsos and Kajabés, on the other Furógatos and Bertódulos. Upon the high table the dainties steamed. The wine sparkled, dark red like blood, in large glasses.

Vendúsos had placed his lyre on his knees, held his ear close to it, and was twisting the pegs and tuning it. Bertódulos, wrapped in his cloak, trembling and happy, under the protection of Furógatos, nibbled ceaselessly. And Kajabés ate and drank: his thoughts were with his wife.

Captain Michales kept filling and refilling his glass and drinking. The wine gave him not the slightest pleasure. He hated it. Every time he raised his glass to his mouth, his lips resisted and refused. But he forced it against his own will into his stomach, to quell the demons within him. Neither woman nor war nor God could overcome them. His demons were afraid of wine alone, and he drank of it freely whenever he felt their rage rising in him. These demons were savage voices: most of them were not human voices but bestial ones, bellowing inside him as soon as the portcullises down below opened, letting ancient images spring forth: a tiger, a wolf, a wild boar, and after them the hairy ancestors out of the caves of Psilorítis.

But now for the first time a new demon announced itself within him. This one did not bellow, did not threaten, it laughed. Its breath did not stink, it smelled sweet. For the first time Captain Michales was afraid, and kept filling his glass and refilling it and drinking.

When the door swung open and Efendína appeared, he raised his head. Efendína rubbed his hands distractedly, jerked a foot forward, but dared not come down the steps. His words, too, fled in confusion. He wanted to say: "Greetings, Captain," but he could not get it out and merely stuttered.

Captain Michales raised his hand and pointed to a low stool opposite him. "Sit down!"

"What am I to play, Captain Michales?" asked Vendúsos, without taking his ear from the lyre.

Furógatos had already stood up. He shoved the benches aside to make himself room. He was eager to start. His soles had caught fire, they were tickling him. For others wine led to song or to joking, or to weeping and slumber. For this clumsy, long fellow, Furógatos, wine led to dancing. He drank, danced and became sober. He did not really become sober, the drinking-fit merely changed its form. It became a keen and fruitless effort to give the body wings, to make it the conqueror of unconquerable laws. But he could not. And Furógatos began drinking afresh, to win fresh power to soar.

Captain Michales took in each of his five guests in turn with a circling gaze. Neither song nor dance nor lyre could lighten his heart to-day. His gaze rested on Efendína.

"Sir," cried Efendína in alarm, "don't ask me to smile and utter blasphemies against the Prophet. Threaten me first! Compel me against my will to eat and drink, then I'll have the courage!"

But Bertódulos, who had eaten and drunk and acquired strength, chipped in:

"Most noble Captain Michales," he began in his drawling, sing-song speech, "may I tell you, to pass the time, a famous old story from Venice? I saw her with my own eyes on the balcony, and since then my heart has been able to find no rest. How often have I forgotten the bitternesses of life, because I bore in my imagination the nobleman's daughter, ignominiously murdered, Dysdemona."

"Who?" asked Captain Michales, frowning.

"Dysdemona, my respected Capitanio, the nobleman's daughter from Venice—haven't you heard of her? A Moor loved her, a tremendous palikare he was, but he was jealous and he killed her from the heat of love. He took a handkerchief . . ."

Captain Michales raised his fist, to stop the shameless mouth.

"In my presence," he said, "there will be no talk of women, Bertódulos."

Bertódulos shrivelled up, and the Venetian tale remained stuck in his throat.

"Well?" asked Vendúsos, raising in the air the bow with the pair of bells.

"Play what the Devil you like!" replied Captain Michales and leaned his head heavily against the wall.

Kajabés empties his glass and wiped his lips. And Furógatos, with his eyes fixed on the lyre, had already raised his right foot to let fly. . . .

But he did not. The house shook, the walls cracked, and Bertódulos grabbed at the cask behind him so as not to fall. The quinces, pomegranates and melons piled on the shelves rolled all over the place and bounced as far as the table.

"Earthquake!" cried Vendúsos, and made to run up into the open. Kajabés had already stretched out his hand to the door. Kajabés's thoughts were rushing to the harbour, pressing into a certain poor hut in search of Garufaliá. And Efendína had fallen on his nose on the floor and was twitching.

On the ground up above, confusion and running and the shrieks of women were to be hard.

"In God's name," Furógatos whimpered, "open the door and let us out!"

But Captain Michales grabbed for the whip above his head.

"Aren't you ashamed?" he shouted.

"Why should we be ashamed?" Furógatos had the courage to retort. "That's an earthquake, Captain Michales. It's not a human being that you can overcome."

As he said this there rumbled from out of the earth a dull, rolling, long-drawn-out thunder, like the bellowing of a bull, and the bells of Ai-Menas began ringing of their own accord.

"Saint Dionysius, help! I am Count Mangiavino!" cried Bertódulos, and hid his head in his cloak.

Captain Michales swung the whip in the air.

"No-one's to stir!" he shouted, "Lift Efendína off the ground. Lean him against the cask."

He whisked the cloak away from Bertódulos.

"An earthquake, Bertódulos, is nothing. Crete is a living thing. It's moving. One day you'll see the way it'll join on to Greece."

Suddenly he was in a good temper, and talked. He had been a youngster when the great earthquake destroyed half his village. Women, men too, were bewildered, they shrieked and cried and were buried in their houses. Only his father, Captain Sifakas, had quietly and without a word braced his hands and arms against the door-frame and held his elbows high, until his wife and children and the two pairs of oxen and their grey mare had got through. Then he himself had sprung out in one bound, and the walls had collapsed. Since then Captain Michales had lost the fear of earthquakes. He knew that a proper man could hold them within bounds. He filled the glasses, they drank, and their hearts returned to their places.

But up above, on the ground, the women of the neighbourhood had rushed out of their houses, buzzing about and screaming. Even Archondula, that stiff, acidulous old maid, had run out into the street with her deaf-and-dumb brother on her arm. She too had mingled with her neighbours and had become one with them. She was chattering and screeching just as though she did not come of an important family.

In the church, at the same moment, the Metropolitan had been preaching. At the start he spoke of God. But soon his discourse swooped away, left Heaven in the lurch and sank downwards to

Crete. The priest stood upright in front of his gilded throne, and his deep voice soared into the cupola, on which was painted the Lord Christ, staring in anger. From there it gained power, sank down and boomed about the church. And the Christians pressed close to one another, as though it really were the Lord Christ, sending down to them His voice from high up in the dome. Trembling they bowed their heads.

"My children," the old man said, "now comes a great time of fasting, the sufferings of Christ are approaching, fear must dominate Man, and he ought to direct his thoughts only to the blood which was shed upon the Cross. And yet God forgive me! I speak of the sufferings of Christ, and I am thinking of Crete."

He raised his hands towards the vaulting of the church, where Christ, the rainbow of hope, gleamed, watchful.

"How long, O Lord?" he cried. "How many generations, how many thousands of Cretans have, like me, raised their hands towards Heaven with the cry: 'How long, O Lord, how long?' We are not stones or pieces of wood, O Lord, we are souls, souls hast Thou given us. We are men and women. How long yet will the blood of Crete flow? The whole sea from the Cretan shore to the Hellespont and to Constantinople is red."

And behold! As the old man, standing upright and gazing up at the cupola, fell silent for a moment, as though awaiting an answer, the whole church shook, the lights swayed, and the bells rang without being touched by human hand.

"Earthquake! Earthquake!" the cry arose. The women ran from the women's side of the church and pressed, trampling on one another, to the doors. The Metropolitan stood stiff with terror, motionless. He gazed at Christ still with staring eyes. Múrzoflos came running, threw his arms round him, and led him from the throne through a side-door into the churchyard.

"Mylord," he said to him, giving him a friendly slap on the shoulders, "Mylord, don't be afraid. It's an earthquake, it's passing."

"I have sinned, O my God," muttered the Metropolitan, and his eyes filled with tears. "I have sinned! I am guilty. Instead of speaking of Thy sufferings, I spoke of Crete."

Captain Polyxigis, as his fate would have it, was gliding through the Turkish quarter. While the Christians were at their service, he had set out for his walk. Shaved, with plenty of lavender-water on his hair, and with his roomy fez cocked to one side, he swaggered along. His boots creaked as they touched the ground, and he felt throughout his body a deep happiness. He was at the height of his strength like a horse, like a gleaming bullock wandering through the fields in spring. His heart, his stomach, his bowels—all his organs were working without friction. Each was fulfilling its duty without quarrelling with its neighbour, and all together in obedient and glad community made up Captain Polyxigis.

He murmured to himself: "It's really a shame, that youth in human beings doesn't last a thousand years! Is God perhaps afraid that we'll take His throne away from Him? Is that why He craftily dismantles us, piece by piece? He pulls out our teeth, screws our knees up stiff, wears out our kidneys, dims our eyes and dribbles slime and spittle out of our noses and mouths. . . . Death doesn't worry me; by my soul, it doesn't worry me. There's something to be said for getting it over once for all. But I can't do with this business of turning gradually into a caricature——"

The phrase was still hanging on his lips as the whole of the Turkish quarter began to stagger. Doors flew to pieces. Screams of women and the clattering of clogs rang out in the courtyards. Ruhéni, the stately Moorish woman who was coming round the corner at that moment, shrieked out "God, have mercy!" and the round platter on her head swayed. The Sesame cakes rolled in the dirt and horsedung.

Captain Polyxigis braced his legs, so as to stand firm and not to fall. He pressed his hand against the wall and, once more as his fate would have it, quite close to Nuri's door.

"Earthquake!" he muttered, and his face became covered with fine sweat. He could fight against anything—against sickness, against enemies, against women. But how was he to fight against an earthquake, how see what he was doing? Captain Polyxigis turned pale. He wheeled round and saw that he was standing in front of Nuri's green door. He could hear high-pitched voices within, and pricked up his ears. He waited: was the earth going to open and swallow up mankind, or was this only a passing terror? All Megalokastro waited, with held breath. Even the dogs, which had begun to howl, stuck their tails between their legs and waited, with their hair standing on end and their necks craning. A dim, yellowish light was spreading, and then an uncanny sound like a piping came from underground. And suddenly the houses were again shaken, the minarets reeled like cypresses, and the wall, against which Captain Polyxigis had leaned, split right down. In Nuri Bey's house there was a crash of glasses, dishes and lamps as they rolled to the ground and smashed.

Suddenly the arched green door flew open, and Eminé Hanum burst out screaming, with her hair down and her feet naked. She fell in a faint in the middle of the street. Behind came running the Christian Moorish woman, carrying her small red slippers. She knelt by her and called to her. But Eminé lay on the stones, with her head thrown back, white as wax.

Captain Polyxigis's eyes flashed. "Eminé Hanum," he muttered, and moved away from the wall. He came closer. His pale face suddenly flushed. For a long time he had yearned to see the wild Circassian. And there she lay before him—what did he care for the earthquake?—with her hair down and her feet naked, just as he wished her to be.

Eagerly he bent over her, but the Moorish woman seized hold of him furiously and pushed him away.

"That's Nuri Bey's hanum," she shouted menacingly. "Don't you come near!" Then she pulled hard at her mistress's scarf, to cover her face.

"If I don't give her lavender-water to smell, the poor thing will die," said Captain Polyxigis, and pulled out of his waistcoat pocket a small bottle of perfume which he always carried on him.

He opened it and, kneeling, held it to the Circassian's nose.

The earth was now firm again, the heart of Megalokastro was beginning once more to beat at its proper rhythm. The dogs, too, plucked up courage again and barked at the earthquake.

The Circassian took a deep breath and opened her eyes. She saw bending over her an unknown man. She gave a cry and with both hands covered her unprotected mouth.

"Go away!" said the Moorish woman to the man, "go away if you value your life. Nuri Bey will be out in a moment."

But Captain Polyxigis was gazing at the Circassian's eyes. How could he decide either to live or to die? At first the black sparkling eyes were fierce and scornful. But the Circassian slowly softened, as she let the man's tumultuous breathing and provocative smell flow over her. She turned to her maid. "Who is the *giaour*?"

"Captain Polyxigis," he himself replied. "Thy slave, mistress. Keep the perfume to remember me by."

But the Circassian threw the bottle in his face and stood up. Her eyes were furious again.

"I'm going," said Captain Polyxigis, and sighed. "Don't be angry."

At that the Circassian tittered contemptuously. "Afraid?" she asked.

"I? Of whom?"

"Of Nuri Bey."

"You are the one and only person I'm afraid of, my mistress. If you tell me now that I'm to kill myself—as truly as I'm a man, I'll kill myself and never come near you again."

But he was scared at his own words and took them back.

"If there's a God in Heaven, I shall come near you one day, Eminé Hanum," he said defiantly, "one day I shall come near you, perish the whole world!"

The Circassian measured him with half-closed, angry eyes. As if she were reckoning up his value. As if she wanted to reckon up his value and buy him. And Captain Polyxigis stood stiffly, with his right hand on his silken sash, and waited.

"My God," said the Circassian at last, covering her face with her scarf without haste, "thinks Greeks are loathsome."

"My God," replied the man, "loves Circassian women and is almighty."

He heard voices and turned. Two Turks were approaching from the corner. Doors were opening. The Moorish woman seized her mistress round the waist and hurried with her into the house. The green door slammed behind them.

Captain Polyxigis wanted to go, but his knees were as though paralysed. "I'm lost, I'm lost," he muttered. "It's as if I'd never kissed, never had any fun, never touched a woman. Where is there a fire, for me to plunge in and get cool?"

He looked about him. He felt giddy. The streets were changed, people's faces were changed, Megalokastro undulated beneath his feet like some mottled net for snaring partridges with houses and minarets and gardens and seas painted on it.

He walked forwards over the net. Anxiously he went home. As soon as he reached the entrance, his fat, spongy sister fell into his arms and cried: "The earthquake!" With all her quivering mass of flesh she longed to hear a kind word from her brother.

But he pushed her aside and flung his fez on to the settee. The house was too small for him.

Meanwhile the party in the cellar had progressed far. At the beginning of the afternoon, Renió had a stealthy look through the peep-hole, to see in what waters her father's foolish guests were swimming.

Furógatos had taken his boots off: his soles were burning, and he danced alone, thoroughly drunk and possessed. At his big leaps his head hit against the ceiling. Blood was already trickling over his ears and neck, but he went happily on with his leaping dance. Efendína had forgotten all shame, and had undone his turban so that his scab showed white. He was leaning against the middle cask. Kajabés was leaning over him, adorning his skull with artichoke-leaves. There were still some eggs left in the clay dish, and Vendúsos was nerving himself heroically to consume them, shells and all. He coughed, and his eyes filled with tears from the effort of swallowing the shells. Poor Bertódulos had taken up position in the corner behind the jugs, with his thin legs braced and his cloak thrown back to avoid soiling it, and was now cautiously shoving his finger down his throat to make himself vomit. After each flood he turned to his companions and bowed:

"Excuse me, most noble Captains," he kept saying in his sing-song voice, "excuse me."

Renió was delighted at seeing how all these toadies demeaned

themselves to amuse her father. And she looked to the far end of
the cellar for Captain Michales.

He was leaning in silence, with his head thrown back, against
the wall, and staring into emptiness. The wine had not affected
him. He was neither drunk, nor talking, nor was he gay. Only his
upper lip quivered slightly, and between the raven hairs of his
moustache his fangs flashed.

Renió smiled. She liked her father. She was proud of his fierce-
ness, his silence, his pride. "If I were a man," she thought, "I'd be
like him. If I take a husband, I want one like him!"

The sun sank. Megalokastro forgot that it lived over an abyss,
and glowed, rosy and happy, under the farewell beams.

The Three Vaults were full of people. As after rain the ants
come out in swarms into the sun, so men and women came out
on to the streets, to see and be seen. They had escaped from a great
danger. For a moment the grave had opened under their feet, but
it had closed again. God be thanked, they were still alive and
beheld the upper world. They came out with their families for a
walk. They greeted one another, raising their hats or shaking
hands heartily. A sudden love united them this evening. They
observed one another tenderly. They went several times up and
down, and gazed, too, at the sea as if they had never seen it before.
A honeysuckle creeper had blossomed on the Pacha's kiosk in
the middle of the square. All stopped and sniffed the air, as though
stupefied by so much sweetness.

"What's that, friend?"

"Honeysuckle."

"Lord bless me!"

Gradually, tired by going to and fro, they sat down at the big
coffee-house of Leonídas Babaláros and clapped their hands.
Wasp-lean, bare-foot waiters came. People ordered cherry syrup
and soda-water, lenten pastries and grape tarts. Turkish children
with pumpkin pies and jasmin came along. Ruhéni too, that
gleaming black mare of a Moorish woman, appeared, with the
glass beads round her neck and those broad drooping breasts of
hers. She had brushed the Sesame cakes clean from the horsedung

in which they had been thrown by the earthquake, and now wandered, all laughter, up and down, swaying and bending. The setting sun drew gleams from her snow-white teeth and roguish eyes.

"What happiness this is," thought the Kastrians, "what a paradise it is. And there comes Ruhéni too, with the Sesame cakes!"

While more and more people from the neighbourhood streamed together and made the Three Vaults gay with their new clothes, the sun had vanished behind Strúmbulas, leaving a soft, violet glow in which the faces of men and women were transfigured.

What man of Kastro was not sought and found, in his Sunday suit, at the Three Vaults? Or what woman of Kastro was there, of any consequence, who did not sit at Leonídas Barbaláros's, buy pumpkin tarts, put back her glass and gossip about all the world?

There was Tityros with his fiancée Vangelio, and with them Chrysánthe, all combed and powdered and wearing a hat for the occasion of a visit to the Three Vaults with her niece and her new nephew. She glanced stealthily from the side at Vangelio and smiled, relieved: "I'm better," she thought, "nicer to look at, and I've got something a man can lay hold of. But this poor creature! Skin and bones! Tityros will find no flesh to get a grip on. But what do I want with marrying? I've got my brother, I don't need anybody!"

The doctor, too, came in sight, with Marcelle. He was a stout, self-satisfied *poseur* with a stiff hat from Paris, a stick and black gloves. Poor Marcelle was thickly painted and smeared with powder, to cover up her misery. She had reddened her lips, too. The women of Kastro turned mocking looks upon her. What a mask, my dear, what airs! Serves that doctor-dandy right! Should have got himself fitted out in his own country!

The sea sank into the dusk, and on its horizon the island of Dia disappeared. A breeze from the shore sighed, set the women's hair waving, and made them shut their fans. A group of Maltese fishermen came by with their concertina. They wore ear-rings, and their open shirts showed their broad, hairy chests tanned by the sea and sun. They sang in raucous voices and did not turn to look at the women of Kastro, but pushed on towards the harbour where, stretched out among trawling-tackle and fish-baskets, the Maltese women were waiting for them.

In the darkness the young gained courage and began again to rove. They drew near to the girls and caressed them with stealthy glances. Over their faces a warm wind of love flickered. On one side the mountains, on the other the Cretan Sea, and up above a dim sky, glimmering blue. And over every unmarried head there danced with a thousand rogueries the evening star, Venus.

While the men and women of Kastro were gathered at the Three Vaults, Captain Michales's son Thrasáki and his three friends were slipping along towards the Pervóla. The Pervóla was an unfenced, unkempt garden at the end of Megalokastro, full of spindly cactuses and nettles. Thrasáki was carrying a rope coiled round his waist, Mastrapas's son Manolios a cudgel, Krasojórgis's son Andrikos a birch and Furógatos's son Nikolas a whistle.

"If we see her father come out," he explained, "I'll whistle, and we all run for it."

"Did you say that Pervóla's always on the doorstep?" asked Andrikos.

Pervóla was not the name of Paraskevás's daughter, but these young rascals had called her so because she was stout and lush and always smiling.

"She stands on the doorstep every Sunday with ribbons in her hair," said Thrasáki. "Give me your whistle, Nikola. I'll whistle when we're to attack her."

He seized hold of Nikolas and took the whistle from him.

"You take the rope," he said. "Aren't I the Captain? Well, I must have the whistle. Let go!"

A few, wretched houses were scattered about. It was the out-of-the-way quarter where poor Turks and Armenians lodged. The Armenians ground coffee in large stone mortars and then sold it. The Turks were porters and labourers by the day.

The four friends, who had till now been running began to move cautiously. They kept close to the walls, in single file, led by Thrasáki with the whistle. Suddenly he stopped. At the door of her house stood the cheerful, lush "Pervóla", with a red ribbon in her fair hair. She was chewing mastic.

Thrasáki turned to his companions.

"Watch out! There she is!" he whispered. "I'll whistle and rush in first. There's nobody coming."

They advanced a little further. The full-blooming "Pervóla" now towered in front of them, still and enormous. She had her face turned away from them and was watching two cats having a noisy fight on the wall above her.

The four pigmies pressed against the wall and held their breath. Thrasáki glanced up and down the street: not a soul. He clapped the whistle between his lips, blew it, and rushed at the girl. Behind him the other three screeched like cats. Thrasáki caught hold of her on one side, Nikolas on the other, Andrikos by the feet, while Manolios stopped her mouth to prevent her from crying out. She did not struggle. Gasping laboriously—for she was heavy—the four lifted her up and did not know what to do with her.

"Into the Pervóla!" Thrasáki ordered. "Hold her fast, so she doesn't escape us! Come on!"

They stumbled through the broken gate and a few steps beyond. Soon they had no strength left and threw her down on the grass. Then they stood round her and looked at her. The red ribbon had come untied and her hair was falling over her shoulders. Her dress was torn to above the knee. Her plump breasts rose and fell frantically under the revealing bodice. The girl had been frightened at first. Now, when she saw who had made off with her, she began to giggle. Stretched on the grass she looked at the children with half-closed, teasing eyes, and waited.

"What shall we do with her now?" asked Nikolas, examining the outstretched "Pervóla" curiously from head to foot and unable to make up his mind.

"Let's spit on her," proposed Manolios.

They all began spitting on her. Yet that did not relieve them. That was nothing. Discouraged, they left off, and stared at her. They must do something else, something else, but what?

"Let's thrash her," said Andrikos, and raised the birch he was holding. They all rushed at her and began beating her—with the

E

birch, with the rope, and Nikolas, the strong one, with his fist. Now the girl was frightened, and cried out.

"Let's stamp on her," Thrasáki proposed, "to stop her screaming."

"What about the cudgel?" asked Manolios. He took out from his belt the thick cudgel he was carrying.

"That comes later," said Thrasáki.

They jumped on her back and on her stomach, while she rolled on the grass to escape their feet. At length she got up and tried to escape, but they fell on her again and dragged her to the ground.

They were now sweating and tired. Once more they paused and looked at the girl and were at a loss what other torment to devise. What else should they do to the girl? They had expected to feel pleasure as they kidnapped and maltreated her. For a whole month they had been thinking over the plan. And now, when they saw the girl lying before them, they got no satisfaction. They gazed at her with hatred.

"We ought to have brought a pocket-knife," said Thrasáki, "a knife to stick into her and make her bleed. That's it!"

"Shall I bite her?" suggested Nikolas. "I can tear off a bit of her flesh."

"Yes, let's take it in turns," said Manolios.

"No, all together!" Thrasáki again ordered.

Nikolas unwound the rope, and they all threw themselves on the girl to tie her up. Manolios also pulled out the cudgel. But they got no further. From the broken gate there came a shrill, furious voice: "You damned ruffians!"

They wheeled round. Signor Paraskevás was standing at the gate of the Pervóla, half-naked and armed with a broomstick. Saturday evening haircuts and shaves for so many Cretans had worn him out. To-day he had slept all day, to get up strength for the coming week. Never had scissors and razor blades seemed to him so blunt as on this Devil's-island. . . . Suddenly he had heard in his sleep his daughter's cries. He had jumped up, grabbed for the broomstick and rushed out, clad only in his breeches, into the street.

"You impudent ruffians!" he yelled, making his voice as manly as he could and raising the broomstick. But suddenly he started back. Among the four figures he had recognised Captain Michales's son. "Oh, that means trouble," he muttered; "be careful, wretched Paraskevás!" And he contented himself with brandishing the broomstick threateningly in the air.

"Let's go," said Thrasáki. "Follow me."

He turned to Paraskevás. "Hey, Mr. Paraskevás," he said, "keep away from the gate and let us through. And throw away that broomstick!"

"Sorry," said the Syrian, and threw the broomstick away.

IV

HOW neatly God has arranged things in the world! During six week-days the hunt for money, and the seventh day belongs to God, good food and amusement. Monday broke, the wheel took another turn, and yesterday's mannerly god-fearing Kastrians forgot the earthquake and God, to plunge once more into "give and take" and "eat or be eaten".

The sun rose, the soldiers took the fat keys and opened the three gates to the outer world. From afar the peasants streamed in shouting, with their laden asses and mules. The harbour gate too was thrown open, and down went porters, boatmen and dockers. Over the mole once more rose the din of many human beings. The same din filled men's ears in the market place, while in the neighbouring gipsy quarter the smiths' hammers began banging. The crier stood in the middle of the square, and his voice was like a bell's. It announced that a calf would now be slaughtered at Ismaili's butchery. Its meat would be as tender as Turkish delight, and those who came in time could choose the best cuts.

In Broad Street the cobblers' shops were opening, one after another. The masters took their places on their high benches and began to cut the pieces of leather. The assistants and apprentices brought out their stools and their tools and set to work. They kept looking out at the street the while, in case any deformed or half-witted person came by, for them to make fun of. That was the best way of passing the time.

The first to come was Captain Stefanés, leaning on his crooked stick. He had heard that the small ship belonging to his friend Captain Jakumes had arrived yesterday evening from Smyrna, and he was going down to greet him. He wanted to know what was happening over there in Greece, what the King was doing and what people were saying about the Union. In Syra there was the Cretan Committee, which thought of Crete day and night. It was collecting money, buying muskets and cartridges, and waiting.

If there was no progress, so they said, Crete would revolt again. So Captain Stefanés hobbled along, to embrace his friend and to learn from him in a tavern something of what was happening in the world.

One of the cobblers' boys whistled: it was the sign. All looked up and stared out. But immediately they turned aside, furtive and embarrassed. Were they to get across that dog-fish who, the day before yesterday, had given a cruel beating to an apprentice who had laughed at him? "You young louse," he had bellowed, "would you snigger at me? Do you know, idiot, where I got this limp— where, when and how? Very well then, find out, you snot-nose!" and struck at him with his stick. The master had not defended his apprentice—on the contrary he had even said: "You're quite right, Captain Stefanés. You are the Cretan Miaúlis.[1] Hit him again!"

So the cobblerfolk kept their heads down, made not a sound and let Captain Stefanés pass by.

"That's a hard nut, children, by all that's holy," said one of the journeymen, when the Captain had gone out of sight in the direction of the harbour. "A hard nut to crack!"

While he was still speaking Mr. Charílaos came in sight—that bow-legged dwarf with his slender stick, his little, twirled and waxed moustache and his triple soles. He swaggered past the shoe-shops, striking the pavement with his stick. The masters raised their hands to their chests to wish him good-day.

Every time the Kastrians saw Mr. Charílaos pass by they felt respect and dread. As if he were no human being, but something between human being and demon. As if this gnome had come out of a fairy story. The children would stop dead and stare at him in terror. He was a guardian of treasure, who kept gold hidden underground. He had command over dark forces. He had the evil eye, and if he looked at you at all long your skin might become green and swell as though a snake had bitten you. The story went that one day in Arcondopula's garden he had stared at a blossoming lemon-tree, and the blossoms had at once faded.

So the cobblers bowed their heads in silence and let him pass by.

[1] A Greek pirate hero (translator's note).

"A bad beginning to the day, children! Nothing to laugh at, to-day!" said the same one as before. "Where's Efendína got to? Where's Barba Jannis? Are they dead?"

"Talk of the Devil!" cried one of them from a shop opposite. "Here *is* Barba Jannis!"

They all leaned forward contentedly, to watch him. Crying up his sherbet with hoarse croaking, carrying the bronze can in his right hand and in his left the little basket with the snow in it, the hideous Barba Jannis with his pointed head approached. Everyone at once got into position. The intention was to bellow and catcall systematically, so as to drown Barba Jannis's voice. And then they would pelt him with lemon-peel, and make fun of him into the bargain. One of them would ask: "Hey, little wife, are all the children in our house mine? Tell me the truth. Think! I'm dying, dear wife." And another from the opposite side of the road would answer in a high-pitched voice: "And suppose you don't die, Barba Jannis?" And the whole of Broad Street would shake with laughter. But now the journeyman stood up so that they might all hear him, and called out: "Children, this time we'll play him a new trick. We won't make a sound, and when he goes past we'll act as if we don't see him at all. That'll send him quite mad. That'll be real fun!"

And so at last Barba Jannis arrived and started to cry up his drink. He looked to right and left at the shoe-shops, stopped still for a moment, waited. What's going on here? Lord, have mercy! Does nobody raise his head to look at him? Does nobody open his mouth to yell at him? Has he sunk so low? Is it all the same whether a dog or an ass or Barba Jannis passes by? Why don't you make a noise, children? I am, after all, Barba Jannis—what's become of the lemon-peel?

Silence. Bent over their leather without a word, they all hammered away, dyed laces, threaded needles, sewed. Barba Jannis trembled. He rubbed his eyes. Was he dreaming? He put his can and snow-basket down on the ground.

"In God's name," he shouted, "say something, children! You're driving me mad! No, no, I can't bear it. Where's the lemon-peel?"

But no-one looked up, no voice made itself heard. Barba Jannis again implored them.

"Have pity on me, children! I'm a dying man, and you don't spare me a look! Am I still alive indeed? Or am I already dead? Say just one word!"

Nothing. The stillness of death. Then Barba Jannis was seized with a strong dread. "Magic!" he muttered. "The world's coming to an end, death is upon us! Either the cobblers are dead, or I am." With a cry of "Help, feet!" he clutched violently at his can and basket and banged them against his feet.

And now Broad Street shook with roars of laughter.

It could be heard as far as the Bishop's Residence. The Metropolitan rose from his bed, where he lay with a cold. Múrzuflos had just taken away the cupping-glass and was now rubbing him with raki.

"What can that row be?" he asked, pricking up his ears. "Is there a storm approaching, or is it another earthquake?"

"It must be the cobblers, Mylord. They're having their fun with some poor unfortunate," answered Múrzuflos angrily. "They're a shameful lot! The world's going to the dogs, but they will bawl away. Curse them, they've interrupted our conversation, most reverend bishop."

The Metropolitan had been telling him about Russia—about Kiev, where he had been Archimandrite for many years: about the snowstorms, the golden cupolas on top of the churches and the subterranean monasteries filled with saints.

"As long as Russia survives," he said, "have no fear, Múrzuflos: the true Faith will live for ever and reign. That is where Christ has now taken refuge. That is where I once saw Him with my own eyes, Múrzuflos, in the depth of winter, at evening. He was striding through the snow, He wore a long leather coat and high boots and thick gloves. He kept knocking at the doors, but no one let Him in. I saw Him through the window and dashed downstairs to open to Him. 'O my Christ,' I cried, but He had vanished."

Múrzuflos made the sign of the Cross.

"I have never seen Him," he said dolefully.

"Go to Russia and you will see Him," answered the Metropolitan, turned his face to the wall and dozed off.

But the Pacha too had woken up in a bad mood this morning. For he had not been feeling well these days. Out of a clear sky there had suddenly descended on him the feeling that he was growing old. The day before yesterday, near the Three Vaults, as he was smoking his long pipe in the Pacha Kiosk and the soldiers were blowing their trumpets and beating their drums, he had picked out among the crowd of Greeks who were streaming idly past the band a girl with luxuriant hair and a voluptuous mouth, who delighted him. He had turned to his groom, the Arab, Suleiman:

"Fellow, who's the Greek girl over there in the red dress?"

"Does she please you, Pacha Efendi? She's no Kastrian. She comes from Kruson, the savage village. Last Sunday she married the grocer Kajabés who's such a good singer. You've heard him. In the Devil's name, let her go!"

"Is she a respectable woman? May she perish if she is!"

"Very respectable, Pacha Efendi, very respectable. And her husband's from Sfakia."

"A respectable woman, a respectable woman," muttered the Pacha, wagging his bald head. "She's respectable because I'm growing old. It's coming to an end. What's to be expected of life, when you can't misbehave any more, when you can't do away with a man when you want to, or kiss any woman you want to? What sort of a Pacha am I? This damned growing old! Ah, what a time I had in other Greek places, when I used to send my executioner along with an apple wrapped in a cloth for the bride and a bullet for the bridegroom. I had them told that they must choose. How could they be expected to choose the bullet? They always chose the apple, and that same evening the bride would come, all tear-stained and dolled up, and would struggle as I like women to do, and then sit on my knee. But now I've grown old. The State, too, has grown old. And it's the fault of this damned Crete!"

He turned to the Arab: "What about it, Suleiman?", and winked at him.

"Do as if you'd never seen her, Pacha Efendi. This is Crete. Here we shall have trouble. Don't sigh. Shall I fetch the Armenian girl?"

The Armenian girl, Marúsia, was famous in Crete. She had even been celebrated in a song. Her husband was an uncouth, broad-boned Armenian, whose shop was situated in the main square. There he stood all day, bent over the deep stone mortar, and pounded the coffee, whose smell spread all around. From the constant pounding his arm had become as thick as a thigh, so that with the heavy pestle he could break through a wall. His wife, a small Armenian witch, looked from behind as if she consisted merely of two half-spheres, which wagged as she went. Her scent— as sensual as a beast's—was caught by the young people even in remote parts of the town. Late in the evening they would slip along to her hut near the Pervóla. There she would stand on the doorstep with her bodice half undone, her cheeks thickly powdered and a delicate little moustache damp with sweat. She would stand there quite still and smile out of eyes almost closed. And late at night, if her tired-out husband was asleep, she would open her own shop and sell love by weight, while in the next room the Armenian snored. She left the door open on purpose. For it enchanted her, at the moment when strangers—Turks, Christians, Armenians, Jews—were embracing her, to feel her husband close by and to shudder with fear.

Every time the Pacha was depressed, every time the Vizier reprimanded him, the Arab brought him this Armenian woman, and the bad mood passed.

"Wouldn't you like me to fetch the Armenian woman?" Suleiman asked again.

"Fellow, I don't want any women," roared the Pacha, and spat with disgust. "The hypocrites, as bad as priests—they make me sick. For sixteen—seventeen years I've done nothing else. Now I'm sighing because I've grown old and Turkey's grown old. We're both of us going to the Devil. . . . What's the name of that one, anyhow?"

E*

"Garufaliá."

"May her dead body rot! Tell Barba Jannis, the sulepi-vendor, he's to come to me in the konak this evening and amuse me. My heart is very heavy, my dear Suleiman. . . . Efendína's to come too."

He knocked out his pipe against a stone. "She loves me, she loves me not," he murmured softly, that the Arab might not overhear. "Allah make me a liar, but I believe Turkey too has reached the stage of saying, 'she loves me not'. . . . Fill my pipe, light it, and don't speak to me!"

A horseman came by: fierce, with a black beard, and his fore-head hidden by a head-band. He struck his mare with a whip, galloped past like a flash and disappeared through the Hospital Gate into the fields.

"Who was that *giaour*, Arab?" asked the Pacha with surprise. "He often plays the hero, it seems to me. Where have we seen him before?"

The Arab stared, as though fascinated, after the horseman, who was now circling the fortifications.

"Where do you keep your wits, blockhead?" asked the Pacha, flourishing his pipe. "Didn't you hear my question?"

"Who was it, Pacha Effendi? Don't you then remember summoning him to the konak last year and dressing him down for having made game of Nuri Bey? He never opened his mouth to apologise, and as he went he caught hold of the stair-rail and nearly wrenched it out."

"Captain Michales!" said the Pacha. He fell into thoughtful silence for a moment. Then he went on: "Listen, Suleiman. One day I shall stand you up by the Three Vaults in front of all the people, Turks and Greeks, and let you fight with him and strike him down. Then we'll be rid of him. . . . Are you listening?"

The Arab looked out towards the sea. The whites of his eyes were all yellow, with a network of red arteries. He did not answer.

The Pacha made a sign. The trumpets stopped. He got up to go and turned once more to his groom:

"If you're afraid of the *giaour*, Arab, then we're lost. You mark my words!"

He had said no more. But for three days his mind had dwelt on the woman in the red skirt and on the chicken heart of Turkey. And to-day—Monday morning—he woke up full of agitation. He had had a bad dream. In the middle of the market place two raging beasts were fighting: Captain Michales and Suleiman the Arab. Both were naked and anointed with grease. Each had in his hand nothing but an axe. The whole of Megalokastro was gathered round them: on the sunny side the Christians, on the other—in shadow—the Turks. They were standing and looking on. No one spoke, all watched with pale faces and open mouths. And he himself was squatting under a red canopy. His heart was shuddering like a reed. If Captain Michales wins, Turkey falls. But if Suleiman the Arab wins, Christendom falls.

The two fought and roared. The earth trembled under their tread and the hollows in the ground filled with blood. Until the sun went down. Turks and Christians were lost in the darkness, and now the Pacha could only make out the two wild beasts as they roared and staggered and rose again, with the strips of flesh hewn by the axes hanging about their bodies. And suddenly the Pacha despaired. "Allah, Allah," he murmured, "it's only a dream. I'm going to give a cry, so as to wake up and not to see the end."

He gave a cry and woke up. And now he sat, depressed and sunk in thought, on his wide bed with its horse-hair stuffing. He clapped his hands, and Suleiman appeared.

"Go, and fetch Captain Michales!" he said.

He did not know what he wanted with him. But he must come! Perhaps some insolent word will escape him, so that I shall get angry and make up my mind! He's not to indulge in any pertness in my realm. I am the Pacha! And he goes riding out on his mare when I'm listening to the soldiers' music!

"Captain Michales?" asked the Arab, scratching his head. "But I'm told, Pacha Effendi, that he's gone down into his cellar with his idiotic drinking-companions and there he's drinking. . . ."

"And suppose he is drinking! He's to get sober and come here!"

The Arab still hesitated. He lowered his voice: "Pacha Effendi, do you want to drown Crete in blood? Have you had orders from Constantinople?"

The Pacha put both hands to his bald head. He felt giddy.

"What's that?" he asked.

"Well, suppose he says to me: 'I won't come.' What do you propose to do with him then? Are you going to send soldiers after him, and have him give them a beating? He's no man, especially when he's drinking. More like an earthquake. When he was drunk last year, didn't he seize hold of the harbour gate, to pull it down? And if, after all, you arrange things so cleverly that he gets killed, then the whole of Crete catches fire! Leave him alone and let him go to the Devil, Pacha Effendi."

"Let him go to the Devil because he's a palikare, and let her go to the Devil because she's a respectable woman—yes, what sort of a Pacha am I?"

He pondered for a while, this way and that. If the wretched island catches fire again and fresh soldiers come from Anatolia, and guns as well and gallows and fresh pachas, the Franks will again mix themselves up in it: curse them too! And it won't do me any good—I shall simply have more trouble.

"Quick, bring me a pot of cream and sugar, and fill me my pipe, you Arab scoundrel," he said at last, tugging angrily at his moustache.

"And Captain Michales?"

"May the Devil take him!"

At the time when the Pacha was talking of him, Captain Michales was observing the rise of the daylight through the small window of the cellar. His head-band had fallen on to his shoulders. His forehead gleamed like bronze in the light, and the hair of his head and beard glittered. His round, deep black eyes were motionless, gazing at the window. All night he had not slept, but had watched, listened and drunk. Each time his heart had tried to calm itself, he had given a fierce, hot cry, and made it clench again. What the Devil do I want? he asked himself again and again. The wine I pour down myself is wasted: robbing Peter to pay Paul.

He was not drunk. It was his secret pride that wine could never bring him down. From time to time he stood up, paced up and down the cellar and again sat down. He despised the wine-bibbers

who reeled about the place, stuttered, made much of their unwashed thoughts or set up a howling. At one moment he turned
to Bertódulos:

"What was that she-demon you were talking about?" he asked,
suddenly.

"Dysdemona, Captain. A prince's daughter in Venice. Her hair
was honey-fair and wound in plaits three times round her head,
like a royal crown. She had a little olive birth-mark, too, on her
cheek. . . ."

"Go on!"

"And so, Captain, not to beat about the bush, this delicately-
bred prince's daughter—what a thing it is, the human soul!—fell
in love with a Moor, a powerful fellow with giant limbs! But, to
give the Devil his due, a doughty palikare! And how do you think
it came about that she fell in love with him? One night the great big
rascal sat down beside her and told her about his life, like a book.
And the girl was so stirred, she was filled with such a strong sympathy for what he had suffered, that she began crying and fell on
his neck. 'Ah, dear Moor,' she said to him, 'don't be sad. I will
console you. I will bring a smile to your lips.' "

Bertódulos drew breath, emptied his glass and sighed.

"Go on," ordered Captain Michales again.

"I'm sorry, Captain, my head's gone blank," said Bertódulos,
scratching his pointed skull to bring the memory out. "Remarkable things happened," he said at last, loudly. "They didn't stay
in Venice, they journeyed to Cyprus. They got married, I think,
and a white officer with gold stripes got mixed up in it. And later
. . . I've forgotten again. It had to do with a handkerchief."

"A handkerchief? Now you're making it up, Bertódulos."

"No, no, I'm not making it up, my lord. A handkerchief, a
handkerchief really. But it was properly poisoned, bewitched—
how should I know? And the Moor became furious with jealousy,
and one night—ah, that night brings it all back to me—he stuffed
the handkerchief into Dysdemona's mouth and. . . ."

A sobbing took hold of him, he pulled his scarf off, wiped his
eyes and forehead and gave a loud cry:

". . . and he throttled her!"

The four drunken men, who had been craning their necks from all sides and listening, burst out laughing. But Captain Michales angrily shouted: "Quiet!" Then he turned to Bertódulos.

"It's not your fault. It was my fault for asking."

He leaned heavily against the wall with his head and closed his eyes. The Moor was right, he was thinking, he acted properly.

Meanwhile those around him had forgotten strangers' sorrows. "Don't cry, my little Bertódulos," said Furógatos. "Those are all fairy tales. Only we are real. Here, Vendúsos, play your lyre, my legs are twitching, I want to dance."

The lyre with the bells on it was itself drunk and sprang on to Vendúsos's knees like a living woman, a newly wedded one, and Kajabés looked at her with a sigh, leaned his utterly fuddled head on his hand and began a long-drawn-out intoning.

And Efendína, with his scabby head wreathed in artichoke-leaves and his belly swollen with wine and pork, clapped his hands and sat up straight as a candle. Suddenly he jumped to his feet, flung his arms round Furógatos's shoulders, and danced like a madman—to the Devil with sainthood!

"Turn Christian, Efendína," Furógatos implored him, "turn Christian, and come to Paradise riding on a pig!"

"I can't, chaps," he replied sadly. "I can't, and you must forgive me. Turk I was born, Turk I shall die."

The eggs had already been eaten, shells and all. Now Captain Michales with a blow from his fist, smashed the pottery egg-cups and distributed them to his guests to eat. Bertódulos was terrified, took his piece and clung breathless to a cask. With goggling eyes he watched the Cretans at his feet bite their bits of clay and chew them until they became sand and grit, which they swallowed with a snigger.

There are three sorts of men, Bertódulos slowly explained to himself: those who eat eggs without the shells; those who eat eggs with the shells; and those who gobble them up with the shells and the egg-cups as well. Those of the third kind are called Cretans. Oh, oh, Conte Mangiavino, what has brought you here? he asked himself, and glanced towards the door.

By grey of dawn they had all laid down their arms. Some

sprawled on the floor, snoring, some leaned with their heads against the casks and strained, groaning, to vomit from full stomachs. Bertódulos, who had done his vomiting, found some water and had a wash. Then he hid his head in his cloak, which he wrapped twice round him, and stretched himself out in a corner. He lay there like a soaked hen with its feathers all over the place. Only Captain Michales, full of drink but unaffected, held his head high and stared through the little window at the breaking day.

As the light entered the cellar and lit up debris of food and pools of wine and vomit, Captain Michales turned and gazed at the five beaten nincompoops as though he saw them for the first time. And suddenly his heart gave a start of scorn. He pricked up his ears. He could hear his wife in the yard—she was up already, drawing water from the well. He could hear the cocks of the neighbourhood crowing. The noise of human beings and animals awakening rose from the face of the earth. From afar the unending roar of the sea came and flocked about him. The mare whinnied in the yard. Charitos was about to bring her her bucket of cold water and her fodder. The whinny mounted into the air as fresh as dew, it spurted like spring water. Captain Michales's soul was refreshed by it.

"I'm beginning to think," he muttered, "that I can only be friends with horses. Yes, if Crete had wolves and boars. . . . Human beings seem to me to be nothing but pitiful idiots."

He stood up, and stretched himself till his bones cracked. He gave each of his companions a kick and threw wine from a jug over them.

"Forward!" he shouted, "get up! To work!"

All through the new day and the following night the carousing went on. The whip whistled when anyone tried to slack. Charitos ran up and down the stairs with dainties. Like brothers, Efendína and Bertódulos crammed each other full. In their mutual tenderness they marvelled that they had lived so many years in the same town and only now got to know and love each other.

"I'll teach you to play the guitar," said Bertódulos, "and then you'll forget your worries. Then you'll play and you'll cross the streets without turning a hair."

"And I'll teach you," replied Efendína, "how to carry flames about with you, Bertódulos my dear, and you'll cool yourself at them."

The Count had got used to the Cretan atmosphere. It made him happy, to love and embrace them all. Only before Captain Michales he remained shy. He, the witty gentleman of Zante, would have liked to crack a joke with him, but at the last moment he felt embarrassed. The story would not pass his lips. He turned to Vendúsos:

"We two, Signor Vendúsos—have you ever realised?—we two aren't men, we're artists."

"Artists? What the Devil's that?"

"A sort of angels. Well, not exactly, there's a little something lacking. Look here: there are animals—asses, mules—and there are human beings. And then, above them, there are the artists, and higher still the angels. We two, my dear Vendúsos, are artists."

"And so—?"

"And so, if you die a peaceful death, don't forget to take your lyre into the grave with you, as I'm taking my guitar. Yes, let's die together, Vendúsos, my little Vendúsos! The angels too play lyres and guitars, and at the gate of Paradise we'll give the great Maestro, whom the unmusical call God, a concert. I'll sing *canzone* and you'll sing Cretan *mantinade*, until the great Maestro comes out to clash the cymbals for us and admit us into His immortal choir."

Vendúsos laughed: "You've said a mouthful, my little Bertódulos," he said. "How do you propose that you should play the guitar, and I the lyre, without hands, without fingers? Have you seen what becomes of hands and fingers in the earth?"

"Be quiet, you wretch! You're making my hair stand on end!" cried the Count, and wrapped himself tighter in his cloak. "Do you mean that even the hands that play guitars——?"

"All, all, my friend in misfortune, all!"

"Well, let's get drunk, while we've still got hands and throats!" shouted Furógatos, filling the glasses. "And women, Vendúsos? Do they too turn——?"

"All of them, all. . . ."

"Even if they're beautiful like the sun?"

"Even then. But what's up with Captain Michales?"

Captain Michales was frowning. "Better let your hands do the talking, Vendúsos. And you your feet, Furógatos. Your tongues should keep quiet."

"At your orders, Captain Michales."

Furógatos jumped up. What more could he ask for? Vendúsos placed the lyre on his right knee, Kajabés raised his hand to his cheek, and dance and song began again. The day outside stood in the fire of the sun, but the life of the boon-companions played itself out in that cellar. Noon came and went. The sun sank, night took possession once more. In the middle of the table and on the casks the fat candles burned. And at the next daybreak there they lay again on the floor like abortions, exhausted, saffron-yellow. Corners and walls were again bespattered, and their clothes nothing but wine- and grease-spots. A stench rose from their mouths and hair.

Motionless, Captain Michales watched over them. At grey of dawn he turned his face to the little window, not to have to look at them any longer. He was thinking of nothing, he was only feeling—had been, now, for two days and two nights—how his entrails wavered and found no firm ground any more. As, on the Tuesday morning, he sat thus with his head leaning against the wall, sleep like a flash surprised him; a flash, no longer. But long enough for the demon to master him. At first it seemed to Captain Michales that he was walking into a cool, vernal cloud. Still dazed from the heat, wine and suffering, he wandered into it, and the cloud embraced him, took him under the arms and raised him up, and from below caressed his body and thighs. But slowly the cloud changed, thickened, became a face: first there emerged two feminine lips, then the twinkle of two wild, shameless eyes, full of mockery and disdain. And lastly two tiny, red-stained soles and two snow-white hands. The lips moved and a voice rang out like gurgling water: "Captain Michales, Captain Michales! . . ."

Captain Michales wrenched himself out of the dream with such a jerk that the table capsized, and everything on it—glasses, plates,

candles, tobacco-boxes—rolled all over the place. The five sleepers
sprang up. Daylight had reached the cellar. They looked about
them and gazed at Captain Michales, who had grabbed the whip
from the wall and now made a rush at them:

"Get out! Get out!" he shouted, as though possessed. "Get out!"
He wrenched the door open. "Get out!"

Kajabés was first: he sprang over the threshold with one bound
and ran across the yard to the street door. He was soon outside.
The third morning only! Garufaliá was surely still asleep. His feet
acquired wings and he ran to the harbour. The other four tottered,
one after the other, clinging to the walls, out of the cellar. As they
came into the daylight, their faces showed greenish-yellow,
sunken, smeared and begrimed. Half-tipsy, they stared across the
yard, at the well, the vine-trellis, the street door, and could not
think where to go. Furógatos went first, depressed, with his
moustache drooping, and was making efforts to get his belt
straight. But it kept escaping him and sliding to the ground, so
that Vendúsos, who was following him with his lyre on his
shoulder, tripped over it. Behind him came Efendína with one
hand holding up his sackcloth breeches whose cord had broken,
while with the other he attempted confusedly to hold his companions back.

"Stop, you fools! Where are you off to? The Captain's only
joking. He'll soon call us back. Just count, if you've any faith in
God: Tuesday, Wednesday, Thursday, Friday, Saturday, Sunday
—six days still to go!"

It seemed to him unjust that they should be dismissed so
quickly, just as one had begun to sink in sin up to the neck. Sins
only began to bring real satisfaction when one was well and truly
up to the neck in them. Then one began to enjoy them, and then
one began to have something to repent of. Sin should be a mountain of pork which had to be mastered, a lake of wine in which
to swim—not just a tit-bit!

He kept counting the days on his fingers, over and over: Tuesday, Wednesday, Thursday, Friday, Saturday, Sunday. . . . A pity
so many days should be lost. "No, it won't do, Captain Michales.
Don't do us this injustice. Call us back!"

It seemed to him as if someone did call him. A hand touched him. It was surely Captain Michales. He turned joyfully. Bertódulos had plucked him by the shoulder. He was whimpering and reeling.

"Efendína, my dear," he said. "I've left my purse behind. Would you go and get it for me?"

Furógatos had got to the street door. His belt still kept slipping down and trailing behind him. He found his hands and feet heavy, as though paralysed, and they refused him their service.

"I'll go and get my wife to give my limbs a rubbing," he said. "Good-bye, chaps. We've got off lightly!"

"Where are you going? Don't leave me alone, Furógatos!" screamed Bertódulos. "Wait for me!"

"Come, little Bertódulos, you support me and I'll support you," said Furógatos, putting his arm round him.

The Maestro clung to the dangling belt.

"I've left my purse behind," he said imploringly. But Furógatos pretended not to have heard. The sun was now reaching into the alleys. The voice of Barba Jannis could be heard, crying up his *sulepi*. And the peasants were shouting: "Logs, good logs!" and driving their laden asses along. Now the two were passing Tulupanas's bakery. They stopped. Two trays, covered with Sesame-rolls, were steaming in front of the oven-mouth.

Bertódulos looked at the Sesame-rolls and stopped dead. Furóogats stuck his hand into his waistcoat pocket and pulled out a small coin. He took a roll.

"Eat," he said to his companion. "I don't want any myself." He had thought of the lepers, and felt sick.

Efendína meanwhile was creeping, with his head scratched bloody by the artichoke-leaves, back to the téké, stealthily so that his mother should not see him and beat him.

Vendúsos went home with his lyre over his shoulder, still all out of breath and yellow in the face. His wife ran to meet him and supported him under the arms. His two daughters also came to his help and the three of them laid him on the settle. They rubbed him with oil from the lamp of the Holy Mother of the Grapes. They swung luck-bringing incense over him. They piled on him all the rugs they possessed, for he was shivering. Finally they ran to their neighbour, Old Flamburiarena, and asked her to come and cup him.

Captain Michales had meanwhile saddled his mare and stuck the thing with the black hilt into his belt. His wife came out into the yard to ask him where he was going and to remind him of the affairs of his house. But when she saw his face, her voice failed her. Captain Michales had turned:

"What do you want?" he asked hoarsely and angrily.

"Should I make you some coffee?" his wife asked.

"I'm going to the coffee-house, I'll have some there. Get in."

Katerina went back into the kitchen, alarmed. Renió had lit the fire and made coffee.

"He's going," said her mother. "He's saddled the mare and is going to ride through the Turkish quarter. He's a wild beast, he is, a wild beast. He has no feelings."

Renió laughed: "He's going to ride into the Turkish coffee-houses again," she said proudly.

Both fell silent. They listened. They heard the mare trample over the threshold, then whinny in the street outside.

"May God hold His hand over him," murmured the mother, crossing herself.

"Did you see the way the fools ran for it?" asked Renió, laughing. "I was looking out of the window upstairs. One after the other, screaming and reeling. And Father standing there, sober and scornful with his whip raised, brandishing it in the air. Why are you sighing, Mother? Would you like to have Bertódulos or Vendúsos as your husband? You ought to be rejoicing over your luck, Mother!"

"It's possible to be a decent husband and a good earner without needing to behave like a fool."

"Yes, it's possible," Renió answered, pouting. "But I don't like either earners or fools. I like captains."

Captain Polyxigis strode past Idomenea's Fountain, and Ali Aga followed him with the heavy basket on his back. He was bringing the wedding presents to his niece Vangelio in good time.

Since the day before yesterday Captain Polyxigis had been out of order, as if the earthquake had upset his mind. He kept running about the streets, would not eat, would not drink, merely smoked and from time to time groaned like a sick buffalo. His wanderings always brought him out at length before a green door. He stopped, measured the high wall with a glance, stood on tiptoe as though he meant to fly over it, but then went away again, made a round and came back.

To remove the suspicions of the neighbours (he was afraid of the hags, with their wicked tongues), he visited a Turkish coppersmith in the quarter and bought first a pan, another time a handbasin and a coffee-pot, or again bowls, cups and coffee-cups. First he could not think what to do with them, and then it occurred to him that his niece was getting married. So he filled a basket with the copper gear, loaded it on to Ali Aga's back, and set off for Captain Michales's quarter, where Vangelio's house lay.

And as he passed Idomenea's Fountain, Captain Michales appeared, riding his mare, with his whip hanging from his wrist and the tassel of his head-band hiding his eyes.

Captain Polyxigis stood still in astonishment, for he knew that on Sunday morning Captain Michales had begun another of his weeks of swilling. Yet there he was, on Tuesday already, on horseback again. Evidently he had broken away and was now making for the Turkish quarter, running straight into the cannon's mouth. Captain Polyxigis shook his head. One of these days, he thought, he'll pay for his audacity with his life, and one of the pillars of Christendom in Megalokastro will come crashing down. But who can restrain him? Neither God, nor the Devil. A man who's not afraid of death—even God is afraid of him.

Captain Michales drew nearer. He caught sight of Captain Polyxigis and spurred his mare on. He wanted no conversation with him. His foppishness got on his nerves, along with his silly jokes and his frivolous way of living. He was one of those men who whistle and sing every morning when they wake up. Captain Michales had no taste for such men. Yet they were honourable comrades when the crack came, when the Christians rebelled and picked a quarrel with the Turks. Then both captains were leaders, both of them felt themselves responsible. But as soon as times grew calm, they ran apart, in opposite directions. He's like a wild boar, thought Captain Polyxigis, I don't like him. He's a barber, thought Captain Michales, not my taste. And so he urged the mare on, in order to pass him without speaking.

But Captain Polyxigis, at the sight of that darkened face, guessed that he was up to no good and that nothing but trouble for the Christians would come out of it. So he whipped up his courage and called out:

"Where are you off to so early, Captain Michales?" And with that he stretched out his arm, as though to bar the way.

"Get out of the way, if you don't want the mare to trample on you, Captain Polyxigis," growled Captain Michales.

But Captain Polyxigis stood in the middle of the street with arms outstretched, and did not budge.

"In Christ's name, brother," he said, "don't throw away that strength of yours. You're a pillar of Christendom. Crete needs you. Your life doesn't belong to you, it belongs to Crete. She may soon want to use you."

But Captain Michales had never felt such a disgust for this Capitanio as now. Yesterday Furógatos has escaped from the cellar for a moment, had gone to stand at the street door to get a breath of air and, while he was there, had exchanged a few words with their neighbour, Krasojórgis's wife. In this way he had heard of Captain Polyxigis's new prank in the Turkish quarter. He had gone back to the cellar and poured the story into Captain Michales's ear. Captain Michales had pretended to be hardly listening, but it had been like a blow to his heart.

And now he could bear it no longer. He bent down from the mare. His lips were bursting with wrath.

"Go and seduce those women of yours! Leave me alone to ride head first at the Turkish coffee-houses."

Captain Polyxigis went scarlet.

"When we're at peace," he retorted defiantly, "I seduce hanums. When we're at war, I kill agas. That's what I call being a man."

He turned to Ali Aga: "Go ahead to Vangelio's house and unload there," he said, and drove him away.

Then he took a step nearer and laid his hand on the mare's hot neck:

"Captain Michales," he said, lowering his voice, "as true as you're a baptised Christian, speak out: what have you got against me? I don't like that look of yours to-day, it bores through me as though I were a Turk."

"Get out of the way if you don't want the mare to trample on you," growled Captain Michales again, turning away.

"Tell me, what have you against me?" Captain Polyxigis asked anew. "Why do you turn your head away?"

"Get out of the way if you don't want the mare to trample on you," growled Captain Michales for the third time.

"No one can talk with you, there's no knowing how to set about you!"

"Very clever, Captain Hanum," roared Captain Michales, furiously. He put spurs to his mare, and she reared high. By a hair's breadth she missed knocking Captain Polyxigis down.

"What can I do against him? After all, he's a Christian and a Palikare," Captain Polyxigis muttered, biting at his moustache. "If not, I'd know jolly well, you madman, how to set about you!" He spat three times, as if to get rid of the evil meeting, and pushed on to the house of his niece.

Vangelio was sitting at her loom. She was just finishing work on the last double width of stubbly cloth from which were to be made breeches for the bridegroom and nightdresses for the bride that would never wear out. She sped the shuttle through in haste. She was in a hurry, for the wedding was getting near. It stood over her like a great dark animal. And Vangelio herself was crouching like an animal, like a bristling boar, to defend herself against it, against that repulsive animal—for so this marriage seemed to her to be, with this half-helping of a bridegroom, with his glasses, his soft priest's voice and his disgusting sheep-like gentleness. Was it then for this bit of a man that she had been born? Was it for his pleasure that she had fattened for so many years, till her breasts and hips grew full and her hair reached to her knees? All this for Tityros? "Marry him," Uncle Polyxigis had whispered in her ear, "say yes, Vangelio, a husband's a downy cushion and keeps you warm." Ah, where was God, that her voice might pierce through the seven heavens and cry to Him: "I won't have him, I won't have him"? For how many years she had seen in her sleep a heroic youth with a woollen cloak about his shoulders, a slim-hipped bully loving wine, women and strife, throwing his money about superbly, somebody matchless, like her brother Diamandés! Ah, how often—indeed every time she lit the lamps in front of the ikon-shrines her parents had dedicated to them—had she begged Saint Nicholas, who looks after orphan girls, and Saint Famurios, who supplies bridegrooms, to send her a husband like her brother! Like her brother, not like her Uncle Polyxigis, that little, dark babbler; and not like Captain Michales either, whose breath reeked of sulphur and before whom even the dogs of the neighbourhood trembled. He should just be like her brother, Diamandés: a body like a cypress, hips like a boxer's, chest like a fortress. Otherwise she would rather stay unmarried, a thousand times rather grow old living with her brother. He too should not marry— a wife would ruin all the sweetness for them. If only they could die at the same time and be buried together—and over their grave there should be two cypresses growing, one of them a manly one, slender like a candle, and the other a womanly one with spreading branches! And under the earth their roots should inter-twine.

But then had come Uncle Polyxigis and said she must take Captain Michales's brother Tityros and marry into an important family and have a man to keep her. For Diamandés had already spent their olive-trees and vineyards, which their parents had left them, so that this house was now all that remained to her, her only dowry. But in a few months that greedy little brother of hers would guzzle and swill it too away. And then?

"It's all the fault of Polyxigis," she muttered resentfully as she went on weaving. "He has got me into this soup. It was he who persuaded me to say yes. But God is just. He will punish him. And if He doesn't, then the unmarried man's sighing will come upon Polyxigis like a flash of lightning. May it strike him and burn him up!"

Captain Polyxigis kicked open the street door and entered. He turned to Ali Aga, who was waiting outside, and signed to him to come in and unload.

"Bless you, Ali Aga! Here, have a good time with this!" he said genially, throwing him a silver coin. Ali Aga caught it, held it tight in his fist as if it were a bird which might fly away, and bent down to kiss the lavish hand. But Polyxigis drew it back with a laugh:

"I'm no pope or imam, Ali Aga! Good-bye!"

He strode across the yard. The dog jumped up in its corner, sniffed, recognised the newcomer and curled up again on the ground.

Through the open door into the house Captain Polyxigis saw the loom—that docile domestic animal with feet, legs, pedals, metal feathers, tongues and combs, with its delicate rigging of warp and woof like a frigate under full sail.

Vangelio turned. She saw her uncle and summoned all her strength together to fetch up a smile of welcome. But from her lips, nose and chin there seemed to drip nothing but poison. She was now perpetually monosyllabic and sour. Some concealed worm was surely gnawing at her vitals. She was growing yellow, and her bosom had begun to turn flabby.

She noticed, behind her uncle, Ali Aga with the basket, and she understood.

"You've been extravagant for my sake, Uncle George," she said, with a stealthy glance at the basket. She made out the copper things and for a moment her face lit up.

"Everyone's got to marry sometime. If the vineyard's lost, it's lost," said Captain Polyxigis with a laugh, trying to set the blood in his niece moving. "People say, Vangelio, that there is no greater pleasure."

"People say. . . ." Vangelio burst out, and broke off.

Captain Polyxigis sat down on the small sofa, took off his fez (for he was hot) and put it on the window-sill. Vangelio went down on her knees and took out of the basket, one by one, the shining copper objects. The house became filled with pans, dishes and jugs, and as Vangelio bent over them a reddish warmth gleamed for a moment from her yellow face.

"Bless you, Uncle," she said half-heartedly, "you take the place of a father to me."

"You say that half-heartedly, Vangelio! You're getting married and yet, my child, you're on the verge of tears. Raise those eyes of yours and let me look at them. . . . Here, smile just for once, let out a shout to make your breath come faster! When brides are weaving their last bit of cloth, they sing as they do it, and make the house tremble—why, the whole neighbourhood trembles as in an earthquake. It's called 'bride's time'! But you behave as if you were weaving a shroud."

Vangelio was furious. Such words in the mouth of a man who had all he wanted outraged her. She thought again of her fiancé. Was she to sing for that pallid face? She felt a foul taste in her mouth. She was on the point of letting herself go, but then immediately hesitated. What should she say? It was all one. If one was happy, why should one cry out? And why cry out if one wasn't? There was no help for it. So better keep quiet.

But Captain Polyxigis could not stand this dumb complaint from his niece. The day of the wedding was drawing near. At Easter the crowning would take place. Before that he had something to get clear with her. He could feel that his niece, ever since he had fixed up her engagement, had looked at him with resentful eyes. He must let her know, before she married, that it had cost him something to induce the bridegroom to say yes. Up to the last moment he had wavered. And so one day Captain Polyxigis had opened his money-chest, taken out five gold pounds and given them to him. "Here, schoolmaster, take these as an extra dowry. No one need know—neither Captain Michales, nor the bride, nor my sister. I'm gilding my niece and giving her to you." That was how he had managed it. And now, if you please, Miss Bride makes a face as if she were drinking quinine. Her bridegroom stinks! She'd like a prince!

Vangelio came out of the kitchen with a round tray on which were the coffee, a glass of cold water and a spoonful of preserved cherries. She put the tray down on a chair in front of her uncle.

"Listen to me, Vangelio," he said with a glance at the door, "isn't Diamandés back yet? Is that swilling brother of yours still gadding?"

"He's young," replied Vangelio proudly, "he's handsome. It's right for him."

"Right for him? What? Was it right for him to ruin you, Vangelio?"

"Oh! He's ruined me, has he? But if he hadn't been there, I'd have died. What would I have had to live for? And let me tell you, Uncle: if I'm bowing my neck now and accepting the yoke you've found for me, I'm doing it so that, even when I'm married, I shan't be separated from my brother. Otherwise, the Devil take Tityros!"

Captain Polyxigis swallowed the glassful of water and suppressed his rage. He purposely took a long time munching the cherry conserve, to prevent himself from stretching out his paw, seizing his niece by the hair and swinging her against the wall.

"Dammit," he said finally, twirling his moustache. "He's your brother, not your sweetheart. He too should marry and found a family. And not turn his mind to the taverns any more!"

Vangelio leapt up from her chair. Her cheeks were glowing.

"Pray God no such thing is written," she screamed. "And if it is written, may He rub it out!"

"What's happened to you, Vangelio?" cried Captain Polyxigis, shocked. "Do you love him more than your husband? But that's disgraceful! And after all the efforts I've made——"

"You've sold me for a bit of bread," Vangelio spat through her teeth.

Captain Polyxigis could control himself no longer:

"A piece of bread—damn it, that seems to you a trifle, does it, my princess? Very clever, it sounds! And what, by God, should a bridegroom find to desire in you? Youth? Beauty? Riches? You're thirty-five, and shrunk to a dried currant, to an old maid with a moustache! And that greyhound of a brother of yours has plundered you. A rag is all you are now! Who's going to look at you now, who's going to want you, you poor thing? God has struck Tityros with blindness, to make him say yes."

Vangelio buried her face in her hands and began to cry, without moving. Captain Polyxigis's heart contracted. How could he have let such words out of his mouth? What was he to do now? How could he console the poor girl?

He laid a hand on the old maid's luxuriant hair.

"There, there, Vangelio dear, don't cry. With God's help it'll all come right. A good man has been found to look after you. You'll see: soon those cheeks of yours will be plump and rosy again. You'll grow young again! And then, if you have fine children. . . ."

"Bah! Little Tityroses!" said Vangelio, wiping the tears from her eyelids scornfully.

"Perhaps they won't just be little Tityroses. They'll have our blood too in them. Perhaps your sons will be like your brother!"

Vangelio was amazed. The blood rose in her faded bosom. "Be quiet!" she said, shuddering.

Captain Polyxigis stood up. He stretched out his hand to caress his niece, but drew it back.

"We'll talk some other day, Vangelio," he said. "I'm going before that swilling brother of yours comes back. I've no wish to see him here!"

He crammed on his large fez and was about to cross the threshold. But at that moment a heavy tread was heard and the street door burst open. Panting and worn out, with a yellowed sprig of basil behind one ear and a cigarette behind the other, the brother stood on the threshold, his woollen cloak thrown round his shoulders. He frowned and pursed his lips as he recognised his uncle in the doorway. "Is he there again, with his match-making? Devil take him!" He jerked himself together, pulled off his cap and crossed the yard. He came in. But he did not see the copper things on the floor. He tripped over them, and cursed.

Captain Polyxigis turned his face away. The sight disgusted him.

"Men drink wine," he said contemptuously, "but don't get drunk. Take an example from me. Men go hunting women, but don't make fools of themselves. Take an example from me."

Diamandés, who could not bear his uncle and knew his vulnerable spots, gave a contemptuous snigger. His tongue was out of his control: he stammered out:

"Men drink wine and don't get drunk, and don't then go to bed like infants but mount their mare and ride—but not into the Turkish quarter to some hanum, but to the Turkish coffee-houses, to the agas. Take an example yourself, Uncle, from Captain Michales!"

These words pierced Captain Polyxigis through the heart, for he felt that the swilling brother was quite right.

"Curses on you, you good-for-nothing! You're well on the way to squandering your sister's dowry on wine and women, watches and chains. If at least you could read the time! But you're not capable of that, you failure!"

Diamandés gave a yell and sprang forward over pans and cans to seize hold of his uncle—but tripped and fell thunderously to the floor.

Captain Polyxigis laughed disdainfully.

"I wish you joy of your little brother, Vangelio," he said, and crossed the threshold.

"God grant I may have joy of him till my death, Uncle!" Vangelio riposted for her brother. She helped him up from among the copper things on to the sofa, brought him a cushion for his head, and stroked him tenderly.

At mid-day young Thrasos came back from school in great excitement.

"Mama!" he shouted, throwing into the air the little red cap his sister had made for him. "Father's mare strikes sparks from the cobbles. I saw him ride along Broad Street, and the shopkeepers and cobblers stood up to gape at him. 'He's come from the Turkish quarter,' one of them said. 'He's going to the Turkish quarter,' another said. I stood where I was, took off my cap and waved to him. But how should he notice me? The sparks were flying from the cobbles, I tell you!"

"Signor Paraskevás was here and has been complaining to me," said the mother, scared at her son's admiration for his father. "The day before yesterday, he says, you and your friends kidnapped his daughter. Aren't you ashamed of yourself?"

Thrasos laughed.

"Why did you do it?"

The insolent boy shrugged his shoulders:

"We felt like it. Yesterday we nearly pulled off something with Tityros. We'd planned to hide behind a door with rope, and just throw a noose round his neck when he came in, like they do to catch wild horses. He'd told us how, himself, the day before yesterday. So now we were playing horse-tamers."

His mother screamed: "Villains! What has that holy man ever done to you? Why did you want to kill him?"

"Kill him? Us? But we like him. It was a game. We wouldn't have made the noose fast. We'd only have given him a fright, to see what he'd do!"

So saying, he took from his shoulder the cord on which the washing was usually hung out, and returned it to its place. Then he clenched his fist and frowned like his father:

"At the last minute the others were frightened. There were too many of them, and too many cowards among them. But it doesn't matter. Another time I'll pick them myself—fewer, and reliable. Perhaps I'll do it alone."

There was a knock at the door, and Ali Aga appeared:

"In God's name, Captainess," he said, "Efendína's playing the madman again. He's run out into the Greek quarter and is coming to your house. Bolt the door. Don't let him in."

He had not yet finished speaking when Efendína burst howling into the yard. It hurt Katerina to look at him. The poor creature seemed hardly human. His clothes were torn, his sackcloth breeches were showing. His eyes were red and swollen from weeping. He had taken off his turban, and his scab was thickly smeared with horsedung. He knelt down in the middle of the yard and began wailing:

"I have defiled myself," he screamed, "eaten pork, drunk wine, uttered wicked words. Men and women, forgive me! May God also have mercy and forgive me! Captainess, if God questions you tomorrow, tell Him that Captain Michales forces me to it against my will." He crawled on his knees towards her, to seize her hand and kiss it.

"Have pity on me, Captainess, I am hurrying round to publish my suffering and my shame, and I am beginning with you. Afterwards I shall hurry to the Pacha's door, and to the other Turkish houses. They must see my scab, and learn of my guilt; they must spit upon me. But I place my trust in you. If God questions you tomorrow, tell Him that Captain Michales forced me to it against my will."

Thrasos watched him and laughed. He had stealthily taken the clothes-line down again and made a noose. Renió came out of the kitchen, glanced at Efendína, and likewise laughed. But Katerina felt her eyes grow wet.

"Stand up, Efendína," she said gently, "stand up, I'll do as you say. I'll bear witness before God that I have seen with my own eyes how Captain Michales compelled you against your will."

"May you be blessed, Captainess! And now I ask you for a favour. Spit on me!"

"No, that I won't, Efendína. Stand up, and go, with the seven-fold blessing of God."

"Spit on me, or I won't go." He turned to Ali Aga: "Next, you will spit on me, Ali Aga—you, as a faithful Musulman. And afterwards, all Megalokastro. Before I left the téké, my grandfather rose up from his coffin and spat upon me. You too must spit, Captainess! Spit on me, if you believe in God!"

The Captain's wife turned away:

"I can't," she said. "I won't. Go, good-bye!"

"I won't go," bellowed Efendína. "Yes, by Mohammed, I shall stay here if you don't spit on me."

The Captain's wife grew angry:

"I shall do as I will, not as you will, Efendína!" she said, and went back into the kitchen.

"Here on these stones will I remain kneeling till dawn." cried Efendína, and beat his forehead against the stones. Then he began his wailing all over again, and howled like a dog.

Thrasos made a sign to his sister. She understood, and took up position near him, behind Efendína's back. And as Efendína beat his breast and howled, with his eyes on the kitchen, Thrasos threw the noose round his neck. Renió too caught hold, and they both pulled.

Efendína gave a strangled cry and fell over backwards. His face went bluish, his eyes started. He wrenched at the noose to prevent himself stifling, but his hands were powerless from terror.

"In God's name, children, you're throttling the poor creature!" cried Ali Aga.

The Captain's wife heard his cry and came running out. She snatched the cord out of her son's hands and loosened the noose. Then she pushed Efendína to the street door.

"Out you go," she said, "poor wretch, out you go! With my best wishes." Then she gave him a shove, so that he stumbled into the street. She bolted the door.

Thrasos and Renió burst out laughing:

"You see, Mother, that's how they catch horses," said little Thrasos and hung the cord up again near the wash-tub. "Tityros won't be able to escape me now!"

Captain Michales stormed through the Turkish quarter on his mare. The wine had not clouded his brain. His knees pressed the mare's flanks powerfully, and in his limbs and muscles he felt a boundless strength. It oppressed him more than the wine he had drunk. He did not know how to shake free from it.

He did not clearly distinguish the men who went past; the houses seemed to him to have got lower and the streets narrower. The Hags heard his horse and rushed to their peep-holes. They recognised Captain Michales, but the sun was dazzling and they could not make out his face well enough to see how it was with him. "What's up with the boar at the height of noon?" Aglaja asked. "Is he drunk?"

"Keep your eyes skinned, there's something going on here," remarked Thalia, sniffing as though she could smell it. "Why has Captain Polyxigis been hanging around our quarter since yesterday? I saw him, just as the moment when the earthquake started—when Eminé rushed out and pretended to have fainted. What a chance that he came by. But was it chance? Or was it arranged? And the person in question woke her up out of her swoon. . . .

And since that day our quarter has been smeared with honey, and he's stuck fast. And now Captain Wildboar as well. . . . That damned bitch! Both those lecherous hounds can smell her a mile away!"

"Quiet, quiet!" said Frosyne, "just listen to how Nuri's horse is neighing!"

From the precincts of the Turkish *konak* the noble steed could be heard greeting the lusty mare.

"Eminé's whinnying," said Thalia with a giggle. But immediately her tongue stuck in her throat, and both her sisters gave a cry; for as the mare heard the stallion's neighing, she reared, as if she wanted to begin dancing.

"That's death for Captain Michales," cried the three.

But as he gripped the rearing beast by the mane and fused to a single body with her. He kept his power over her unyieldingly and put the spurs to her. She felt her pitiless master on top of her, lowered her head and moved on.

"Damn you, with that hot blood of yours!" he muttered, and struck the mare's head with his fist.

Outside, down by the sea, he gave her her head, to run freely along the broad ramparts. His chest filled with sea air. High up on a bulwark overgrown with weeds he reined her in. He gazed out over the deep-blue foaming sea sparkling in the sun, and lost himself in the mist to the north, towards Greece. He sighed:

"With Thee I can endure life, my God," he muttered, "with Thee, not with men."

He rode on. Always when he thought of Crete, abandoned by all, he disputed with God. A violent blasphemy pressed forward to the tip of his tongue. He did not lament before God, he was angry with Him. He asked for no sympathy, he asked for justice.

A dark cloud, no bigger than a water-bottle, rose up from the south, became larger and larger, until it darkened the sky. The sun smouldered. A damp, sultry wind came sighing from the sea over Captain Michales's haggard face. He raised his eyes to the sky.

"But I can't fight it out with Thee, my God," he growled between his teeth. "So I shall fight it out with men."

F

He dug his heels into the mare and shot along Broad Street
again like a flash. The Christians stood up, the better to see him.
He reached the Kanea Gate, where the big Turkish coffee-house
with the distinguished agas lay. In this coffee-house, every time
there was a rising, the great consultations took place, and from
here the Turks went forth with knives between their teeth to
every slaughter. When, on spring afternoons, the sun's heat
diminished, the pavements were sprinkled with rain and the earth
was fragrant, in this coffee-house the handsomest Turkish youths
sat enthroned on high benches and sang their languorous refrains.
And here in winter the most gifted story-tellers made the agas
laugh. The Muezzin, too, resorted here, searchingly examined the
Turkish youths, listened to their languorous melodies and joined
in their yearning. Soon he no longer knew whether this was
Mohammed's Paradise or a coffee-house. Nothing was lacking,
neither good tobacco for his nargile nor a fresh little breath from
the gardens.

Midday was already past. The agas had eaten and were sitting
at ease, with legs crossed, on the straw mats of the coffee-house.
They had ordered nargiles and, half dozing with eyes half-closed,
were sipping their coffee. They were happy.

Everything had arranged itself pleasantly for them. Generations ago their forefathers ahd divided up Crete, and its fat vineyards, olive-orchards and acres were their heritage. The arid ones
had been left to the Greeks. From time to time the Christians
raised their heads, but the soldiers from Anatolia struck at them
and made them bow again under the yoke. Beautiful were the
hanums, and each man could have as many of them as his purse
allowed. Beautiful too were the Turkish boys, and if one only
pampered them properly they acquired downy, blossom-white
flesh. Also their Mohammed was no puritan: he liked what the
agas liked. He did not worry them to become saints. He carried
no cross and did not ask them to carry theirs. In his pocket he
always carried a phial of scent, a small mirror and a comb. For the
pleasure of Musulmans he was no God, but a man. And death,
for the faithful, had nothing about it of worms or stench, but was
a green doorway to a wide, everlasting garden.

Nuri Bey appeared, freshly shaved, handsome as a lion, and his thinly pointed moustache, dyed with black pomade, flashed like iron. He bowed to right and left in silent greetings and went to sit right inside near the serving-table, to be quite alone.

Since the day when his horse had stumbled between the tombs, and when his father had risen up before him in the air with wild and bloody hair, Nuri Bey had been able to get no pleasure from sleep or food or conversation. The blood of his father was hankering for vengeance. Sons, brothers and nephews of the murderer were alive. They were marrying, breeding, carousing, swaggering. And had not one of them recently brought an ass into the village mosque to pray? How long were all these insults to be endured? How long was his father to wander barefoot up and down the underworld? The moment had come for him to take a decision, if he was a man.

"Pass me the nargile, Hussein," he told the proprietor, "and don't let anybody come near me."

In the distance dull thunder was heard. The agas turned their faces towards the door. The sky was now entirely covered. Sulphur-yellow lightning flashed. The wind hissed like rending silk.

"That's because of the heat," said one of the agas. "It'll rain." "That'll be good for the crops," said another. "And for the olives and the almonds—make 'em ripen quick," said a third, and went as far as the door to observe the weather.

But as he reached the threshold, and before he could raise his hand to protect himself, he sprang back terrified. Captain Michales appeared on horseback at the entrance of the coffee-house. He bent down, saw the agas sitting comfortable round and sleepily smoking their nargiles. The blood rushed to his head and the world swayed. He spurred the mare and she reared and crashed into the coffee-house. This was not the first time. They knew this gentleman's moods. Inside, the mare smashed several stools and upset a table, so that there was a sound of china breaking. She got as far as the serving-table, where the proprietor, as usual, stood in front of the coal fire, putting the coffee-pots on and taking them off. There she came to a halt.

The coffee-house was in a turmoil. The agas flung their nargiles aside and stood up. The bolder ones felt hastily for their knives in their red sashes. The old men raised their hands and cried:

"Be careful, Captain Michales, don't plunge us into bloodshed!"

But he remained unmoved by this and swung his whip in the air:

"Out with you," he shouted, "I want to drink my coffee alone!"

The muezzin, though an old man too, jumped up from where he had been sitting, cross-legged, on the platform, and yelled, as loud as he could:

"This time your game won't succeed, Captain Michales. You can't make fools of us every year. This time you won't get out of here alive, unbeliever!"

A Turkish hot-head was sorry for the old muezzin and stepped forward to protect him. He wrenched from his sash a broad, two-edged dagger and rushed at the rider. But Captain Michales bent down and seized him by the wrist, so that the young Turk's arm was paralysed and he let go of the dagger. Captain Michales stuck it into his pocket and again raised his whip.

"Out, out," he bellowed, "out!"

"Allah, Allah," cried the old men, and did not know what to do: send a messenger to the Pacha for soldiers, or sugar the bitter pill and give in to avoid bloodshed.

Nuri Bey had not stirred. With bent head he smoked his nargile. But out of the corner of his eye he surveyed the coffee-house, until everything before him vanished. Now he saw only the sweating chest and belly of the mare and Captain Michales's black boots. The first rain-drops were falling outside. There were heavy claps of thunder and the glass of the doors tinkled. The muezzin screamed:

"If you believe in Mohammed, let me pluck him to bits like a sardine!"

But several old men seized him round the waist and under the arms, and dragged him out.

Nuri Bey bent his head still lower, smoked puff after puff and blew the smoke through his nose. The hour has come, he thought. I have given my word to my father, I prayed for an occasion, here it is! The murderer's brother has come, my father has brought him, straight in front of the muzzle of my gun. Now for it!

To make sure, he sought to rouse his heart to fury. "Now stir yourself, my heart; up, and strike! Or are you perhaps afraid?" His fists burned him, as in a fever. He raised his eyes and saw Captain Michales's gaze directed at him. Nuri Bey put away the tube of the nargile and stood up slowly and heavily. He walked down from the platform and took hold of the mare's reins. Then he turned to the proprietor, who had crouched down behind the serving-table.

"Hussein," he said, "make a coffee for Captain Michales. I will pay."

He raised his hand authoritatively and signed to the young people, who were standing round the mare, to go.

"Nuri Bey," said Captain Michales, "I want to drink my coffee alone. I want no company. Clear the coffee-house."

"Haven't I too a want? A small want, Captain Michales?" said Nuri Bey, and tried hard to make his face look gentle. "I ask you one favour. Don't insult me."

The white head-band slipped from his head, he groped for it and set it swinging, so that the air smelled of musk. At once Captain Michales's nostrils quivered. The veins of his neck grew swollen.

The scent of musk pierced his vitals like a knife. It bewildered him: night, the lemon raki, the partridge, the laughter behind the lattice, the creaking stairs, and suddenly in the door-frame a body, which swayed and filled the air with the scent of musk. . . . And this same Nuri. . . . Captain Michales's brow spat sparks. He shoved Nuri aside, put spurs to the mare and very nearly rode him down. He came to the middle of the coffee-house:

"Out, out," he shouted again, as though possessed. "Clear the coffee-house!"

Nuri Bey wound the head-band tightly about his hair. He bit his lips hard, drawing blood. The agas had left the settles and were pressing round him. A couple of them were waiting, crouched behind the door, with knives. The more prudent of the old men had already slipped out of the door. The coffee-house was beginning to empty.

Nuri Bey felt ashamed. "Go out," he said quietly to the agas.

"He's drunk. Don't argue with him. I'll stay. To see he doesn't go too far. To see we don't need to be ashamed."

The agas stood still. Selim Aga, who till now had been smoking a nargile unmoved and without a word, got up: the best-balanced mind in Turkey, an old man blessed with everything—rich, cultivated, of good family, the father of fine sons, still handsome in his old age as he had been long ago in his youth. He signed to the agas:

"Control yourselves," he said, weightily. "It serves no purpose to bathe Crete in blood. The hour will soon come—I see it already marked in Allah's book—when this Greek will have to pay. I can already see his head nailed up over the Pacha's gate. Be patient. Let's go!"

He stepped forward with measured gait, and the agas followed. The coffee-house was empty.

Captain Michales twirled his moustache and looked down at Nuri. He laughed—his fang jutted out. His heart gave a bound of pleasure. He turned to the proprietor, who was now venturing out from behind the serving-table:

"Hey, Hussein," he said, "put the pot in the fire and make me a coffee. Without sugar!"

V

THE storm had broken. The sky fell, Megalokastro seemed to rise and become part of it. The falling water flooded the streets and the world grew dark. Everywhere lightning played round the minarets, and down below, in Broad Street, Captain Michales's face flared harsh and undismayed as he rode home. The mare's broad, white chest glittered with wet.

It was a "bora" that lasted scarcely half an hour. Then came a wind from the mountains, the clouds were rent, and through them gleamed the deep blue sky, while slanting, new-born shafts of sunshine fell upon the drenched town. The cobbles seemed to laugh, and the sparrows on the roofs shook their soaked feathers. Megalokastro emerged from the storm freshly washed and young again. From the courtyards came the scent of rain-wet honeysuckle, marjoram and basil.

With one blow Captain Michales opened the door. His wife took the mare by the rein without a word, while he himself strode into the room and hung the Turk's dagger up on the shrine, in front of the ikon of Saint Michael. Captain Michales was steaming with scorn, sweat and rain. Clean, dry clothes were brought him, and he put them on. With his body refreshed he stretched himself on the bed, closed his eyes and was immediately embraced by soft, merciful slumber.

But while he rested, the Kastrians gathered, Turks and Christians alike, early in their homes that evening. The men whispered together, while the women sat about, listening and sighing, but saying nothing. So Crete, abandoned by all, was not to have repose? Were the massacres going to begin again, would we once more have to lose our men? So they pondered. And where shall we go? Once more with the infants, the pots and pans and the linen on our backs? The most prudent of the Christians, likewise the owners of shops and vineyards, cursed Captain Michales's drunken exploits which dragged so many men with him into trouble. The others on the contrary, the palikares, were proud of this fresh flouting of Turkey.

The Turks had gathered, some of them in the tékés, some in Nuri Ney's konak. They cursed and threatened, but could not think how to wash away the disgrace. The muezzin kept poking up the fire in them, and the more reasonable of the elders tried to put it out again, while Nuri Bey sat thoughtful in a corner and said nothing. At length they grew tired of the noise, and of slaughtering the Christians in their thoughts. They chose three spokesmen to go next morning to the Pacha and to urge him to tighten the reins upon the Christians. Is he a Pacha or a piece of halva? How long has it been since he stopped hanging Christians from the plane-tree or putting them in the pillory? If this goes on, the *giaours* will venture anything and—God punish us if we are lying—that mad Captain will soon ride even into the mosques and drive us out of them with his whip. He must hang or be stuck in the pillory, even if only to warn his followers to keep within bounds. That's how Turkey would act! But this Pacha deals too softly with the Greeks: the weak-witted creature talks of justice! He plays draughts with the Metropolitan, they drink mastic, eat baklava and sit up all night together whispering secrets!

Next day, early in the morning, the three spokesmen proceeded to the konak. Their ears were still buzzing from the stormy instructions with which they had been charged. In the middle walked the muezzin, on his right Selim Aga, and on the left, sunk in thought, Nuri Bey. Their gait was measured, and they did not speak to one another. Each was weaving the web of his thought—what he was to say at the Pacha's and how. Selim Aga had a large yearly income in oil, corn, almonds and grapes; he was for peace. The muezzin was pressing the Koran to his chest, next to the skin, and it was burning him. Nuri Bey kept his head bowed and was undecided. That night his father had again appeared to him in his sleep, still in rags and covered with dirt, and had slipped his costly, black-hilted knife under the pillow. But in the morning, when Nuri Bey picked up the pillow, he found no knife. His heart was on the point of breaking: the old man doesn't trust me, he sighed; he's taken it away from me again. He's afraid I'll dishonour it.

Heavy and morose, the Pacha sat waiting for them on the big divan. More trouble, the dogs and the cats are fighting again. These *giaours* want freedom—curses on them! The Musulmans are pressing me to slaughter all *giaours*—curses on them too! Servitude, my respected *giaours*, is a thing ordained by God! The bondsmen too, my agas, are ordained by God: they till the fields, they keep trade going, they bring in taxes. Who wants to kill the goose that lays the golden eggs?

The Moor appeared. "Pacha Effendi, they've arrived."

"Show them in," replied the Pacha, his voice rising.

They came in, one after another, made their bows, and without a word took their places cross-legged on the large divan.

First the muezzin opened his wide mouth. Lanky and bony, with sunken cheeks, sparse, whitish wisps of beard and a hairy wart as big as a horse-fly which sat between his brows and made him look three-eyed, he spoke and spoke. The longer he heard his own voice, the fiercer it made him. Foaming with wrath, he pulled the Koran out from his bosom and began rocking to and fro and reading. The Pacha felt giddy; he raised his long pipe.

"Hodza Effendi," he said, "you've made me giddy. Speak simply, so I can understand. I'm an Anatolian, a slow mind. In a word: what do you want?"

"Action," the muezzin answered, and the hairs on his wart stood out.

The Pacha sighed and turned to Selim Aga:

"And what's your opinion, Selim Aga?" he asked. "Is that also your view?"

"We need peace, Pacha Effendi," replied the grey-haired property-owner, "not a massacre, peace! We're having a good year: March has brought us plenty of rain and given the crops strength; the olives, too, are promising. We shall have a rich harvest and excellent oil this year, God be praised. So peace, Pacha Effendi! This Crete is a great savage beast: let's not wake it up—it devours men! What does it matter that a madman broke into our coffee-house? After all, he was drunk. Let's shut our eyes

F*

—it's in our interest to do so. If we pig-headedly give blow for blow, we're lost. Pig-headedness turns to wrong-headedness, Pacha Effendi. Open your records and enter the *giaour* in them: his name is Captain Michales. His hour will come. You are the Pacha, you bear the scimitar, you strike off heads."

He turned to the muezzin: "That is my opinion, Hodza Effendi," he said, "I'm sorry. You own no trees, vineyards or fields, and you don't know the distress of the earth and of men and women. But ask me. Ask the trees and the crops. Do they want a rising? No, they don't."

"I don't ask among trees, crops and human beings," the muezzin bellowed, thumping the Koran, "I ask Allah."

He again took the Koran out from his bosom and opened it. But the Pacha stretched out his hand.

"The Koran says whatever its reader has in mind," he said with a yawn. "You want a slaughter? You open the Koran and find a justification. If Selim Aga opens it, he'll find another word— peace—and that too comes from God. Both are from God, so be quiet!"

He turned to Nuri Bey: "And what's your opinion, Nuri Bey?" he said. "Massacre or peace—which does your Koran say?"

Nuri Bey rubbed his fist several times along his hairy, crossed legs, as he sought the right answer. He took a long time to weigh his opinion. He certainly did not want peace. Turkey had already been patient too long, the Greek had grown too insolent. The moment had come to knock him on the head. But he also wanted no massacre—he was not bloodthirsty, nor was he a hodza who read the Koran and fetched his fire from there . . .

"Well?" asked the Pacha, annoyed by his hesitation. "I'm asking you again: do you want peace, Nuri Bey, or a massacre?

"The straightforward, simple way has become lost to us, Pacha Effendi," said Nuri Bey, trying to gain a little more time.

"It's not lost, young man, but we've grown blind and can't find it. Or has your lordship found it?"

"I think so, Pacha Effendi."

"I hope so for your sake! Speak, then, and free us from our blindness."

"Neither peace, nor a massacre. The guilty one must pay."

"Captain Michales?" asked the Pacha. "Do you mean him?"

"Grant me the liberty, Pacha Effendi, not to say whom I mean. You are Pacha. If you intervene, weapons will speak and we shall swim in blood. Let me undertake the vengeance on behalf of Turkey. Who the guilty man is you'll soon learn."

"Will you kill him?"

"I shall kill him, but no one will find out who the murderer was. Trust me."

The muezzin jumped up, furious. "There isn't one man guilty, thousands are. They all deserve the pillory. *That's* what keeping the peace means. The Greek understands nothing else. Cut off his head, if you like, then he'll be quiet."

But Selim Aga's brain was full of trees and vines. He too jumped up and began to shout. Yet the muezzin's voice was like a bell—how was he to silence it? So they came to blows. Nuri Bey came between them, to separate them. The Pacha remained sitting unmoved on his divan. These Turks of Crete made his head whirl. All were right, all were wrong: how was he to unravel it? Above all, he was sleepy. He had not had a good night—had overeaten and drunk too much. He was in a hurry to have done. He shook off his fatigue and shouted:

"Hey, you, aren't you ashamed of yourselves? Stop fighting, I tell you! Nuri Bey, you are right. That is the camel's way, the correct one. So do as Allah enlightens you. I give you freedom to do so!"

Selim Aga picked up his white head-band from the floor and turned to Nuri Bey:

"You have my blessing, Nuri Bey," he said in a tone of entreaty, "if you proceed cautiously, kill with moderation, don't make the Greeks wild, keep the peace for us."

"I shall not let my law be trampled underfoot," bellowed the muezzin. "I shall preach in the mosque and awaken Turkey!"

But that brought life into the Pacha, and he raised his fist:

"Hodza," he shouted, "I am in command in Megalokastro. By the beard of the Prophet, I'll make you wear a muzzle, like a dog

that bites! Listen! There will be no masascre—get the idea out of
your head—as long as I receive no order from Constantinople."

He stood up, turned his face away (for he had a pain in his
stomach) and yawned again.

"Go, I am busy. Do as we said, Nuri Bey, but be careful. Careful,
children, for these are Greeks, damn them! If they had not been
in our path, Turkey would already have swallowed up the world."

He clapped his hands, and the Moor came in. "Show the Beys
out," he said.

While this meeting was taking place, three other distinguished
heads, Greek this time, were making their measured way to the
Metropolitan. They were Hadjisávas, Captain Eliás and old
Mavrudés, known as Rose-bug.

The first, a pale hobbler and stutterer with a grey beard stained
yellow by cigarette-smoking, had in his time travelled into the
land of the Franks to become a doctor, and had come back with
his head turned. His madness consisted in paying workmen to
dig up the earth for him in places where there were ruins, or on
deserted bits of the coast, and even in the caves of Psilorítis. He
dug and dug, and found hands and feet of marble, dishes covered
with odd lettering, and pottery vases. And all this he took into
the bishop's residence. He had already stuffed a huge room with it.
That was now not enough, and he had begun to spread out his
treasures in the churchyard. The Christians grumbled that they
could no longer send their wives and daughters to church for
fear of their seeing those shameless ancient demons, stark naked.
. . . It had been good advice that had been given to old Hadjisávas
the father, not to send his son to the land of the Franks, for he
would get his soul damaged there. Quite right! Back he had come
with a shovel, and dug and dug and dug. It was said he was
looking for the golden sow with the nine piglets. But how should
he find her? All he possessed he spent on workmen's wages. Now
he ran about in a shabby suit and worn-out shoes. He talked to
himself in the street, and soon, for sure, he would begin throwing
stones. Only—look—the Metropolitan respected him, gave him
a seat near his own at church, and on Sunday handed him the

consecrated bread before anybody else. And whenever the Christians found themselves groping in the dark, they sent him as spokesman to the Metropolitan and to the Pacha. And once, when Frankish warships anchored in the harbour, he had gone and chattered with the Franks. He had talked and talked and none of the Greeks could understand him. Poor thing!—or did he really speak foreign languages?

Captain Eliás was another relic of 1821, a crumbled, weed-grown tower without door or window. His body, pierced like a sieve with bullets, was square-built and big-boned, and his voice was like a clap of thunder—anyone to whom he said good-day received a shock. His right eye had been put out by a Turkish Pacha with a fork. But the Athenian National Committee had sent him a glass eye, the first glass eye to land in Crete. And Captain Eliás wore it and shot sparks from it at those he could not hurt. On official occasions he took it out and kept it in a glass of water. Then he came into the presence of Metropolitan or Pacha with one eye, to remind them of 1821. The two other elders had now placed him in the middle and, bowed over his cudgel, he was on his way, once more one-eyed, to the Metropolitan.

The third, old Rose-bug Mavrudés, was a hideous, sour bachelor and miser, who went hungry and moaned when he ate, shivered with cold and cursed when he had bought himself a warm coat. He had thrown widows and orphans on to the streets when they owed him money. He had collected and collected: gold pounds, vineyards, fields, houses, steam-boats. But if anyone asked him why he did not eat regular meals, he would whine: "What should I eat? Where am I to get it? Nothing's mine; all this belongs to the nation. I won't touch it!" In the 1871 rising he went to the Metropolitan with a sealed document. "Bishop," he said, "take this paper. I am giving all my fortune to the Senate of Megalokastro. An insurrection is an expensive thing, it requires money. Sell what I possess, and put it into arms." "And you— how are you going to live, Mavrudés?" the Metropolitan had asked with tears in his eyes. "Why are you worrying about me, Bishop? I shall knock at the doors and beg." The Metropolitan took care of him and set apart a monthly allowance for him. But he at once began stinting again, would not eat, would not drink, would not dress respectably any more, lent money at high rates of interest and extracted their capital from widows and orphans. He had got together a new fortune. Old now and with one foot in the grave, he had made a will leaving all again to the nation. But his brain was like an axe, and in difficult moments it hewed to right and left and opened up a way. So the Christians sent him too as their spokesman.

The Metropolitan was waiting for them on a soft divan in the Bishop's Residence. Before him, on a stand of cypress-wood in the form of a dove with outstretched wings, lay the silver-clasped Gospel. Above it hung three lithographs: to the right the Patriarch of Constantinople, to the left the Czar, in the middle Hagia Sophia. The sun came in through coloured panes and threw a blue and violet light on the opposite wall, which was crammed with photographs of living and dead metropolitans and bishops. They had snow-white or pitch-black beards, mitres and amulets and chains and croziers. Some of them looked out with gracious and benevolent eyes and were as hairy as unshorn rams. But others had protruding eyes, wide mouths and stubborn necks, and clutched the crozier to them like a police cudgel. There was also, among them, the present Metropolitan as a young Archimandrite in Kiev. How powerfully he gazed out, what a noble force he showed! This young hero was created by God to be a great leader or a prophet, or else a terrific wencher and enjoyer of life. But Christ had wooed him for Himself, with words which to him were sweeter than honey and had led him slowly on the way to what he was—a Metropolitan.

He glanced at his picture as a young man and sighed:

"I've grown old, I've got yellow like a cabbage, and the day is drawing near when I shall stand before the Judgement Seat with empty hands. How many Metropolitans of Crete will take their places before the Incorruptible Judge, bearing in their hands the gear of martyrdom—knives, axes, whips, and stakes. And I shall stand there with empty hands. O God, grant me to die for Thy honour and for the honour of Thy poor daughter!"

Múrzuflos came in with drawn face:

"The elders have come, Mylord," he said. "They're waiting."

"Show them in. And take the large silver salver, to hand round. These are gentlemen, you know."

Múrzoflos hesitated on the threshold. The Metropolitan looked at him in surprise.

"Is there anything else you want, Múrzuflos?"

"Do you forgive me, Mylord," said Múrzuflos, and his face was anxious again, "do you forgive me for what I've done?"

The Metropolitan smiled:

"Don't worry, Múrzuflos," he said. "The Crucified One will forgive you. Build on His mercy!"

"My guilt is great . . ."

"But His mercy also is great. Go now!"

The three elders came in, kissed the Metropolitan's hand and sat down on the divan. They pulled out their rosaries and waited for the Metropolitan to speak first.

"Lovely weather, my children," said he, looking out of the window. "What pleasant days these are! What sunshine! God's own good cheer! The spring! Saint George! How goes it now with the crops, old Mavrudés?"

"God be praised," he answered.

"With the crops it goes well," said Captain Eliás. "With men, not well. I'm for heroic deeds when they're needed. If not, they're idiocies!"

"The men of old used to say . . ." began Hadjisávas, but Captain Eliás raised his hand angrily and interrupted him:

"Let the men of old alone, Hadjisávas, they're dead and done with. We're talking about the living. At the moment," Captain Eliás went on, "the big agas are having a conference with the Pacha. God alone knows what the dogs are up to now. Let's be on our guard. What do you think, Mylord?"

"I too have heard of Captain Michales's new exploit," said the Metropolitan. "I'm sorry for the palikare, sorry for the man. Wine will be the ruin of him."

"He'll be the ruin of us! We must curb him. Otherwise . . ."

"In God's name, no rising!" said Hadjisávas. "We've much work to do in Crete. Our soil is blessed, it hides great treasures—

statues, inscriptions, royal palaces. How can one carry on excavations in the middle of a rising? Therefore we must . . ."

"Leave the men of old alone, I tell you," Captain Eliás interrupted. "Devil take 'em, let them leave us in peace! Speak, Mavrudés. My poor brain is blunt. Yours is an axe and cuts. Cut away!"

The old Rose-bug was pleased, and laughed.

"If you will allow, Mylord," he said.

"What are you thinking of, in Heaven's name, that you laugh?" asked the Metropolitan. "Your brain's like a woman. The welfare of Christendom is now in labour."

"Alleluja is a short psalm," replied old Mavrudés. "Now, this minute, rise up, Mylord, and go to see the Pacha. He's a kindly man, an Anatolian, good-natured. He doesn't like trouble. Tell him whatever truth and lies God inspires you with; soothe him down, say that he must forgive us for Captain Michales having been drunk, that we will call him to order and that he won't do it again. Take him some sort of present, too—let's say, a fine tobacco-box, or a big piece of amber for his long pipe. The bishopric has precious things for difficult times. Give him something: he's a dog, throw him a bone to gnaw. Then he won't bark. And our renowned fighter here will have a talk with Captain Michales, and may God protect him as he does so!"

"At the deaf man's door you can knock for a long while," shouted the Captain, wagging his scarred head. "He listens to no one, he's like a wall. All the same I'll speak with him. I'm an old man, fought in the 1821: perhaps he'll listen to me. . . . Apart from that, Mylord, I think our respected councillor is talking sense. Take your crozier and go to the Pacha. Quick, though! Before the blow falls!"

The round salver came: coffee, cakes, conserve. The elders fell silent. Through the window came the scent of the lemon-tree in blossom. A bee flew in, circled round the four heads, saw that they were no trees in blossom, and made off. Now the three spokesmen could be heard drinking their coffee in great gulps and smacking their lips. They had despatched the business quickly, and had easily hit on what was to be done. The cream and the sesame-cakes too came at the right moment. Hadjisávas asked the

Metropolitan for permission to roll himself a cigarette. The other two did the same. They half shut their eyes, and clouds of smoke rose and veiled the Patriarch, the Czar and Hagia Sophia.

The Metropolitan stretched out his hand and opened a drawer.

"My children," he said, "I'm going to show you a remarkable picture. Don't be carried away. You know our friend Múrzuflos. It's his work. He is god-fearing, but a visionary. He sees things that we don't see—not because they are not there, but because God has put blinkers over our eyes, as we do to horses, so that they may not be distracted to right and left, but may remain fixed straight upon the work. But God—who knows for what secret purpose?—has taken the blinkers off the visionaries."

He took out of the drawer a picture wrapped in a piece of white linen. He unwrapped it and handed it to the three spokesmen.

Captain Eliás took it, placed it on his knee and stared at it with his one eye.

"That's the Crucifixion," he said, "the Crucifixion. But I can't quite make it out."

Mavrudés bent over it, looked at it, and gave a cry:

"God forgive me, my eyes are flickering. But should . . .?"

"Extraordinary," cried Hadjisávas, who had taken a magnifying-glass out of his pocket and was eyeing the picture. "A wonderful idea! Bless those hands of yours, Múrzuflos! It is the Crucifixion. By my honour, I tell you, if I were a bishop, I'd hang this ikon up on the ikonostasis in the church."

The Metropolitan gave a bitter laugh and shook his kindly lion head.

"But," said old Mavrudés, "that's not Christ on the cross. I am a sinner, my God, it's a woman, wearing cartridges and silver pistols."

"It is Crete, it is Crete," said the Metropolitan in a voice stifled by emotion. "The cross is raised upon a heap of skulls and bones. The sky is full of dark clouds, and a flash of lightning reveals a monastery in the background to the right. Look at its bell-tower, the windmills in front of it, the domes, the walls with towers all round: that is Arkadi. And Crete is nailed to the cross in the form of a tortured mother in black, whose blood is running down on to the remains of her children. And below the cross, to right and left, stand two captains, one grey-haired and the other a young man with a broad fez . . ."

"There's a scroll coming out of his mouth," said old Mavrudés. "It says . . ."

"What does it say?" asked Captain Eliás, and bent forward, but could not read it.

Hadjisávas moves his magnifying-glass slowly along and read: "Eli, Eli, lama sabachthani . . ."

"My God, my God, why has Thou forsaken me?" the Metropolitan translated.

For a long while nobody spoke. The four men gazed at the new Crucifixion and sighed. At last Mavrudés opened his mouth:

"Isn't that a sin, Mylord? Crete as Christ?"

"It is one, it is one," replied the Metropolitan with a sigh. "But . . ."

"But what?"

"But she is worth it," murmured the Metropolitan, gazing at the crucified woman, at Crete.

The way Múrzuflos had painted her! The suffering that lay over her face! Her cheeks were furrowed, her huge, tormented, deep black eyes were overflowing. And her thin, half-open, twisted lips could be heard sighing. Her naked feet were sprinkled with shining blood, and at the bottom of the picture hung a pair of cream-coloured boots.

Suddenly, with a fierce jerk, as though making a great decision, Captain Eliás threw his black fez aside, seized the ikon and pressed his lips to it. For a long time, as though they could not tear themselves away. His broad chest rose and fell violently. At last old Mavrudés could hold out no longer. With tears streaming from his eyes, he snatched the ikon out of the hands of the grey-headed warrior, bowed over it and kissed it, weeping. Hadjisávas wiped his eyes, stood up and looked out of the window at the blossoming lemon-tree.

The Metropolitan took the picture and crossed himself.

"We worship thy sufferings," he murmured, and kissed the

blood-spattered feet of Crete. And all together they yielded themselves up without restraint to their sorrow.

The Metropolitan recovered first. He wrapped the ikon in its
white linen, pushed it to the back of the drawer, gathered his
strength together, and stood up.

"Go with my blessing," he said. "May God stretch out His
hand over you."

"We must stretch out ours first, Mylord," said Captain Eliás.
"If God sees no human hand, He doesn't stretch out His either.
Remember that!"

"Quite right, quite right, Captain Eliás! I'm going to see the
Pacha at once. God grant I find him in a good mood!"

They bowed, and kissed the Metropolitan's plump, white hand.
Captain Eliás took his cudgel at the door and went out. They
passed into the churchyard. The Captain shook his head. He saw,
strewn all over the yard, marble hands and feet, severed heads,
and dishes with unintelligible inscriptions.

"The men of old," he muttered angrily, "the men of old."

Hadjisávas bent down and began reading from the stones.

"Let's go," said Captain Eliás to his grey-haired companion.
"Leave him there. . . . There are seventy-seven sorts of folly. I'll
go and look for Captain Michales. And as for you, you've Turkish
friends. Selim Aga especially, Have a word with them at once.
God grant we don't have another rising breaking out before it's
time. Crete has already had too many losses. That's enough now!"

But at the Metropolitan's street door Barba Jannis stood waiting
for them. He had placed on the ground his basket with the snow
wrapped in straw and the copper can filled with sherbet. From
time to time, if anyone came past, he would cry up his wares:
"Cold as snow, cold as ice! Buy the drink of Paradise!"

He was a miserable little old man with a bald head, grey, round,
bright little eyes, and a long stork's neck, seamed with wrinkles
and cavities. His piercing falsetto voice tore people's ears. Turks
and Christians considered him daft, because he feared neither
Turks nor Christians and openly said what he thought. He cursed
and blasphemed, now against Christ, now against Mohammed,

now against the Sultan. And one Easter, some years ago, he had stood in front of that blood-stained Mustapha Pacha and prepared him a sherbet with plenty of snow for his refreshment; and at that moment his spirit had become embroiled, and he had begun to bewail the Christians killed at Arkadi and to leap into the air as though tormented by flames. The Pacha and the Effendis sitting beside him in the kiosk by the Three Vaults smoked their long pipes and enjoyed the diversion. People heard the wailing and ran up, Turks and Christians together, and this excited him still more. He bent down, picked a blade of grass and brandished it about him in the air, like one possessed. He wanted to provoke the Pacha, to tear out his eyes from his head, to menace him. Suddenly he began shrilly singing: "O my supple, gleaming sabre, oh you'll slaughter the Turks . . ."

Christians and Turks were dumbfounded; they did not know how to take it, and gazed at the Pacha to get their line from him. Surprisingly, the Pacha clapped his hands and burst into peals of laughter. What a piece of fooling—this human ruin who would menace Turkey with a grass-blade!

"Bravo, Captain Barba Jannis," he called out to him. "Come here!"

The Effendis, too, burst out laughing. And the people also joined in. And Barba Jannis danced and sang and howled on.

"That's enough, though," the Pacha shouted, "now you've done for us all; Turkey is lying on the ground! Come here, I tell you, you idiot palikare, I like you. I'm going to present you with a real sabre, and pin a high decoration on your chest: the open hand, Mohammed's seal. And now listen carefully: I give you the freedom, every Easter, to gird on the sabre, wear your decoration and strut like a Pacha through Megalokastro from the Kanea to the Hospital Gate, and from the New to the Harbour Gate. And you've the freedom, every day, to say whatever comes into that silly head of yours, and even to curse me. You're a Fool, your words are free of duty. For years, Barba Jannis, I haven't laughed so much as to-day, and for that I give you thanks."

Since that day Barba Jannis had plucked up courage, and the Turks bore with him and had their fun with him. And so it had

come about that Barba Jannis was the only free man in Megalokastro. If there was unrest in the air, Barba Jannis was the first to
scent it. And what the Christians had in mind but dared not yet
express, he shouted out loud with the sherbet in summer and the
salepi in winter and brought relief to Christendom. From many,
when he went too far, he got a box on the ear, and the Turks
threw lemon-peel and rotten tomatoes at him, but this did not
stop Barba Jannis from letting that tongue of his work on.

Since yesterday he had smelt powder in the air. He saw, too,
the three elders going thoughtfully into the Metropolitan's residence in the early morning. That had put a flea in his ear. He took
up his position by the street door of the residence and waited. He
must find out what was going on. Easter was near. He would have
to put on his sabre and his tin decoration, and vent his rage outside the Three Vaults when the Pacha and the Effendi were
listening to the band. In that way he would give the poor under-
dogs, who might not say a word, some satisfaction.

As he saw the two elders emerge, he took his snow-basket in
his hand and the can under his arm and approached them.

"Good-day, elders," he said. "Wait a moment, while I make you
a sherbet to cool you. It's getting warm."

"Leave us in peace, Barba Jannis," said Captain Eliás. "We
don't want your sherbet."

"Don't be so rude, Captain Eliás. I'm not afraid of you. I'm a
Fool, you know, and I'm not afraid either of Pacha or of Sultan,
while all you clever gentry and captains are p——ing in your
breeches. But Barba Jannis has his sabre and his letter of freedom
and his folly. What comes into his mind, that he says without
fear."

"I wish you well, Barba Jannis," said old Rose-bug gently.
"Curb that tongue of yours, the time hasn't come yet."

"When will it come?" asked Barba Jannis, likewise gently. "I
want to know."

Captain Eliás raised his cudgel. Barba Jannis collected his gear
together and moved on.

The Metropolitan hung round his neck the golden talisman—

one side of which represented, in many-coloured enamel, the
Crucifixion, and the other the Resurrection—and put in his pocket
an old silver tobacco-box from the celebrated workshops of
Janina, whose Metropolitan was a friend of his and had given it
to him. He picked up his crozier and went on foot, with the
Deacon following him, to the Pacha's entrance-gate.

Meanwhile the Pacha was slumbering, stretched out on soft
cushions, and was having a dream. He had gone for a walk in the
garden of his home town, Broussa. The trees stretched over him
their branches laden, some with blossom, others with fruit. As he
smoked his long pipe and wandered about, he thought he was in
Paradise, so that at any moment Mohammed, with his little mirror,
comb and phial of perfume in his red sash, might come out to
bid him welcome.

But as he turned for an instant to one side, what should he see?
A sturdy olive tree, scorched by lightning and twisted, without
either leaves or blossom. On its branches there hung fruit of a
strange kind: guns, and cartridges, and daggers, and black head-
bands. . . . What sort of an accursed olive-tree was this, that bore
weapons instead of fruit? cried the Pacha in terror, and shrank
back, to return again into his garden of blossom and fruit. But it
had sunk away, and round about him the Pacha saw nothing but
wild deserts, cliffs and, beyond them, bushes of muskets and silver
pistols.

"Crete! Crete!" yelled the Pacha and sprang up.

At that same moment Suleiman the Arab opened the door:

"Pacha Effendi," he said, "the big Pacha of the Greeks has
come. He's coming up the stairs."

"I've had a bad dream, Suleiman," said the Pacha, wiping the
cold sweat from his forehead.

"Shall I tell the great beast to take himself off?"

The Pacha reflected for a moment:

"No, let him come in, you blockhead. These *imams* of the
giaours are good interpreters of dreams. He'll explain me this one.
Let him come."

The Metropolitan entered, and the greetings took place. So
the two highest dignitaries of Megalokastro met together. They

were like two grey-headed kings in this community, and their kingdoms, the Turkish and the Greek quarters, execrated one another. Cross and crescent were intertwined.

They sat down side by side on the broad divan. The Pacha lit his long pipe, the Metropolitan pulled out his rosary from Mount Athos and began to tell its black ebony beads, and to ponder how the conversation ought to begin. Through the open window were visible on the left the buildings of the guard, on the right the old plane-tree with its young leaves. Anyone leaning out could have seen also, near the plane-tree, the famous Venetian fountain with the marble lion, and have felt the warm wind.

The Pacha yawned and began:

"Summer is here, Metropolitan Effendi. O Allah, how time passes! It is a wheel and never stops turning, and we turn with it. Summer comes and one says: 'How hot it is! I'm stifling!' and while one is saying so, the thunderstorms and the rains set in, and one wraps oneself in one's cloak. What does your religion say to these mysterious things?"

But before the Metropolitan could frame an answer, the Pacha, in whose inside a worm was gnawing, asked him:

"Do you believe in dreams, Metropolitan Effendi? Where do they come from? Who sends them to us?"

"Some are sent by God," replied the Metropolitan, "others by the Evil Spirit."

"And how can you tell the difference? Which are from God? Which from the Evil Spirit?"

"You have surely had a dream, Pacha Effendi. It still lies on your eyelids, I can see it."

"Yes, that is why I am asking you."

"May it have been a good and blessed one, Pacha Effendi. Let me hear it."

"Do you understand something about dreams?"

"God sometimes grants me enlightenment. Well?"

The pacha sighed and recounted the dream. He added a little decoration on to the olive-tree. He said he had seen several heads also hanging on its branches.

The Metropolitan lowered his lion head thoughtfully. He was seeking to use this dream to attain his aim.

"Well, is it from the Evil Spirit?" asked the Pacha uneasily.

"From God," the Metropolitan answered. "But how can I interpret it, Pacha Effendi? Perhaps it disturbs you?"

"I be disturbed?" exclaimed the Pacha. "Don't you then know that a true Musulman is never disturbed? For he knows that everything that happens in the world was already written, and no one can strike it out. And if at this moment the Sultan were to send me a *firman* and demand my head, I might well bewail, I certainly would bewail, but not be disturbed. It stood written so. Shall I put my hand into God's plan? So speak out without fear, Metropolitan Effendi. But beware of lies. Tell the whole truth!"

The Metropolitan collected himself for a few moments, then said:

"The garden which you saw in your dream is the good man's heart. Your heart is a garden, Pacha Effendi: it is opened at night, to let you go in and walk about. What you saw in your sleep was what answers to your nature: to wander tranquilly and at peace beneath blossoming trees in Broussa, the town where you were born. . . . Your heart is a garden, but behold, for you it was written that you should become Pacha and undertake this office here in Crete . . ."

The Pacha sighed:

"What can I say to you, Metropolitan Effendi? It is true, as if you were reading in my heart. But go on."

"When a man's village lies before him, Pacha Effendi, he needs no guide to it. The olive-tree hung with weapons, which you saw, is Crete. You went and stood under the lightning-scorched tree, and your face darkened. Here your destiny begins to be troubled. . . . It is a great pity that you woke up and do not know what followed. Perhaps God wrote for you, further on, that He gives you freedom, from now on, to do as you will. The responsibility is yours."

"Yes, may it be as you say, Metropolitan Effendi," said the good Anatolian. "By the sun which shines over us, Christians and Turks could live as brothers; the Greeks work, the Turks eat, and both lead a happy life."

"It lies in your hands!" the Metropolitan exclaimed, having now found the starting-point he had been looking for. "It is in your power to bring love to the island. God sent you the dream at the right moment!"

"What do you mean by that, Metropolitan Effendi? I don't understand."

"You have heard, no doubt, that Christians and Turks in Megalokastro are beginning once more to be stirred up, because, so they say, a drunken horseman forced his way into the Turkish coffee-house."

"And does that seem to you a trifle? The *giaour* has put Turkey to shame!" the Pacha exclaimed, his eyes coming to life.

"Turkey is not so easily put to shame. She is a mighty realm, Pacha Effendi!" said the Metropolitan in a studiously mild tone of voice. "Let's leave the drunkard hero on one side. You were asking me about your dream. I believe that God is enlightening me, and I will interpret it for you. Though if it bores you——"

"No, by the Prophet!" said the Pacha emphatically and placed his hand entreatingly on the Metropolitan's knee. "By you faith, go on."

"The seven heavens opened. God came down to you in your sleep, Pacha Effendi, and showed you the way."

"What way?"

"The way you will choose. There are two: one green and the other red. I can see them clearly marked in your dream. You can choose which you will."

"No, not as I will," protested the Pacha, "but as it is written by God!"

"But it may be, I tell you, that God has written for you a free choice. You can decide on the red road and start the executions and set Crete in a blaze. Or you can equally well decide on the green road, and then everything turns to milk and honey: Turks and Christians make friends again, and the world blesses your name. Now choose!"

So saying, and without giving the Pacha time to think, he pulled out of his pocket the precious tobacco-box.

"You are a connoisseur, Pacha Effendi," he said softly, "you

know something about treasures. This tobacco-box is a master-
piece from Jannina. On one side it has a two-headed eagle, on the
other a crescent, engraved with the finest art. Just what you are
working for: Musulmans and Christians living together in
brotherhood. Knowing your heart, I have long wanted to
give it you as a present. The time has come. May it bring you
luck!"

With that he laid the silver box in the Pacha's open palm.

"By Allah," said the Pacha, admiring the present, "you Greeks
are an immortal race. You catch the flies, sometimes with honey,
sometimes with vinegar."

He bent forward and stroked the tobacco-box delicately with
his thick fingers.

"Yes, let me tell you, Metropolitan Effendi, what a rain of
sweetness this box from Jannina brings to my heart. My first
wife—may she be happy in the underworld, where she now is—
possessed five-fold beauty like the Lady Phrosyne; she came from
Jannina." With a sigh he added: "But how can you understand
that? For you know no woman."

They fell silent. The Metropolitan played with his rosary and
looked through the window at the great plane-tree, which slowly
moved its leaves under the blue sky. At length he opened his
mouth to bring the conversation back to earth:

"The crops promise well, Pacha Effendi," he said, and looked
out of the window again at the green fields.

And the Pacha tore himself away from the sweet past and came
back to Megalokastro.

The Metropolitan stood up. The Pacha also stood up, and held
out his hand:

"Goodbye, Metropolitan Effendi," he said. "Both of us are
god-fearing men. We have deliberated wisely and divided Crete
wisely under us. You keep a tight hand over the Christians, and
I will do the same with the Turks."

He was silent for a moment. Another sentence came to the tip
of his tongue. He coughed, scratched his head and at length
decided to say it:

"Noisiness at weddings is common," he said, "but even if, in

these coming days, you hear a noise that sounds like a killing,
pretend it never reached your ears."

"A killing, Pacha Effendi?" asked the Metropolitan, glancing
uneasily at the grey-headed Turk with the deep-set eyes. "God
forbid."

"Come, come, a drunken Turk might also one day kill a Greek
palikare. Such things do happen. There's no lack of fools in the
world. But you, Metropolitan, you act deaf. . . . Just as we acted
blind, when we didn't see a certain Greek ride into the Turkish
coffee-house and flout us. So you act deaf now, Metropolitan
Effendi. My best wishes."

A snake wound itself about the Metropolitan, but he pretended
not to understand.

"God is great," he said. "He judges even Sultans and
Pachas."

"And Metropolitans, Effendi," said the old Anatolian, and his
lips smiled cunningly.

And on that the two highest dignitaries of Megalokastro parted,
before they could fall to disputing.

Days came and went; April reached its middle. More and more
trees covered themselves with blossom, while others were already
developing their fruits. Megalokastro squatted in the spring sunshine. Within its walls the men and women were suffering. They
had fallen into two angry bands, each with its God. And men and
Gods were whetting their knives. They did not notice the cool
sea, which smelt like a peach, nor the sun, which blossomed like
a heliotrope every morning, nor the stars.

Captain Michales went back, taciturn and sombre, to his shop.
For the first time a carouse had failed to lighten his heart. After
the drinking-bout he had risen up still more unconsoled, more
angry, than before. Now he avoided every drop and would only
eat a piece of bread, then at once leave the table. At home he
never opened his mouth all day long. Also he refused to sleep.
He sat on his bed and smoked and looked through the narrow
window at the night. He kept his eyes open, because he knew that
in sleep dishonouring dreams would overcome him. No. One

dream, one demon, which fell upon him every night. Was wine powerless to stifle this demon and his shame?

Nuri Bey also could not sleep. He was not only gnawed by the thought that he must keep his word to wash Turkey clean of the disgrace and avenge his father's blood. To this was added the anxiety about his wife. Ever since the day when Captain Michales had been to his house, Eminé had refused to take him in her arms. "He's put you to shame," she said obstinately, drumming on the floor with her little slippers. "Captain Michales has put you to shame, so I shall put you to shame. That's the custom among Turkish women."

To distract himself, Nuri Bey had turned to his country estate. The weather was warm: soon the hanum would come out, as every year, to spend the summer among gardens and flowing water. And God is great: perhaps her thoughts would grow mild here and her love rise afresh. So he spurred on workmen to paint doors and windows and to construct little pavilions of brushwood. Also he ordered canaries from Smyrna and parrots from Alexandria to pass the time for Eminé. This will soften her mood, he hoped.

But she reclined on soft cushions behind the lattice of the balcony on the street, drinking sherbet, chewing mastic and eyeing the passers-by. She made no distinction between Greeks and Turks, they were all men to her.

"What's a Turk, a Christian or a Jew, Maria?" she asked her old nurse. "There are only two kinds of men—old or young, white beards or black beards. I like the black ones."

Every evening, as the sun sank and the alleys grew shadowy, a Greek with a large fez and jaunty boots came and went down below and cast loving glances at the latticed balcony above.

"Who is that Greek, Maria? Where have I seen him?" Eminé asked the Moorish woman one day. "It seems to me as if I'd seen him in a dream."

"He's the one who roused you out of your faint, when there was the earthquake," answered the Moorish woman. "Captain Polyxigis."

"He looks handsome, by my soul. He has gaiety written in his face. He sways and stretches, and his boots creak. Listen, the poor man's sighing like a calf."

Eminé laughed, chewing mastic and sipping sherbet, and felt eager for him. She half closed her long-lashed eyes and smiled contentedly. I'll do as I want, she thought. If I want, I'll fetch him into my bed. If I want, I'll leave him in the street, to wander about like a dog. Am I not a woman? I'll do as I want."

Once, at midnight, when the street was empty of people, Captain Polyxigis took up his position beneath the latticed balcony. The moon was shining, honeysuckle and jasmine were fragrant, and in Nuri's garden the nightingale twittered a hopeless love-longing. From the harbour, too, the sea could be heard—it too was sighing and kept rubbing its breast against the fortress wall.

Eminé could not sleep. She was hot. She threw off her night-dress and peeped out, and saw in the moonlight a man, exhausted, leaning against the pillar of the street door. She recognised him at once. She laughed and nudged the Moorish woman, who was asleep, curled up like a hare.

"The poor thing," she said giggling. "Come, you have a look at him. He's almost fainted, I think, and I should love to go down and rouse him. The way he roused me! What do you think, Maria? Nuri Bey is at the estate."

"Eminé, my child, it would be a great sin."

"For you," retorted the hanum, "for you, because you're a Christian. But I'm a Moslem. I've a different God and different laws. You eat pig's flesh and aren't defiled. But if you nibble at a strange man, you are defiled. With us it's the other way round: pig's flesh defiles us, a strange man doesn't. Go, tell him to come up."

"Eminé, my child . . ." the Moorish woman pleaded, bewildered.

"See first if the Moor at the door is asleep."

"He's asleep," said Maria with a sigh. "I heard him snoring."

"Is the dog tied up too? Go on, you silly hen, don't shiver. Show some zest in the thing. God made men and women for this, you poor creature! Ah, what a moon there is tonight, what a warm wind! The jasmine is in blossom, and the nightingale is mad.

Go on, fetch him up. I've often thought: in winter a woman can be respectable, but in the spring . . .?"

Eminé, leaning forward, saw Captain Polyxigis still at his post, staring up at the lighted lattice. "I don't care for Nuri, and Captain Michales is not to be had: this one here is good enough for me!" She reached for her comb and mirror, hastily tidied her hair, rubbed musk under her armpits and gave the nurse a push: "Go on, I tell you!"

The Moorish woman seized her head in both hands and stumbled down the stairs.

Eminé splashed the rest of the musk over her bosom and body. She stood up and pulled the lamp back behind the door. "I wanted a different one," she murmured, "but he is wild and unapproachable. Doesn't matter, this one too suits me."

She pricked up her ears. She heard the street door slowly open, the dog barked once, steps became audible in the yard, in the men's part, on the stairs. . . . She leaned back on the cushions and made to put on her nightdress again. But she thought better of it and let the moon shine unhindered on her breasts and body. Boots squeaked on the floor, the smell of a man came in, Eminé's nostrils quivered. She passed her tongue several times over her lips. Then she half closed her eyes and waited.

Captain Polyxigis stood now on the threshold. She gazed at him through her long lashes. He raised his hand to his eyes as though giddy; his heart was beating as though mad. The Circassian flung her arms wide open in the moonlight and lay back. As if this were the agreed signal, Captain Polyxigis at once gave one bound towards her and extinguished the lamp.

April was nearing its end, and full of fear the Christians entered Passion Week. In the whole of Christendom there was no people that shared so deeply, so bloodily, in so special a way, in the sufferings of Christ as the Cretans during these decades. In their hearts Christ and Crete were mingled, the sufferings of both were the same: the Jews crucified Christ and the Turks Crete. The Christians felt in themselves how the sufferings of Christ mounted from day to day, as they grew weak from watching and

fasting, until in their hearts an angry accusation sought to find
vent for itself by force. They eyed the Turks with wild looks, and
could only with difficulty hold themselves back from striking
down the few Jews—tinsmiths and money-changers—who lived
huddled in the Jews' alley near the harbour. These always shut
and bolted themselves in early during the sacred and dangerous
evenings of Passion Week.

This time the atmosphere in Megalokastro was even more
threatening than before, for over against the disturbed Christians
the Turks had not got over the injury done them by Captain
Michales. At night they crowded to St. Menas's church, where
the Christians were mourning for Christ. They hurled curses and
tried with noisy singing to insult and dishonour the Christians.
These waited hourly to know where, when and how the agas
would strike. The subterranean excitement grew stronger and
stronger.

So passed, in incense, watching and fasting, the Monday,
Tuesday and Wednesday of Holy Week. The evening hours were
soft and blue. Violets bloomed in all the courtyards, and on the
next day but one—Good Friday—the girls would pick them, to
set them along with the elder-blossom and the last April roses
upon the cloth with the picture of the dead Christ. Immediately
after sundown the Christians shut their shops, went home to their
houses and rapidly ate the meal prescribed for a time of fasting:
baked beans, lettuce, raw artichokes, red fishes' roes, olives and
sesame-soup. They paced round their yards, listening and waiting.
St. Menas's bell rang out, hesitant and mournful in the mild
twilight. The Christians crossed themselves, opened their doors
and streamed, bowed down and silent, through the alleys of
Megalokastro, to learn once more, this evening, how God would
suffer at the hands of men.

As Passion Week went on, the excitement of the Cretans rose.
On Maundy Thursday, as the reading of the twelve gospel lessons
began, and as now the Metropolitan, now Pope Manolios, now the
Deacon read, in harsh voices on one note, how Judas had betrayed Christ and how the Mohammedans of those days had begun
to strike, to mock and to scourge him, it affected them as if they

themselves were running breathlessly with Christ from Annas to Caiaphas and to Pilate, as Omer Vrioni had run to Mustapha Pacha and to the Sultan, to demand justice.

With growing impatience, they managed to listen to the first seven lessons; but then they rushed headlong out into the church-yard, where early that morning a Judas of daubed clouts and straw had been set up. They fell upon it with knives and burning torches, pierced it through and set it on fire. This relieved and cheered them all a little, so that they then went back into the church, to hear the remaining lessons.

On Good Friday morning the bells rang still more sorrowfully. Over the holy tomb in the middle of the church the cloth bearing the image of Christ was spread. The doors of the church stood wide open, and Christians kept going out and in.

In the churchyard stood Múrzuflos, exhausted from watching and fasting. Round him stood Demetrós, Kajabés, Vendúsos, and Signor Paraskevás the barber. They were all listening with bent heads to the words of Múrzuflos. He was telling them how yester-day the Pacha had sent his Arab to the Metropolitan with the present of a hare. But the Metropolitan had been angry and had sent the hare back and had a message conveyed to the Pacha:

"We are fasting. The Jews have killed Christ, and we are mourning."

"He ought not to have sent it back," said Paraskevás. "That was an insult."

"He oughtn't to have sent it," said Kajabés; "*that* was an insult. Didn't the dog know that we are in Passion Week?"

"It's pure madness," said Demetrós with a sigh. "Are we now going to get up against the Pacha? Hit the egg with a stone and it goes to the Devil. Hit the stone with the egg and again it goes to the Devil. That's what I think."

During all these holy days Captain Michales did not go to church. He honoured and prayed to God, but could not abide priests. His custom was to wait till the church emptied and the priests' vestments, women's skirts and men's breeches were out of the way. When the place was pure he would visit it and light his candle. But always on Maundy Thursday morning, whether consciously or without thinking, he would come to church when the popes were still there, and receive communion. He would cross himself, open his mouth and receive the body and blood of Christ. He would feel a great fire die down within him.

But this year, for the first time in his life, he rode out into the countryside on his mare, aimlessly. He got as far as the estate of Nuri Bey, but stopped short and turned. He breathed in the sea air, but he did not go to communion. "As long as the evil spirit is in me," he said to himself again and again, and breathed heavily, "as long as the evil spirit stays in me, I won't go to communion."

There was no longer day in the year than Good Friday: it stretched over five afternoons, lost its way, stood still, took one step forward and two back and would not let evening be reached. The Christians, hungry from their fast, could feel themselves growing weak as they passed by the fragrant bakeries. The women went about their housework as though possessed. They cleaned the rooms. Great fires were kept going. The courtyards were freshly scrubbed. Hearts were expectant, they were waiting for the setting of the sun, and then for the merciful, dark blue night to rise up, fulfilling the cry: "Christ is risen!"

Krasojórgis's wife kept looking out at the sun and measuring the time. The star of blessing, it seemed, would never come forth in the sky. The smell of the chicken cooking and of the custard cakes which her son Andrikos had brought from Tulupanas's bakery, made her nearly faint.

Penelope had been painting eggs since Maundy Thursday. They had come out very well. Now she was gaily preparing the tripe soup in the kitchen. Mr. Demetrós ran about at her orders with pots and pans, to and fro between house and bakery. "Up, my Demetrós! Courage, my hero! This evening Christ rises; this evening I shall need you, my treasure! Are you listening? All this meat and these custard cakes must not be wasted."

God granted Krasojórgis's wife her prayer at last and made the sun go down. Easter smells spread over Megalokastro in the dusk. The Christian quarters were filled with loud gaiety. The women began to make themselves look nice. Vangelio too dolled herself

G

up and then sat in the courtyard waiting for her brother. Would he come? Or not? Would he take her for the last time alone to the Easter service? Next year they would have Tityros with them.

Midnight drew near. The Christians went out into their yards and listened for the chimes to begin. Already Christ was stirring in His grave, already He was gathering Himself to heave the heavy stone aside. All Christians stood on tiptoe in the courtyards and at their windows with their ears pricked and waited. Only two in all Megalokastro were not with God in their thoughts. One of them, on this holy night, held a Circassian woman in his arms. The other sat upright on his bed in the dark and smoked one cigarette after another. Like a dog his thoughts ran through the narrow alleys and stopped, barking, in front of a green door.

The Christians collected in the forecourt of the church gazed at their Metropolitan. They had not yet lit their candles. The Metropolitan, in his Easter vestments, had gone up to the laurel-decorated platform under the blossoming lemon-tree, and now opened the heavy, silver Gospel. The faces showed light, and the night breeze played over them. And as the thundering cry rang out: "Christ is risen from the dead," the holy light flared up and all the candles were lit: all Christians rose with Christ. The leading people fired their silver pistols, and Múrzuflos, with his joy foaming over, set the three bells—Saint Menas, Freedom and Death—swinging, and they announced: "Crete is not dead. Crete lives!"

Barba Jannis girded on his long sabre and his tin decoration and strutted up and down. It was his day of rest, on which he sold no sherbet. Turks and Christians laughingly bowed before him, and he returned every greeting with the dignity of a Pacha. He had hired a street-boy and daubed his face with soot: so now he had a Moor, who followed him step by step.

The gnome Charílaos, with his moustache freshly waxed, went out visiting in a carriage. He wore the straw hat which somebody had recently brought him from Athens, supported his chin on the lion head of his stick, and observed the people with spiteful looks. He could not forgive them for having shapely bodies while he had not.

Towards evening Christian men and women dressed for Easter

were milling round the Three Vaults. The silk ribbons in the girls' hair fluttered in the wind. To the north the rose-coloured sea lay at peace, to the south the fields were green, the mountains glittered and the olive-trees shimmered silvery. And over all a violet, silken, very soft sky held its shield. Then slowly the evening shadows grew, the faces of the richly-fed Kastrians became peaceful as they strolled for their digestion, and suddenly Venus hung in triumphant laughter high above the heads of the people.

VI

RICH in strong manhood, Captain Michales's family rose at gray of dawn in the four villages where it had struck root since the times of his ancestors—Petrokéfalo, Ai-Janni, Kruson and Redtower—and set out for Megalokastro, to be present at the wedding ceremony of the youngest brother, Tityros. They all came together in the mother-place of the family, Petrokéfalo, where the hundred-year-old grandfather and father of them all, old Captain Séfakas, lived. He was to lead the procession. Some came on mules, some on horses, on which red cloths had been laid and wedding presents loaded: cooked lambs and sucking-pigs, hard and soft cheeses, leather bottles of wine and oil, pots of honey, raisins, figs and little bags of almonds.

With a great stride old Séfakas came over the threshold, in his best suit of heavy wool, in black boots, with a black head-band and his long, double-handled stick. His beard streamed over the whole of his chest, deep-set eyes sparkled under thick eyebrows, and out from the wide sleeves of his snow-white shirt there stuck two arms, lean and furrowed as the stems of ancient olive-trees. He looked about him. The whole street was motley with sons, grandsons and great-grandsons. He was glad.

"A thousand times welcome, children!" he shouted to them, throwing his arms wide open. "A field full of flowers and grasses!"

A single shout of joy answered him out of the human swarm which had come from his loins.

"We're happy to see you again! Rejoice in your kingdom, old man!"

Two of his grandchildren led up to him an old mare. One of them held the reins, the other a stirrup. They placed the beast near the rim of the fountain in the yard, to make it easier for the ancient to mount. But with a laugh he shoved his grandchildren aside:

"Do you think I've got old, and would you hold the stirrups

for me?" He seized the mare by the mane and with one heave was in the saddle.

"Health and joy to you, old man! May you live a thousand years!" they yelled at him.

"A thousand years are a long time, children!" replied the grey-beard, pulling his head-band tight. "Five hundred will do!"

He had begotten eleven sons and four daughters, regular wild beasts! Only the straggler was no good. He was lean and lanky, wind. How the Devil had such a product sprung from his loins?

"What are we going to do with him?" he had debated with his wife. "He'd be no good as a shepherd, he hasn't the pluck for stealing. He'd be no good as a farmer, he hasn't the strength for ploughing. He'd be no good as a sailor, the sea makes him sick. He's no good for anything!"

"He'd make a good pope," suggested the old woman, to whom her youngest son was especially dear.

"A pope or a schoolmaster. In the village we've got a pope, but not yet a schoolmaster. So let's make him into a schoolmaster."

He sent him to Megalokastro, to study, and so a son of Captain Séfakas became the schoolmaster Tityros.

Old Séfakas had been relieved at getting him out of the house. He was ashamed to call him son, and remained on his roomy farm with his ten wild beasts. He was proud of them. "When my sons are eating," he used to say, "the house trembles, so that strangers ask: 'Is it an earthquake?' 'Oh no, Séfakas's sons are having a meal!' "

But Charos[1] had come, posted himself on the threshold and looked over the wide yard. Here, it seemed to him, were far too many palikares growing up. He sought out his share. Some he took honestly and in manly fashion, in war; others he stole cunningly from their beds. And yet enough remained, thought Séfakas, and they had given him grandchildren and great-grand-children. One leaves a hundred behind him, and these a thousand,

---

[1] One of the many survivals of ancient religion among the Christian Greeks. But, as Nilsson (*A History of Greek Religion*, Oxford, 1925, p. 303), points out, Charos or Charondas is greatly changed from Charon, the ferryman of the Styx. He "is the strong and cruel robber, who mercilessly snatches men away from their life in the light of day" (translator's note).

and in the end Crete will be full of them. How many will Charos
devour by means of the Turks? Yet enough yeast will remain to
make the dough rise.

"In God's name, children!" he said, raising his hand, "forward,
let's marry the last son."

At the head of the procession rode the old man. A step behind
him, to right and left, came the two eldest sons, with years upon
them already, but strong: Manúsakas, the passionate farmer from
Ai-Janni; and Fanúrios, the guerilla leader and great herdsman.
He was a man of the grasslands with a fierce face and smelling of
cheese and goats. All the Lasithi mountains were his province.
When the mountain loneliness oppressed him, he would come
down from the bald heights to the plains. He would seek out the
bull belonging to Hadjinikolés in Petrokéfalo. If he found him
tied up to an olive-tree, he would untie him and fight with him
to get rid of his depression.

Yet he was afraid of one wild beast in the world: his wife
Despoiniá. She was a yellowish bit of flesh with light blue eyes. If
you blew on her she would fall over. But the wild Fanúrios
trembled before her. Every time he came down to the village and
stayed a few days at home to beget a child on her, he behaved
decorously before her and adopted human manners. He wanted
to drink and did not drink, wanted to curse and did not curse,
wanted to spit against the wall and did not spit. He controlled
himself and waited for the night, till his wife had gone to bed.
Then he would stick his paw out of the window, grab by the neck
anyone who came by and drag him in. He would sit down opposite him and they would set to work softly drinking, without
making a sound. If another came by, the same fate befell him.
They would lay their fingers on the rims of their glasses so that
they could touch glasses without a sound. They drank until
Fanúrios decided that they had had enough. Then he took them
again by the neck and bundled them out. Only then did he
visit his wife in bed. In this way his many children had been
begotten.

The dust on the road whirled high, the sun was scorching.
From time to time old Séfakas turned his heated face back and

cast a swift glance at his followers. Behind Manúsakas and Fanúrios came the grandsons—stately men, all of them, some married. After them the great-grandsons, with fair or raven-black down on their cheeks. And right at the end the noisy, cackling womenfolk.

Then he looked to the front again, towards Megalokastro. He made no conversation with his sons, nor did he smile. His heart was satisfied and at peace in its right place. He no longer needed anything or anybody. In the last times the words had remained hanging within him. If any secret anxiety still gnawed at him, he could not speak of it with anyone else. Only with God.

And in fact, since not long ago, strange meditations had been revolving in his brain. For the first time old Séfakas was thinking of death. The day was drawing near when he would stand before God, and the grey-haired man of authority shuddered at it. His picture of death was a dark mountain, with rushing waters for which he was thirsty and wild beasts of which he was afraid. He remembered how once, during a rising, he had slipped out all alone at night on to Cruel Mountain, outside Megalokastro, where the Turks lay. He had gone forward slowly, bent double, with his knife between his teeth. Then he caught soft sounds of speech, saw cigarettes glowing, heard weapons clinking together and saw them gleaming in the darkness. Trembling he had gone on further. God now seemed to him like that mountain.

Vangelio, meanwhile, had returned from the hot bath. Renió was combing her hair with the ivory comb given her by her godfather, Idomeneas. She put rouge on the cheeks to hide their yellow tinge, and powder on that nose to make it look less large, while the bride sat in silence before the mirror. Penelope and the wife of Krasojórgis were decorating the bridal bed—trilling wedding songs and strewing it with lucky lemon-blossom. Both women were already slightly tipsy. Down below in the kitchen those two good housewives, Katerina the wife of Captain Michales and Polyxigis's sister Chrysánthe, were preparing the dainties. Ali Aga was bringing all the plates, knives and forks of the neighbourhood.

Diamandés entered, with his cloak draped foppishly over his shoulders, gave off-hand, sleepy, dissipated greetings and stared with his round eyes at the disturbed house. He pursed his lips and played nervously with his watch-chain. All this was not to his liking. They had done very well without a brother-in-law. Why the Devil was that fellow with the long coat-tails and the sagging glasses intruding on them? With heavy tread he stumped up the stairs. Krasojórgis's wife looked at him knowingly. She knew he had only bought his watch to show off and was quite incapable of telling the time, so that his friends teased him about it. So she asked him, mockingly:

"What time do you make it, Mr. Diamandés?"

"It's stopped, woman," he snapped back angrily. "It isn't going."

He turned away from her and saw how they were adorning his sister. They're adorning the victim for the sacrifice, he thought, and made to go back down the stairs. But his sister felt his gaze and turned towards him. Her eyes filled with tears.

Penelope broke in:

"We're adorning the bride. Men are in the way here."

The handsome man pulled a hair out of his moustache and threw it on to the bed:

"May it bring luck," he said, and stumped downstairs, sighing.

Neighing and the chink of harness in the evening twilight, then the narrow street filled with horsemen. Captain Séfakas with his train had arrived. The doors of Vangelio's house swung open and immediately the manliest smell of sweating bodies, cooked meat and cheese poured through the house. The old grandfather took the bony Vangelio in his arms and kissed her. And the whole of her new kindred fell upon her and enveloped her in the stink of sweat and goats and vinous breath. The bride's cheeks were rubbed almost raw by the bristling whiskers and beards which pressed against them. And she ran back into the bedroom upstairs to put on more rouge and to powder herself afresh.

There was not enough room for the guests in the downstairs room, so the women went up to the bedroom, some of them also into the kitchen, and spread out the presents. Many of the men stretched themselves out in the yard. The house hummed.

"Don't make such a row, children," shouted Captain Polyxigis, as he ran up and down greeting his new sisters-in-law. "Don't make such a row, we're in Megalokastro, here, not in the mountains."

Tityros and godfather Idomeneas soon got away from the embracings and greetings and began whispering together on a corner of the sofa. Tityros told him enthusiastically how many old marriage customs were still alive among the people. These Greeks were immortal. And he was glad, not because he was getting married, but because he was being married according to ancient custom. And Idomeneas answered that he had yesterday sent a pressing ultimatum to the Queen of England. In a few days without any doubt he would have a reply, and a favourable one too. "God grant, godson," he said to him peacefully, "that your wedding may be a day of good fortune and Crete may be set free."

Captain Michales appeared, with serious countenance, took off his cap and kissed his father's hand. Then in the courtyard he shook hands with his brothers and nephews, pretended not to see Captain Polyxigis and, going back into the house, sat down on the settee beside his father. The old man bent over his son's ear:

"The bride looks to me a right sorry sight, Michales."

"She suits the looks of the bridegroom", replied Captain Michales.

The old man shook his head and laughed drily.

But their conversation was interrupted. Manóles the pope with the capacious pockets, the Deacon with the wild boar beard, and Múrzuflos with the silver censer, entered. All rose. The freshly painted bride came down, her godfather took the bridegroom by the hand, Múrzuflos filled the censer, and the intoning began. The bride kept her head bent, and the wild clan, massive and breathing deeply, all full-bloodedness and moustaches, stood round about and stared at her. This spindly woman was now entering their clan and would mix her blood with its. Would that work out well? They were all hersdmen and ploughmen, they knew a thing

G*

or two about cattle: which goat or bull to couple with which she-goat or cow, to get the strongest young and make the herd thrive. And the women knew a thing or two about cocks, hens and rabbits, and sized up the young couple uneasily. "The bride's very thin. She's no breasts. How's she going to nurse children?" "Don't you worry. She'll give milk. Do you remember, last year, the she-goat Mavrada. Skin and bones she was, and you could hardly see her udder! But she was fruitful and had kids and yielded—you won't believe it!—a quart of milk at every milking!" "She hasn't any hips either. How'll she bear a child?" asked another. And her neighbour reassured her: "Don't get worried, she'll broaden out now. They all fill out when they marry." The women went on whispering, and Pope Manóles sang the wedding words: "Isaiah danced . . ."

When the service was over, the godfather carried out the exchange of crowns, and the relatives fell upon the young couple yet again, wishing them long life and an honoured old age. Then at the loaded table the chewing and gurgling began. The bridegroom, later, could no longer remember when all this happened. A cloud sank over his thoughts, and it was only dimly that he distinguished faces and voices—and his father enthroned on the sofa, holding a roast sucking-pig on his knee, while on his right sat Captain Michales and on his left Captain Polyxigis. And later—he could remember this a little—in came Diamandés, his wife's brother, and greeted no one. His cap was drawn right down to his eyes. He went straight into the kitchen, to drink and celebrate there. Then Captain Polyxigis leapt up from the sofa and went out, and immediately after there could be heard voices in dispute and glass breaking.

Captain Michales gnashed his teeth and made as if to jump up too. But he thought better of it. He remained seated, but his blood boiled. His daughter Renió came up to him with the salver and offered him fresh cherry-juice. He became calmer as he drank. He gave the girl a friendly look. He had seen her somewhere already. Who could she be? All the evening she had attended to him and unobtrusively brought him whatever he wanted: water, wine, something to eat, a cigarette. She ran at once and brought it to

him. He signed to his wife, who was carving the meat for the
guests:

"Who's that nice girl?" he asked her and indicated Renió with
a glance. "I've seen her somewhere. But where?"

Katerina sighed:

"She's your daughter."

Captain Michales bent his head and made no sound after
that.

Captain Polyxigis came back sweating. All eyes were turned on
him. He managed to put on a smile, and said:

"He's drunk. You must excuse him."

He sat down next to Captain Michales, as if he wanted to put
him in a friendly mood and make him forget the behaviour of
his unmannerly nephew. Captain Michales's nostrils twitched in
spite of him: his friend smelled of musk. But Captain Polyxigis
went on trying to soften him. For days Captain Michales had been
been repulsing him roughly. Why? After having recourse several
times to wine to give him courage, he burst out accusingly:

"What have I done, Captain Michales, to make you dislike
me?"

"You smell too Turkish to me," came the answer.

"How do you know?" asked Captain Polyxigis, and blushed.

Captain Michales stared him straight in the eyes. Suddenly his
heart leapt high in his throat and seemed about to stifle him. He
understood. He seized hold of the chair which Renió had brought
him to put his feet on, the chair cracked as though its joints would
give.

"Now I know," he said through closed teeth. "Aren't you
ashamed? With a Turkish woman?"

"She's going to become Christian," said Captain Polyxigis.

Captain Michales jumped up. The house was swaying before
his eyes.

"Instead of her turning Christian, why don't you turn Turk?
Then we shall be rid of you," he said softly, and went out into the
yard to get some air.

The next day was already trying to break, but everyone still ate
and drank. The song-lovers brought out bag-pipes which some-

one played, while in the yard others danced the dance of the five rows, and sang. The newly-married couple sat silent and listless on the end of the sofa, and neither of them was eager to go up to the flower-strewn bridal bed. The old grandfather squatted near them with his eyelids lowered, but was not asleep. He was listening to the noise of his grandsons around him, to the voices, the songs and the bursts of laughter, and was glad, as though he were a huge plane-tree with rain falling on it and its happy roots drinking up the water.

Captain Michales, with sombre eyes, signed to his wife: "Let's go!"

God began a new day. The sun shone over the wedding court-yard. It found it full of gnawed bones and breadcrusts and men sleeping doubled up in their beards and wide woollen cloaks. It rose over Megalokastro where to-day, the Wednesday after Easter, the shops would open and the masters gird on their aprons. It touched caressingly the olive-orchards and fields, and stood over the estate of Nuri Bey. It rejoiced over the newly-painted window-frames and over the jasmine in bloom. To-day too, there had arrived from Alexandria four parrots, two dark green ones and a pair that were sea-green with yellow breasts. Nuri Bey had also engaged old Braimis, the blind drummer, that Eminé Hanum might not be bored. For two weeks he had not gone to Megalo-kastro and had been preparing, like a love-lorn bird, the nest where the beloved woman was to spend the summer. He longed to see her, and the day before yesterday he had sent her a message to say he was coming to her—he could bear the separation no longer. But she answered by the Arab that she thought she was pregnant: she had attacks and could see no one. Only, every evening, Hamidé the wise woman came and practised her healing arts. Then the pain went away. If he loved her, he would not come before the birth.

This anxiety was not the only one. He had had to do without the sight of his beloved for two weeks, and now, into the bargain, the Pacha had sent him word yesterday evening by his Arab that he was taking too long to fulfil his word. The disgrace had still not been washed away, and the agas were murmuring. Whatever he had in mind to do he should do at once.

His father now visited him in his sleep regularly. He did not speak and no longer remained standing over him. He went past him with bare feet and long, dragging steps, in his rags, and did not turn to look at him. He went and yet was never out of sight; all night he was there with averted face, inexorably present.

And it chanced that precisely that morning the accursed tribe which had killed his father came past on its way back from the wedding. Furiously he shut the door, went upstairs to the bedroom and watched through the wooden lattice the hundred-year-old leader of the family proudly riding past, and behind him his following: a whole host.

As they rode past the door, Manúsakas reined in his mare, pulled out a silver pistol and fired into the air:

"I'm shooting at your shield, Nuri Bey," he called out.

But behind the lattice Nuri Bey bit his lips and did not take up the challenge. Manúsakas turned to his companions:

"The dog made a row because I took the ass into the mosque to prayers. The day after tomorrow, at their Bairam festival, as sure as my name's Manúsakas, I'll take my sow!"

The wedding guests roared with laughter and vanished in the dust.

Nuri Bey's eyes grew bloodshot. He came downstairs, uncorked a bottle and sat down outside, in front of the door, to quench his rage by drinking. But he could not remain sitting down. He noticed the mess those accursed mules and horses had made of the ground in front of his door. He went to the middle of the road and looked towards the sun, where his enemies had vanished in the dust. He tipped the bottle up and spilled five or six big mouthfuls on the ground.

"So may my blood be spilled," he muttered, "if I don't do what in this hour I have decided!"

He threw back his neck and drank without pausing, till the wine splashed over. Then he went in, laid the pistols on his pillow and loaded them. He fired two shots. They were in order. He pulled his large two-edged dagger out of the sheath and tested it against his wrist. It cut like a razor-blade. All day he ran up and down his place or went out and followed the tracks of the mules and horses on the road. He returned full of renewed rage. At nightfall he killed a rabbit and had it prepared in his favourite way. He ate with appetite and plucked a handful of jasmine blossoms, which he strewed over his pillow. For the first time for a long while he fell into sweet, unbroken sleep. Also, that night, his father did not visit him.

In the morning he woke up cheerful. He whistled. The cocks in his yard also woke up and greeted the sun. Light dropped from the sky on to the leaves of the trees, and the fountain in front of the door made a sound like a cackling hen. The stallion came out of his stable and neighed excitedly to the day, as though he saw a mare. And Nuri Bey too exulted at the young day.

He went down into the yard. His old dog Kartsomis barked his welcome. He stroked the horse in the stable. He ordered a groom to wash it with warm water and himself brought it a pail of water from the well to drink. Then he shook out for him plenty of fodder. Back indoors, he told his cook to get ready for him some good things and to fill a bottle with lemon-raki. But quick, for he must set out at once, before the sun grew hot.

"Are you going to Kastro?" the old woman asked, "and are you bringing our mistress?"

Without replying he went up to the bedroom. There he spread dark pomade on his moustache, put on his ceremonial suit, and dashed musk over his hair and ears. In his sash he stuck the silver pistols and the two-edged dagger. Then he went down to the yard again and stood at the door, radiant like the sun.

An aged Turk came by, with a sack on his back. He was Mustafa Baba, who collected herbs, prepared ointments for wounds and also dealt with jaundice, shingles and evil spells. He journeyed through Greek and Turkish villages crying: "Good doctoring, good medicines, long life!" He distributed from his sack, according to the illness, juniper berries, hellebore, rue, wormwood, mandragora: a holy man, who journeyed about as a healer and would not take any pay. He would eat a piece of bread, drink a mouthful of water, and live on that. As he caught sight of Nuri Bey in front of his door, he stopped dead and stared at him in terror.

"What's the matter with you, Mustafa Baba? Why are you looking at me in such a startled way?" Nuri Bey asked, holding the dog back by the scruff of its neck.

The old man bowed.

"You're very handsome to-day, Nuri Bey," he answered admiringly, "Handsomer than is right," he added in a subdued voice.

Nuri Bey laughed.

"Don't laugh, Bey," said the old man. "To men and women there are limits set, and to cross them means sin."

"Too great handsomeness, too great kindness, too much honour —is that sin?"

"It is sin, Bey," the old man sighed.

"Why? I don't understand that, Mustafa Baba."

"Neither do I, my child. But such is God's law. Be careful, Nuri Bey!" Once again he raised his hand to his chest, lips and forehead. "Fare well, Bey," he said. He took several steps and again stopped. Nuri Bey watched him and laughed.

"Would you like something, Mustafa Baba? Have some breakfast at my table."

"I'm not hungry, Nuri Bey. Excuse me. Only . . ."

"Only? Speak out freely, Mustafa Baba."

"I would like to say something to you, but you will laugh."

"You're a holy man. I'm not laughing. Speak."

"Rub a smut upon your face, put on your everyday suit and your patched boots if you have any. Lay those silver pistols aside. Diminish your handsomeness, Nuri Bey!"

The Bey burst out laughing again, and sorrow spread over the kindly, thin old face.

"As God is above you, don't laugh, Nuri Bey!" he muttered and, bent double, passed on his way.

Proudly Nuri Bey went back into the yard, where his saddled horse stood glittering. The old maid was hanging a saddlebag with the dainties and lemon-raki from the saddle. Nuri Bey looked about him. The house shone like new, the olive, almond and pomegranate trees were showing fruit, the fig-trees were spreading broad, dark-green leaves and the parrots were preening themselves in the cages between the trellised vines. Not a breath of wind.

For an instant Nuri Bey's heart hesitated. Where was he going? Why was he going? Why was he leaving all these comforting gifts of God? His estate was a paradise, nothing was lacking here. The woman too would soften—she would come, and this courtyard would echo with her sparkling laughter. And the pomegranates would ripen and the figs grow sweet, and the parrots would lay eggs the size of almonds, concealing yellow, green and rose-tinted wings.

He sighed! The old servant observed her master. She had reared him, day by day, hour by hour. He had grown up under her hands. She had never married or known a man. She did not regret it. This man was her husband, her son and God. Never did she raise her eyes to question him. What he did was well done, what he ordered was right, and to obey him was a joy. She had no other joys. But to-day her heart was heavy.

"Where are you going, Master?" she asked him again.

Nuri Bey turned in surprise:

"What's the matter with you, little mother? Why do you ask?" He placed his toes in the stirrup and swung into the saddle. The old woman laid her shrivelled hand on the horse's shimmering neck.

"Where are you going, Master?" she muttered once more, fearfully.

"Look after the place!" he replied, and put spurs to the horse.

"God be with you, my child. . . ." She saw her master use the spurs again and vanish between the silver-leaved olive-trees.

She felt a lump in her throat, yet her heart was hard as a stone.

"He's drunk the immortal water and knows no fear!" she said out loud, and bolted the door.

After the Easter days Manúsakas had gone up to the pens on the slope of Mount Selena. The heat was already oppressive, the shearing had begun. That was a tremendous festival in the mountains. With their clumsy shears the herdsmen were shearing the goats and sheep and cracking jokes as they worked. The women too came out on to the mountain, and kindled fires on which to heat kettles of water for cleaning the wool. Manúsakas's sons and young herdsmen had dug a hole that day, outside the pen, and stuffed into it a dead lamb in its skin. They had covered it with plenty of glowing charcoal and were waiting till the meat was roasted in the earth.

Manúsakas had got the big ram firmly between his knees and was clipping off chunk after chunk of the thick, matted wool. On his right stood about twenty sheep shorn to the skin, on his left as many unshorn. And in front of him the mound of wool, smelling strongly of grease, was growing. Manúsakas was humming. He was in a good mood. A little, cool breeze was blowing from the mountain. It was a good year. The flocks and herds were increasing. In the hut close by the pen his two eldest sons, Thodóres and Jannakis, were arranging cheeses in deep copper jars, and in the cool cheese-cellars there were masses, God be praised, of hard cheeses and soft. Down below, in Ai-Janni, the crops and vines were thriving. And his mare had brought forth a foal.

He let his shears rest for a moment and took a long look around him, and down as far as the plain. "Yes, the earth is like a rabbit," he murmured. "She's always bearing and bearing. The animals bear, the trees bear, the women bear. . . . Hey, Christiniá, be a good girl and bring me a raki to cool me down."

His wife Christiniá was poking the fire in the middle of the pen. She was still a woman with strong muscles and firm bones, but dried up. She could bear no more children, and about that she now complained to God. Only when a woman was over seventy should she be past bearing children—such was the advice she gave, in monologues, to God. Then one would manage to bring two dozen children into the world, and one's longing would be stilled. Two dozen children would be enough: twenty sons and four girls. And on the day when she received her first great-grandchild a pleasant giddiness, like a sleepiness, would come over her; then she should cross herself and die. "My God, if only I had been at Your side when You were making the world!

I would have revealed to You some secrets which only we women know . . ."

She heard her husband call and answered at once:

"With pleasure, Manúsakas dear. Would you like something to eat as well? I've cooked some sheep's kidneys."

"Bring them over!"

And as he ate and drank and was content with the world, hoof-beats and rolling stones were heard.

What demon can be coming up the mountain on horse-back? Manúsakas wondered, and with his mouth still full he rose on his knees and looked over the stone wall of the pen. He shielded his eyes with his hand against the blinding sun and recognised a black horse, which was climbing upwards with short steps and sending stones flying to either side.

"God punish me for lying, but I believe it's that dog Nuri!" he muttered, and jumped up. He strode over the space in front of the pen and came to a standstill at the entrance. "He's looking for me!"

With one bound he was inside the pen and took his bag from the wall. His wife was again kneeling by the kettle and making up the fire. She did not see him. He pulled out of the bag his broad, short knife and stuck it by his hip, at the same time tightening his belt. He picked up his shepherd's staff of oakwood and went back to the entrance and stood there.

The horseman had now passed the huge oak with the thick leaves, which stood darkly in a hollow. He was wearing a white head-band, and the silver pistols glittered in the sun. Manúsakas could not clearly make out the very round, very light face of Nuri, with his black waxed moustache.

"He's looking for me!" he muttered afresh. "Welcome to the dog, if he comes this way."

He called to his wife:

"Hey, Christiniá, lay the table. We've got a guest."

"Who?" he heard his wife's surprised voice say from inside.

"A devil," replied Manúsakas. "Get the table ready, I tell you!"

He went to meet the horseman. Nuri saw him and raised his hand. From a distance his drawling, mocking voice was heard:

"Good day, Captain Manúsakas."

"Welcome, Captain Nuri Bey. Where are you bound for?"

"For Captain Manúsakas's pen. Do you know him?" Nuri asked with a laugh. His teeth flashed, his fresh cheeks rippled.

Manúsakas's eyes sparkled with rage, but he controlled himself.

"Who has not heard of his heroic deeds?" he answered, and tried to laugh, but only his upper lip moved, laying his teeth bare. "Only a few days ago he brought an ass into the mosque to join in the prayers."

"I heard that too. A mischievous bird flew by and told me. And I've come to see what shoulders they are that carry an ass on them."

"You won't see any shoulders, Nuri Bey. Get that out of your head. Manusakas doesn't show his shoulders."

"If he sees danger ahead, he'll show his buttocks as well, I think!" laughed Nuri, and tickled the horse's ears with his whip. The proud beast reared powerfully and leapt forward at Manúsakas.

Manúsakas did not stir. But the blood throbbed wildly in his wrists. He held himself in. Nuri Bey had come to visit him. Patience! He clenched his fist, and could not curb his tongue:

"No dog has bitten me yet, unless he was mad, Nuri Bey," he said thickly. "Look out for yourself!"

"But I am a wild beast, Manúsakas," the Turk retorted. "So I don't like singing my own praises. I keep silent."

"Well?" Manúsakas asked. "Why do you come to my kingdom? What do you want?"

Nuri bit his moustache and said nothing. Manúsakas, from the stone on which he was standing, looked at him and likewise said nothing. But both their hearts were storming, trying to jump out of their chests.

At length the Bey's voice made itself heard:

"Manúsakas," he said calmly, slowly, weighing each word, "you have insulted Turkey gravely, you must pay for it."

"I've amused myself. Let the tax-collector come and tell me what I owe."

"He has come."

"You?"

"Yes, I. Turkey, flouted by you, has sent me. From the under-world I received a letter from my father, whom your tribe mur-dered. I have many accounts to settle with your tribe, Manúsakas. Only a day or two ago your brother rode into the Turkish coffee-house and turned the agas out. Megalokastro is shouting and demanding vengeance. I may not touch Captain Michales—he is my blood-brother. I'm touching you."

Manúsakas stealthily felt round his belt. He found the dagger.

"Let's go a bit further on." he said, "so the wife doesn't hear us. My sons are in the hut, too."

Nuri Bey dismounted. He considered it unmanly to ride while his enemy went on foot. He wound the reins round his arm.

"Let's go," he said.

The two moved forward. The horse set stones rolling and neighed uneasily.

The mountain lay lonely, for the sun stood at its noon height. Outside the pen Manúsakas's sons and the shepherd boys had opened the hole, taken out the lamb, now perfectly done and tender, and had posted themselves round about it, some squatting, others leaning forward on their knees. Their jaws were working like mill-stones. The wooden bottle passed from mouth to mouth. Not a soul paid attention to the mountain. The sheep, too, dis-burdened of their wool, were lying under the oak-trees. And near them the sheepdogs had stretched themselves in the shade with their tongues hanging out, gazing in amazement at the shorn flock.

At the tall heavily-leaved oak in the hollow the two halted. They glanced over the flat ground about the god-like trunk.

"Here is all right," they said, "the place will do."

Nuri tied his horse to a less tall oak a little to one side, where it could not see. Meanwhile Manúsakas cleared the space of stones and slender fallen twigs. Nuri came back and was pleased at finding the field swept.

"You've cleaned it up nicely," he said. "We've room enough."

"Yes, room enough," Manúsakas replied. "We could have a feast here if we wanted. But if we want to, we can kill one another. What's your choice, Nuri?"

"That we fight," he answered calmly. "Honour demands it, Manúsakas."

"The one doesn't exclude the other," said Manúsakas.

"Let's fight," Nuri Bey repeated calmly.

"As you will." He pulled his belt tighter and rolled up his sleeves. Nuri Bey pulled his white head-band closer about his locks, drew the pistols out of their leather holsters and hung one of them up on a branch of the tree. The other he held in his hand. Manúsakas watched him.

"Hang it up properly," he said, "I like those pistols of yours. As soon as I've killed you, I shall take them for myself as a remembrance."

Nuri Bey cocked the pistol. Manúsakas stood in front of him without moving.

"Manúsakas," said Nuri Bey, "yesterday afternoon your tribe came past my estate and you halted. You pulled out your pistol, fired in the air and called me out with the cry: 'I'm shooting at your shield, Nuri Bey!' I'm taking up the challenge, even if Charos gets me!"

With that, he fired a shot in the air over Manúsakas's head.

He stood on tip-toe and hung the still smoking pistol by the side of the other.

They took their stand opposite each other, with their legs wide apart and firmly planted, and eyed each other. Their blood was not yet inflamed. They waited. They tried by means of crude mockeries to rouse themselves to rage and bloodlust.

"Damn the beard of your Mohammed!" said Manúsakas, spitting in the air.

"Damn your Christ, the bastard!" swore Nuri Bey.

They flouted their Gods, but their blood would not catch fire. Then they tried with the Saints and circumcision, with the Sultan and the Greek race. But that did not provoke them to kill each other. At last Manúsakas thought of something:

"Captain Michales should be here to settle with you. Remember how he caught you by the belt and flung you on to the roof? But I'll throw you in the same way."

He rushed forward to catch the other by the waist. But Nuri

eluded him nimbly. He took a step backwards and pulled from his sash the two-edged black-hilted thing. Now both pairs of eyes grew bloodshot.

"*Giaour!*"

"Dog!"

Nuri sprang forward with raised dagger. But Manúsakas bent instantly aside, so that the Bey nearly fell. Manúsakas from his crouching position butted his head with full force into the other's stomach. Nuri nearly fainted with the pain. Yet he mastered himself and gathered his strength again. While his opponent was still bent down, he plunged his dagger deep in his side. Bones cracked. Hot blood spurted out and spattered Nuri as he wrenched the dagger out. He gave a shout of joy and licked the blade greedily, till his lips and beard were smeared with blood.

"That's for my father," he cried. "I'm avenging his blood."

Manúsakas leaned swaying against the trunk of the tree.

"Dog," he muttered. "You've got me."

"The account's settled," Nuri answered.

He began to approach with slow zig-zagging steps, like a lion. His nostrils were quivering.

"You just come here. . . . You just come here," muttered Manúsakas, who felt his strength going and could not make a rush at his enemy.

The hoarse, masterful voice provoked Nuri. He glided closer, with his dagger raised.

"One more," he bellowed, "one more stroke, to the heart, *giaour*, for Turkey which you flouted, you and your brother Captain Michales."

When he was quite close, he leapt forward like a flash, to pierce his enemy's heart. But Manúsakas dodged sideways, and the dagger struck the trunk of the tree. It broke. Manúsakas collected his last strength together and plunged his short knife deep in the other's body, low down.

The Bey bellowed like a buffalo, but managed to overcome his pain. He tore the knife from his enemy's already limp hand.

"For Turkey!" he yelled, and plunged it in his heart.

Manúsakas collapsed over the roots of the tree. In a flash his wife Christiniá, his children, the pen and the half-shorn ram passed through his mind. And suddenly a thick, black cloud covered his eyes. He saw nothing more— and fell forward in a pool of blood.

Nuri crouched beside him. Blood was running from his breeches and flowing to the ground beside Manúsakas's head. A sharp, unbearable pain tortured him. He put both hands to his wounded testicles and bellowed. He looked around. The sun was sinking. The mountain was again ringing with the bells of the sheep, and a wind arose.

"Allah, Allah, help me to reach my horse and get away!" Nuri groaned, and tried to stand up.

He held on to the trunk of the tree tightly, pulled down the silver pistols, and stuck them in his sash. He picked up Manúsakas's shepherd staff to support himself, and looked at the dying man, who was rattling and convulsed. He tried to give him a kick. The pain prevented him. He spat on him.

"I've kept my oath," he muttered. "But you've got me too, *giaour*!"

He put his left hand between his thighs and groaned:

"It would have been better if you'd stabbed my heart, *giaour*."

Manúsakas half opened one eye. It was dim and bloody. His lips were dark blue; they moved to speak. But they stiffened and remained half open. Nuri Bey crawled, howling with pain, to his horse. From afar the noble animal heard his groaning and turned round. The white of its eyes flashed.

O, if I could only get on and ride away, thought the Bey. Mustafa Baba knows herbs that will cure me.

Blood made a trail behind him. Darkness was before his eyes as at length he reached the horse and collapsed in front of it. It bent its neck down and snuffed at its master—his neck, his hair, his back. Finally it raised its intelligent head and neighed, as though calling for help.

Nuri tried to lift his foot as far as the stirrup. He could not. The pain brought him again near to fainting. He collapsed close to the horse's front legs and clung to them. It looked at him, with lowered head. Suddenly it understood. It moved forward and

bowed its knees over a stone until it was kneeling. Again it looked
at its master. When he saw the horse kneeling, he stumbled, face
foremost, and placed his arms round its neck. Then he heaved
his body and both legs up, till he was fast in the saddle. He clenched
his teeth, to be able to bear the pain. But he could not open his
severely wounded thighs, and so he rode woman fashion.

"On, on, brother! Away from here," he muttered. "Slowly,
slowly . . ." and he stroked the beloved animal's neck.

And it moved forward, watching the ground carefully so as not
to stumble, skirting holes and precipices, slowly downhill in the
evening twilight.

The sun had sunk, blood-red, over the mountain. A few women
were coming up the mountain to visit their men. When Nuri saw
them, he clenched his teeth and held his head high. But the blood
was running in thick drops over the saddle and the horse's belly
and was painting its track on the stones.

It was a most gracious hour, now that the heat was past. The
face of the earth grew fresh. Two or three big stars already hung
in the sky. In a hut at the foot of the mountain a lamp was burning, and a song could ne heard from within: a mother was lulling
her child tenderly to sleep. Nuri Bey had shut his eyes. He saw
nothing, and heard only the awakening insects, loud as bells. He
clung to the horse's mane. Where was it going? It knew its way
unerringly. Its master trusted it.

It stopped before the door of his country house. Nuri opened
his eyes and shouted. Servants came running and carried him in.
The old nurse made him up a bed on the sofa. Scarcely was he
stretched out before the sheets were covered with blood. Nuri
moved his hand and whispered:

"Mustafa Baba . . . Mustafa Baba."

Then he fell back on the pillows.

It was deep night before Mustafa Baba arrived at the house,
breathless, with his sack of healing herbs and ointments on his
shoulder. The servants brought lamps and candles. He bent over
Nuri Bey and shook his head.

Nuri Bey lay unconscious, with his eyes shut. The old man put
some drops of rose-vinegar into his nose, and rubbed his temples.

The Bey opened his eyes, looked at him, and asked in a trembling voice:

"Shall I live?"

"You are in Allah's hands," the old man answered. "He can heal you."

"Noone else?" asked Nuri in terror. "Can't men? Can't you, Mustafa Baba?"

"The wound is severe, Nuri Bey, and in a bad place."

"Damnation!" groaned Nuri Bey.

"Don't blaspheme," said the old man. "Allah guided the knife where He willed it to go."

"Why, why, why?" whispered the Bey miserably, and gazed with fear at the old man.

But the old man did not answer. He had known since this morning, when he had seen the Bey so radiant on his threshold.

"Keep still," he said. "Don't ask questions, if you want to get well."

Raki was brought. He washed the wound, stopped the blood and put on a bandage. From his sack he took a handful of herbs and gave them to the old woman to boil. This was for a sleeping draught. He turned the servants out and opened his bag again, to take out a small bottle and some ointment. Weeping, the old woman watched him.

"Mustafa Baba, is the master badly wounded? Can he get well?"

"He can get well," muttered the old man. "But what will he do with life then?"

"What will he do with life? Why do you ask, Mustafa Baba?"

The old man looked about him. "He will never be a man again," he said softly.

The old woman shrieked, and covered her face with both hands.

Next day, just as the sun was beginning to set, Captain Michales stood on the threshold of his shop and stared out at the Harbour Gate. Ships were again loading and unloading, while the waves of the sea were a deep red. He stared, but saw nothing: his gaze was directed within. His body had grown slack in the last few days, and his mouth was bitter and firmly shut. Passing Turks cast evil

glances at him, and many of his Christian friends avoided him.
They guessed at a dark power in him, and dared not come near
him.

Captain Michales took his tobacco-box from his belt. Neither
wine nor a ride on his mare now brought him any relief. Above
all, not this wretched cigarette. He lit it, took a few puffs, and spat
furiously. It poisoned his mouth even more. He threw it to the
ground and stamped on it. "To the Devil with you too," he
muttered, and turned to go back into the shop, to sit there and,
as soon as the day came to an end, shut it up and escape.

But now appeared—covered over and over with dust and bathed
in sweat, and with his tongue lamed by terror—Thodóres, the
first-born son of Manúsakas. He stopped in front of his uncle with
his mouth open, and stared at him. He tried hard to speak, but
his heart was too full and stopped his breath. Captain Michales
seized him by the arm and shook him:

"Speak!" he told him, and bent over him. Full of evil foreboding
his thoughts rushed to his brother Manúsakas.

"They're killed my father, Uncle!"

"Who, young 'un?"

"Nuri."

Captain Michales let his nephew's arm drop, stuck his thumb
between his teeth, and bit. He could taste hot, salt blood on his
lips.

"When, young 'un? Where? Find your breath."

Thodóres found his breath and told, in between tears and curses,
how that afternoon they had found his father lying under the
big oak. He had two knife-wounds, one in the side, the other
through the heart. Two women who had come up the mountain
in the evening twilight yesterday—Hadzijorgos's wife and
daughter—had met Nuri clinging, pale and exhausted, to his
horse, and had found tracks of blood all along the cliff path.

For a few moments Captain Michales said nothing and did not
move. He stared at the ground and listened to his nephew, who
now fell silent. And he could see the thick-leaved oak in the
hollow, and at its roots a majestic body dabbled in blood. When
he had had his fill of this picture, he raised his head and seized his

nephew by the shoulder. "Are you a woman, howling like that? The gates are still open, you've time to get back to the village. Tell them to wait and not to bury him. I'm coming!"

When he was alone, Captain Michales went into the shop, and threw Charitos out. Nobody must see him. He gave the chair on which he usually sat a kick, so that it smashed in pieces, and flung himself upon a coil of rope, pressing his fists against his head. The shop sank away from him, Megalokastro sank, and an oak spread itself out in him, a darkly gleaming one, surrounded by thorns. And at its foot lay his brother Manúsakas. He was not dead; that was not blood streaming over him, but wine! He was clapping his hands and singing: "The Muscovite will soon be here!"

He shook his head and stood up. His decision was suddenly made. He shut the shop and stuck the key in his belt. He did not go into Broad Street, but took his way through the narrow alleys. Out of the Greek quarter he came into the Turkish. The Hags were not yet at their peep-holes and did not see him. In front of the green door he halted. Like a falcon his gaze shot up to the high, blind walls and perched on the tiny balcony with its close lattice. But suddenly he wrenched his gaze back from there, with rage and disgust in his heart as though he had defiled himself, and let his eyes once more sweep over the rough walls. This evening he was not concerned with women and balconies. The falcon of his spirit swept over the head of Nuri and longed to strike its claws into his eyes and his brain.

A strange, inhuman rejoicing filled him. His spirit suddenly shook free and rose. A different body now occupied him, and it was a man's. It did not deck itself, it did not paint itself, it did not smell of musk. It smelt of male sweat. Now Captain Michales went home. His eyes were blazing.

"Manúsakas, my brother . . . Manúsakas, my brother . . ." he murmured as he went.

Night fell, and the stars came up, while a doleful, half-eaten moon hung in the sky. The doors in Ai-Janni were bolted, the lamps went out one after another, and the village plunged into darkness. Only the door at Manúsakas's stood wide open, the

lamps were burning, and in the middle of the main room, on a
bier, was the corpse of the master of the house, laid out for the
funeral ceremony. It had been washed with wine and veiled in a
linen shroud. A cross of wax lay upon the lips, and a small ikon
of the Redeemer had been placed in the crossed hands. Two huge
lamps were burning, one at the feet, the other at the head. His
eyes had remained open and were glazed: since no one had been
there to close their lids when they were still warm, they would
not shut. Ever since morning the relatives and friends had been
coming. With mourning strokes the bells announced the dread
presence of death. From Ai-Janni, from Petrokéfalo and all the
neighbouring villages the Christians had been coming, to kiss the
dead man and take leave of Manúsakas.

His wife Christiniá had flung herself over him and was sobbing
and beating her breast. The neighbour women also had come—
the widows, the mothers whom Charos had robbed, and the orphan
girls—and at the sight of others' grief theirs had welled up, as they
loosened their hair and joined in the keening. Old Séfakas came
on foot from Petrokéfalo, armed as though he were going to war.
He carried old-fashioned pistols, a long knife with a white handle,
and his father's heavy muzzle-loader with its wide muzzle. He
halted, stood motionless on the threshold, saw his son lying on the
bier, came forward and stretched out his huge hands to clasp
both the dead man's hands.

"All's well, Manúsakas," he said. "Only you've been in too
much of a hurry. It was MY turn. Now greet the people below
for me. Tell them I'm coming too."

After these words he sat down on the threshold for a while.
Then he stood up and went back, silent and dry-eyed, to his
village.

Slowly the keening tolled on. The bodies of the mourners grew
weary and found consolation and sweetness in weariness. One
after another, the friends and relatives got up to go home, to
feed and sleep. They were still alive, and tomorrow work was
waiting for them. Other people's grief was still other people's.
It could even secretly bring pleasure, because Fate had struck their
neighbour and not themselves. And so there remained in Manú-

sakas's house his three bosom-friends only: his brother Fanúrios, the man of the grasslands; his godson Stratés, a sturdy young man of thirty-five, of healthy stock, with a pointed beard, slender hips and an open forehead. He was a stranger from Kísamo, who five years ago had fetched up in the Lasíthi district for the Krustalénia fair. There his fate lay in wait for him in the shape of a girl from Ai-Janni whom he saw dancing. His soul desired her, and he took her. Manúsakas set the wedding crowns on their heads. Nine months later he had his first-born christened. That was how they had become godfather and godson. The third was Patasmos the lyre-player, a but of ill-leavened bread the witches had licked at. His father had begotten nine sons, and he was the last—a grey-beard's work. But he was a man in whom the wrath of God moved. No one could challenge him when at the fair the jeering mantinades[1] began to ring out. In the flick of a wrist he was out with the scornful rhymes. He knew everybody's weakness or secret anxiety. Fear seized men and women when, enthroned in the middle of the dancing-space with his lyre on his knees, he stabbed one after the other with his eyes and at last opened his mouth, to dart out the mantinade. He lived alone as an old palikare, without a care. He was the first and best at every fair, wedding, christening and drinking-bout. Everyone competed to have him to stay or to meals, so as not to be sung of. He was known as Patasmos and Beelzebub and Spear and Captain Wasp. Yesterday he had come to Ai-Janni for the christening. Stratés's third child was to be christened. But now here was an evil re-union with Charos, who was also making a stay there. Patasmos had been an inseparable friend of Manúsakas. They had emptied whole casks of wine together, devoured whole sheep to the bones together. He had loved him and never made fun of him.

He bent down, looked at the corpse, and sighed:

"Yes, a man's no more than a bladder—it swells and swells and suddenly—poof—it bursts and goes to the Devil . . . I mean, to Paradise," he corrected himself quickly, for he was ashamed in front of the corpse.

Stratés bowed his head and said nothing. He took his kerchief

[1] Rhyming couplets, usually topical or personal (translator's note).

and flicked the flies away from the dead man's nose and lips.
Fanúrios stood up, put his arm round Christiniá's shoulder and
raised her to her feet. Then he lifted each of the other keeners up
in turn.

"Out with you women, that's enough! Out with you, and be
quiet, sisters of misfortune. We three are taking over the watch
for the night."

The women united in an outcry and tried to resist. But the
herdsman raised his paws and drove them like a flock into the
inner part of the house. Then he came back and sat down at the
foot of the dead man.

For a while the three gazed at the murdered man without a
word. Each had his thoughts elsewhere: Stratés with his wife, and
with the mule he had bought the day before yesterday. It had
turned out to be very wild; it kicked, and might one day kill one
of his children.

Patasmos was building in his mind a new poem, a dirge, a
mixture of truth and lies. How Manúsakas had fought with seven
Turks and had killed six of them.

Fanúrios was hungry. He had seen, hanging on the wall of his
brother's cellar, some pork sausages, and in the corner a little cask
of raki. Also Christiniá had done the baking yesterday, and the
wheaten bread still lay in the tray, giving out fragrance. . . . His
mouth filled with saliva, and while eyes remained bound to the
corpse, his mind was pondering how he could give the conversation a turn towards sausages and raki.

It must be midnight. A light north wind was making the leaves
of the lemon-tree in the yard rustle. It cooled the brows of the
death-watchers. Now that the women were quiet, an owl could
be heard hooting up above in the loft. And in the neighbourhood
the dogs had scented Charos and were howling.

Fanúrios could feel his innards growing tense with hunger. He
could not see how to guide the conversation cunningly. So he
burst out:

"Chaps, what do you think? My eye caught sight of some
strings of sausages and a demijohn of raki in the cellar. Shall we
drink to his salvation?"

"Why shouldn't we drink?" asked Patasmos, rubbing his belly. which was beginning to rumble. "Only the dead don't drink. Go, Fanúrios, with God's help! Go to the cellar! What do you think, Stratés?"

"Isn't it wrong?" said he, "in front of the body . . ."

"In the first place, we'll drink outside, Stratés. And then only to give us the strength, my boy, to go through with the watch till morning. Besides, we'll be drinking to his well-being. . . . Go, Fanúrios, please, to the cellar."

Fanúrios had already grabbed the lamp which burned at the dead man's feet, and made for the cellar. He emerged carrying a string of sausages and the demijohn. Also, in his belt, three tumblers.

Patasmos jumped up, cut some lengths of sausages off and went out into the yard. There he made a fire and roasted them. The world smelled sweet.

"For God's sake, shut the doors, Fanúrios, so that the women don't notice the smell!" said Patasmos, as he wrapped the delicious-smelling morsels in lemon leaves.

Meanwhile Fanúrios had filled the glasses with raki to the brim. Stratés had gone to the cellar, to get a loaf of bread.

They gripped the glasses, and touched fingers to avoid the clink.

"God bless his soul . . ." said Stratés.

"His health, chaps! Ours too!" cried Patasmos.

"Drink it all up in one gulp," said Fanúrios, "The demijohn— God has sent it to us—is half full. Brother Manúsakas, fare well!"

They drank to the last drop. Then they seized hold of the sausages. Fanúrios pulled out his herdsman's knife and cut the bread into three. Appetite was whetted. They roasted the remaining sausages as well. Fanúrios brought a white cheese from the cellar. He placed the demijohn on his lap and doled out.

"Let's drink to the health of the widow," Patasmos proposed. "I'm sorry for the poor thing. I'll make a mantinade for her."

"To her health!"

They drank. "And to Captain Michales's health!" said Stratés. "He will avenge his blood. To his health!"

"Come, chaps, to the health of all the people we know," suggested Fanúrios, "whether they're alive or dead."

They went through the relatives, the friends, the dead parents, the neighbours, all in turn, and drank. Then they took the great fighters of Crete—Kórax, Hadjimicháles, Kriáres, Daskalojánnes, and drank. Next they came to Arkadi Monastery and drank three large glasses to its health. Then they moved on to 1821 and drank to the health of Kolokotrónes, of Karaiskákes, of Miaúles, of Odysseus Andrútsos. The demijohn was nearly empty.

"Let's drink to the health of ancient Hellas," proposed Patasmos, who laid claim to a couple of grains of education.

"Too dull," said Fanúrios.

"Well then we'll sing . . ."

"In the name of Christ, that isn't right!" Stratés objected.

"Quiet, quiet! In a whisper. Not a soul can hear us. Like this . . ."

And he began, imitating the motion of a fiddle-bow in the air, to sing softly:

> "*Faithless one, in you the red*
> *Of dawn was at its prime——*"

The other two quickly sang after him:

> "*Of dawn was at its prime:*"
> "*When I kissed you, and you said*:
> '*It's night, and loving-time!*' "

"Is that the mantinade you've composed for the widow? Have you no fear of God?" cried Stratés, and stopped his mouth. "Don't you know any sacred songs?"

"Sacred songs is it you want? With pleasure!"

He turned to the dead man, crossed himself, and began: "Come to the final kiss . . ." and hardly had be begun, when they all three took up the hymn of mourning, and collapsed upon the dead man, and with tears kissed him.

The house droned with the litany. A door half opened, and a woman stuck out her head, wound in a cloth. But Patasmos made an angry sign at her, and the woman vanished.

Then they felt that the hymn of mourning had gone on long enough, and stood up, the three in a row, before the dead man,

and looked at him. They felt lightened. There was in them a surge
of strength renewed by raki, sausages and weeping. Fanúrios
spat on his hands:

"Chaps," he said, indicating the dead man with his eyes, "shall
we jump over him?"

"That's it! let's jump over him!" cawed Stratés and Patasmos
together. They pulled their sagging breeches-ends well up, so
that their legs should be unencumbered, seized hold of the bier
and placed the corpse in the door to the yard, so as to give room
for a run.

"I'll go first!" said Fanúrios, "because I'm his brother!"

He took up position by the street door, spat on his hands, took
a run, and let fly. As he came up to the dead man he gave a mighty
leap. His skull hit the lintel with a crack, But Fanúrios did not
notice, and landed on his feet in the middle of the room.

"I've jumped over him," he said proudly. "Your turn,
Stratés!"

Stratés too took a run and with his supple, slender body sprang
in a low arc without touching the corpse. He landed lightly on
the tips of his toes.

"Your turn, Patasmos," he said.

But Patasmos's heart flinched. He gazed at the bier. How the
Devil can one jump so high? "I'm not jumping," he said, discouraged.

"Aren't you ashamed of yourself, Captain Wasp," Fanúrios
chided. "Are you a Cretan or a mainlander? Jump!"

"I'm not jumping, I tell you. I'm a lyre-player."

"Have you no sense of the honour due to the dead, you heathen?
It's an insult! Or is that all your friendship with Manúsakas?
Jump, even if you fall down dead!"

Patasmos scratched his bald spot. He remembered how much
he had really loved Manúsakas. His sense of honour awoke.

"All right, I'll jump!" he exclaimed, then: "Hop! Hop!" to give
himself courage.

He took the run and got up speed. But as he came to the dead
man, it seemed to him that the bier reached to the ceiling. His
legs caught the feet of the bier, the impetus was communicated to

H

the corpse, and it rolled to the ground—Patasmos, with hair all over the place, beyond it.

"You've disgraced us," said Fanúrios, "Get your beard shaved off." He gave him a kick. "Come, Stratés, help!"

They lifted the dead man from the ground, wrapped him in his shroud again, bundled him into the open coffin and pressed the ikon once more into his hands.

"There, brother, you're dead. It doesn't do you any harm. It hasn't hurt you," said Fanúrios, stroking the dead man's hair and beard.

He bent down, picked up the demijohn and tipped it up. There was a little raki left in it. They drank. They sat down once more about the dead man and gazed at him. Their eyelids slowly drooped, their heads sank on their chests, and sleep embraced them.

Next day, before the sun was well up, Captain Michales arrived at Manúsakas's yard. Black shirt, black head-band, black boots, like Charos. He shoved the women aside as they crowded wailing round him, went in, bent down, kissed the dead man and stood for a long time gazing at him. The women of the neighbourhood had brought from the fields that morning basil, marjoram, mint and yellow marguerites by the armful and had decked the corpse with them.

For a long time Captain Michales gazed at his brother. He made no sound. The dead man, too, gazed at Captain Michales with his open eyes. Christiniá, the sons and daughters, Fanúrios his brother and Stratés and Patasmos and the neighbour women stood in a circle and watched the two brothers, how they spoke together without a word.

This mysterious conversation lasted a long while. When Captain Michales had had his fill of grieving, he went inside the house, into the kitchen—then out into the yard; visited the stable, touched the dead man's cattle and his mare; went up to the bedroom, saw the wide bed and the working gear and the holy pictures; looked out of the window at the roofs of the village with the little church of St. John in the middle; then over it and be-

yond at Petrokéfalo, the substantial village of his father at the
foot of the towering mountain. Captain Michales was embracing
his brother from all sides with his mind and placing him in pro-
portion within himself.

"Farewell, brother Manúsakas," he whispered over and over,
as he examined, touched and took leave of the things the murdered man had loved.

The pope came. The bier was lifted high. The women clung to
it and tried to prevent it from being taken out. Christiniá fell
down in a faint, and while she was being brought round with
water and perfume, the corpse and bearers had already crossed
the threshold and were nearing the green cemetery at the edge of
the village.

From Petrokéfalo and the neighbouring villages they had come
—the men armed, the women in black—to take leave of the fallen
pillar of the village. No Turk went out from the villages of the
district on the day of the burial. The women tore their hair and
extolled with ever fresh tales the virtues of the murdered man. Old
Séfakas, gripping the double handle of his stick, walked first
behind the head of the dead man, dry-eyed. He knew what Charos
meant, that it was not becoming to human beings, and could do
them no good, to sink so low as to supplicate him. He was Charos,
a collector of dues, a slave, sent out by the Sultan who sits in
Heaven and raises the poll-tax. And so he went along without
words or tears, striking the stones with his stick, and stood
impassive before the hole in the earth.

The pope intoned the last words at the grave hastily, raised his
hand and gave the blessing. He took a handful of earth from the
ground and threw it into the grave. The corpse was lowered. All
bent down, took each a handful of earth, and threw it after.

Captain Michales stepped forward to the edge of the grave:

"Farewell, brother Manúsakas," he said, in a calm voice and
with burning eyes that could bring forth no tears. "Listen to what
I am saying to you. Don't come into my sleep to accuse me and
make me wild. I know my duty. Have no anxiety." He was silent
for a moment, pondering. But he could think of nothing else, and
repeated: "I know my duty. Have no anxiety. Just be patient!"

Suddenly his heart swelled. He shouted:

"Farewell, Manúsakas!"

Before the escort broke up he returned alone to Manúsakas's house and there mounted his mare. At that moment Thodóres, the eldest son, came running to the street door.

"What orders have you got for me, Uncle?" he asked, catching hold of the reins of the mare.

Captain Michales bent down and looked at him.

"I mean, how am I to avenge his blood?" asked the son.

"How old are you?"

"Seventeen."

"Stay in your nest."

He put spurs to the mare and took the wide main road to Megalokastro.

VII

PRIL went by with its burden of human pleasures and fears
and the Passion of Christ. May came with its sunny con-
sequences—the melons and cherries, the swelling clusters
and the first, still unripe, gleaming vintage-grapes. The heat became oppressive. Turks and Christians poured out their sweat
and dried in the cool breezes. Nuri still lay consumed with pain
on his bed, and Manúsakas hidden in Captain Michales's heart. In
Megalokastro revolt was brooding, still covered up. At night
the elders gathered in the Metropolitan's residence, to take counsel
about the threatened position of the Greeks, while at midday in
the Pacha's *konak* the beys and hodzas discussed measures for the
repression of the Greeks. The fate of Crete hung once more on a
hair.

One one of the last days of May—it was the 29th—the bells
were heard beginning to toll dolefully through the dim twilight.
The Christians rose from their sleep. They knew that day's sombre
meaning for Christendom, and they set out for church. In the
middle of the church, on a huge tray, there stood a memorial cake,
flanked by two great lamps swathed in black. Inscribed in almond
kernels and cinnamon on the thin sugar coating was the
name of the dead man: KONSTANTINOS PALAIOLOGOS. This was
his death day. On a dark morning like this one, the Sultan's
myrmidons had brought him low and put Constantinople under
their yoke.

The Christians stood round the cake and listened to the funeral
service. The prominent Kastrians had gathered. There were the
three elders—Captain Eliás, Hadjisávas and the Rose-bug. With
them had come Captain Polyxigis, Charílaos the gnome, the
learned Idomeneas, Stefanés the ship's captain, Kasapákis the
doctor and the grocer, Mr. Aristoteles. Behind them stood less
important people: Demetrós Leanbottom, Krasojórgis, Mastrapas,
Kajabés, Vendúsos, Furógatos, Bertódulos, and Signor Paraskevás

the barber. And to them was joined the throng of the insignificant.

Even Captain Michales had appeared—but had not entered the church. He stood in the narthex, looking darkly, in his black shirt and with black heart. Since the funeral of his brother he had spoken to no one. His blood was full of unrest. His mind was busy —devising a thousand arts of malice, turning over a thousand occasions by which he could catch Nuri and avenge the crime which had been committed. To him he was no longer a blood-brother. That blood had turned to water, and the red thread which had bound them together was cut. He had heard that Nuri too had been severely wounded and was at his country estate, at grips with death. Captain Michales had sent Ali Aga there to spy. He was to eavesdrop the servants and find out if he really was seri-ously wounded and lying on his bed. Ali Aga had come back that same day with his tongue hanging out and had brought the news: "It's true, Captain Michales, the poor man is badly wounded." "Where? Have you found that out?" "In the testicles, Captain. Your brother, it seems, stabbed him with his knife between the thighs. Mustafa Baba has anointed him and bandaged him, but the pain is torturing him and he bellows day and night. I heard him myself from the gate, Captain." Captain Michales was dismayed. As long as he was ill, he could not touch him. He would have to wait till he recovered strength. How long might that be? He was in a hurry!

Every night he racked his brains. When, this morning early, he heard the mourning bells, he decided to go to church. "Tityros is to make a speech; he'll make us all ridiculous," he thought. He dressed impatiently. He pulled the tassels of his head-band over his eyes. He did not want to see and greet anyone. Could that cheese of a little schoolmaster have the least idea of what the fall of Constantinople and heroism and struggle meant?

Leaning against the window at the entrance, he could see, over the crowd, the Metropolitan standing, clothed wholly in black, and with a long, black scarf wound round his hat.

All of a sudden the ritual was at an end. The Metropolitan signed to Tityros. Captain Michales grew agitated. He watched his brother mount the high platform and pull from his inner coat-pocket a bundle of papers. He began speaking. At first he stammered and coughed, so that he could hardly be understood. But gradually he warmed up, and his voice filled with power. He caused the towers of Constantinople to rise before his hearers, and the bells of Hagia Sophia tolled in passionate entreaty, as in the midst of the church the last, fate-laden battle pursued its course—that battle which had filled the graves of the vast city with blood. And in the incense cloud above the tray with the cake there appeared the blood-stained head of the Emperor Constantine. Everyone saw him.

Captain Michales dried his eye, which had suddenly become wet. He observed his brother thoughtfully. How could such a flame dwell behind those glasses, above those narrow breeches and under those crooked shoulders?

When Tityros had done, he cleaned his glasses and looked among the women, who stood behind the men, for Vangelio, his wife. As he did not find her, he sat down, sighing.

After the ceremony Captain Michales went over to his brother.

"You brought no shame on us," he said.

Tityros hardly heard what his brother said. The flame was still burning in his heart.

"What did you say, Michales?" he asked.

"Nothing," came the answer.

They walked a few steps together. The schoolmaster was tired. Slowly and listlessly he started homewards. Captain Michales looked at him from the side. How he had changed since his wedding! His hump seemed to have increased, and he was beginning to be bowlegged.

"How are things at home?" he asked softly.

Tityros did not answer at once. But he heard his brother's question. Suddenly the sacred flame went out.

"It's no life at all, Michales," he said at last.

"Why? What do they do to you?"

"Nothing. They don't speak to me, they don't swear at me, they say nothing. And when I turn my back, I hear them laughing."

"Aren't you then master in your house? What sort of a man are you? Kick him out!"

"If I throw him out, she goes too."

They had reached Tityros's house. Captain Michales stood still. "Are they both in?" he asked.

"They're inseparable He didn't want to go to church, so she didn't go. Is that any sort of a life, brother Michales?"

Captain Michales felt sorry for him.

"Listen, schoolmaster. I'll go in with you and play the two of them a tune to make them dance."

"For God's sake!" cried the teacher, in terror. "Don't do that! If you do, I'm done for! Be patient a bit longer . . . . I'm going to do something . . . and then we shall see."

"What shall we see?"

"We shall see," he repeated, looking to one side.

He approached the door and took hold of the knocker.

"What? Have you no key?" exclaimed Captain Michales in astonishment.

"No. They won't give me one. I have to knock."

Captain Michales wrenched the knocker off at one go and flung it into the street.

"I want you to have a key by tomorrow," he said, and went off with heavy tread towards the Harbour Gate.

In Captain Michales's shop Captain Polyxigis was waiting for him. He had come there immediately after the memorial service, to speak with him. Only, what he had to explain to him was so difficult to express, that he kept pacing uneasily up and down. He sent Charitos out for coffee, lit one cigarette after another, only to put it out at once. How could he so much as begin, without provoking a burst of fury from Captain Michales? He liked and respected him and did not want to lose his friendship. On the contrary, he was anxious to strengthen it. That was why he had decided to speak to him to-day. He had tied a piece of black crêpe to his fez, to show that he too was in mourning for the loss of Manúsakas, his brother-in-law at one remove.

"Quick, Charitos. Run to the house and see if your uncle's there. Tell him . . ."

Before he had finished, Captain Michales was on the threshold.

Tityros's fiery speech was working in him still. But even more his rage about the key which had been refused to his brother.

He stared at the early, unexpected guest and pressed his lips together, but then said coolly:

"Good morning, Captain Polyxigis."

"I'm glad to see you, Captain Michales."

Captain Michales threw aside his head-band and took his coat off. He picked up an account-book from the table and fanned himself with it. He said nothing.

"How hot it is!" said Captain Polyxigis, beginning to be oppressed by the silence.

Captain Michales obstinately said nothing. He took his tobacco-box from his belt and began, slowly and clumsily, to roll a cigarette, as if he would never be done. Captain Polyxigis threw his cigarette away, coughed and pushed back his chair.

"Captain Michales," he said, "I've something to say to you."

"I'm listening."

"I adjure you, by our old friendship, Captain Michales, listen to me patiently. I must speak at some length, so that you may understand the whole thing."

"I'm listening," the other repeated.

"I tried to tell you once before, but you at once went up in flames and wouldn't let me say my say. But now, it's necessary. Listen to me patiently, brother."

"I'm listening. I've said so already. Drop the preliminaries!"

"Hey, Charitos, young man, get me some tobacco and some cigarette-paper," Captain Polyxigis exclaimed, to get rid of the rascal, who had clambered on to a roll of ship's cable and had his big ears pricked.

Charitos slid reluctantly down from off the cable and made off.

"I've something to say to you, Captain Michales . . ." Polyxigis began, hesitating again.

"Well, get on with it!"

"About Eminé . . ."

"Drop this shameless talk, Captain Polyxigis. You know I don't like it. Love stories and women's gossip are your business, not

H*

mine. You've come into my shop, so I can't throw you out. But change the subject!"

"I'm not shameless in talking about this. Calm down, Captain Michales. Let me go on . . . Eminé wants to become a Christian."

An almond which happened to be lying on the table, was seized by Captain Michales and reduced to dust between his fingers.

"If you were a Frank, she'd turn Frank. If you were a Jew, she'd turn Jewess. Are you making even christening an amusement?"

"But it's Christian she wants to become, and I am going to marry her," Captain Polyxigis went on.

"Marry her?" He gave a convulsive movement and tore the solid leather binding of the account-book.

"Congratulations!" he said at last, malevolently, and spat on the floor, as though he felt sick.

Captain Polyxigis took off his fez—anger made his head feel too big. He crushed the fez together in his hands. He looked at Captain Michales, whose face kept changing colour meanwhile. "Storm away inside, you old boar," he thought. "What I have to say you shall hear, whether you like it or not."

Captain Michales stood up, as though to give his guest the signal that it was time to go. But he did not move.

"I am here, Captain Michales, to ask you to give the bride away."

"Me?" He clutched at his beard. "You make me ashamed of my beard. Get Efendína Horsedung to give her away. He's just right for you!"

That brought Captain Polyxigis to his feet. He could no longer contain his rage. He put on his fez on one side, picked up the chair and dashed it to the floor.

"You're going too far, Captain Michales," he shouted. "You're a man, that's true. But so am I a man. You fought in the war. So did I. You break into the agas' coffee-houses on horseback. I into their houses. In both of us it's daring. And if you never laugh, that doesn't mean you're a brute. And if I do laugh, that doesn't mean I'm a buffoon. When I talk to you about the woman I intend to marry, I expect you to show me some respect."

Captain Polyxigis curbed himself. But he still had not relieved himself enough. Rancour still reigned within him.

It was otherwise with Captain Michales. He looked hard into Polyxigis's eyes as he listened. He did not raise his hand to stop his mouth. He listened. And the longer he listened, the more his scorn subsided. As long as Captain Polyxigis was merely making wretched requests, calling him—Captain Michales—brother and flaunting the mourning crêpe.in his face to appease him, he had felt the impulse to seize him by the scruff of his neck and throw him out with coarse insults. But now that he heard him speaking strongly like a man, his old brotherly feeling for this foolhardy captain awoke in him. The memory arose of how on horseback they had charged the Turkish soldiers and had not looked round to see if anyone was following them. Then also they had not resembled each other at all, but they had become friends. "You want to free Crete with roaring, and I with song," Captain Polyxigis had said to him one day, laughingly. But after the war had ended, they had parted all the same. If Captain Michales saw him coming from a distance, he either avoided him or abused him. But now he saw him raising his head high and resisting. So the old friendship arose afresh. He put out his hand and took hold of him with two fingers by his waistcoat.

"Captain Polyxigis," he said, "you're a palikare. I know that. All right. I don't want to quarrel with you."

"Nor I with you, Captain Michales. Only sometimes you force my soul into my nose, and I have to snort."

"Well, all right," Captain Michales repeated, and pushed him gently but firmly, with those two fingers on his waistcoat, towards the door.

"You're turning me out?" Captain Polyxigis shouted, and stamped on the floor. He would not go. Something still unsaid was burning on his lips. "I've still something to say to you, Captain Michales. One thing only. Then I'll go."

"Say it, but be quick."

"Eminé herself sent me. To ask if you would please give her away."

"She herself, that——" Captain Michales broke off. He was disgusted. He clenched his fist against Captain Polyxigis's chest. His voice was suddenly hoarse:

"Enough! Enough! I tell you. Not a word more!"

They were standing at the door of the shop.

"God grant you may be sorry for to-day, Captain Michales!" said Captain Polyxigis, raising his head towards the sky, which at that moment was glowing white in the sun's blaze.

That same evening, when the people of Kastro had shut their doors and were at table, a stoutly hanum, who had approached with firm tread and open parasol, knocked at Nuri's green door. The Moorish woman, who lay hid behind it, opened it like a flash and let her in.

"Eminé's still ill," thought the Hags, watching at their three peep-holes. "Hamidé Mula has come to do her doctoring."

Meanwhile the Moorish woman advanced across the courtyard. She was gay and sprightly. Her soul was in a garden. The watchman was down at the estate, looking after his master, and the red and green lamp was not burning. In the dark the flowers and fruits gave out their scent, and the Moorish woman danced with pleasure because her mistress had now recognised the true light and wanted to become a Christian. One day she would enter Paradise. And if God in His mercy should turn His eye on her and ler her also through the golden gate, she would be able to serve her mistress through eternity.

The stoutly hanum threw her mantle, veil and parasol on to the divan, and revealed herself as Captain Polyxigis.

"The mistress is upstairs and is longing to see you, Captain. She's something amusing to tell you," the Moorish woman announced. But this evening Captain Polyxigis was not in the mood. On other evenings, as soon as the slave woman rushed up to him, he would laugh and joke and have brought her something: a silk headband, embroidered slippers, or even a box of

Turkish delight or almond cakes. This time he was empty-handed, and his mouth was bitter and shut.

He went upstairs slowly—usually he took the stairs three at a time—and followed the scent of musk to the mistress's small bedroom.

Eminé heard his step. In the great heat she was lying half-naked on the divan, and had opened the window on the garden to let in a little fresh air. She lolled on the cushions nervously, now sighing, now laughing. What answer would she receive from Captain Michales, the terrible boar? The question made her uneasy; then once more laughter overcame her, as she thought of the news that had been brought her this morning by Mustafa Baba. "He'll not be a man any more. He'll still wear a beard, but all the same not be a man. He's unmanned. Nuri's been turned into Nurina." Eminé could not stop laughing. "Will he get a woman's voice as well, Mustafa Baba? And in time will he grow breasts?"—"Perhaps," the old man had said, disconcerted by the woman's laughter: "all the same he won't be a woman."—"Poor Nuri Bey, you wonderful hunter of women, you lion of Turkey, what has become of you?" Eminé had shouted; "A mule!" She had gone on laughing. Mustafa Baba had looked at her, terrified. He had picked up his little sack and gone.

Now Captain Polyxigis stood before her.

"Welcome, my captain, my evening star," Eminé exclaimed, and unsheathed her perfumed shoulders. "Welcome, my husband. I've something amusing to tell you."

"I've got news for you, too," said Polyxigis, and lay down beside her. He embraced her ardently and breathed in the fragrance of her bared breast. The world vanished. But he was very heavy and solid. The woman felt the weight of him and rebelled. Forcibly, though tenderly, she pushed his head up.

"First I want to hear your news," she said. "When you came in you were depressed. Does he refuse?"

Polyxigis drew away from her. The world came back, and with it his cares.

"Yes, he refuses."

"The damned wild boar! And why?"

"That he wouldn't say. He tore an account-book he was holding in his hand, and took me by the waistcoat to throw me out of his shop. But I was overcome by rage and told him what I thought. I didn't spare him!"

"That's not enough!" Eminé shouted, stamping with her rose-tinted heels on the floor. "No, Polyxigis, that's not enough. You ought to have killed him!"

Captain Polyxigis shuddered: "Killed him?"

"Of course! Killed him! That's what being a man means. Not answering an insult with another insult. Women do that. Men kill."

"Captain Michales?"

"Is he a God? He's a wild beast, and you're afraid of him. Aren't you ashamed?"

She seized her nightdress and with a single movement tore it from top to bottom. Her firm, erect body gleaped in the lamplight and there was a little rill of sweat trickling between her breasts.

"That's how I'd tear him, my God!" she whispered, and suddenly burst into tears.

Captain Polyxigis was dismayed. He tried to take her in his arms and to calm her. But she stiffened her arms against him and would not let him come near her. She crouched, like a wild beast, in the corner. She was not crying now. Hard, dry laughter shook her body.

"Polyxigis," she said, beating against the wall obstinately with her little fist. "Nuri disgusted me from the time when I saw Captain Michales break the raki glass apart with his two fingers, which Nuri couldn't do. Take care you don't make me loathe you too. The man who embraces me must have nobody that's like him."

"I won't."

"You can't."

"I won't," Captai. Polyxigis repeated, and it was he now who stamped on the floor. His face became distorted, his eyes pointed at Eminé like a knife.

The woman saw his fury. It gave her pleasure. A heavy smell streamed from the man's sweating, raging body, and Eminé's nostrils quivered delightedly.

"My captain," she said, "my treasure, stamp and be angry—that's how I like you!" And she opened her arms.

With Captain Polyxigis the whole world collapsed on Eminé's bosom. And when, with extinguished eyes and wet hair, the man rose once more, it was as though he emerged, with stifled breath, from the depths of some dark sea.

"My beloved, my husband, my hero," Eminé cooed, reconciled, stroking his hairy thighs.

Captain Polyxigis lay with his back leaning against the wall and observed the woman out of half-closed eyes, which were full of profound joy. At the same time he could hear the rumour of the town, the barking of dogs, the far-off serenades of nocturnal revellers. "There's nothing in this world above," he thought, "to equal Woman."

And so, happily lovelorn, he rejoiced that God had arranged for their bodies to be in such harmony. He laughed with satisfaction, stroking her firm, round arms.

"Eminé," he said, "don't worry. We'll find another, better man to give you away."

"You haven't asked me what the news was, I had to tell you. Have you forgotten?"

"How should I remember when you're lying there before me and it will soon be day?"

Eminé laughed. Then she whispered something into his ear.

"God!" exclaimed Captain Polyxigis, with his eyes starting out. "Oh, the poor fellow!"

He felt profound sympathy with the wretched man. Eminé's laughter made his heart contract. She sat up and extinguished the lamp.

But he sat upright where he was, and stared into the dark.

Mr. Idomeneas was on his way home from the memorial service. To-day he was in black, with a black band on his hat and an even wider one round his sleeve. He was in mourning.

It was getting on for midday as he came in. He sat down at his writing-table and told his servant, Doxaniá: "I'm not eating to-day, either now or this evening. I'm fasting." Then he sent her out of the room. He picked up his pen, took a large piece of paper, sighed, and began to write. To-day every letter was a capital in red ink. The Sovereigns in the great cities also wrote in red ink, and to-day it was as though Konstantinos Palaiologos, in whose memory the service in the church had been held, were himself turning to address Victoria, Queen of England:

My dear Cousin Victoria,

Four hundred and thirty-six years have now gone by since I was killed. I lie beneath the earth and await justice at the hands of the Christian Queen of the upper world. Beloved Victoria, how long?

Two fat tears dripped on to the paper and spotted it. He could not send it to the Queen like that! He took another sheet and wrote with one hand, while with the other he held his handkerchief and wiped his eyes to prevent them from dripping. He wrote, and wiped his eyes, and fasted . . .

When it was time to light the lamps, his friend Tityros came.

He had a bad day behind him. After Captain Michales had left him, he had found his wife and her brother sitting in the court-yard. They had laid the table and were drinking their morning coffee and milk, eating the last of the Easter biscuits, and laughing. He greeted them. They looked at him without answering. His wife did not get up, did not bring him a cup. Brother and sister winked at each other and laughed again.

Tityros shut himself up in his room. The thing had got to come to an end. To-day, after his heroic oration in the church, he was feeling brave. He would go at it with energy and turn that parasite out. "This house is my Constantinople," he muttered. "He's the Turk, I'm Constantine."

He ran noisily downstairs and out into the yard.

"Why are you laughing?" he shouted, and his chin quivered. "Shut up!"

The woman turned and put her hand in front of her mouth, so as not to burst out laughing again. The brother looked at him sideways, yawning. He was still in his nightshirt, unshaven and barefoot.

"Is laughing then forbidden, teacher?" he asked mockingly.

"You have nothing to say here," replied the schoolmaster. "I'm

master of the house here!" He plucked up courage and stamped.
"And I demand the key of the house. The master of the house
keeps the key."

"What will you say next, teacher?" said Diamandés in a tone of
amazement, putting his long leg up on the chair. He turned to his
sister and pointed with his thumb at the schoolmaster, who was
standing behind him, greenish-yellow in the face.

"Just look at him, the fly!"

Vangelio applauded him with a peal of laughter.

"What are you laughing at, you shameless creature?" shouted
Tityros, beside himself, and rushed at his wife to stop her mouth.

But the brother, who had kicked the chair aside, jumped up to
help his sister.

"Down with your claws, schoolmaster, " he bellowed, "or I'll
knock you down."

He swung his fist over Tityros's head, and Tityros started back.

"Get out!" bellowed Diamandés, shaking his fist menacingly.
"Get out, or I'll pound you to pulp, Tityros. What impertinence,
trying to play the master and demand the key. Hey, you snake in
spectacles, you lean bottom, take yourself off! If not, I'll give you
legs!"

He seized him by the coat, shook him and pushed him against
the wall. Vangelio undid her long hair, took out her ivory bridal
comb and began combing voluptuously. Smiling proudly, she
looked at her brother—at his broad, hairy chest exposed by the
open nightshirt, at his cypress-like form—and at the same time,
with disgust, at her sickly husband.

Tityros had torn himself out of the hands of his brother-in-law
and ran to the street door. But before opening it he called out to
his wife:

"This is no life at all! It's got to end!"

"Yes, end," shouted Diamandés, puffing out his chest, "I can't
stand any longer having you, Tityros, stumbling over my feet,
morning, noon and night, The house isn't big enough. There
isn't room for both of us."

He turned to his sister. "Vangelio, choose."

Tityros's breath stood still. He stared at his wife. He waited.

Vangelio was holding a green silk ribbon between her teeth. She did not hurry with her reply. She smoothed her hair with both hands, tied it up and shook it, so that it fell over her neck and down to her knees.

"I'm not parting from my brother," she said, "not if it means the end of the world."

"That means I . . ." Tityros began, and stopped.

Vangelio shrugged her shoulders. Diamandés laughed drily and again stretched himself out with his long legs up on the chair.

"She's given you the go-by, you poor thing," he said. "Haven't you got there yet, teacher?"

It was the sight of the sea that first calmed Tityros down. He sat on a rock near the wall and spent several hours there motionless, gazing at the expanse of waters.

The sun was already sinking when Tityros got up from the rock. He looked about him in surprise. His agitation had subsided, his eyes were dry. During all the hours he had been gazing at the sea, he had been wholly without thought. But inside him something was stirring. He came at last—his blood did, not his understanding—to a decision. He had not been able to make it in any way explicit, but he felt himself safe within his own certainty. "All will go well," he whispered, "I am the master of the house."

He turned into the crooked alleys near the harbour, passed through the Jewish quarter and stopped in his own part of the town, in front of the grand house of Idomeneas. There was a light still in his friend's window. He's certainly writing to the Queen again, he thought, what a waste of letters! I'll go and chat with him for a bit. It will distract me, and him too.

He knocked. Old Doxaniá's face showed pleasure as she saw him.

"Since early this morning he's eaten nothing," she said. "Get him to eat, and God bless your honour for it! God has sent you."

Mr. Idomeneas too was delighted to have a guest. He had just finished his letter-writing and pressed upon the envelope his seal—Athena armed. Tomorrow the letter would go to London.

"Others fight with weapons," he said, pointing proudly at the

sealed letter, "we two—and Hadjisávas as the third in Megalokastro—fight with our brains, and we shall set Crete free."

The schoolmaster shook his head. He did not believe that Crete
could be saved by writings and letters and marble fragments.
Tired and hungry, he sank on to a high, half-sat-through chair.

"And who will save *us*, Idomeneas," he asked with a sigh.

"Who? Crete, as soon as we have freed her, schoolmaster! Our
personal happiness is bound up with that. In the fight for the
saving of Crete we are fighting also for the saving of our souls."

But the schoolmaster shook his head. At the same time he wiped
his glasses, which were spattered with spray from the sea.

Idomeneas stuck to his opinion. Wandering about excitedly he
cried: "What other way to happiness can you see? To be sure—
what's the good of my talking to you now? You're newly married,
so drunk with bliss. But the first rapture will pass, and then you
will follow any way. For men like us there is no personal happiness. We find it only in the fight for the happiness of the community."

He paused. He wanted to roll himself a cigarette. But then it
occurred to him that he was mourning and fasting to-day, and he
put his tobacco-box aside. So he drew pleasure from this sacrifice,
which he was making to the community.

"That's the secret, schoolmaster!" He raised his kindly, prema-
turely shrivelled face with pride. "In Megalokastro I am the only
one who knows it. Perhaps Hadjisávas as well. Later you too will
understand."

He paused again. But his heart was overflowing. To-day he
must speak. The day demanded it. His friend must at last learn the
secret which he had been meekly keeping to himself for years.

"Why do you suppose I write to the Queen? Why do I stay here
in the half-tumbled-down grand house of my father like a living
corpse, and cry out. No, I don't cry out. Crete cries out. Because
she has no mouth she uses mine. You, unbelieving Thomas, carp,
and say: 'Your crying's useless, no one hears you.' And I tell you:
a cry is never wasted! Before the ear came voices. With their
calling and crying the ear was first created, Mr. Teacher! All the
Kings and the Mighty of the Earth, to whom I write, will one

day hear. And if not they themselves, then their children and grand-children. And if not these, then God. Why is God there? Why, do you think? To hear! Don't laugh. Yes, yes, I know, everyone thinks I'm crazy. Behind my back I hear them whispering: 'What a waste of letters!' Let them say it. What do they understand about God and Crete and the Duty of Man? I cry out from among these ruins to God, and one day He will hear. He will bend down from Heaven to Crete. Ashamed of having left her in slavery for so long, He will ask me, Idomeneas, for forgiveness. Suddenly Saint Menas's Easter bells will start ringing loudly, and the Christians run out like mad into the streets, which are strewed with myrtle and laurel. Men and women stream to the harbour, to greet the Greek King's son. While he is stepping from the ship, they kiss one another and shout: 'Crete is risen! Really risen again!' "

He wiped his eyes, which had become wet. He had relieved his heart.

But the schoolmaster's mind was elsewhere; his friend's flame did not warm him.

"You and I, my dear Idomeneas, will by then be withered leaves. We shall die slaves, and not live to see that resurrection."

Idomeneas laughed at his friend pityingly:

"You're still not capable of understanding me. I have no need to see and to test, in order to be set free. I am free even in the confusion of servitude. I enjoy the freedom of the future, genera-tions in advance. And when I have fought for freedom my whole life long, I shall die a free man."

"That I really don't understand," said the schoolmaster, who was thinking of his wife and her shameless brother and the key of the house which he had demanded and had not got.

"But you will certainly understand it one day," said his friend. "For the moment you are ensnared by small things, which feast on the souls of men. The soul is a lioness, worries are her lice. But you will shake them off!" he said, giggling at his own wit.

Doxaniá appeared on the threshold. As Idomeneas had his back to her, she made a sign to the schoolmaster. He was very willing to eat now, for all day he had had nothing between his teeth.

"A hungry bear doesn't dance," he said. "You speak of great

ideas, but my mind is revolving round food. Ever since this morning I've had nothing to eat, and I spent last night writing."

"I haven't had anything to eat either," said Idomeneas. "What harm does that do? Nourishment too is a louse."

"But the lioness would die," said the schoolmaster with a laugh, "if that louse were missing."

Idomeaneas clapped his hands. Doxaniá came running up, delighted.

"The schoolmaster's hungry, nurse," he said. "Lay a tray with what we've got, and bring it."

"With pleasure," exclaimed Doaxniá, hurrying off.

"We'll eat together, won't we?" said the schoolmaster. "I can't eat alone. You can endure fasting; but now you must also show that you can endure eating. Fasting, bad living and asceticism—those are lice, too, I think."

The two friends laughed. This mixture of joking and great thoughts cheered them up. The full tray came, and Doxaniá's wrinkled face was lit with good humour. Since the sun had gone down, the hungry Idomeneas was not breaking his vow either, as he now entertained his friend. And so they tucked in with a good appetite, and drank some old wine from a cask which had long been in the house.

"To Freedom!" they cried, clinking glasses.

When it had grown quite dark outside, the schoolmaster's thoughts returned shuddering to his home.

"Why are you depressed?" his friend asked him. But the schoolmaster did not answer.

"How do you like your new existence? Is it easy to live with a woman?"

The schoolmaster went over to the window. "It's night. I must go."

The waxing moon, under which Tityros had married, had already waned, and the fourteen days of mourning for Manúsakas were also nearing their end. His first-born son Thodóres had spent them in violent agitation in that village rich in gardens. His Uncle, Captain Michales, had insulted him badly. He had treated him like a boy not yet capable of using a knife and killing Turks. "How old are you?"—"Seventeen."—"Stay in your nest!" Did seventeen years seem to Captain Michales too few? He was a grown man, he could manage the plough with their ox, Russos, and till their field. He was a match, too, for Hussein, Nuri's nephew, the young Turkish palikare-leader in Petrokéfalo. When they wrestled, he could throw him—and could easily plunge his knife into his neck.

"Uncle insulted me," he told his mother, Christiniá, who, dressed in black, had gone to her husband's grave and there, with her face pressed to the ground, set up a keening for the dead. Tomorrow was the fourteenth day. She had come like that each day and had called him, scratching at the earth with her nails.

"You're still too young, Thodóres," his mother replied. "Leave the revenge to your uncle."

"But when? When, mother? Tomorrow is Father's fourteenth day, and we still eat and drink and sleep and the deed remains not done. Doesn't Father appear to you in your sleep? Doesn't he complain to you? Every evening he reproaches me."

He bound the black head-band round his head and looked across to the foot of the mountain, where the head village, Petrokéfalo, shone bathed in sunshine. It was full of Turkish masters and oppressed Christians. The sun had burned the young man's powerful body brown. Thick down was sprouting on his cheeks, with already a good many goat-hairs. His chest too had already a pelt. He lived among the mountains with his father's sheep and with the rams. He seldom came to the village to see human beings. But since last year his lonely existence had begun to lie heavily on him, and so he went every Sunday to the village church to come in contact with women. The blood was beginning to drive him. Since the day of the murder he had not returned to the mountains. His brother Kostandis, the next in age, stayed there as herdsman. Thodóres, on the contrary, had donned the boots, jacket and head-band of his father, adopted also his tobacco-box and hazel staff, and gone back from the big oak to Ai-Janni. He often went into Petrokéfalo, always sullen and silent.

"I'm going," he now said, taking the hazel staff and standing up from the grave.

"Where, Thodóres, my child?"

"To Petrokéfalo. Didn't you say you wanted pomegranate-kernels tomorrow to strew over the funeral cake? I'll get you some. There are some hanging in the loft at Grandfather's."

Out of his black belt stuck his father's knife, with the dried blood still on it. His mother wanted to clean it, but he would not let her. "Blood isn't washed away with water, Mother, but with blood." He always had that knife about him. By night he placed it under his pillow. "Give me the knife, my child," his mother begged him; "as long as it lies under your pillow, your father comes and torments you in your sleep."—"That's just what I want, Mother," the son replied; "him to torment me." And he crossed himself.

Now he left her, striking the stones with the hazel staff.

"Be careful, Thodóres," his mother called after him, as she watched how he kicked the stones aside with his powerful strides. "My blessing go with you!"

But her son was already out of sight. A hare ran through the heather. Thodóres hurled the staff after it and caught the animal's paws, knocking it over. He picked it up and hit it against a stone, smashing the head.

"I'll take it to Grandfather as a present," he said. "A good sign, the hare brings me luck. That's how I'll pick up Hussein and hit his head to pulp against the cliff. But he's no hare. It'll mean a hard fight."

Two days before, he had challenged him to a fight, in front of the threshing-floor. At Thodóres's whistle, Hussein had come out to him. "Hey, Hussein," he had called to him, "the day after tomorrow ends the fourteen days for my father, who was murdered by your uncle, Nuri."—"Pitch and sulpher on his corpse," said Hussein with a short laugh. The gall rose to Thodóres's eyes. He trembled with rage and could not speak. "What are you goggling at me for, *giaour*? Why did you whistle for me? Have you gone blind? Didn't you see I was busy winnowing?"—"If you are a palikare, come and fight with me. I'll die a Turk if that back of yours doesn't rub the ground!"—"My back, you infidel? When and where?"—"At the same place where my father was murdered—at the big oak. The day after tomorrow, his fourteenth day. Early in the morning, so that nobody catches us."—"Do we bring knives?" —"Yes!"

They separated. Hussein went back to his winnowing, while Thodóres returned home. He knelt down on the threshold and took the knife out of his belt, to sharpen it. But then he wanted the blood to remain on it, and so stuck it back. Later he went to the great oak and leaned against its trunk.

Now, at the entrance to Petrokéfalo, near the well, he saw a girl, and went fiery red. She had taken hold of a jug by the handle, to lift it on to her shoulder, but when, already from a distance, she saw Thodóres coming, she stood still, waiting for him. What a radiant girl! Her body was taut, and yet supple in its lines. Above her gleaming almond eyes the brows bent like curved blades. She was like an animal that had caught a scent and now snuffed it tensely.

Thodóres eyed her from afar. "Everything's turning to good, to-day," he muttered, while his heart leaped. "There's Frosáki!"

He looked about him: nobody. . . . The other girls had done some way from the well with their jugs. The peasants on the threshing-floor were flailing, winnowing and piling the corn. In the whole world there was only Frosáki. And above her head, like a crown, the sun.

He felt a delicious weakening at his knees. He stopped by the well.

"Good day," he said in a trembling voice. He lowered his gaze. The girl's slender, bare ankles gleamed as the sun poured over them.

She surveyed him boldly and laughed at him mockingly:

"Why are you carrying a hare, Captain Thodóres? Are you going a-hunting hares?"

"I'm going a-hunting Turks," replied the young man, raising his eyes. "I've been getting my hand in on the hare."

For a moment their looks crossed like daggers, then in agitation the young man again lowered his head.

The girl corked her jug with a wooden peg. Then she too looked hastily about her. There was no one to be seen. "Are you thirsty, Thodóres?" she said.

"Yes, I'm thirsty, Frosáki. But who'll give me, an orphaned son, water to quench my thirst?"

The girl looked down and remained silent, but her neck and ears went a deep red.

Thodóres whispered:

"Tomorrow is my father's fourteenth day. Come to our house and help my mother with the funeral cake. The other girls of the village are coming too."

"If my mother'll let me, I'll come," said the girl. And immediately afterwards: "Even if she won't let me, I'll come, because you've invited me. Captain Thodóres is someone to whom we don't refuse any wish."

She said it with mocking laughter, to hide her inclination. She looked at him, she devoured him with her eyes. Each night she remained awake, to think about him. She would have liked to be earth, to spread herself beneath his feet. But now that she saw him in the flesh, she teased him and provoked him—yes, she would have like to scratch him, to hurt him.

Thodóres rested his chin on his staff and, gazing at the ground, reflected that tomorrow he would have to fight with Hussein.

"Ah, Frosáki," he said, "if anything happened to me, would you weep for me?"

Then the girl could control herself no longer. Tears flowed over her cheeks, as she whispered:

"I've nobody but you in the world, Thodóres!"

"Well then," cried the young man joyously, raising his head from off his staff, "you mark my words, Frosáki: nothing bad can happen to me!"

Two girls with pitchers appeared. Frosáki quickly wiped her eyes, bowed her shoulder under her pitcher and pretended to be looking into the distance. But she could not restrain the throbbing of her heart. Thodóres ran into the village, whistling loudly and swinging the dead hare in his hand.

Next day—a Sunday—when the liturgy was over and the

memoria .service for Manúsakas began, Gregóres the pope went up on to the platform in the forecourt. Beside him stood a black-bearded shepherd-boy holding, on a heavy dish, the funeral cake with its thick icing, its almonds and pomegranate kernels. Manúsakas's name, traced in cinnamon could be read there. One peasant after another walked up and stretched out his palm, which the pope filled. Each one murmured: "God be merciful to your soul," and, as he moved on, buried his face in his paws to eat greedily and adorn his own moustache with cinnamon and icing.

Because the fourteen days were gone by—in reality it was men and women who had gone on, not the days—the virtues of Manú sakas were receiving particularly loud praise. He had actually appeared to old Katerinió, mother of the watchman of the pen, as she returned last night to the village. Her dog, too, had seen him, and his hair had stood on end. He had tried to bark at him, but his muzzle had remained open, and it could not yet be shut.

"The man we've lost is walking as a ghost," said one of the grey-beards, crossing himself. "He was killed at the height of his strength and is still going on. He won't die."

"He wants blood," said another. "Why is Captain Michales hesitating such a long time?"

While they were still chatting Kokoliós, the watchman of the pen, burst into the forecourt with his tongue hanging out. In his trembling hand he held his horn. The distribution of the funeral cake had just ended, and the pope was descending from the platform while, on their knees, the shepherd-boys were licking the dish.

The pope came over to the watchman, while the congregation crowded round them both:

"Hey, Kokoliós, get your breath. Have you got more bad news for us? God have mercy on us!"

"Hussein, Nuri's nephew, has been found dead!"

"Where?"

"Under the big oak."

"Who . . .?"

"God knows. Petrokéfalo is in an uproar. The gates have been shut. The Christians are arming. The Turks have laid the body in the courtyard of the mosque, and one Turk after another bows down in front of it. All the while, they're firing off pistols. And they're threatening to burn down Ai-Janni."

"How can we help it?"

"Someone from Ai-Janni is the murderer, they say. Someone of Manúsakas's family. They're demanding Thodóres as a victim."

"Someone go to the widow and tell her the news!" the pope ordered. "Thodóres must escape to the mountains! Quick!"

But Thodóres had already taken possession of his father!s musket and pair of silver pistols. Also he filled his sack with cartridges and shot and, opening his father's trunk, took from under its double bottom the Greek flag. He quickly folded it together and, without washing the blood from his hands and chest, fled to the mountains. He passed by the pen and gave instructions to his brother Kostandis. Remembering that he had not taken leave of his mother, he left for her a message that all was well with him and she should please give him her blessing. He put a lump of cheese into the sack and went off to climb Selena, the highest of the Lasíthi mountains. There were shepherds there from whom he had often stolen sheep—and they from him. This had made them fast friends. I'll sleep in their pens, Thodóres had decided, and if soldiers come hunting me, I'll raise the flag, place myself at the head of the shepherds, and we'll fight and shout: "For the union with Greece!"

Towards evening two armed agas came to the widow Christiniá's door. They knocked. Not a soul! They knocked again, making the house ring. Nobody!

An old Turk, who had gone up to the mountain in search of wood, was coming back with his load. "Welcome, sirs," he said. "You're looking for Thodóres? The bird has flown. He's made for the mountain."

"Be careful what you say, old Braimis. Did you see him with your own eyes?"

"Yes, by Mohammed, with my own eyes. The *giaour* was running as though he was a horse. I fell to the ground in terror. When I looked again, he'd vanished."

The agas cursed and stabbed the door twice with their knives.

On their way back they met, in the ravine which divided the two villages, old Katerinió—the same to whom the ghost of Manúsakas had appeared. She had been collecting wild lettuce and asparagus, and had filled her small sack. Now she was going contentedly home to prepare supper for her son.

The two agas rushed upon her and murdered her cruelly.

In the neighbouring villages Turks and Christians now collided. The killings began. One time the corpse of a Christian would be found in the middle of the street, another a dead Turk, hidden in his garden or in a dried-up well. The tidings flew about like sparks and set village after village on fire. And so they reached Megalokastro too.

One midday Suleiman, the Pacha's Arab, was drunk. Not of his own accord. He had been pumped full of raki by the agas and then sent out into the Greek quarter. "Do your best, Suleiman, to find Captain Michales and finish him off—if you're a man." He drew the dagger which the Pacha had given him at last year's Bairam festival, and rushed bellowing through the Greek streets. As the Christians heard him they snatched their children out of the streets and shut their houses.

"The Arab! The Arab!" shrieked the women, banging the bolts to.

The Christians who met the Arab as they were going home to the midday meal, dived for the first door that would open for them.

"Crete, abandoned by all, is catching fire again!" they told one another, some with fear, the others with rage. From the cases where they had hidden them they pulled out their rusted muzzleloaders, to clean them.

At Idomeneas's Fountain the Arab stopped. Heated by raki and by the midday sun, he had his brow, neck and legs trickling with sweat. He shoved his head under the fountain to cool himself, bellowing like a buffalo. The whole quarter trembled. And while he still had his head bent right down, he saw between his legs Captain Michales approaching from the far end of the street. With a wild shout he grasped his dagger and made a rush for him.

Captain Michales stood still. For a moment he thought of

turning back, but then was ashamed. To his right a door opened, and Krasojórgis's wife put out her head, with her hair all coming down.

"For God's sake, Captain Michales, why are you standing there? Come in!"

But he had now taken his broad handkerchief from his hip and wrapped it about his fist.

The door of Captain Michales's house also opened, and Katerina rushed out.

"Michales, Captain Michales, have pity on your children," she cried, and ran to his side.

She saw a monster facing her husband, with flashing teeth and rolling eyes.

"Now I'm going to gobble you up, Captain Giaour!" the Arab yelled, with his dagger raised.

The woman tried to come in front of her husband, but he had already, with all his strength, planted his fist in the Arab's belly. With a roar he fell, Captain Michales wrenched the dagger from his clenched fingers. As he turned, he saw his wife.

"Your place is in the house," he said. "Go!"

Captain Michales, with his wife behind him, went in. She brought him a fresh shirt. As he changed, his body cooled down, and he smiled under his moustache, gazing at the sharp dagger.

"Wife," he said, "give Thrasáki that dagger, to sharpen his pencils with."

That same evening two young Turks, the sons of the muezzin, beat up the harmless Bertódulos in the Pervóla and trampled on his straw hat. They were about to tear his cloak too, but he cried out, and that made them run away. Next day, early in the morning, the muezzin was found tied to the great plane-tree, frozen blue and stark naked. Over his mouth his green turban-cloth had been bound, to prevent him from crying out. He was set free, his legs were rubbed, and he was given a hot infusion to drink. As soon as he could speak again, he described how two Christians, one of them with a wild moustache like a mountain goat, the other a lame man, had taken him prisoner, stripped him and tied him to the plane-tree with the gallows-rope. They had meant to cut off

his beard too, but had forgotten the shears. So they merely spat
on him and ran off towards the harbour.

The Pacha was beside himself. He ordered that all the lame in
Megalokastro should be arrested and thrown into prison. Search
was also made for Captain Stefanés, but he was not to be found.
The police put the lame men in the stocks and dosed them with
castor-oil. But they all behaved like palikares and revealed nothing.
After three days the Pacha had had enough of feeding them and
plying them with castor-oil (there were some thirty of them), and
he let them go.

But he had Suleiman the Arab put in irons when he heard of
his failure.

Two or three days went by. A strong south wind came from
Arabia and loosened flakes from the walls of the houses. Thick,
hot dust was whirled up and got into people's noses, ears and
mouths. Megalokastro groaned as in a fever. At noon the dogs
huddled in the shade, with their mouths open the men and
women gasped. They did not stir from their shops, where they
fanned themselves with straw fans and gulped down cool sherbet.
Barba Jannis stood at his height of glory. He ran through the
heat, selling the snow-cooled drink. That weakling of an old man
feared the fire of summer as little as the frost of winter. His
profit-making cooled him in summer and warmed him in winter.
And so he remained, all the year round, evenly tempered.

In the gardens the watermelons swelled to the point of bursting.
Every morning the gardeners brought to the main square near
the great plane-tree, and to the Three Vaults, mountains of watermelons, gherkins and cucumbers. The vine-trellises were showing
their first coloured berries, and the first sour-sweet figs were venturing to market. The earth was exploding with fruitfulness—
how could the fruit-dealers keep pace with it? Turks and Christians
stood before the piles of fruit, the vendors sang full-throatedly,
and at evening they gave away what was left over. Then from all
sides children, old men and destitute old women rushed up, and
each one collected what he could.

When the sun sank, the earth breathed. It grew cool, and tender shadows settled over Megalokastro. The housewives sprinkled

their yards and then gathered, now in one house, now in another, to gossip. On Sunday they were in the courtyard of Krasojórgis's wife. While they were enjoying themselves, nibbling dainties and cracking jokes, suddenly Penelope rushed in, pale and with staring eyes, wearing her patched and spotted house-dress, and wailing. All jumped up and led her to a chair. Krasojórgis's wife gave her a drink of cherry-juice. She drank and moaned at the same time.

"What's the matter, Penelope?" they asked, "why are you crying?"

Penelope swallowed what was left.

"Demetrós. . . . Demetrós . . ." she cried.

"For God's sake, is he ill?"

"He's gone off."

"Gone off? Where?"

"With his umbrella!"

"Where, my dear?"

"Into the mountains again."

"But why, Penelope? What's up with him?"

"Ah, I'm so worried! . . . He ran out with his umbrella. . . . He's run away from me once before. With his umbrella that time too. During the 1878 rising."

"O, that's a bad sign! You mark what I say, my dears!" exclaimed Chrysánthe, Polyxigis's sister, slapping her knee. "That means another rising—God punish me if I'm lying!"

"Don't say such a thing, my dear! May the Devil's ear be deaf!"

"God punish me if I'm lying!" Chrysánthe repeated. "How does the mouse get wind of an earthquake and escape? In the same way Demetrós gets wind of the rising and runs out with his umbrella."

"And he has no money," Penelope whispered. "And who'll cook his meals for him, who'll do his washing for him and his mending, and make his bed and cover him up at night? I know he'll come back to me, like last time, with his breeches in holes!"

"Don't make such a fuss, my dear," said Krasojórgis's wife, "I'm well on my way to being sick of my husband, with his cushions of fat."

But Penelope was not consoled. She again opened her mouth to wail, but the mistress of the house popped into it a spoonful of halva with almonds.

"What's Captain Michales doing, neighbour?" she asked quickly, to change the conversation. "For days and days I haven't seen him."

"Things are well with him, God be thanked," replied the Captain's wife. "But he leaves the house at grey of dawn and does not come home till night. How can you expect to see him?"

She sighed and fell silent.

And in truth things were well with Captain Michales. Only the world was too small for him, like a prison. He was rattling his chains. He rode over the fields as far as Nuri's country house. He saw it lying there among the olive-tree and cypresses, and his heart growled.

"Patience, patience, my heart, don't be in too much of a hurry. Wait till he's well." So he muttered, and turned away.

Every evening, late, Ali Aga came, covered with dust from Nuri's country house with his news:

"To-day he tried to get up, but the pain overcame him and he rolled back on to his bed."—"To-day he got up. His Moor supported him and guided him out to the yard. I stood in a corner behind the water-trough and watched him. . . . By my faith, Captain, I didn't recognise him. He's so pale, so thin! And where have those cheeks of his gone, and that well-kept moustache? His skin is full of furrows."—"To-day he came out into the yard without the Moor. He looked at me, and I went up to greet him. But he waved me away—he didn't want to speak. I left."— "To-day the Moor got him on to his horse, and he went for a ride. The Moor ran behind, in case he should faint and fall from the saddle. . . . And the horse went carefully, as if it understood everything!"

Finally, one evening, after days and weeks, Ali Aga came panting into Captain Michales's shop, where he sat waiting in the dark.

"He's well," said the old man. "To-day Mustafa Baba left the house. 'You don't need me any more, Nuri Bey,' he told him; 'the rest lies in Allah's hands.' And with that he went. The Bey rode out this afternoon without the Moor accompanying him."

"What does he look like? Fresh and ruddy as before? Strong? In his stride again?"

"He's still pale, Captain. Yellow as a bit of lemon-peel. Gloomy. He keeps his lips shut. He doesn't eat, the old nurse told me, he doesn't drink, he doesn't sleep. He's always sighing. And yesterday, when the old woman asked him when Eminé Hanum was to come out to the estate, he caught hold of the stair-rail to prevent himself from falling. He was near to fainting. He looked at the old woman with staring eyes, and did not answer."

"You talk too much, Ali Aga."

But Ali Aga stayed where he was. He wanted to say something more, but hesitated.

"Why are you scratching your head? Is there a piece of news you're still keeping back?"

"They say, Captain . . ." He broke off again.

"Speak out, you blockhead! What do I pay you for?"

"They say the poor creature is maimed."

"What do you mean?"

He lowered his voice still more.

"He's no longer a man. And Eminé Hanum has heard it . . ."

"Go!"

Ali Aga reeled back. Stumbling between ships' cables and paint pots, he found the way out and vanished.

Captain Michales started to his feet.

"That must not be!" he shouted, rushing up and down in the darkness of the shop. "I won't stand it! It isn't possible!"

He would not believe that such a misfortune could befall a man. He kept saying to himself again and again, biting his moustache convulsively:

"It can't be! But supposing it is? Suppose it's true? How can I take vengeance on a maimed man? What sort of vengeance is that? What does death mean for him?"

Suddenly he made a decision: I'll go and see him myself!

He let a few more days elapse. The man must rest a bit longer, he thought—get back to his old strength. And one Sunday he mounted his mare. The plain lay in the blaze of summer, the vine-trellises were heavy with clusters, the sky burned.

I

"Summer, vintage, war . . ." he whispered. "Ah, Mother rich in sufferings!" His spirit embraced Crete, full of pity.

He loved Crete like a living, warm creature with a speaking mouth and weeping eyes; a Crete that consisted not of rocks and clods and roots, but of thousands of forefathers and foremothers, who never died and who gathered, every Sunday, in the churches. Again and again they were filled with wrath, and in their graves they unfolded a proud banner and rushed with it into the mountains. And on the banner the undying Mother, bowed over it for years, had embroidered with their black and grey and snow-white hair the three undying words:

FREEDOM or DEATH

Captain Michales's eyes grew moist. When he was alone he was not ashamed of tears.

"Luckless Mother!" he whispered. "Luckless Mother!"

Between the olive-trees gleamed the Bey's country house. Captain Michales put spurs to the mare.

The door stood open. He rode through it. In the yard he dismounted and looked around—after so many years! Here, in this yard, near this gnarled olive-tree, the two of them had kneeled together, and their blood had flowed. They had had the choice between death and brotherhood: they had become brothers. And now that, after so many years, he was returning to that same yard, it looked as if God had repented and they must kill each other. . . .

A servant ran up and recognised him. "Welcome, Captain Michales," he said.

"Where is the Bey?"

"Upstairs."

"Go and tell him I've come and would like to see him."

Nuri's stallion scented the mare and stuck its noble head out of the opening in the stable door, neighing. But the mare did not answer, for she was pregnant.

The servant came back. "The Bey says: Welcome, Captain. Would you have the kindness to wait until he is dressed? . . . Shall I give the mare some hay, Captain?"

"No."

He went out to the fountain and took down the brass cup from its hook. He drank. There was an inscription in Turkish lettering round the rim of that cup, in which their blood had once been mingled. That evening Nuri Bey had translated it: "Raise thy head, O traveller, and drink. Even the hen raises her head when she drinks, and thanks God!"

The servant appeared. "Will you be so kind as to come in?" he said. "The Bey is waiting for you."

Captain Michales pulled his black head-band tighter, concealed the bone handle of his knife, and went in.

Nuri Bey was sitting at the most shaded point of the divan, dressed up like a bridegroom. He knew with what purpose this guest had come, and was ashamed to appear before him pale and lowered. He had put black pomade on his moustache and rouge on his cheeks. His eyelashes too had been coloured with charcoal, to enhance the sparkle of the eyes. He too had pushed his black-hilted dagger deeper down into his sash, to make it invisible.

"Welcome, Captain Michales," he said, stretching out his hand. But the other had buried his hands deep in his belt, and would not touch the hand which had killed his brother. Nuri Bey, ashamed, leaned back against the wall.

Captain Michales did not sit down. He was trying, in the half-dark, to measure the strength which remained to Nuri, and to weigh his words accordingly.

"Are you in such a hurry, Captain Michales, that you won't sit down? And you've come all this way . . ."

"Can't you stand up, Nuri Bey?" Captain Michales asked. "The business that has brought me to your house is not discussed on divans."

"I know. Why do you remind me, Captain Michales? Only don't be in a hurry. Let us first drink a coffee, smoke a cigarette, and talk a little. And then what you want shall happen, Captain Michales."

His voice was tired and full of bitterness.

"Right, Nuri Bey. Since you wish it, I won't be in too much of a hurry," said Captain Michales, and sat down opposite him. At the same time he examined the other's face ever more closely, and involuntarily the other drew back still further into the half-dark.

"You were wounded, Nuri Bey—they say, severely . . ."

"I'm very well, like before, Captain Michales. Don't worry," the Bey riposted defiantly. "My bones are still where they ought to be."

"I'm glad," said Captain Michales, and fell silent.

The coffee came. Each of them rolled himself a cigarette, and they both sat in silence, with bent heads. He has come to kill me, to avenge his brother's blood, reflected Nuri Bey, without any excitement. He's dressed in black, like Charos. Welcome to him! What good is life to me now? For me life and shame are one.

"Welcome," he said suddenly, aloud. "Day in, day out, I have waited for you."

"I have drunk the coffee you gave me and smoked the cigarette, Nuri Bey. We have nothing to talk to each other about. Stand up!"

"As you decide." The Bey stood up with a great effort. He bit his pain down. Then he walked with a slight limp to the threshold of the courtyard, where the light of the sun fell on him.

When Captain Michales saw him in the sunlight, he fell back, appalled. So that was the handsome Nuri Bey, the moon countenance, the lion of Turkey? His cheeks were hollow, his eyes dim; his under lip receded, shrinking as though before a perpetual pain. Behind the rouge and the pomade Captain Michales discerned the complexion of death. He frowned. How can I fight with this cripple? What a dishonour for me! So thinking, he stood still.

"Nuri Bey," he said, "you're still not right again, are you?"

"Do I look pale to you? A cripple? Come! On the threshing-floor the truth will appear."

With trembling knees he limped further. In the middle of the yard he turned. Captain Michales was still standing at the threshold and watching him.

A chill overcame Nuri Bey. The *giaour* sees through me, he thought, and is refusing me. He tried in vain to speak strongly. His voice remained plaintive.

"Captain Michales, how long I have been waiting for you! For no one else, all this time. Only for you. And now that you've come, do you mean to go away?"

Captain Michales said nothing. His feeling of pity grew stronger.

"Why do you keep looking at me? The illness has devoured my cheeks, but my strength has remained. Don't listen to people's gossip, Captain Michales. My strength is as before. Come, go with me."

Captain Michales did not move.

"Shall I have my stallion brought, so that you may see how I ride? Shall I fire my pistols at a target? Draw a circle—I'll shoot at it. Come with me to the threshing-floor. There we shall see who is a man."

He pushed his headband to one side and laid his hand challengingly on his sash. But a cold sweat trickled from his forehead and his belly hurt. Captain Michales's heart was full of pity.

"Nuri Bey," he said calmly. "Speaking loudly is a strain to you. Come inside."

Nuri Bey caved in. Two heavy tears rolled suddenly from his eyes. He turned towards the outer door, to hide his pain. "He's sorry for me," he thought. "So low have I sunk. Nuri Bey, you move nothing but pity now."

"Let's go indoors," Captain Michales repeated. "Another time . . ."

Nuri Bey ceased to pretend. With a gloomy look at his swarthy guest he whispered, so as not to be heard by the servants:

"Captain Michales, you came to kill me. Why don't you kill me?"

"Let's go indoors, Nuri Bey. We can be heard."

He went over to the Bey, took him by the arm, and felt how the weakened body shuddered. Nuri made no resistance and followed, hobbling. As he did so, he moaned:

"You are my blood-brother, don't forget. In this house of misfortune we mingled our blood. I beg you for one favour: kill me!"

"Don't be angry with me, Nuri Bey. Some other day . . ." replied Captain Michales

"You're sorry for me?" He sat down again on the divan, in the shadowy corner. He asked once more: "You're sorry for me?"

But Captain Michales made no answer. He could bear this shape of woe no more. It was driving him away. What business had he in this Turkish *konak*? With this poor creature he had no account to settle. What did death mean to him?

He stood up. The sun was already sinking.

"Nuri Bey, good-bye. I'm going."

The Bey's hoarse voice sounded now as if from a great distance, doubtfully: "You're right, Captain Michales. God guard you."

Standing up, motionless, Captain Michales watched this man and thought of his former handsomeness, of his heroic bearing, of the sparks his horse used to strike from the roadway, and of his breeding.

"Captain Michales," came the unearthly voice again, "if I ever was a man once upon a time, give me your hand. If I was not, farewell."

Captain Michales stretched out his hand and gripped—softly, so as not to hurt it—the other's hand.

"God guard you, Nuri," he said.

"Perhaps this means good-bye for ever, Captain Michales. Do you understand what I mean?"

"I understand," he answered, and stepped over the threshold. And that wild beast suddenly felt a painful cramp in the back of his neck.

Nuri Bey waited, crouched there on the corner of the divan. He listened to the hooves of Captain Michales's mare trampling over the stones. Then all was silent. The rays of the setting sun penetrated into the room and turned the walls golden. Soon they vanished, and the walls became black.

He glided slowly from the divan and went over to the mirror. In front of it he washed with musk soap, changed his shirt and sprinkled the whole of a small bottle of lavender-water over himself. He spent a long time combing his hair. Then he went out to the stable and with long, delicate movements stroked the beloved horse from its fine, pointed ears to its slender legs. The stallion bent its neck down and passed its mouth caressingly over it's master's head and neck. It neighed joyfully.

"Farewell, my child," the Bey murmured, in tears.

They parted. He went up to his bedroom, took a sheet of paper, and wrote: "When I am dead, I wish you to kill my horse over my grave." He placed his seal underneath.

He sank on both knees upon the ancient Anatolian carpet on which his father, seven times a day, had carried out his observances, facing towards Mecca. He looked through the open window at the starry sky. A strong wind had got up, and the dog in the stable was barking. In the far distance the song of a passing waggoner could be heard, calling with longing to his wife. Nuri Bey thought of Eminé, closed his eyes and sighed.

"Treacherous world, farewell!" he whispered.

He pulled from his sash the black-hilted knife, raised it high in the air, and with all the strength that remained to him plunged it into his heart.

VIII

EARLY next day, when the Kanea Gate was thrown open, dark news entered the town: Nuri Bey had been found dead in his country house! In the Turkish coffee-houses there was a humming as of swarms of wasps. Some affirmed at the tops of their voices that the Greeks had murdered him, others said it was a case of suicide. It deprived the muezzin in the mosque of coherent speech: all he could do was, foaming at the mouth, to stammer confused words—"Massacre! *Giaour!* Mohammed!" The Greeks left their work in the lurch and took counsel secretly all day by twos and threes in their houses.

The atmosphere was oppressive, and faces were distorted. The soldiers shoulders their arms and ranged through the streets and over the markets. The Pacha appeared in person in the cemetary for the burial of Nuri Bey. Behind him paced the imam and the muezzin, and after them, in a noisy swarm, the armed agas. Even Suleiman the Arab was present escorting the Pacha, who had freed him from the irons, having had enough of his bellowing. The servants had brought the body to the tomb. The horse had followed, stepping lightly and neighing. It opened its eyes wide and snuffed the air.

The Turks gathered at the place of burial. The imam recited the last words in a high monotonous voice and consigned the dead man to the other world. The muezzin took from the dead man's head the blood-stained white head-band and stuffed it into his own bosom. With deep obeisances all took leave of Nuri Bey, who was lowered into a cavity next to his father's monument. Then the Pacha gave a signal that the horse was to be brought to the grave. He held in his hand the paper which Nuri's Moor had delivered to him. "Agas," he said, "I hold in my hand the written and sealed last wish of the dead man. Open your ears!"

He lifted the sheet of paper to the light, and read: "When I am dead, I wish you to kill my horse over my grave."

The agas were appalled at these words. They gazed at the horse. It had bowed its head over the grave, so that the bluish mane hung down, and was sniffing at the earth. Then it stamped on the ground with its hoof and called to its buried master with a doleful neighing.

"A pity it is, before God and men," voices could be heard saying on all side.

"Pity or not," the Pacha retorted, "it is the dead man's wish. It rends my heart too, God knows, but it is the will of the dead man to take the horse with him. I would do the like. Which of you will harden his heart and draw his knife?"

All stood as though turned to stone. They looked, horror-struck, at the slender body of the horse, gleaming in the sun. That was no Greek one was killing, no ox or sheep one was slaughtering, to preserve one's own life. It was an ornament of the world, the pride of Megalokastro. Connoisseurs came from Rethymuo and Kanea to admire it. Who could raise his knife against such a neck?

The Pacha breathed heavily with anger:

"Who is ready to draw his knife?" he asked once more, looking about him.

No one stirred. The horse had now crouched over the grave and was sniffing frantically. Its neighing sounded like a human voice wailing over someone who has died.

The Pacha turned to his Arab:

"Suleiman, you slaughter it!"

The Arab drew his knife and took a step forward. Then he stumbled and fell on one knee. The horse leapt up and gazed at him without a sound. The Arab hesitated.

"Courage, Suleiman. Shut your eyes and jump at it!" The Pacha ordered, while his tears welled up.

All fixed their gaze on the Arab.

"If he kills him, I'll pound him to a pulp, by my father's corpse," muttered one of them, with his eyes sparkling.

The Arab approached the horse with his knife raised. He began to curse and swear, to get up his courage. The horse again lowered its neck and neighed dolefully, and the Arab let his arm drop.

I*

"Pacha Effendi," he said hoarsely, "I can't."

"Bravo, Suleiman," came the cries of approval and relief.

"I can't," the Arab repeated.

"Take the horse for yourself, Pacha Effendi," cried the agas; "save it, if you believe in God!"

"I'm afraid of the dead man," said the Pacha, gazing at the famous stallion with longing.

He raised his hand to stroke it. But the beast reared threateningly, and would let no one come near.

"Let's go," said the Pacha. "Let it appease its grief over the grave. It too had a soul. And later, don't worry, hunger will compel it. The dead man's Moor is to remain close by and keep watch. Let him give it fodder and water. And when it has calmed down, he's to bring it to me."

They all moved off towards the town. The Pacha went contentedly at their head. Allah was great and good and a friend to the Pacha. How often had he desired that horse! He had longed to grip it between his knees and to remember his youth! If he were to be offered all the women of Megalokastro and then to be given the choice: these women or the horse—he would choose the horse; the Devil could take the women! And now, my God, Thou art munificent! Thou killest Nuri Bey and makest me a present of his horse!

They passed the old fortifications outside Megalokastro, where fruit and vegetables were now planted. In the sunset light a Venetian lion glowed red above the stone battlements. A swarm of ravens was returning soundlessly to the ruined towers from the day's hunting. Through the evening stillness Megalokastro was barking, neighing and shouting in the distance, and still further off roared the sea.

The Pacha halted, and spoke to the agas gathered about him:

"Remember, the fate of Crete is hanging by a hair. Nuri—this I swear by God—killed himself. Do not make him the banner of a Turkish campaign that would mean a fresh beginning of the slaughter. By the Prophet, I shall hang not only *giaours* from the plane-tree but—mark my words—Musulmans as well. Beware!"

Then he cried: "Come, Suleiman," and together with his Arab rode away from them, breathing heavily.

The muezzin shook his head. The great ones quickly exchanged stealthy looks. This Pacha was a man with no backbone, a Greek bastard—what business had he in Crete? Was there ever an Anatolian wedding at which no lambs were slaughtered?

The Pacha had not yet disappeared through the fortress gate before the muezzin pulled Nuri's bloodstained head-band from his bosom and raised it on the tip of his staff as a banner.

"Down with the *giaours*, children, down with them!"

With this shrill cry he placed himself at the head of the crowd of agas.

Down below in the moat two greyhaired Christians were drawing water from the fountain and watering their beasts.

"There we have two of them already," cried the muezzin. "Palikares, at them!"

Two palikares drew their knives.

"With my blessing," shouted the muezzin.

The two slid down the slope through reeds and tall sunflowers and reached the fountain. They seized both the little old men and held their heads over its rim.

The two heads rolled into the fountain.

"Forward, brothers!" cried the muezzin. He raised his staff, and the sea-breeze swelled the bloodstained head-band. Then the troop poured over Megalokastro.

The Christians, who had heard the noise of the returning funeral company a long way off, felt their hearts throbbing hard. They hastily shut their shops and workshops and ran to find shelter behind the doors of their houses.

The muezzin placed himself in front of the big Turkish coffee-house at the Kanea Gate and, raising his staff high, cried:

"Allah, Allah, let the *giaours* taste your knives!"

But old Selim Aga and other sage men of property led the muezzin into the coffee-house and ordered for him coffee, Turkish delight, and a nargile, to calm him down. And later they had Efendína fetched and installed him on a stool in the middle of the room. He was to tell a story from the Halima—about women and handsome boys—to deflect the muezzin's mind from blood and massacres.

A few days went by. Hourly the Greeks trembled, lest one noon the fortress gates might be shut and they then caught in the trap. There were not many of them, and the Turks in their over-whelming numbers would easily finish them off.

Then came fresh Job's tidings. The Turks had broken into Agaratho monastery and murdered the brave Abbot Agathan-gelos. They had come on him as night, sleeping on the roof. He had been to Thrapsamos to consecrate a church, and now lay full of food and drink in a heavy slumber, from which he did not awake when they hacked off his head. One murder led to another: four days later Agathangelos's cousin, a monk from Vrondisi, the well-known monastery at the foot of Psilorítis, came down to the rich Turkish village of Suros and killed its bloodthirsty Aga, just as he had bound two Christians to the treadmill of the well in his garden and was making them turn the wheel.

The Turks in the Greek villages took fright and loaded their asses and mules with all they could carry in the way of household goods—clothes, coppers, cradles, cooking utensils—and their hanums, children and babes in swaddling clothes, and fled to Megalokastro, to the protection of the military. The peaceful and fearful among the Christians, for their part, fled with their families and household goods into the mountains.

The Pacha was at his wits' end. For the first time he found him-self in a Cretan revolution. He was not the man for such an up-heaval. A good-natured Anatolian from Broussa, he loved amuse-ments, fine cooking and sleep. Why the Devil were these Cretans brawling with one another? And why just now, when he had taken possession of Nuri's famous stallion? He wanted to feed it with sugar and give it water to drink out of his hollowed hands, so as to get it used to him. And now this damned Crete must go and have a revolution! He could not think what to do. Now he went to the Metropolitan and implored him: "Metropolitan Effendi, pronounce an anathema, say that anyone who kills a Turk will find no peace in the grave." Now he rushed out to the Turkish villages: "Don't run away and leave your houses, you idiots," he told them at the top of his voice. "I swear, not a nose shall bleed. I have already sent a report to Constantinople, and soon troops will arrive and restore order."

But he did not succeed by these means in stamping out the fire. That same Sunday, there came another piece of news: "Captain Thodóres at noon to-day set fire to a Turkish village in the Lasíthi." The big agas, full of rage, went armed to the Pacha.

"Pacha Effendi, the mischief is spreading, the *giaours* have lost all shame. They're burning our villages. Have you heard what has happened in the Lasíthi?"

"Who is this Captain Thodóres? It's the first time I've heard of him," the Pacha asked, playing peevishly with his beads.

An aga from Petrokéfalo jumped up.

"A young stripling from an accursed stock! It was his father, Manúsakas, who maimed Nuri. His uncle, Michales, is that Captain Wildboar. This downy-chin has the impertinence to attack us! If you don't have him caught and pilloried, we on our side shall set fire to the Greek quarter of Megalokastro. We just wanted to tell you that, Pacha Effendi. Think how you can put it right with the Sultan afterwards!"

"In the name of the Prophet, don't commit such an outrage, you devils!" yelled the Pacha. "My head's whirling! When the Sultan hears of what you've done, I shall be finished!"

"Then catch Thodóres and put him in the pillory. If not, we'll lay Megalokastro in ashes."

"How can I catch him? Where is he?"

"In the Lasíthi. Send soldiers."

He sent soldiers, who tramped through the Lasíthi mountains. Thodóres heard of them and gathered his friends about him. They were most of them young fellows who wanted to have their fling.

Thodóres had been luring the agas of Petrokéfalo from mountain to mountain. They had sworn his downfall, to avenge the blood of Hussein. For the most part Thodóres had been alone, sometimes he had had a few daring comrades with him. They had begun shooting, and when things got too hot they escaped over the precipices. He had his father's gun and was wearing his father's boots and torn, sweat-stained head-band. He felt himself one with his celebrated sire, whose manhood passed to him from his clothes. His father had risen again, father and son were now one, and Thodóres grew stronger and riper from one day to the next. His words, too, acquired weight, and his dealings were now properly weighed.

More and more Greeks gathered round him, at this hard time when soldiers were thrustung into the mountains. About twenty palikares had followed his call.

"Turkey is out for our blood," Thodóres cried, "that is why I have appealed to you, brothers! Do you know what has happened? From our villages the apark has now flown to Megalokastro. From there it will reach Rethymno and from there Kanea. Soon all Crete will be burning. Don't lose courage! Simply remember that those dogs are not just hunting a murderer. Even if they catch him, they won't lay down their weapons. They're hunting the whole of Christendom! Our grandfathers and our fathers knew that already. Now OUR time has come. Before I fled I opened my father's trunk and took the Greek banner with the inscription: FREEDOM or DEATH. For the union with Greece!" And with that he unfolded the flag.

When the Pacha heard, he was seized with rage. He hurried out to seek the Metropolitan. The *giaours'* big pope would have an account to settle with him. He took the Arab with him and growled about his ill luck all the way. The anxiety about Crete was not the only one. To-day, first thing in the morning, they had brought him another piece of bad news, Nuri's servant had come running from the cemetery: "Pacha Effendi, the horse is lying dead on the grave!"—"Didn't you then give him any fodder or water?"—"I gave him it all, Pacha Effendi. But he wouldn't touch it. He wanted to die. Now he's dead."

The sun was high. The muezzin craned his neck out from the minaret and announced the great virtue of prayer and the mercy of God. The Metropolitan was sitting on the broad divan, with his rosary between his fingers, conversing with the learned Hadji-sávas in low tones. In his thoughts he was back once more in the years of his youth, when he had been Archimandrite in Kiev and Representative of the Holy Sepulchre. His lion head was full of Russia. What a blessing of God that country was—what a soil, what corn, butter, smoked fish and caviar it possessed! And then the golden domes on top of the churches, the silver ikon shrines, and the pearls, sapphires and rubies on the gospels! "As long as Russia survives, Hadjisávas, I am afraid of nothing. One day it will open its mouth and swallow Turkey. And then Crete will see freedom. We have no other hope."

But Hadjisáavas was looking absent-mindedly out of the window. A sultry "bora" was blowing, these days. Hadjisávas had been down on his father's land near Aja-Irini, an hour's distance from Megalokastro, and, whether it had been a message from God, or put into his mind by the old times he had been studying—anyhow the idea had occurred to him that this soil might be concealing a celebrated ancient city. And there, in the field, by the bank of a brook, as he was scratching about with the iron tip of his stick, a glittering thing had rolled out from the moist earth. A golden ring!

He had just shown it to the Metropolitan. Two figures were graven on the ring: a woman with exuberant hips holding a double axe in her hands, and near her a naked man of slender build—just like the Cretans of to-day—with his foot raised to dance. Above them both was placed a seal, a half moon.

He laid it on the Metropolitan's palm and said: "In God's name, Mylord, hide it. No one must hear of it. What treasures there must be in the soil down there, what golden ornaments of the dead! But we are slaves. If we reveal the treasure now, Turkey will rob us of it. Let us be patient. As soon as Crete is freed, may some other Greek dig up the ancient city and win the renown."

The Metropolitan shook his head. All that was very nice, but he had many, many souls to care for. What concern of his were things which the earth had swallowed up thousands of years ago? He listened politely, but tried to lead the conversation back to present-day Crete and to Moscow.

Hadjisávas was put out.

"Your Reverence expects freedom from Moscow, the people expect it from guns, and I from this ring, which you, Mylord, despise."

Múrzoflos opened the door:

"The Pacha, most reverend Bishop," he said.

Hadjisávas rose with a laugh:

"The Anatolian has not done with the Cretans yet?" he said, kissing the Metropolitan's hand, and made his escape through a concealed side door.

Already, as he entered, the Pacha began angrily shouting:

"Metropolitan Effendi, I don't understand. The Cretans have raised the flag and are demanding freedom. What freedom? I don't understand. If you obey God, in Whom you believe, and do what He commands you, do you then complain of being a slave and raise a banner and demand freedom? No! No, isn't it the same with God's representative on earth, the Sultan? What Devil's game is going on here in Crete, and robbing me of peace?"

"What happens, though, if you obey a God in whom you don't believe, Pacha Effendi?" asked the Metropolitan in reply. "The Cretans don't believe in the Sultan. That's why they feel they are slaves and seek freedom."

The Pacha put his hands to his temples—he could not understand that. He kicked the door open and went out. Home again, he sat down at the window and gazed through a small telescope at the sea, to see if the Turkish ships with the soldiers were coming yet. They would make everything clear and restore order . . .

Captain Michales waited with held breath and two loaded pistols behind his door. Every evening he sent his wife with the baby in her arms, accompanied by Thrasáki and Renió, to spend the night with one of the neighbours' wives. He remained all alone in the house. But after a few days he said to Thrasáki: "You will stay here with me, you must get used to it." So now father and son kept watch together. But for several days it remained calm, and Captain Michales could sleep in his bed and was even, this Sunday, enjoying a rest. While he was entangled in reflections, there came a heavy knocking at the street door. Someone entered, and immediately a screaming and a howling were heard. He recognised the voice of old Marjora, a relative, whom Tityros had recently brought in from the country to help his wife with the marketing and cooking. It was a consolation to him to have one of his own people in the house. Captain Michales peered through the little window. Old Marjora stood in the middle of the yard, shrieking and tearing her hair.

"Hey, Marjora, what's all the screaming about? Come up!" he ordered.

With her jaws trembling she stood before Captain Michales's bed. She tried to speak, but her words remained unintelligible.

"What are you saying?" Captain Michales shouted. "Diamandés? What the Devil's the matter with him?"

"He's dead!" shrieked the old woman. "We found him just now in his bed. Stiff! Vangelio is screaming and beating her breast. She's shaken him, taken him in her arms, rubbed him with oil of roses and with vinegar. But he remains stiff! He's been poisoned. He's dead."

"Poisoned? How do you know that? Who gave it him?"

"He's dark green in the face."

"Go."

"Don't you breathe a word about it!" he told his wife, as he went out through the street door and followed old Marjora.

At the end of the street, close to Idomeneas's Fountain, lay his brother's house. He went through the door, which was standing open. From the bedroom Vangelio could be heard wailing and beating her breast. Tityros was cowering in the lower room, on a corner of the divan, with his teeth chattering.

Captain Michales went up to him. The schoolmaster raised his eyes and at once lowered them again.

"Schoolmaster," said Captain Michales, "look me in the face!"

Tityros raised his head. Frightened eyes flickered behind his glasses.

"You killed him," whispered Captain Michales. "It was you!"

"Me?"

"Yes! If a man had killed him, it would have been done with a knife. But you've done it with poison, like a coward."

"I couldn't stand it any longer."

"I don't blame you a bit for killing him, but I do blame you for killing women's fashion, with poison. You can't deny that."

"I couldn't bear it any longer," said the schoolmaster again. "I couldn't have done it any other way. He was the stronger."

"Does your wife know?"

"She may. She doesn't speak to me, and when I go upstairs, she pushes me away. Now I'm sitting here and waiting."

"What for?"

"Nothing. I'm waiting."

Captain Michales went out into the yard. Vangelio's lamentation sounded monotonously and tonelessly like running water. He went in again.

"What are you waiting for?"

Tityros became suddenly more cheerful.

"Come what will! Come what will! I'm not afraid any more."

"But your wife may denounce you."

"Let her do what she will. I've done what I wanted. Now it's up to her."

"Stand up. Keep quite calm. If she does denounce you, tell the truth, even if it means prison for life. If she doesn't denounce you, say nothing! And don't let the dead man weigh on your conscience. Are you listening? A proper man kills once for all! Stand up!"

He hoisted his brother up and said:

"Let's go and arrange for the funeral."

When the body was carried out next morning, nobody saw the dead man's face. It was covered over and over with flowers. Vangelio had pillaged her small garden. The neighbours' wives too had sent armfuls of rosemary, basil and roses. Only the dead man's uncle, Captain Polyxigis, shoved the roses aside and looked at the dead man's face: it was swollen. He hastily covered it up again and cast a dark look at Tityros, who was standing opposite him.

When Vangelio saw the Pope entering, she came down from her bedroom and, with her hair loosened, threw herself upon the corpse. She allowed nobody to come near him. Without weeping or wailing she lay stretched out over it, motionless, as though asleep. But when the four bearers laid hold of her, she offered no resistance. She stood up and cut off her tresses near the roots. She wound them into two thick braids and knotted these round the dead man's hands. Then she let him be carried out peacefully and at the threshold raised her hand as though to bid him farewell. Going back into the house, she brought out her brother's clothes, heaped them up in the yard and set light to them. Then she cleaned the house, made herself tidy, and sat down in the yard, with her staring eyes fixed on the flames.

After the interment her uncle, Captain Polyxigis, came and sat down beside her. He took her by the hand and asked her if anyone suspected murder. She looked at him without answering. She merely moved her head to right and left and pressed her lips together defiantly.

Tityros was afraid to sleep in his own house or in his brother's. He spent the night with his friend Idomeneas, and they talked about death and the immortality of the soul before they went to sleep.

Three days went by. Vangelio paid no attention to Tityros when he passed her, moving like a shadow in the house. She bolted herself into her brother's room, lit the lamp of the dead, and placed near it a glass of pure water, in case his soul might be thirsty. She knew that a dead man's soul roamed the house for fourteen days. She could feel its presence on her hair and on her neck and on her shrivelled hands. At night it fluttered like a butterfly over her lips. The world had never given her anything more beautiful.

For three days her mouth remained shut and her gaze fixed and tearless. She wore black: only the ribbon, which she bound about her hair, was yellow.

Her aunt, Chrysánthe, begged her to come to her small country house by the sea—it would make some slight change for her; but she shook her head and bolted herself into her brother's room. She did not go to the grave. She was completely quiet, and rummaged in her trunk among her scanty dowry. Then she cleared the house, as though she were going for a journey.

On the third evening she said to old Marjora:

"Lay the table. Get out the white, embroidered cloth, and the

262 Freedom and Death

good dishes and knives and forks, and tell your master that I will eat with him this evening. And don't light any lamp, except the two lamps for the death watch."

The schoolmaster was ready to faint with fear when he saw the burning death-lamps. He sat on the extreme edge of his chair and dared not look his wife in the eyes. She sat opposite him, pale and stiff like a corpse, and barely tasted the dishes, without saying a word. A thick coating of powder lay like chalk upon her skin. She had put on her white wedding-dress and stuck the faded lemon-blossoms in her hair.

They remained like that for a long time, sitting opposite each other without making a sound. Sometimes Tityros opened his mouth, but every word remained stuck in his throat. Sweat poured over him. Through the open window giving on the court-yard the night breeze came in gusts, making the two plumes flicker.

Suddenly the woman stretched out her hand and filled the two glasses to the brim with wine. It was a red throat-scraper from Kisamos, a wedding-present from Manúsakas, God rest him.

She raised her glass and with a violent blow smashed Tityros's glass.

"I drink to your health, you murderer!" she said in a deep, almost masculine voice, and did not bring her glass to her lips.

She went out into the yard for a short while, then climbed to her brother's room, where she shut herself in. In the night no one heard anything. In the morning they found Vangelio hanging by the clothes-line from the roof-beam.

The news reached Captain Polyxigis in Eminé's room, early in the morning. The widow was ready to be christened, but had decided to wait patiently till Crete should have calmed down again, in order not to provoke the agas. She was delighted at the thought of becoming a Christian and going into the streets with-out a veil. She looked forward to being able to gaze about her in church, and to being seen. Air and sun would play about her freely, she would wear Greek blouses and ruched skirts, and would show her raven-black hair for the world's pleasure. Christ for her was a door which she could open, to go out through it without a veil into the streets.

While she was musing, stretched out on her bed beside Captain Polyxigis, about all these advantages of Grecian life, her black nurse entered with dishevelled hair. She had run across, first thing, to the Hags, to learn the day's news; and now back she came with her tongue lamed.

"Captain," she stammered, "your niece Vangelio has hanged herself."

Captain Polyxigis let go of Eminé's hand and started up.

"Hanged? When? Who told you?"

"The Hags. Last night, in her house. With the clothes-line."

Meanwhile Eminé had pulled out her little round mirror from under the pillow and was examining tongue, teeth and eyebrows.

"Hoo! My tongue's not red to-day. Where's my mastic, Maria?"

"She's left her husband, they say, and followed her brother," the Moorish woman went on, while she searched for the mastic.

"How my race has fallen!—and I have no children," thought Captain Polyxigis, sighing.

He bent over Eminé, who without a care was admiring her beauty in a mirror, and caressed her body tenderly.

"Our son will be half Cretan, half Circassian. That means, immortal!"

As if he had realised this for the first time, his breast filled with confidence. He had stood up to go out, but his knees were trembling, and he sank back on to the bed. That he should produce a wild son, drunk with Circassian blood, who would ride horses before he could spit!

He had long ago ruled that brother-and-sister pair out of the book of his race. They had been degenerate: the one a good-for-nothing and swiller, the other a sour, ageing, infertile maid. He had no other nephews and nieces. The line was near extinction. But from this Circassian, who sat chewing mastic in front of her mirror, and whose mouth smelt of musk, his son would come— the immortal man—and would glorify the seed of the Polyxigises to all eternity.

Then he remembered once more the Moorish woman's tidings,

and felt ashamed. He murmured: Eminé, my child, I must go,"
stood up, put on his belt and donned his fez.

Eminé raised her naked arms and stretched, making her joints
crack.

"Go," she said peevishly, and looked at him out of half-closed
sickle eyes. She yawned.

During those three days between the death of Diamandés and
the suicide of Vangelio, events in Crete grew more turbulent. In
the villages the Christians killed several agas one after another,
and the Turks in Megalokastro raged accordingly. For one man
killed in the country there fell two Greeks that same night in the
alleys of the town. The reins had slipped from the Pacha's hands.
All he had left was his telescope, with which, from the window of
his seraglio, he searched the sea for Turkish frigates.

On the third day, suddenly, at noon, the fortress gates were
closed. No one could go in or out.

And with that day began Ramadan. The Turks touched neither
bread nor water nor cigarettes all day. But as soon as night came
and the first star shone, they made up for everything. A big drum
stood in front of each wealthy aga's *konak*. Dully and heavily it
sounded, like a signal for war. The Christians gathered in their
houses trembled at it, lest the agas after their evening feast should
rush into the streets and beat the Christians' doors in.

All his neighbours came to Captain Michales's in the evenings,
hoping for protection from the wild palikare. Since it was summer, the men lay in the yard and on the veranda, while the women
stretched themselves in the bedroom. Captain Michales kept
watch in his little room, with his gun above his head.

One night there was a secret gathering of the spokesmen and
leading people in the Metropolitan's residence. Captain Michales
was there, and so was that bear of the sea, Stefanés. He had put
on his sea-boots, as though he were going on a voyage. He was
thinking of old times and had forgotten that he was lame. The
Metropolitan spoke briefly and cautiously. Crete was once more
passing through dark and uncertain days. Christendom was in
danger.

The Rose-bug had again a suggestion: "Go, Mylord, to Athens, seek out the King. They must send us supplies and munitions. If not, we are lost. But go yourself. The face of a man is a sword."

But the Metropolitan shook his head:

"I do not leave my lambs at the hour when the wolf breaks in. Let Captain Eliás go."

But Captain Eliás said angrily:

"My dice still roll, Mylord. I'm not an old man. I can still command in war. I'm not going. Let the quill-driver Hadjisávas go."

He turned to Hadjisávas, with his bushy eyebrows still twitching with wrath.

"Let us not drag our poor, unhappy Mother, Greece, into this with us. It will only damage her," said the Metropolitan. "Let us trust in the Great Powers, above all in Russia, which is of the true faith."

"Let's trust in the small powers—in our own strength," said Captain Michales. "That is my opinion."

"Mine too!" shouted Captain Eliás. "Why has the wolf a strong neck? So that he can seize his prey by himself!"

"Let's each of us throw a stone into Suda Bay," suggested Mr. Idomeneas. But nobody was listening to him. They separated at about midnight without any decision.

Day and night alternated, each with its terrors. All day the hungry and excited Turks ran out of the mosques inflamed by the muezzin's harangues, and rushed about with glassy eyes like blind people. At night they reeled, full-fed and drunk, into the coffee-houses, then swirled into the Greek parts of the town and fired shots into the air, to terrify those who were crouching behind closed doors.

Every night, at an agreed time when the agas were still at table, Ali Aga slid along the walls to Captain Michales's house and brought news: this is what the imam said to-day in the mosque, those are the words which were uttered in the coffee-house; the muezzin demanded violence, but this or that bey opposed him— all scalding hot, evening by evening.

Three soft knocks, in close succession, on Captain Michales's door. In came Ali Aga, very depressed. He sat down on his stool near the water-trough, and all the neighbours gathered round him.

"That damned telegraph!" said Ali Aga with a sigh. "It's a dog with its head in Crete and its tail in Constantinople. Someone pulls its tail in Constantinople and an hour later it barks in Crete and causes trouble."

"Trouble, Ali Aga? Speak plainly! What do you mean?" asked Krasojórgis anxiously.

"The Pacha received a telegram to-day, saying that tomorrow soldiers will arive in Megalokastro! With cannons, they say, and cavalry, and the green flag of the prophet!"

"O my Demetrós, what hole will he creep into, so that the soldiers don't catch him?" screamed Penelope, flinging herself down on her swollen knees.

Ali Aga then described the jubilation in the coffee-houses. It had been decided there to go down armed to the harbour next day and pay homage to the flag of the Prophet. The longer Ali Aga spoke, the more his depression disappeared: he was carried away. He was no longer the humble old man in the corner to whom nobody paid attention, but had become a person of consequence.

"Let's call Captain Michales. Let's hear what he says." suggested Mastrapas, whose kindly eyes looked frightened. "I shan't set foot outside, tomorrow."

"Neither shall I," said Chrysánthe. "Not even to evening service, God forgive me."

She placed herself every evening under Captain Michales's protection, like the other women, since her brother now spent every night with Eminé. "Instead of her becoming a Christian, he has turned Turk, God forgive me." So she thought, but never said it aloud.

The neighbours slept that night like hares, with their eyes hardly shut, and pondered how they could force the bars of their prison and get out.

In the morning trumpets sounded from the harbour. The Turks stood there, fez to fez, and covered the walls with red. Thrasáki, who had escaped from home, climbed up on the rocks at the harbour entrance and let his insatiable eye range far and wide. The rusty steamer lay at the quayside and was disgorging from its entrails bristling Anatolians with pock-marked faces, cannons and horses. Right at the end came a swarm of clamouring Dervishes in green skirts and pointed white hats, and with daggers in their belts. They clambered on to the mole, unrolled the green flag of the Prophet in front of the Harbour Gate, and began dancing round it, slowly, clapping their hands.

Thrasáki drew nearer. Suddenly the dance of the Dervishes became wilder, each of them spinning like a top, so that their robes stood out like bells. Their eyes began to redden. They drew their daggers and wounded themselves, so that blood spurted out. They howled loudly—but then their wildness subsided, they stuck their daggers back in their belts and moved more calmly. Their bellowing became half song, half speech, then speech, then a whispering, a soft and tender moaning.

At noon Thrasáki came home in great excitement and told his astonished listeners what he had seen.

"Weren't you frightened?" his father asked him, frowning.

"I wasn't frightened of the soldiers."

"The Dervishes?"

"Not of them, either."

"Of what, then?"

Thrasáki hesitated.

"Go on, say!" his father urged, tilting the child's bent face up by the chin.

"Of the green flag, Father!"

Megalokastro sank into darkness. In the first days after the landing of the troops a disquieting stillness reigned. The Christian elders went in and out of the Metropolitan's residence, the agas held secret councils now at the Pacha's *porte*, now in the noise-filled barracks. For one hour a day the three fortress gates were opened, and in came Turkish peasants with their hanums and worldly goods, excited and fearful. There was no more room for them in the mosques and tékés. They broke open the doors of Christian houses and took possession of these, after throwing the Christians out.

The Metropolitan sent Hadjisávas to Athens with letters in which he adjured the Greek brethren to send ships and save the

Christian Cretans from the knives which had already been drawn
by the Turks.

One evening the neighbours gathered early at Captain Michales's,
to come to a decision. No one was missing. Even Captain Polyxigis, Idomeneas, Tulupanas the baker, the black-clad grave-digger
Kolyvas, and Dr. Kasapákis with his French wife, had put in an
appearance. Only Archondúla and her deaf-mute brother were
absent. They had been told, but had not come She stood under
the Pacha's wing, and had no need of a Captain Michales. Her
brother had just, these days, done a portrait in oils of the Pacha.
He purposely kept the window on the street open, so that the
passers-by might admire the Pacha in the gold frame on the wall.
It was an unsurpassable likeness. Nothing was missing. Not even
the wart on his nose or the pig's bristles in his ears.

The gathering was taking place this time not in the yard but in
the house, to be secure from eavesdroppers. Captain Michales
was sullen. It displeased him to see that Circassian-Turkish fellow,
Captain Polyxigis, in his house.

Thrasáki sat with the men. "You sit with us," his father had
told him. "You're a man."

The silence lasted a long while, since the master of the house
did not open his mouth. Captain Polyxigis could bear it no longer.

"To what end have all the neighbours come here this evening?"
he asked, with an angry glance at his sister, who had dragged him
along. "The neighbours are going to decide," she had said, "what
they should do to save themselves from the Turks." But he, after
all, could decide nothing without Eminé. What these people here
did was no concern of his.

Captain Michales wanted now to raise his head and ask: "Why
are you here, Polyxigis Bey? Your neighbours live in the Turkish
quarter, your home is at the green door." But he controlled himself. The man was a guest in his house. It was against good manners
to provoke him like that. So he kept silence.

Then Tityros stepped in. He had been gaining in strength and
courage since the death of his wife. He now no longer felt in-
ferior to other men. He had proved that he too could kill, and
kill properly, so that the murdered man did not visit him at night.

His wife too had never troubled him in his sleep. The school-children had been the first to perceive his new strength: he stood no nonsense from them and beat them soundly. So now he spoke in place of his brother.

"We have gathered to decide how we propose to save ourselves from the Turks. Three courses lie before us. Either we stay quietly in our houses, and perhaps in that way prevent a massacre. Or we escape through the fortress gates and distribute ourselves among the villages. Or we wait to be fetched away by the Greek ships which the Metropolitan has asked for in Athens by Hadjisávas. Let us therefore examine which of the three courses is the most hopeful. And then let us adopt it, and may God come to our aid!"

Their chairs creaked, their heads bent, each one weighed his opinion. But they saw obstacles to each course, so the decision was hard.

The first to break the silence was Kasapákis the doctor—the fat, pock-marked peasant's son who had gone to Paris to study medicine. There he had attended lectures on law for three months, because he mistook them for lectures on medicine. When he had discovered his mistake and frittered away his father's vineyards, he had returned to Megalokastro with a broad-brimmed hat and with the daughter of his Parisian landlady, and had opened a grocery. Now he talked down at Tityros.

"There is a fourth course also, schoolmaster: that we should take refuge in the Consulates of the Great Powers!"

"Where will there be room enough for us, doctor?" retorted Krasojórgis. "You say 'consulates' and seem very pleased. But even a consulate is only a house with four walls. How many people will it hold? Perhaps two families. And what becomes of the rest?"

Mastrapas, that holy man, opened his mouth—but shut it again immediately from nervousness.

"Speak out, neighbour," Tityros encouraged him.

"What you decide . . ." stammered the bell-founder and went red.

"Listen to my view," said Krasojárgis, and stood up. With his belly filled and body unwashed, he had sweated with anxiety all

day, and now his body reeked of every smell a man can exude.
His wife gazed at him with pride. She liked to see her husband
excited like that.

"We're listening, Krasojórgis," said Tityros.

"Listen, then, to what I think. The safest course leads to the
villages. Are we to squat here as in a mousetrap? The Turks have
often slaughtered Greeks before now. Why wait for the ships?
Or shall we perhaps look for four-leafed clover? I put no trust in
Athens. The poor chaps there would like to, but they can't.
They're afraid of Turkey, they're afraid of the Franks. How often
have the Greeks not been——"

"But how escape, neighbour? Tell us that!" snorted Kolyvas.
"We've a heap of children."

"I put no trust in Athens," his neighbour went on. "But I do
trust Krasojórgis. Let me take command and, by the bread I eat,
I'll bring you all into the mountains—with your wives and children, your gear, your beds and your pots and pans!"

A murmur arose. All drew closer to Krasojórgis. He was now
silent, observing with pride the excitement his words had provoked among the neighbours. Just look! They had always despised him, because he was awkward and had no training and wore
patched boots. Now he would show them!

"Let's hear your plan!" said the doctor, who was injured because not enough consideration had been given to his proposal.
"Those are big promises, neighbour. I don't like that."

"Neither do I, doctor. But listen: I'm on good terms with the
soldiers who guard the Hospital Gate. Don't ask how and why!
A tiny bit of smuggling—two or three demijohns of raki, two or
three packets of tobacco, a string or two of sausages that I present
them with, so they'll keep their eyes shut. . . . Let's not go too
deeply into that. I'll grease the wheel again, and out we all slip,
unmolested."

"Long may you live, Krasojórgis," exclaimed Kolyvas. "I entrust you gladly with my children."

"Me, too," said Mastrapas, peering uneasily at his wife, to see
if she was in agreement.

At this moment there were three soft taps at the door.

"Ali Aga," said Tityros, and got up to open.

But Captain Michales raised his head.

"Throw him out!" he said.

Tityros opened the door. "Ali Aga," he said, "don't be angry with us, this evening we're having a meeting. Come tomorrow."

Ali Aga, however, stayed where he was, standing in the street door.

"I came to tell you that the agas are planning to kill you."

"For God's sake! When?"

"Soon. During the Bairam festival."

"Come in."

The little old man crossed the yard and leaned against the door-post.

"Good evening, neighbours," he said, in arrogant tones. To-day he was breaking a fearsome piece of news and was pluming himself with it. But suddenly he discerned Captain Michales on the corner of the settee, and collapsed.

"Forgive me," he said, "I'm in a hurry. But it was necessary to come. If you believe in God, neighbours, look out! The agas are planning a massacre before Bairam is over. They've already allotted the different parts of the town. The best palikares will come to ours, on account of Captain Michales."

"Good. Go," said Captain Michales, raising his hand. Here Mastrapas interposed: "Try to find out what you can, Ali Aga, and come here again tomorrow evening. Good-bye!"

The old man went across the yard and out through the street door, and glided off to the Turkish coffee-houses.

Captain Polyxigis stood up: "Excuse me, I have business this evening. My sister will tell me what you decide. All I wish to add is this: I shall go to the mountains—that is what honour demands."

"A good thing you remember it," growled Captain Michales.

Captain Polyxigis ran off at high speed. It was late. Eminé had certainly gone to bed already and was chewing mastic to prevent herself from going to sleep while she waited for him.

And now all turned to Captain Michales, to hear his opinion.

He was feeling relieved, now that the air was free from the scent of musk and Turkey. He raised his head.

"Neighbours," he said, "all of us here are men and have weapons. It would be shameful to leave Crete in the lurch in these most difficult days. So let us take the women and children into safety. Krasojórgis has said well. And after that, there is only one course for us: to arms! The schoolmaster, too, will come with us, and Mr. Idomeneas—all!"

Old Tulupanas had been twiddling his thumbs all this time, his head bent, and thinking about his son, whose face now had no nose, no ears, no lips. Where was he to go? Who would take him along? His appearance caused terror. And whoever touched him might be infected. The day before yesterday police had come to take him away to the lepers' village. The poor mother had screamed. The old man had pressed some silver coins into the hands of the sergeants and made them go away again.

Against his will a deep sigh escaped old Tulupanas, so that all turned towards him.

"What's the matter, neighbour? Why are you sighing?" they asked in astonishment.

"Nothing. . . . What should be?" he answered, while tears streamed from his eyes. "I'm not going out with you. Where can I go? Who will have me?"

He got up. No one raised a hand to hold him back. Stumbling, he found his way to the street door and disappeared.

"Agreed," said Tityros, "We've come to a decision. What is your view, Mr. Idomeneas? You haven't opened your mouth yet."

"You know my view. You all know it. I've expressed it again and again: everything you are saying and doing is froth and frills. . . . As long as Suda Bay remains . . ."

"Agreed!" exclaimed the doctor, suppressing a laugh. He grabbed for his enormous hat with a view to leaving, for it was nearly midnight.

"Doctor," said Captain Michales, "you are coming with us to the mountains . . ."

"But——"

"There's no 'but'! You're coming. That's what you're a doctor for. There'll be wounded."

The doctor looked at his wife. She was sitting at the other end of the divan and not understanding very well what was being said. She pressed her handkerchief to her mouth and coughed. The poor woman had become shrivelled and yellow. She was weary of seeing, time and again, the "Cretan railways" passing her door and fouling her doorstep. Paris was now no more than a far-off legend to her. Ah, if she could only get a aboard a steamer, a pinnace, a nutshell—anything to get away, anything to get away. . . .

Captain Michales stood up.

"What has been said will be carried out," he said, and went up to his small room. He had spoken too much and longed for solitude.

The neighbours breathed with relief. Tongues were loosened. The women, too, joined in the conversation. Renió appeared and brought the salver with raki, conserve and coffee.

"God guide this thing aright," said Krasojórgis, raising his glass. "To your health, Captainess. May you have joy in those you love. And your health, Renió!"

They clinked glasses. All drank. Renió poured out again. They were happy.

"What a drop of drink can do!" exclaimed Krasojórgis, smacking his lips. "A glass of raki, no bigger than a thimble, my soul upon it—but the whole of Turkey drowns in it! I can see, at the bottom of my glass—there lies the fat Sultan, dead!"

"It's not the raki that does it, it's the company," Tityros suggested.

"You're right, schoolmaster," said Mastrapas, his tongue too being at last loosed by the drink. "Men are like bells. If they are in tune, death has no terrors for them."

The bell-founder's ear was sensitive. Last summer he had been unable to sleep in his village during the first night: the bells of a flock, outside on the mountain, were not properly in tune together, and this set his soul jangling. Already at grey of dawn he got up, climbed the mountain, found the flock, tuned the bells, went home, lay down and slept.

"Like bells, so are men," he repeated. "Whether they're wooden rattles, or sheep-bells, or church-bells, small or large—each one has his own sound. A joy it is for the flock when their ringing got properly in tune by the master! It no longer fears the wolf."

But Mr. Idomeneas shook his head: what concern have I here? he thought, what sense has this talk?

He got up and beckoned to Tityros:

"Come, godson. Sleep in my house and keep me company."

He felt a strong need for some elevated conversation. The two of them would again discuss the stars and the immortality of the soul. No other questions existed for him in the world, only these two. At most Suda Bay could be placed beside them. All the rest was noise and smoke.

And now they all broke off. Some, to whom all those rakis had given courage, returned to their houses like palikares. Others stretched themselves out in the yard and on the veranda at Captain Michales's, and the women lay down in the bedroom. It was after midnight.

Thrasáki had listened all through the evening, without uttering a sound. But all the gestures of the neighbours had stamped themselves deeply in his brain—the frightened ones to begin with, then the calmer ones and finally, after the raki, the happy ones. The deepest impression was made on him by his father, who kept his head bent all the time and only raised it for a moment, when he uttered a sentence, to lower it again at once. This meant that he had no wish to imitate the garrulous heads around him. Through all these observations Thrasáki was ripening, without knowing it, into a man.

The schools had closed. Thrasáki rose early and joined his father in the shop. He liked to watch for every breath from his mouth. He was realising, gradually, why Captain Michales was so sparing of gesture, did not speak, did not laugh, despised men and women. One day he would be just like that. And not like Captain Polyxigis, or Krasojórgis, or Tityros. While all this was rumbling darkly inside him, he ran down towards the harbour. There he heard shouting and cursing. He quickened his pace and

came to the barber's shop of Signor Paraskevás. A crowd of
Turks was standing before it. In the middle of them he saw the
unfortunate man from Syra, whom they were abusing and spitting
at, at the same time drawing their knives. The poor man stood
there trembling, with his shirt torn and bloodstained, and his face
was covered with rotten eggs and tomatoes. He was assuring the
Turks that he would flee, go back to Syra and never set foot in
Crete again. Only they must have mercy on him and on his daughter, for whom he had to find a husband.

Thrasáki felt sorry for him and ran back to his father, whom he
found sitting at his table, bent over a letter to his nephew Kosmas
who had turned Frank: "If you are a man, if you have any feeling
of shame, leave the land of the Franks and think of your own
country. It needs you, the hour has come. What were you born
for? Why are you called a Cretan? Come at once, take up arms
like the other young men. There is another thing I must tell you,
nephew . . ."

At this point Thrasáki burst in, in great excitement:

"Father," he shouted, "they're trying to kill Paraskevás—in
front of his shop. Save him!"

Captain Michales rose and looked at what was happening from
his doorstep. A crowd of raving dockers had now pinioned
Paraskevás. Not a Christian was to be seen in the street. The
Greek shops round about were shut, their proprietors had
vanished. And Captain Michales could see several knives gleaming in the sun.

"Father, help him! You're not afraid?"

Captain Michales stared in front of him. The Turks were in
overwhelming numbers, to attack them meant certain death. But
he was ashamed before his son. He was sober-minded and did not
admire rash deeds. But now . . .

"Aren't you going, Father? Are you afraid?" his son asked
again.

"I'm going," said Captain Michales and approached the knot
of men.

He walked slowly and calmly forward, with a dispassionate
face, showing neither anger nor fear.

K

When the Turks saw him coming they stood still. What did the *giaour* want? Had he no fear of them?

Captain Michales reached them and raised his hand to bid them let him through. They moved aside, amazed. What was he going to do? Even the roughest of them lowered their knives.

Captain Michales went up to Signor Paraskevás and seized him by the ear, his expression suddenly scornful. He twisted the ear and shook the man:

"March! Home! Don't let my eyes catch sight of you any more!" he said peremptorily.

Paraskevás ducked his head between his shoulders and staggered forward. Captain Michales went with him, still twisting his ear. The Turks let them pass without a word.

"Back home!" Captain Michales repeated scornfully. "Quick!"

Paraskevás began to run, turned into the first turning, and vanished. The Turks remained where they were, staring after Captain Michales without doing anything, as he went slowly, with the same calm stride, back to his shop.

Thrasáki watched him in astonishment. He wanted to ask his father a question, but remained speechless. Captain Michales sat down again at his table, picked up the pen and bent forward to finish the letter:

"... nephew, that your Uncle Manúsakas ..."

IX

A T the end of the month of fasting came the festival of Bairam. The agas put on their best clothes and filled the coffee-houses, sitting enthroned there on soft cushions. The Turkish boys craned their slender necks and sang their long-drawn-out melodies. Because of the great heat Barba Jannis had ordered three ass-loads of snow from Psilorítis, and went running up and down with his bronze can to bring the agas refreshing coolness.

In the barracks near the Three Vaults the soldiers' trumpets resounded from early morning, and salvos were fired at the sky. The Pacha and the profusely braided officers betook themselves to the New Mosque, to prayers. The rings of lamps still burned on the minarets. In Hamidé Mula's téké the Saint's tomb was adorned with rosemary and basil. In front of it sat Efendína, cross-legged, singing verses from the Koran and swaying the upper part of his body to and fro. Round about the Saint, grey-haired worshippers knelt on mats. They had brought their nargiles with them and were smoking as, with eyes half-closed, they took up the responses from the Koran in a soft, bee-like hum.

These old people were profoundly happy and had already entered Paradise while still alive. They lacked none of the good things of life. Through the cracks in the door and the latticed wibdow in the wall the noise of Megalokastro came like a murmur of water and in the distance the sea roared. Old Hamidé Mula ran tirelessly hither and thither on bare feet, bringing now a piece of Turkish delight, now a small heap of glowing charcoal with which she carefully warmed the nargiles, so that they bubbled cheerfully like cooing doves in a circle round the Saint.

But while they were all sunk in this paradisal stupor, suddenly loud shouting rang out, doors creaked, women screamed and pistol-shots tore the air. Fled was divine blessedness. The grey-beards jumped up.

Efendína laid the Koran on top of the flowers and rushed to the

door to open it. Turks with knives between their teeth ran bellowing past. They had their chest and arms already spattered with the
blood of *giaours*.

Suleiman, the Pacha's enormous Arab, was hurtling along,
ahead of them all, with naked chest and naked feet. A yellow
burnouse waved about his shoulders. His eyes flashed, his full,
hanging lips foamed.

"Down with them! Down with them!" he bellowed, and made
his scimitar whistle through the air.

"Where are you off to, brothers? cried Efendína, craning his
head fearfully out of the door.

"To slaughter that wretched rascal, to drink his blood!" roared
the Arab.

"Whom, Suleiman?"

"Captain Michales."

Efendína blenched and cried:

"Have you no fear of God?"

But his voice was lost in the din that was rising from all the
Christian courtyards and houses. There doors were being batttered
in, women were climbing on to the flat roofs and some, in panic,
threw themselves off, with their children in their arms. Men stood
to arms for a moment—but then shots and blows and cries were
heard, and all had gone by.

Captain Michales was standing armed behind the door. He had
sent his family up to the bedroom and kept only Thrasáki with him.

"Come here," he said to him, "and listen carefully to what I
say. If they manage to smash our door and force their way in, I
shall kill you all, so that you shan't fall into their hands. And you
first, Thrasáki. Do you understand?"

"I understand, Father."

"And do you agree?"

"I agree."

"Don't tell them. They're women. They'll be afraid."

"I won't tell them anything."

The two men fell silent. They stood bolt upright behind the
door and listened intently to the noise from the street.

Some of the neighbours had already escaped some days before.

First of all Krasojórgis, Mastrapas and Kolyvas, with all their children. On the next day Penelope and Chrysánthe, Polyxigis's sister. They had disguised themselves as hanums. Tityros too had dressed up as a Turk, in baggy breeches and a white turban. He had stuffed his glasses down his chest and reeled out to the Hospital Gate. Tulupanas had stayed with his son. The doctor had hoisted the French flag, and Idomeneas had declared that he would not run away: he had placed the flags of the Great Powers above the fountain.

"When are we going, Father?" Thrasáki had asked, yesterday. He longed to get out to the fields and mountains.

"We're staying to the last of the whole neighbourhood."

"Why?"

"Think it out for yourself," his father had answered, and said not another word.

It was now mid-day. The cries of Megalokastro shrinking under the Turkish knives grew more and more hoarse. The muezzins climbed the minarets for the midday prayer and announced the lovingkindness of God.

Precisely at that moment five or six Turkish dockers came running to the Pervóla Garden and rammed Signor Paraskevás's door with an iron bar. They stormed into the house and found his daughter under the divan. They hauled her out and threw her on her back. . . . A couple of others discovered the unhappy barber hidden behind some jars, dragged him by the neck to the threshold and slaughtered him. Then they bundled up "Pervóla", who was streaming with blood, and rushed out with her.

Captain Michales heard shots from the direction of Idomeneas's fountain, at the end of the street.

"Here they come," he muttered, and cocked his gun. He turned round and looked at his son."

"Here they come," he said.

"Here they come," said Thrasáki likewise, and he too cocked his little pistol. In the last few days his father had taught him to shoot.

"Looks to me as if you're not afraid," said the father, gazing hard at his son.

"Why should I be afraid? I've learnt to shoot."

He straddled his legs, planted them firmly on the stones of the yard, and waited.

More and more shots went off. The Turks had now halted at Idomeneas's fountain. They leaned with their shoulders against the decayed door of the grand house, to burst it open.

Mr. Idomeneas had been sitting since early morning bent over his writing-table, composing a letter to the Great Powers:

"O ye Mighty of the World! In this moment, as I commit these lines to paper, the Christian population of Megalokastro is being slaughtered. Once more the air is ringing with shots; Turkish bandits are breaking open the doors of the Christians; they are dishonouring their women, they are killing the men, they are laying hold on the infants and smashing their heads.

I raise my voice. I am nothing, a man without consequence, lost on the rim of Europe, far away from you, ye Mighty of the World! Yet God stands close to me! He is angry, He is striding up and down the lonely room in which I write. He does not speak, He presses His lips together and waits to see the answer you will give me. You should know—I shall not send you another appeal after this. I have had enough of crying in the wilderness. If this time you send me no answer, I shall turn to God and—"

Here Mr. Idomeneas broke off. He heard the shots and craned his head far out of the window. He looked at the Turks straining against his door.

"What do you want?" he shouted. "Have you gone blind? Can't you see the flags of the Great Powers over the fountain?"

There were shouts and cat-calls. A stone grazed his ear and cheek, then smashed to fragments an old Venetian mirror on the wall beyond.

Mr. Idomeneas jumped back and put his hand to his ear. It was covered with blood. He smeared blood over the whole of his hand and pressed it upon the letter which he was preparing for the Great Powers.

"There, there, there!" he shouted, "That's how this letter ends. May the blood of Crete be upon your heads and upon the heads of your children and your children's children, England, France, Italy, Austria, Germany and Moscow!'

The door was now burst in, and the Turks rushed across the yard with their knives between their teeth. They knocked down old Doxaniá, who stood on the threshold of the door into the house and tried to bar its entry with her arms outstretched, and they trampled on over her. Yelling, they ran up the stairs. The tottering mansion trembled to its foundations.

Idomeneas, from his study, heard the wild horde approaching. The moment is come, he thought. Idomeneas, do not dishonour yourself!

He looked about him—he wanted to choose the manner of his death by his own free will. There were no weapons hanging on the walls. He needed none. He was not fighting with the sword but with the brain. The pen was his weapon. His decision was made. "I shall stay at my post, here," he muttered and struck the table with his fist. "Here's where I fight, here's where I shall die!" He sat down and grasped the pen. . . .

The Turks broke the door in with a kick and came to a standstill, amazed. They found Idomeneas calmly bent over a large, blood-stained sheet of paper.

"*Giaour*," they yelled, "where've you hidden your treasure?"

Idomeneas raised his head from the letter. "Here," he answered calmly, and pointed to his forehead.

One of them laughed:

"Is your head a money-box?"

"Slash it in two, Brainas—then we'll see what it's got inside!" yelled another.

And before Idomeneas had time to reply, the Turk split his head from brow to throat with one stroke of the scimitar.

They stormed through the whole house and flung old clothes, rags, chairs, tables and mattresses into the street.

As they turned the corner they met Suleiman the Arab, who with ten barefooted ruffians was on his way to Captain Michales's house.

"Where are you coming from?" asked Suleiman, stopping, breathless.

"From Idomeneas's fountain."

"You leave Captain Michales alone, or I'll drink your blood. He's reserved for me!"

He went to the fountain, splashed himself over with water, and drank greedily like a bull-calf. His sweating comrades also drank. One of them looked through the splintered door and saw an old woman stretched out on the stones of the yard, keening for the dead and tearing her hair.

"Shall we kill her?" he asked a comrade who had joined him.

"Too dull, Mustafa."

"On!" the Arab now shouted.

They rushed down the street, clashing their scimitars against one another arrogantly.

Behind the door Captain Michales heard the crew approaching and recognised the wild voice of the Arab.

"They're looking for me," he thought, and kneeled down behind the water-trough, using it as a parapet. He pulled down Thrasáki to kneel beside him.

"Christ will conquer," he whispered, crossing himself.

He turned to his son: "Courage, my child," he said.

It was the first time Thrasáki had heard his father speak gently and call him "my child". He went all red with pleasure.

The rabble was now before the door. The Arab was distributing instructions: one man was to climb on to the bent backs of two comrades and so on to the wall and then jump down into the yard, while the others smashed in the door. "But no one's to lay a finger on Captain Michales! He belongs to me. He's unsulted me. I'm going to have my revenge on him—drag him to the plane-tree, hack him in pieces and throw his flesh to the dogs of Megalokastro to eat."

Thrasáki heard the threat and looked at his father, who had already aimed the barrel of his gun at the top of the wall.

"Did you hear, Father?" he asked.

"Silence!" whispered Captain Michales through his teeth, without turning.

Outside, silence had fallen for a moment. A scraping on the wall was heard, and heavy breathing. Someone was climbing up.

Captain Michales ducked down completely behind the trough. Only his gun-barrel showed. With his left hand he had pushed Thrasáki behind him.

Suddenly a wild, shaggy head emerged above the wall. Between the teeth a broad-bladed knife flashed. The man glanced stealthily over the yard. Now a hand was stretched out. . . . Captain Michales pressed the trigger. The bullet struck the man full between the eye-brows.

Up above, in the bedroom, crouching behind the window-sill, the Captain's wife was giving suck to her baby, while Renió watched her father and Thrasáki in the yard through the cracks of the shutter. When she saw the Turk's head vanish, she thrilled with delight.

"Hail to those hands of yours, Father!" she whispered, full of admiration.

"Renió, my poor child," said the Captain's wife, "our life is hanging by a hair. Do you know what your father's thinking of doing?"

"If the Turks get in, he'll kill us. And he'll be quite right."

"You ought to be a man," said her mother, looking at her daughter with terror. "Aren't you afraid?"

"We've got to die sometime, Mother. Let's die without dishonour."

Their conversation broke off. But what was happening down in the street? A violent rushing to and fro, fresh shouting, fresh cursing.

"Isn't that Efendína's voice?" said Renió, and cautiously opened the shutter.

It was in fact Efendína. When he had seen the raving Arab rushing in the direction of Captain Michales's, his heart had contracted. He loved Captain Michales, even though he compelled him twice a year to debase himself. Perhaps he loved him just because of that. What would Efendína's life be without this monster of a Greek? "What other pleasure have I in the world, wretch that I am?" he wondered. "My mother beats me, the people of Kastro—Turks and Christians—pelt me with lemon-peel. I've no money, no wife, no hero's courage, nothing. Nothing, except

K*

Captain Michales. I count the days and the months. Every six months a great pleasure comes round to me again, and a great sin. And who knows? God is merciful, God is bountiful: perhaps I too may become a saint the day after my death. And they will erect my tomb by the side of my grandfather's. God bless Captain Michales! Without him, would I have any chance left of becoming a saint?"

His heart rebelled. "No, no, I won't let them kill my Captain Michales! What a noble, what a lusty man he is! What wine he has in his casks! What sausages, what chickens and sucking pigs!"

Efendína's head caught fire. He leapt up and darted in pursuit of the Arab. He even forgot that the streets were broad streams, and crossed them without hesitation, to rescue his friend. On Broad Street a band of booty-laden Turks called out to him: "Where are you running to, Efendína? Who's after you?"

They formed a chain and barred his passage.

Efendína halted, out of breath and bewildered. The Arab would by now surely have arrived before the house—he would now be smashing the door in and killing Captain Michales.

"Do you recognise no God above you?" he whimpered. "Let me through! It's urgent, brothers!"

A flash passed through Efendína's brain. He looked over his shoulder and screamed:

"Saint Menas!"

The Turks burst out laughing.

"You godless people, why are you laughing? Can't you hear his horse's hoofbeats? I saw him ride out of the church. And he terrified me. Can't you hear him? There he is! There he is!"

The Turks' hair stood on end. Did they really hear the jingle of harness? Was that a horseman approaching?

"There he is!" screamed Efendína afresh, with his eyes starting. "There he is!"

But the Turks did not once turn to look. They ran away.

When Efendína saw them running, he stood transfixed with dread. Had he become so powerful that he could make it true? he wondered. Had he not already, in the last rising, seen him chase away the Turks who were trying to force their way into his church?

He broke out in a cold sweat. Now he could distinctly hear the horse approaching.

"Allah! Allah!" With this cry he gathered up his clothes and ran for all he was worth.

As he came past Idomeneas's fountain he saw how they were just on the point of bursting open Captain Michales's street door. He rushed up to them.

"Look out, children!" he screamed. "He'll gobble us up! He's coming on horseback."

"Who, you idiot?" roared the Arab.

"The neighbour."

"What neighbour?"

"Saint Menas. There he is!"

They all wheeled round. Everything was dancing before their eyes. They could distinguish nothing.

"There he is! There he is!" Efendína cried, turning away. He clung to Captain Michales's door like one possessed, as though he wanted to hide, so as not to be found by the eyes of the Saint riding by. He must already be past Idomeneas's fountain. He could recognise him distinctly, with that never-changing form of his, just as the ikon showed him: sunburned, with white hair and beard, on a purple-red horse with a golden saddle. The air round about Idomeneas's fountain was all filled with white hair, red horse and golden harness.

"There he is! He's in sight!" he whispered, and his jaw was quivering.

"Where is he? I can't see properly!"

"Can't you see him? There he is! Dark, with white hair and a red horse. . . . He's seen us. Now he's making for us!"

With a leap he left the door and was running for the harbour. Behind him, panting, the Turks followed, as fast as they could. They too heard the horse now—it was after them—and the Arab, turning round for a moment, made out, on the horse, in the air, a rider.

"Run, children! Run!" he yelled. His yellow burnouse fluttered away from him, but he had no time to pick it up.

Out of breath, they reached the harbour. They wiped the sweat off, crouched down in the shade, let their tongues hang out, and sniffed like dogs. Efendína had collapsed with his face to the ground and lay there twitching.

Megalokastro groaned under the knives of the Turks. The Christians raised their hands in entreaty to God. The Metropolitan crossed himself. He could no longer sit and listen to the slaughtering of his flock. "God be with me," he murmured, and stood up. He clapped his hands, and Múrzuflos appeared.

"I'm going to the Pacha," he said. "Bring me my great robe."

"Are you going out in the streets, Mylord?" asked Múrzuflos. "The Turks are raging. I'm coming with you."

"I shall go alone, Múrzuflos. Help me to robe myself."

He wrapped the golden stole about him and set the imperial mitre on his lion head. He grasped the tall crozier with its two intertwined loops. . . . "In God's name," he said.

Múrzuflos gazed at him, full of admiration. A marvellous apparition, a towering form, the beard a stream of snow, the eyes blue, benevolent and flashing. It would be like the Metropolitan that Múrzuflos would paint God the Father, clothed with golden clouds and in the act of plunging down upon Megalokastro to put an end to the massacre.

The main door of the Residence was thrown open. Upon its marble lintel was inscribed in large black letters: "In this doorway the Turks hanged the Metropolitan of Megalokastro in the year 1821. Everlasting be his memory."

"Everlasting be his memory," murmured the Metropolitan, as he crossed the threshold.

Múrzuflos's eyes were wet. "God and Saint Menas be with you, Mylord," he said, in a trembling voice.

"Be of good cheer, Múrzuflos. I am neither the first nor the last," replied the Metropolitan, pointing at the black inscription.

He crossed the forecourt of the church and greeted Saint Menas with bowed head as he passed his door. Then he strode off with masterful bearing in the direction of the Pacha's *porte*.

Múrzuflos watched him departing to his lonely battle with death. He felt ashamed of having let him go alone. "This is the moment," he muttered, "when it will be seen whether you, Múr-zuflos, have a soul in you, or only a stomach." He crossed himself and slipped off after the Metropolitan.

Megalokastro was filled with din. The Christians were scream-ing, the Turks were roaring and laughing. In between, one could distinguish the keening for the dead.

The Metropolitan strode onwards, and his heart contracted at what he heard. "How long will the people of the Hellenes," he sighed, "hang from the cross. We are men, Christ, we are not gods like You. We cannot bear it. Bring the resurrection at last!"

He could feel Megalokastro with its walls, houses and human beings like his own body, and wherever a door was smashed in, wherever a woman beat her breast, his heart jerked and hurt.

From the market-place a crew of bloodstained, very drunken Turks was approaching. When they caught sight of the gold-clad Metropolitan, they halted amazed. "What sort of a beast is that," they growled. "Where's he going? Draw aside, God help you, or he'll trample us down!"

The Metropolitan was going with even steps to meet death. His eyes, filled with sorrow and anger and thirst for martyrdom, saw nothing. Neither streets, nor men, nor—to right and left—the Greek shops. He was dominated by one thought: "O the sweet happiness, if I should be killed to set my people free!" How did it go—that word of agony of Christ on the Cross, of which the Gospel told? "Eli! Eli!" That means: "Joy! Joy!" in the language of sacrifice. "Eli! Eli!" whispered the Metropolitan likewise, and the nearer he came to the Pacha's seraglio, the more he quickened his pace. And behind him glided Múrzuflos like a dog.

He reached the huge plane-tree, glorious in cool, rustling green. Its trunk was flecked like a leopard-skin. The Metropolitan's eyes were dancing, and he saw thousands of Christs dangling from it like fruit.

Two soldiers before the Pacha's gate crossed their rifles and would not let him through. Then came Múrzuflos running, who understood Turkish and spoke to them. They raised their guns, and the Metropolitan entered. Now Múrzuflos went ahead, to open the doors.

When the Pacha caught sight of the Metropolitan, he made a peevish face. He had been leaning out of the window to listen to Megalokastro bewailing the dead. Even he, the good-natured Anatolian, had gone savage. Perhaps it was the ancient Turkish thirst for Greek blood that had awoken in him. And yet he felt ashamed that he, as Pacha, had not the courage to order a halt, to strike the knife from the hands of the agas.

The Metropolitan stood on the threshold, filling the doorway.

"Have you no fear of God, Pacha?" he shouted.

"Why have you dressed yourself up in gold for me, *giaours'* priest?" replied the other, angrily. "Are you hoping to terrify me?"

"Have you no fear of God?" the Metropolitan shouted afresh, and raised a finger threateningly towards the sky. "Does the shedding of blood not concern you? And where will it fall, do you suppose? Upon your head!"

"Hey, don't yell so, Metropolitan! The plane-tree stands before you!"

"God stands before me. I am not afraid."

The Pacha moved away from the window, paced to and fro and at length stopped in front of the Metropolitan. He looked him up and down and could not think what line to take with him. He imagined him in all his gold and crosses dangling from the plane-tree, but dread seized him. And yet this insolent Greek mouth must be stopped, he thought. It was not to be endured! He barked at the Metropolitan:

"Don't make me lose my temper. Go! I'm telling you out of kindness. I'm not afraid of anybody!"

The Metropolitan left God on one side and brought the Sultan into play.

"Very well, you have no fear of God. But what about the Sultan? You know that Crete causes him anxiety. He means to have peace here, and that is why he sent you. And what has your Worship done? Allowed a massacre! And the massacre will bring a rising in its train. And the rising will attract Moscow. Forgive me, Pacha Effendi, but I see your head on the point of falling."

The Pacha froze. He too saw his head on the point of falling.

"What am I to do, then?" he asked, fearfully.

"Don't lose a moment, order the soldiers to sound their trumpets, as a signal that the slaughter is to stop. Give orders! Threaten! You're the Pacha! Show it!"

The Pacha clutched his head with both hands as if it needed propping up:

"Cursed be the hour in which I first set foot on this Devil's island of yours!" he shouted at length.

He looked imploringly at the Metropolitan.

"My lord Metropolitan," he said, "why are you standing there on the threshold? Come in and sit down, so that we can discuss how this thing can be brought to an end."

"While we are talking, Christians are being slaughtered. I cannot sit down. First call the soldiers and give the orders! Until I hear the trumpets I shall not sit down! Neither shall I go away."

"The Devil take you! Damn the lot of you, you Cretans! Bad and good together!"

Furiously he went out into the ante-chamber. His oaths could be heard, and the noise of officers rushing past with their scimitars and spurs.

The Metropolitan, standing there on the threshold, sighed: "God has not found me worthy to hang in the doorway of the Residence. Never mind. It is enough that the Christians will be saved."

The Pacha came back, mopping his brow: "Now you'll hear the trumpets," he said. "Go! I've had enough of this business. I don't want to see anyone now. Is it earth I'm standing on, or a powder-barrel?"

At that same moment Captain Michales turned to Thrasáki. He had been kneeling close to his father and listening to what was happening in the street—Efendína's cries, the Arab's curses, the steps of the men running away, and now the sudden stillness, which settled over the whole quarter. Only a sound of keening came from Idomeneas's fountain.

"Are you hungry, Thrasáki?"

"Yes, I'm hungry, Father."

"Then tell your mother she's to come down and get a meal. I think our work's done for to-day."

He propped his gun against the step of the trough and felt for his tobacco-box, to roll a cigarette. He heard the keening again. His fingers stopped where it was. He listened.

"They've killed poor Idomeneas," he thought, "and now his old nurse is keening for him."

He shook his head. Was that a man? What resistance could he have put up? He must have yelled and been slaughtered by them like an Easter lamb.

And as he stuck down the cigarette, now rolled, there was a sound of trumpets, and heavy, measured steps became audible. Captain Michales stood up and cautiously opened the door. About twenty soldiers with shouldered arms marched past, on patrol. A crier ran at their head, calling out: "Peace! Peace! Come out of your houses, Christians!"

Next day the Pacha issued a command: "What has happened has happened. Destiny so willed it. But now peace is to reign, not a nose is to bleed any more! The fortress-gates are to be opened, the Christians may come back from the villages, the Musulman farmers may go back to the villages. And those who have gone out into the villages to resist are to lay down their arms and take up their work again. Not a hair of their heads will be touched. The Sultan is merciful and pardons. Musulmans and Christians, by my good will, listen to the words of the Pacha. For in my fore-court stands the plane-tree, and the noose is waiting for the disobedient!"

The Turks wiped their knives clean and once more sat cross-legged in the coffee-houses, smoking their nargiles and listening with half-closed, sunken eyes to the chubby-faced Turkish boy as he sang the long-drawn-out melodies in his womanish voice. The Christians ventured out from their houses, gathered up the murdered and summoned Kolyvas from his village. Múrzuflos too, and Kajabés, Vendúsos, Furógatos and others set their brawny arms and compassionate souls to the picks, and began to make big trenches in the cemetery before the Kanea Gate. Others dug in the churchyard of the Sinai Church of Saint Matthew, hard by the Pervóla.

Manóles the pope, panting and with his shirt-sleeves rolled up, laid the dead together by fives, spoke the prayers in haste, commended them to Heaven and turned his attention to the next five.

During three days the men dug graves, during three days the women washed doorsteps and bedrooms clean of blood and mourned in silence, that the agas might not hear and be enraged afresh. For in their glance and gait one could discern the after-tremors of the massacre.

On the fourth day Captain Michales called his son into his small room and said to him:

"Thrasáki, the time for the rising has come. Let the Pacha say what he will, he's an Anatolian, he understands nothing. Once Crete has caught fire, it isn't easily put out. Do you understand?"

"I understand, Father. It isn't easily put out."

"So tomorrow, first thing, we men must get the women and children out of Megalokastro. I'll go at the head, you bring up the rear. Understand?"

"Can I keep the pistol?"

"What? Do you suppose we shall be unarmed? We're going to your grandfather's. Tell your mother to get ready."

In the afternoon Captain Michales rode on his mare to the Hospital Gate and out, and reached the widow's inn. He dismounted and called for the merry widow. She emerged, plump, bowing and scraping.

"I'm leaving my mare here this evening. Feed her well. I shall fetch her tomorrow morning. Get ready for me three asses as well."

"You're taking to the open, Captain Michales?" the widow asked, slowly and ostentatiously buttoning her bodice. "Does that mean the massacre isn't over?"

"It's only beginning now," he answered, and without lingering started on the walk back, striding swiftly so as to find the fortress-gates still open.

It was now full summer. A south wind was blowing from the Libyan desert and whirling a blinding dust along the road. Cap-

tain Michales kept his face turned to the right, towards the sea,
to get some cool. Over there he could see the uninhabited island
of Dia, quite bare, rose-pink and shaped like a turtle swimming
in the sea. Some time ago, in a mood of depression, he had taken
a boat, set the sail, and after some hours reached the deserted
island, all alone. He had landed there, at the little, stony All
Saints' Harbour. He had made his boat fast and climbed upwards
in the oppressive heat. The cliffs glowed, the air danced. Two sea-
gulls flew over his head, swooped down and screeched in amazement, almost grazing him. Between boulders the frisking rabbits
sat up and eyed him. Captain Michales strode right to the peak
and looked about him: loneliness, the island a heap of stones, and
on all sides the sea, deep blue, with wild waves. The air pure—
human breath had not yet spoiled it.

"That's where I'd like to live," he thought. "On those cliffs.
I'm sick of fresh water and green grass and human beings."

Quickening his pace he reached the fortress-gate and passed
through. A few corpses were still lying in the alleys; there was a
stench of corruption. He stopped in front of Furógatos's small
house and pushed the door open. He went into the miserable
hovel and looked around. No one. "Hey! Anybody there?" he
called.

From one corner he caught a high, timid little voice, like some
bird's. And slowly, out of a large, bulging cloak there arose,
gleaming in the dusk, the little, bald head of the terrified Bertódulos.

"Who's there? Who's there?" he asked, as though blinded by
fear.

"Don't be afraid, Mr. Bertódulos. It's I."

The man recognised Captain Michales, and his heart went back
into its right place.

"Welcome, noble sir!" he said, raising his hand as though to
take off his hat and greet him.

"Are you ill, Mr. Bertódulos? Your teeth are chattering. Are
you cold?"

"No, Captain. I'm frightened."

"Aren't you ashamed?"

"No, Captain, I'm not ashamed."

He wrapped himself in his cloak, sat upright and leaned back against the wall.

He crossed himself. "*Kyrie eleison*," he said. "It passes my understanding how a man can take a knife and kill another man! I don't understand it. I couldn't even kill a lamb. Did I say a lamb? Would you believe it, Captain? Cutting up a cucumber makes me shudder."

"Where's Furógatos?"

"God protect him, Captain. What am I to say? A heart of gold. When the massacre broke out, he fetched me from my little room. I couldn't walk for terror. He took me on his arm, and with his lyre over his shoulder we set off. In the streets what Turkish ruffians there were, Captain! What moustaches! What legs! I hid my face in my cloak, so as to see nothing. He didn't put me down till we reached the water-trough in his yard. His wife rushed out, saw the lyre, looked at me and shrieked like a demon: 'They're trying to murder us, and you carry lyres about with you?' She regarded me too as a lyre! But God was merciful to us. Next day she went off to her village and we were rid of her."

Furógatos now appeared.

"Welcome, Captain Michales, to my poor hovel. I know what you want from me. I've come direct from your house. When?"

"Tomorrow. Call Vendúsos and Kajabés too. War, too, is a feast. I'm inviting you."

"That's fine, Captain. But what about him?" said Furógatos, pointing to Bertódulos.

Bertódulos was listening with his eyes wide. He understood what these two Cretans were talking about: guns, mountains and hiding-places. His teeth began to chatter again.

Captain Michales looked down at the good-natured old man, who had now muffled himself up completely.

"We'll take him too," he said. "One human being more won't do any harm. He'll come as a guest."

The Count stretched out his head, and the last five or six hairs on it were standing on end.

"Into the mountains?" he screamed. "With the guns?"

"No. With the women and children. You'll gossip with them and make them forget everything," said Captain Michales, and strode to the door. "Till we meet again."

"Where are we meeting, Captain?" Furógatos asked.

"Up on Selena, above Petrokéfalo, in old Séfakas's sheep-pen."

He went out and passed through a narrow alley. Barba Jannis was on the way home with his empty bronze can, tired and depressed. When he saw Captain Michales he stopped.

"Captain," he said, "a deal of blood has flowed. Let's think how we are to avenge it."

But Captain Michales shoved him on one side. He had no taste for idiots and half-idiots.

He halted once more by Captain Stefanés wretched dwelling. The self-willed ship's-master was sitting by himself on his small sofa, darning. As an old palikare he was well up in all sorts of woman's work. Every day he swept his little house as if it were a ship's deck, and filled Saint Nicholas's lamp with oil, although in the hour of stress the saint had not stirred a foot to come to his help and save his *Dardana* from going to the bottom. "The poor thing can't always get to all the ships that are in distress at sea! He's a right, all the same, to the oil he consumes." So he said, and filled the little lamp, every morning, to the brim.

Now he raised his eyes from his needle.

"Welcome, Captain Michales," he said, bowing. "What wild north wind has blown you here?"

Captain Michales gazed at him in silence.

"I understand," said Stefanés. "You're getting ready to take to the open and you're getting your band together. . . . But if you were thinking of adding me to your list, cut me out."

"You too are getting ready for the open, though, I think. Come with me, Captain Stefanés."

"Cut me out, I tell you. I'm no good on dry land. The base earth requires legs, and I'm a hobbler. I'm going to Syra, to the Cretan Committee. They're giving me a ship."

He turned to the ikon: "Are you listening, Saint Nicholas? Don't play me another trick, like last time!"

"Good-bye then, Captain Stefanés. If I don't ever see you again, forgive me, and may God forgive you."

The sea-wolf laughed:

"That's just what Polyxigis said to me the day before yesterday. . . . You fool, I'm not going to die yet. I don't need any farewells."

His mocking old eyes twinkled as he called after Captain Michales, who was on his way to the door:

"Hey, Captain Michales, Polyxigis has beaten you to it. He has already hoisted the banner and set up his headquarters in the big Turkish village, Kasteli. He's got his little hanum with him too, so they say."

Captain Michales stood still. His face darkened. The world swayed around him. He had gripped the iron latch, and the nails with which it was fixed to the door gave. As if the house was falling, he gave a leap and rushed out into the street.

"Hey, Captain Wildboar, just call: 'Eminé!' and she'll come to you."

Next morning they started. At their head Captain Michales with the pistols and knives stuck well down in his leather belt. He had also flung his thick woollen cloak about him. Behind him the Captainess, erect and fearless, with the infant in her arms. By her side Renió, with a cloth in which were wrapped her best clothes and her mother's trinkets. Bringing up the rear Thrasáki, straining to appear taller than he was. Ali Aga had gone ahead, an hour earlier, with two asses, and was waiting by the Three Vaults.

The soldiers were standing with dark faces and watching the fortress gate, with their arms shouldered. Noisy bands of peasants were pressing in, and the vault of the gate was ringing once more with shouting and neighing. Captain Michales opened out his cloak and held it before his face, as if to shield it from the dust. He slid close along the wall and escaped in the crowd. "Hurry up! Hurry up!" Thrasáki ordered the women, and himself squeezed through, playing the indifferent meanwhile and whistling.

Towards evening they arrived at the patriarchal farmhouse of Captain Séfakas, the grandfather.

They found in the front yard a seething mass of grandchildren,

male and female. Here, during the bloody days in Megalokastro,
they had been getting on with the vintage and had gathered the
grapes into the huge winepress in the yard. And now sturdy lads,
naked to the waist, were treading the grapes, tipsy with the smell
of the must.

Captain Michales's nostrils quivered joyfully. This scent of
grape-juice seemed to him sweet as blood. "Greetings, nephews,"
he shouted, and the Captainess turned in amazement towards her
husband. His voice had sounded gay to her.

They walked into the middle of the yard. The grandfather came
forward to greet them. He stretched out his lean arms from his
wide-sleeved white shirt.

"Welcome, children, and grandchildren!" he said. "Eat and
drink. All is yours."

"I'll hand over to you your daughter-in-law and grandchildren,"
said Captain Michales. "I'm going into the mountains.'"

"All right, Michales! You were a wild colt from a child. You
still haven't grown prudent."

"I shall grow prudent only when Crete is freed."

"Then," said the grandfather, joking. "it were better not freed.
If you become prudent, it'll make no difference whether you're
alive or dead!"

Father and son jested so, with affectionate hard hitting, until
the huge table had been laid inside the house. The old man's
daughters-in-law and grandchildren, left him by dead and living
sons of his, went in and out. The ground floor, the yards, the bedrooms upstairs and the flat roofs were full of his family. In these
perilous days they had all gathered from the neighbouring villages
under the old man's magnanimous protection. With them also
their asses and mules, cattle and dogs and sheep. Now Captain
Michales's mare joined them.

The neighbouring villages were astir when the arrival of Captain Michales became known. Next day he rode out on his mare
and made the round of his command, to stoke up the rebellion.

"A lot of blood has flowed in Megalokastro, brothers!" he
cried from his horse in the centre of each village. "A lot of blood!
Honour demands that we should avenge it. Forward! To arms!"

He left the villages behind and climbed up Selena. In front of his father's pen he planted his banner—a piece of black cloth with red letters: FREEDOM OR DEATH. He sent two palikares up to the peak of the mountain, to light a fire there. And they did not come down until they had passed the signal on to the other crests to east and west, so that the message was taken up and the fire carried further.

Thodóres too heard from his sentinels that his uncle had arrived. When they met, he kissed his hand.

"Thodóres, you madcap, didn't I tell you you were to stay in your nest? But you, a beardless lad, were in a hurry and disobeyed me. Take your banner down, fold it up and hide it in your breast. Unfold it only if I'm killed."

The captains of eastern Crete saw the beacons, understood the message and gathered in the sheep-pens of old Séfakas. Captain Michales sent his father a message, asking him for permission to slaughter his sheep to feed the leaders.

"It is great luck for my sheep to be fodder for captains," answered the grandfather. "Only don't touch the big bell-wether —the black one. I'm keeping him for my funeral."

On the fifteenth of August, the royal festival of the Assumption of the Virgin, the captains sat down together in a row in the open space of the large pen, while the sheep were being turned on the spits. That day the grandfather also had climbed the mountain on foot, to take part in the national assembly.

In all they were fourteen. Each one of them had his story, which surrounded him like an aura. There were three immortals in this assembly. A throne had been erected for them. A wide bench covered with sheeps' fleeces. To right and left of them, on stones, sat the younger ones—those under seventy.

On the big bench in the middle sat the grandfather. A hundred-year-old lion with a flowing beard, which now covered his open, shaggy chest and wound-scars from the great rising. Thick, bristling eyebrows shaded his eyes—so that he had to stroke them back if he wanted to see. In spite of his many years his cheeks had remained fiery red, and when he grew angry one could see the blood throbbing in his temples. His arteries had nowhere gone chalky; tirelessly they gave drink to that aged body. And it was still thirsty and drank, full of eagerness. He had not yet had enough of the world. He touched, heard, saw, tasted and smelled it with the same longing as a twenty-year-old. He saw men and women as tiny creatures swarming about his feet. He was sorry for them and laid his hand on their heads to instil courage into them. It was no pleasure to him that human blood should be shed. But, as soon as it came to a fight, his eyes grew troubled and he forgot that the Turks too were human beings—his hands never wearied of slaying them.

The peasants honoured him like an oak, and would come on Sundays and high feast-days to the village square, to sit at his feet. In his old age he resembled one of the ancient gods, the immortals. When the elders of Crete assembled to deliberate about freedom and death, they made him sit in the centre, and when the captains stood up to speak, they looked at him.

To the right of the grandfather, in to-day's assembly, sat yet another wild beast, Captain Mándakas. His hair and beard were short, his neck thick, his bone-structure clumsy, his face furrowed with scars from Turkish scimitars. He had an ear missing, bitten off by a Turk in the year 1821. He had also two fingers of the left hand missing, having himself as a young man hacked them off with his axe, because a poisonous snake had bitten them. To him it was a pleasure to see Turkish blood flow. Every time Crete took up arms again, he had hurled himself blindly on the Turkish soldiers. He had stormed through the Turkish villages—plundered, burned and escaped. He killed Turkish women too, but would have nothing to do with them. He had been a tremendous wencher, but as long as war lasted he had kept away from them. He would not even touch his own wife, as long as he was carrying a gun. If he saw her coming from a distance, bringing him food or cartridges, he would shout at her: "Don't come near me, damn you! Don't inflame me! Put it all on a dish and go away!" But when the war adventure was over he would rush in festive delirium from village to village, and into many embraces. Now, though, as a greybeard, the one pleasure remaining to him was that he could swagger along to an assembly of the captains with his silver pistols and with the scars on his chest.

On the left of the grandfather lolled Captain Katsirmas, the pirate. Tall and thin like a ship's mast, clean-shaven, sunburned, squinting, he had neither the mighty, lordly style of the grandfather nor the heroic verve of Captain Mándakas. He was a difficult man to get on with and full of bitter accusations against God. He had always played a lone hand and relied only on himself. But his strength too was now gone.

The other eleven captains sat in a single row on the boulders. They were still young—only seventy or under. One of them was an abbot from the Monastery of Christ the Lord, with blue eyes and a flowing beard. Another was a schoolmaster from Embaro. This was a misshapen, shrivelled bit of a body which no one could set eyes on without asking: "What's that rabbit doing in the gathering of the beasts of prey?" But he had to be seen in battle, when his spirit caught fire. He had to be known at a drinking-bout, when he played the lyre so as to set the stones a-dancing. And when people heard him speak, they felt like praying to God: "Give me ten ears, that I may hear it all."

Captain Polyxigis too had come, good-humoured and self-contented, with his silver pistols and with a silk scarf smelling of musk, a present of Eminé's. He sat down next to Captain Michales. Their eyes met, but they did not speak to one another.

Some had said that Tityros also ought to be invited, for he too had become a wild beast. He had put away his books and now swept through the villages, to speak in the churches on Sundays and set men's hearts on fire. But the grandfather had opposed this: "He's never done a thing in his life, only talked," he had said. "Captain's work is hard. Besides—and that settles it—he's still too young."

All eyes were now turned upon the ancient. He rose, stretching out his bony arms in their white sleeves. His voice boomed darkly:

"Welcome, Captains, to my mountains. Two things a Cretan has, and they are all he possesses: God and his gun. In the name of God and our guns I open this meeting to-day. Once more we have to speak about Crete. Let each man stand up and say freely what he thinks. But first, will the holy Abbot of Christ the Lord give the blessing?"

The Abbot had already donned his priestly stole. He went over to a boulder, in a hollow of which there was still some rain-water. He bent down and plucked a sprig of thyme. With this he performed the sprinkling of the holy water. Then he began to say the prayers, while the captains rose to their feet and took off their fezes and head-bands. They heard, without precisely understanding, the words in church language: God, victory over the barbarians, justice, mercy. They had no need of such ideas, for in Captain Séfakas's sheep-pen they saw Crete in the flesh: a mother in mourning, barefooted, starving, bloodstained. They raised their hands to Heaven and prayed for their children.

They crossed themselves and sat down again. For a while no one managed to speak. Their throats seemed swollen and speech bitter—it would not come forth. Once more the grandfather was the first to raise his head, and looking to his right he said:

"Captain Mándakas, you ate powder out of your spoon as a child. You've been fighting all through two generations. Your spirit may have been a bit giddy at first, but with age it's grown clear. Speak, then! Let's know what you've got to say."

"The younger ones should speak," he answered.

The grandfather turned to his left:

"What have you got to say, Captain Katsirmas? You too have been fighting for two generations, at sea. You've seen and suffered a great deal. Your opinion has weight. Speak."

"I have no word to say," came the answer, sullenly. "When a man's no strength any longer, he's no longer anything to say. The young ones should speak."

"Very well, then, the young ones!" the grandfather exclaimed, folding his hands over his pistols and preparing to listen.

The Abbot of Christ the Lord stood up. He was short and square-built. His cheeks, his forehead, his muscular arms and his throat had been scored with scimitar-strokes and pierced by bullets. He directed his gaze at Captain Michales:

"Captain Michales," he said, "I think the first word is yours by right. You have called us together. You have escaped from the massacre and you at once sent out the invitation. What, then, have you to say to us?"

Captain Michales stood up. His blood was racing. He leaned on his gun:

"Brothers, captains, you know very well I can't spin speeches. So I'll speak bluntly, drily and soberly: forgive me. Once again the noose is tightening around Crete. Soldiers and dervishes have come by ship; the Turks are growing arrogant and are slaughtering our brothers in Megalokastro. We are no lambs. The blood of the killed is crying out. Arise, captains! Freedom or death!"

So he said, and sat down.

The captains wagged their heads, and by two and threes put them together. The aged Kambanáros, the first of the elders of the communes, rose. The murmuring died down. The speaker was well known for his clear reasoning. He was a man of measure. As soon as he stood up in an assembly to speak, the hot-heads frowned in expectation of the cold water he would pour over them, while the respectable ones breathed again.

"Kill the king, but don't threaten him!" he exclaimed, and threw a severe glance at Captain Michales. "When, in God's name, shall we learn discretion? How often have we uttered threats, but never have we had the strength to carry them through and to force the Sultan out of Crete! Curses on him! But it's we who pay. Men and women and vineyards are destroyed each time the fire flares up in us. And we, the leaders, bear the responsibility for thousands of souls! And what are you aiming at this time, Captain Michales? Do we want to plunge Crete again into a bath of blood? You are a shrewd man. Tell us, then: how many shiploads of guns and ammunition and food and tents and horses have you already obtained? How many cannons to storm the fortress? Tell us, please, what understanding you have reached with Greece and with Moscow so that we may all fall upon the Sultan with one blow. Give us the facts! Reveal to us your secret, Captain Michales, that our hearts may rejoice!"

All turned towards Captain Michales, but he did not stand up to reply. He had stuck his moustache into his mouth and was chewing it. What sort of a secret was the old man there drivelling

about? He had no secret. Neither the Muscovite had sent him an
envoy, nor the Greek. He had come. He had come on his own
decision, he was sent by Crete, crying and wailing within him.

But at this point the short, pale, bent schoolmaster jumped up
from the boulder in which he had been sitting, and rolled his
tongue like a wheel:

"Old Kambanáros wants secure facts before moving: ships and
provisions and weapons, and the Muscovite to send soldiers to
get themselves bloody heads, and our poor mother Hellas to join
in too with her three bits of regiments. But when have great deeds
ever happened in the world with security, old Kambanáros? When
has discretion inspired men to leave their houses and their property and take to the mountains in search of freedom? That is
just the art of the palikare: to break out without security. The
soul of a man, Captain Kambanáros, is not a dealer, she's a fighter.
Fighters are what we Cretans are, not shopkeepers. The heart of
Crete is a powder-ship, that lets fly at the Sultan's fleet and blows
it sky-high. So 'forward in God's name' say I too, with Captain
Michales. To arms, brothers! That's what I had to say, you leaders,
and he who has ears to hear, let him hear!"

"My blessing on you, schoolmaster," murmured the Abbot,
and raised his right hand in the teacher's direction, as if to bless
him. He repeated aloud, so that all could hear: "My blessing on
you. The soul of man carries no pair of scales—no, it carries a
sword. You are right."

"Better an hour of life in freedom than forty years of slavery
and prison," Captain Trialonis from Jerapetra threw in as his
advice.

Old Kambanáros shook his discretion-filled head.

The leaders had now risen to their feet, excited by the speeches
and counter-speeches. They were chattering and arguing together in twos and threes and fives. The prudent were in the
minority; the palikares—those who would stake all—outweighed
them. Captain Katsirmas watched with angry, squinting eyes this
band of captains foaming round him like the sea. Captain Man-
dakas sighed, remembering his youth: "Ah! These people here
take pencil and paper and add up for and against. In our time we

had one cry: 'Freedom or death', and our brains reeled, and we charged the ramparts of Kastro to breach them. Man is spoilt, he's grown small, Captain Séfakas!" But the grandfather looked with warm sympathy at the younger men assembled around him, and he smiled. "Everything's in order," he thought, "I have confidence. The old go under the earth and come again out of the earth. Made new. Crete is immortal."

He stood up.

"Hey, children," he shouted, "this is an assembly of the elders, not a Jewish school. Sit down, and let's reach a conclusion. Captain Kambanáros on one side, the schoolmaster-captain on the other—two courses. We have met together in these mountains to decide. So choose!"

Captain Polyxigis rose. He twirled his fair, musk-scented moustache and bowed his greeting to the three eldest. His shirt was open, and on his white throat could be discerned a red mark—a bite of Eminé's. Coolly he looked the captains up and down, and paused for a second at the sombre countenance of Captain Michales, whose glance, like that of some steer, came up at him.

"Brothers, captains," he said, "leaders of Eastern Crete! Whoever speaks in your presence is in duty bound to weigh his reasons. I have weighed mine. Leaders, listen to me. If we wait, Captain Kambanáros, for the shiploads you demand to be landed and for the Bear to set his bow legs in motion and bring us help from the north, we shall never free ourselves. And besides we shan't—God forgive me!—be worthy of freedom. To judge by my experience in the few years I've lived and worn this belt of mine, freedom is not a cake that drops into one's mouth and is there for the swallowing, but a citadel to be stormed with the sabre. Whoever receives freedom from foreign hands remains a slave. So it's fire to the villages, the axe to the trees, the tramp of men at war, streams of tears and blood! And even if we fall with our skulls split, fresh men will stand up in our place. Strife and mourning have far to go yet in Crete. A hundred, two hundred, three hundred years—I don't know. But one day—there's no other way, don't listen to people like Captain Kambanáros—one day, yes, by the royal sun that circles over us, one day we shall see freedom!"

Captain Polyxigis had taken off his fez, and his fair-haired head steamed in the sun. Many of the captains were fired, leapt up and shouted aloud: "Freedom or death!" Captain Michales went over to Polyxigis. With his heart bursting, he gave him his hand:

"Captain Polyxigis," he said, "a devil has got between us and is trying to separate us. But Crete is again at stake! Here's my hand!"

"Brother, Captain Michales," the other answered. "Here's mine too. And let the devil go to the Devil."

So he said with a laugh. But Captain Michales was already sorry. He went back to his place, and his countenance changed again.

The meeting lasted another hour. They tied up all the details of who were to meet, and where and how, in order to occupy the cross-roads, blockade the Turkish villages, gather the multitudes into the high-lying monasteries.

Wine was brought them. They sprinkled it on the ground, taking oaths. The three eldest rose from their large bench. The sun was setting as the meeting came to an end.

In God's name! The leaders dispersed to their realms and gave orders to their companies: young and old fetched their weapons from the lofts or dug them up out of the earth. These were all sorts of muzzle-loaders from the 1821 period, which they now cleaned of rust and tied together with cord. The poorest shaped themselves clubs and made plans to fall upon Turkish soldiers and seize their weapons.

In the courtyards of the monasteries, girls and women tore up old manuscripts and folios and made of them cartridge-cases. Skilled monks pounded up in mortars ointments and balsams for wounds. Others stripped the roofing of the churches and turned its lead to the making of bullets. Crete became a workshop of freedom, working day and night. The August moon shone, the cruel sun had already grown a little less harsh. It tenderly stroked its dear Crete, which had again given birth to wheat and barley, maize and grapes, and was now longing for the fresh rain. The first autumn clouds were already appearing in the sky—all white and downy. A tiny, light breeze urged them along, till they had formed themselves anew and gently covered the face of Crete.

The must was fermenting in the casks. But who will drink it? The Cretans asked themselves. Who will bake the bread from this year's harvest? Who will live to celebrate Christmas? The mothers gazed at their hero sons, the wives at their husbands, the sisters at their brothers, and saw Charos staring over their shoulders. But they said nothing. They knew that these were Cretans and had been born to die for Crete.

Eminé too had joined the Cretan ranks, and now, unveiled like the Christian women, helped to make cartridges in the churchyard in front of the church of Kasteli. She put together the cases, but her mind wandered. It was wholly unmoved by the fate of Crete, by Captain Polyxigis, and by Christ and all the Saints. It kept flying into the mountains, to the wild man who was hunting there. In a few weeks—on the 14th of September, Holy Cross Day—she was to be baptised. Fat, heavily moving Chrysánthe stayed at home, in the *konak* of Ali Aga which the Captain had taken over, and prepared the bakemeats for the great day when the Moslem woman was to become a Christian.

Seven captains, each with his train of palikares, were to come as godparents. Tityros would be asked to make an oration. The people of the neighbouring villages also were expected in crowds, to witness with their own eyes the baptising of Nuri's wife. It seemed to them a good omen—that Turkey would return to Greece. They took pride in pampering the beautiful new Christian woman. Eminé accepted everything with a smile.

On the evening of the assembly of elders, Eminé was sitting at the window and waiting for the return of her friend. She had washed and combed herself and dyed her meeting eyebrows. How she would have liked to go with him and to see those fourteen mighty captains like eagles on the cliffs! And then she would have met the wild, stiff-necked Captain Michales! At the thought her bosom rose passionately. Why, my God, did she think of him? What did she find in him? He was no man, but a wild beast, lone, ugly—she did not like him! She had done rightly in choosing the gentle, attentive, sweet-speaking Captain Polygixis. And yet—if only she could, even for a moment, see Captain Michales up there on the mountains.

She lifted up her slanting eyes to the rosy peaks of Selena. Nuri Bey had completely vanished from her mind and body, as if he had never lived, as if he had not been superb as a lion, as if he had never embraced her. Her flesh was like the sea. A ship would glide over it and scratch it for a moment. Then it would draw together again, maidenly. How should she still think of the cretinous pacha who had bought her from her father? That had been her father's trade, by which he lived: he begot lovely daughters, fattened them well, displayed them and sold them. . . . Or should she remember the beardless palikare, the young Circassian, who one summer night had fallen upon her in a garden by the river bank and thrown her down among tall sunflwoers? She had thought he wanted to murder her and had struggled against him, but he had not killed her. After the embrace he had become tame, bent tenderly over her and smiled at her. "What's your name?" he had asked, "mine is . . ." How should she remember his name? All those men and many others had glided over her and lost themselves in nothingness. Now it was the turn of Captain Polyxigis. Now he was gliding over. But alas! She could feel that, on the day of their wedding, he would depart from her, and a three-masted pirate frigate with black sails would suddenly rise up from below the horizon.

While Eminé, sighing, gazed out of the window, Captain Michales was riding, all alone, down to his father's house. His heart was beating hard, full of angry shame. "You fool, you're fighting for freedom and yet you're still a slave," he cried within himself. "My lips say one thing, my hands another, and my heart means another! Why do you prattle, Captain Michales you hypocrite, and beat your breast because of Crete? A different demon has fixed its claws in you and is your master, you man without honour! And evèn if you fall in battle and if you storm Megalokastro and set Crete free, you're without honour. Your heart is after something else, your purpose dwells elsewhere!"

He had sent his best palikare, Thodóres, ahead with the flag,

and was wholly absorbed in argument with himself. He had seen
Polyxigis again and on him smelt that accursed Turkish musk. He
had spied the red bite on his throat, and his blood had shuddered.
"Curse her," he whispered, "curse the bitch! As long as she's
alive, I am dishonoured." He had the picture ceaselessly before
his eyes, of how the bridegroom had sought out his godparents
in the assembly, how he had invited them to the crowning-day,
how he had also approached him and only started back before his
glance. "I can't stand it any more," he cried out loud, "this is no
life. I must make an end of it."

Captain Polyxigis, Eminé and Chrysánthe were still squatting at
table and eating their evening meal, when there was a knock at the
door and in came Tityros. Captain Polyxigis was astonished.

Since the day when his nephew Diamandés and his niece Van-
geiio had met so swift a death, he had not seen the schoolmaster
again. At first he had been angry with him, because he suspected
him of having poisoned Diamandés out of jealousy. But he had
soon changed his mind. It was unthinkable that such a lamb of
God could kill. And so he put the blame on destiny. It had been
written that. . . . He no longer had anything against the schoolmaster. And as he now heard that he was travelling through the
villages and arousing men's hearts, he forgot the whole business.
He was delighted at seeing him come in so unexpectedly.

"Welcome, schoolmaster," he cried, and moved to one side to
make room for him.

The schoolmaster greeted him gaily and squatted down, so that
his face was lit up by the lamp. Captain Polyxigis was struck with
amazement as he looked at him. Was this Tityros—that half-
helping with glasses on a string, with the tight breeches and
crooked back? Beside him there sat a different man!

Tityros had in fact become a different man. Since the day when
he had murdered the pretty boor, a transformation had been going
on in him. He plucked up courage and saw that the whole
secret of manhood did not consist in possessing a great strong
body. One must have in one's soul the strength of decision! A
horse-fly with decision could fell an ox. Manhood was soul, not

body. Ever since he understood that, Tityros had been turning
into a different man. Gradually his body, too, gained strength. He
no longer held himself with a stoop, he ate with appetite and drank
wine. His cheeks grew red. And—greatest surprise of all—he
caught fire and went after women. Now that with his sack on his
back he was going from village to village speaking about the
fatherland, he had made himself godfather to various children and
established a family tie with their parents, to be able to count on
shelter for the night from them. And it fell out that one of these
new relatives of his, a woman in Kasteli whose husband was absent, had a sense of fun. One night, after a gay conversation, they
found themselves—not knowing how—in bed together aud in
each other's arms. Since then, Tityros had passed through Kasteli
often and slept with his relative—whom God, so he hoped, would
protect!

"You too are at war, schoolmaster, so I hear," said Captain
Polyxigis, filling his glass for him. "Your learning has begun to turn
captain, and carries a flag with the alphabet embroidered on it."

"I hope I'll soon get hold of a gun as well," answered the schoolteacher with a laugh. "The alphabet is good as an appetiser. But
the meat course is the Turk."

Eminé propped her apple cheek on her hand and gazed at him.
"That's Captain Michales's brother." she thought, "A schoolmaster like that. . . ." And she tried hard to discover in his face the
fierce, cruel features of the other.

Chrysánthe got up and went out. She could not look at him.
The two corpses rose from the earth and sat down opposite her
at the table.

"Will you have the kindness, schoolmaster, to come to the
baptism, on our crowning-day?" Captain Polyxigis asked. "Eminé
is going to be baptised and become Eleni. That same evening
there'll be the wedding, too."

"That's just why I've come, Captain. About the baptism. Old
Mavrolias, as he was digging in his field near Kasteli, found a
splendid pottery basin. He asked me to come and see it. He thought
it was old. And truly God alone knows how many thousand years
old it is. On the outside it's covered with decorations—a grape

and coral design. I couldn't be sure what they all were. And in the bottom of the basin I found a handful of Egyptian beans, which had become like charcoal through age. . . . By my soul, that basin comes from the time of Minos!"

"Well . . . ?" Captain Polyxigis asked. "What's your idea?"

"Don't you see, Captain? A font! The village pope couldn't think what vessel he was to baptise her in! The church font is much too small. And now God, in the moment of need, makes a splendid basin rise up out of the earth! A good omen, Captain! By my faith, soon Constantinople will be Christian again!"

He stood up, for he was in a hurry. At his godsister's the table was laid and she was waiting for him.

Captain Polyxigis said, with a laugh:

"Your brain is pregnant, schoolmaster, it brings forth. Eminé, what do you think?"

But she said nothing. She gazed at the schoolteacher, and her soul meanwhile had shaken free from her body and swept away far from Christ and fonts.

The godsister had in fact already laid the table and filled the wine-bottles. She was waiting for her godbrother. She was a man-woman, square-built, with long white teeth and a thick black moustache. Her broad face was sown all over with pock-marks. It was just this ugliness that had made the schoolmaster lose his wits. Strange world: if she had not been freckled, she would not have kindled the schoolmaster's blood, and he would have remained for some time longer too timid to embrace a woman.

Tityros wished her good evening. His godchild, still a baby, was lying in the cradle. Another small son was asleep on a little sofa. The husband was a pedlar, making the round of the villages. Godbrother and godsister were quite alone in the house. They ate hastily, emptied their bottles, crossed themselves, covered up the ikons to prevent them from looking on, and hurled themselves into the heaped-up bed.

Next morning the schoolmaster stumbled upon an excited crowd in the village square with its three gnarled poplars. Hearing the shouting, peasants were rushing barefooted out of the houses.

A monk had just arrived. His chest was bare, he was gasping, and blood trickled from his feet.

"Brothers," he shouted, "I've been sent by the Fathers of the Christ the Lord Monastery. Hassan Bey, the General, has marched out from Megalokastro with a strong force of soldiers. They've invested the monastery! Where is the captain of the village? Help us, brothers! To arms!"

The captain was lying in Circassian arms. When he heard the noise, he leapt up. But as captain he must not go out without breeches. He dressed and stuck his pistols into his leather belt. Then he ran in the direction of the voices. He seized the monk by the arm.

"Don't shout like that! Don't upset my people!" he said, and shoved him along into his house. He shut the door and gave something to eat and drink. The monk regained his breath.

"Now speak," Captain Polyxigis ordered. "And none of your whimpering before me. They're only Turks, you silly monk. The Devil will get them!"

X

GOD made it be day. The heights were touched by the torches of the light. It glided down the slopes and flooded over the plains. Then it shot shafts over the indigo clouds and poured down upon the tortured body of Crete. If God had been pleased to look at Crete, He must have felt pity at the sight of the burning houses, wailing women and orphaned children round the feet of the naked and hungry mountains. And of the men who—too wild to pray—hung on to the passes and the peaks and, holding up a bit of cloth with a cross embroidered on it, went into battle. Without bread and without ammunition, barefooted. With nothing but a miserable gun. For how many generations had they raised their hands and implored God? When did God ever lean down and listen to them? Heaven was deaf, God had changed faith. So they set their hands to their guns.

The first gleam of morning found Captain Polyxigis busy with preparations to set out for war, and saddling his mare. The evening before, he had sent a runner to Captain Michales with the news: the Turks are besieging the celebrated monastery. Now let him let fly the banner: freedom or death! Speeches and debates should be ended; the real mouth of Crete, the gun, must speak.

"Now, Captain Michales," he had added to his letter, "to the Devil with out little feuds and concerns. They've eaten into both of us. 'Who are you afraid of,' someone once asked the lion; 'the elephant? the tiger? the buffalo?' 'No,' he answered; 'the louse'. The louse has bitten both of us, Captain Michales. Sometimes we called it pleasure, sometimes care. But it was always a louse. The Devil take it. Crete calls. Give us your hand, brother!"

Eminé came out and leaned against the door-post. Her eyes had blue rings round them, her lips were bitten. The captain turned to her at last. His mind was still stirred by the proud words he had

311

sent to Captain Michales yesterday evening, and his face remained severe.

"Where's your mind strayed to?" asked the Circassian woman, fiercely. "I'm here and you don't give that a thought."

He was just hanging from the saddle a double bag embroidered in colours. He filled one part of it with cartridges, oil-cloth and balsam, and in the other put a loaf of bread, a soft cheese and a bottle of wine. How should he answer the woman who was standing there in the doorway and watching his setting-out? Since he had written those words yesterday evening to his wild comrade in arms, it had become clear to him, as never before in his life, where Woman belonged and where Crete, and what were the real duties of a man.

"I must reveal you a secret," said the Circassian, and she walked up to him. She stroked the mare's neck and bent her head, until her hair fell over her neck like the mare's mane and nearly touched the ground. The yard filled with the scent of musk.

"A secret?" asked Polyxigis, and his hands stiffened and remained motionless in the air.

"Yes, and I'm telling it to you so that you may not complain afterwards that I never told you. Sometimes I get news secretly from Megalokastro. Nuri's relatives mean to fall upon Kasteli one day with soldiers and seize me. And if I don't return to my faith they'll kill me. So go to the monastery of Christ the Lord! But keep your wife in mind also, Captain Polyxigis!"

He stood there for a moment undecided. Outside, a multitudinous din was audible. Wives were bidding their husbands farewell, old women were weeping and men tearing themselves loose. "Good-bye," they shouted, and gathered by the three poplars in the village square, around Captain Polyxigis's flag.

When the Circassian saw that her man remained silent, she said: "A woman's a citadel, too. She has to be taken."

"I'm not forgetting," the man answered at length. "Good-bye."

He folded her in his arms, he felt her firm bosom, and his senses reeled. The world could come to grief, if only this thrilling body might never leave his arms. The woman closed her eyes, raised herself gently on her toes and tried to reach his mouth. The man's knees gave way.

The mare whinnied. The captain broke out of his dizziness and leaned against the doorpost. Softly he pushed the woman from him, freed himself from her mouth, caught hold of the horse's mane and swung himself at one go into the saddle.

"Good-bye!" he said, and without turning again he rode through the outer door and galloped to the village square.

That same early morning Captain Michales, surrounded by his best palikares in the grandfather's huge yard at Petrokéfalo, was confiding to the hands of Thodóres his banner—the black cloth with the red letters. Beside him, armed, stood his sometime drinking-companions, Kajabés and Furógatos. Vendúsos had gone out to make arrangements for his family. Bertódulos had stayed with the women.

Captain Michales turned to his wife, who stood silent on the threshold with folded arms:

"Good-bye, wife," he said.

"God be with you, Captain Michales," she replied calmly. "God be with you, palikares!" she added, while her eyes glided earnestly over her husband's young comrades-in-arms.

The grandfather came out. His cheeks glowed red in the early morning light.

"Forward, children, with my blessing!" he cried, raising his heavy paw. "Go with God's blessing! You're fighting for Crete, and that's no joke! Happy the man who lays down his life in the service of Crete!"

He fell silent. But soon he went on:

"On this day that's breaking now, it seems to me better—I couldn't say why—to be killed in her service than to live in her service."

The noise forced its way into Thrasáki's sleep. He guessed that his father was setting out for war, and leapt from his bed, to appear on the doorstep wrapped in a red, embroidered rug. His father looked at the boy, still half encompassed by dream as he bobbed up between his grandfather and his mother—and laughed.

"Good-bye, Thrasáki, till you're old enough!" he said, and jumped on to his mare.

He crossed himself: "In God's name!"

The banner moved forward, and the village emptied itself of men.

The celebrated monastery of Christ the Lord had been founded in ancient times, before the fall of Constantinople, before the coming of the Venetians to Crete, when the Byzantine emperors still ruled in the East and far into the West.

The story went, that it had been built by the Emperor Niki-foros—that great, dark soul who had been led astray by a woman's beautiful body and had by a hair's breadth missed plunging to Hell. But he had managed to grasp hold of God. And God had heard him and placed him in Paradise, together with the other sinful and sorely tormented emperors.

He had gained mastery of the world, landed in Crete, stamped down the Saracens, overthrown the Crescent, and set up over the scorched fields and plundered towns the banner of Christ. And one evening, the story went, he was passing through a ravine. Here, under a lemon-tree, he would sleep, and as soon as God made it be day again, press on towards Chandaka (that was the name of Megalokastro then). It was in the month of May: the moon was full, and the night air was quivering with the song of the nightingale. The Emperor saw Christ the Lord approaching, barefooted, faint from long journeying. He stopped under the lemon-tree, did not see Nikiforos, and stretched Himself on the ground with a sigh. He took a stone as pillow and said: "How tired I am." Then He folded His arms, shut His eyes and went to sleep.

All night the Emperor felt a sweet, ineffable happiness. It was the gift neither of the moon, nor of the nightingale, nor of slumber. He had entered Paradise.

Waking up at grey of dawn, Nikiforos said: "This tree, where Christ has slept, is hallowed." He commanded that the holy lemon-tree be surrounded by a monastery. And that, they say, is how the Monastery of Christ the Lord was founded.

The Byzantine emperors died, the Turks took Constantinople, the Venetians over-ran Crete, later the Ottomans subdued it. The "Christ the Lord" was destroyed, built up again, destroyed again. And now, beleaguered by the Turks, its bells rang mournfully and cried their message to the countryside: "All you believers, come and help!"

The Abbot was arming himself in the church, the monks were digging up the guns from under the sacred altar. The Abbot knelt down before the huge ikon of Christ near the ikonostasis.

"Lord Christ," he cried aloud, that all might hear him, "forgive me, the fault is mine, I am the one to blame! And now the dogs have come to avenge the blood."

He was in fact the one to blame. On the first of September, the beginning of the ecclesiastical accounting year, the Abbot of Christ the Lord had been on his way back from Megalokastro. He had gone there to be confessed by the Metropolitan and to lay at his feet the monastery's yearly contribution. He had also begged him to take the monastery under his protection: he must please use his influence with the Pacha to make him prevent the Turks from attacking it once more. How many times more would they burn the monastery down? "Have pity! I've grown old, My-lord. My wounds hurt. I haven't the strength left for defending it!"

"How old do you suppose God has grown—yet He can still lay fresh burdens on ten Saints!" answered the Metropolitan with a laugh. "Go with my blessing, and stop worrying."

The Abbot had taken the Metropolitan's blessing with him on his way home. He rode on his mule to the Hospital Gate and out of it, and in the sunset light he looked at the blue, shimmering mountains in front of him, at the harvested fields, the vineyards generous with clusters, the olives loaded with fruit all round him, and at the sea. His heart flew upwards.

"It's beautiful, this false world," he murmured, "Crete is beautiful, God is great."

He kept close to the seashore, crossed the red sand of the river-bed, drank a raki at the widow's inn, then set off up Cruel Mountain. His mule trod with the greatest care the narrow goat path

L*

along the precipice. A light breeze was sighing. To the left the
Abbot saw the sea down below, darkening as he looked at it. He
crossed himself and repeated out of a heart filled with happiness:
"It's beautiful, this false world. Crete is beautiful. . . ."

He had not finished his sentence when three powerful young
Turks, who had been lying in wait for him hidden behind a rock,
rushed on him with their knives. For there were many greying
hanums still living whom the warlike monk had widowed in the
1866 rising, and the orphaned Turks had sworn they would one
day get rid of their fathers' murderer.

The mule started back and very nearly threw the Abbot into
the abyss. But he forgot he was an old man covered with forty
scars, and leapt to the ground with the suppleness of a wild
cat.

"In Christ's name," he shouted, drawing his knife.

Above the abyss the four bodies whirled entwined. The small,
bony but very agile Abbot laid about him with his fists. His blood
kindled, his youth came back, and all his forefathers who had
fallen in battle against Turkey rose up in him. It was not one who
was hitting out, but all Cretans together.

Night broke over them, and down below the sea lay dark. The
stars stood in the high heaven, inhumanly gay. A night bird
squatted up above on a cliff, watching the dance of death of the
four hairy forms, and sang its song.

"In Christ's name," shouted the Abbot again, and he contrived
with an immense effort to free himself from the clutches of the
six pairs of limbs. Then he hurled himself with all his strength
against the human bundle, to ram it over the precipice. It began
to slide. For a moment it still managed to hold on, but a fresh,
mighty push broke the last resistance, and the three Turks fell
bellowing into the abyss, into the sea.

The Abbot leaned against the mountain and crossed himself.
Blood was streaming over his head and chest; his monk's habit
was torn. He bound his wounds with strips of stuff, and called
his mule.

"Give me strength, O Christ," he said, "to get to the monastery.
After that, do what Thou wilt."

He clenched his teeth and with great pain climbed into the saddle.

"God is great," he murmured and rode on.

Next day Megalokastro echoed with the fresh deed of the Turk-gobbling Abbot. Three old women, new victims of Charos, united in the wailing for the dead. They hurried—with them many Turks—to the place of the fall, climbed down to the wild shore, picked up the bodies and buried them in the sand. The men struck their knives into the grave-mound and swore that they would build the monument out of the ashes of the accursed monastery. And that was how, one morning, the ravine before the "Christ the Lord" filled with red fezes.

On the same morning fresh bands set out from the Hospital Gate against the besieged monastery and against the big Turkish village of Kasteli, which the *giaours* had occupied. The nephews, cousins and friends of Nuri, with the ferocious muezzin at their head, pressed forward as if possessed. In Megalokastro the Christians through shuttered windows watched them streaming by with pistols and daggers and plunging their knives into Greek doors.

That same morning, under the same sun, on the other side of the sea, Athens awoke. From the columns of the Parthenon the light gradually spread to the plain on which the city made famous by intellect and beauty was beginning to awake with yawns from heavy sleep, powerfully assisted by the throats of the milkman, the newsboy and the vegetable-vendor. Out from vacant school-buildings, store-rooms and cellars where they had been given scanty quarters, there emerged, silently, the Cretan refugees. They held tins and casseroles in their hands and took up position in front of an open door, through which one could see into a yard with some large cauldrons. They waited for an hour in the queue to get their couple of spoonfuls of lenten soup. At first they had been ashamed, because they were not used tost retching out their hands to beg, but then hunger had compelled them.

Mother Hellas, though likewise haunted by Charos, was going short of many morsels in order to give them to the starving

Cretans. Miserly householders opened their purses, newly married couples sacrificed their wedding presents, popes raised their hands to God, and ships put off from places on the coast nearby to smuggle ammunition, food and volunteers into Crete.

On the island of Syra, rich in ships, Captain Stefanés limped about the back alleys of the small town and stretched out his hands in entreaty.

"A ship for me, too, Christians, a ship for Crete!"

And God did arrange that, precisely on that same day when the two leaders who were his friends were marching to Christ the Lord Monastery, Captain Stefanés was able to hop aboard the ship which the patriots of Syra had entrusted to him. It had a cargo of flour, belts, muslin bandages and cartridges.

Captain Stefanés crossed himself, took the ikon of Saint Nicolas and placed it well forward in the bows. He whispered to it: "I'm placing you in the bows, well forward, Saint Nicolas, my Saint, because your eyes see better than two pairs of men's eyes. Never say, after this, that you were in the cabin and saw nothing!" The sea saint with the short beard looked at him in silence. In his hands, eaten away by salt, he was holding a toy—a ship with tiny men on board. He was smiling. Captain Stefanés bent over him and kissed him.

A small cloud appeared in the sky to the south, like a smoke-cloud. It grew, and other clouds like sheep came frisking behind it, driven along by a hot south wind as by a shepherd. By midday the whole sky was covered. The first, luke-warm drops of autumn rain fell, the first claps of thunder boomed over the sea.

Captain Stefanés turned his flashing eyes to the south and smiled. "Up, south-wind, master of waters, pour your floods down, so that neither sun nor moon appears and I can bring Crete's dowry to land in pitch-black darkness, in the turn of a hand."

Vendúsos, too, heard the thunder as he climbed the mountain. He was alarmed as he raised his head and the sky hung dark above him. "Wait, sky," he muttered, "till I've got to my godfather, Jorgaros. Then you can let your temper go!"

He quickened his pace, to reach the mountain village of Anapoli.

He wanted to ask his godfather to look after his wife and two daughters until Crete should be at peace again.

He arrived in pitch-black night. He knocked on the door. Not a soul! He knocked again, and his godfather came to the door, with reddened eyes, dishevelled hair and pale face. "Greetings, godfather Jorgaros," said Vendúsos. "May I lie down in your house tonight?" "Ask for my head and it's yours," answered the godfather, "welcome!"

Vendúsos went in. The wife did not appear. Subdued voices came from the bedroom upstairs. Soon they ceased.

"And godmother?" Vendusos asked.

"You must excuse her, godson Vendúsos," Jorgaros answered. "She's not been well, these last days. She sends you her greetings and bids you welcome."

The godfather laid the table, brought food and wine and lit a second lamp.

"Excuse me, godson," he said, "I've not much to offer you. But how was I to know you'd do me the favour of coming this evening. Tomorrow I'll kill you a chicken, God willing."

The south wind raged, the rain slapped against door and steps.

"Tomorrow, first thing, godfather, I must be gone, God willing," Vendúsos replied. "I've given Captain Michales my word and I'd be ashamed not to keep it. I've come, godfather Jorgaros, to ask you a favour."

"Anything in my power," replied Jorgaros, nodding his head.

"If you had a room to spare, to shelter my family, till the weapons are silent . . ."

Jorgaros drank a gulp of wine, as if his throat needed widening.

"It happens a room has fallen vacant," he said, lowering his eyes, "just these last days. Take it, godson Vendúsos!"

He stood up, to open the door and go out into the yard. He came in again at once, wet through.

"God be thanked," he said, "it's raining. The soil will be soft for the ploughing."

He pushed the table to one side and made up a bed for his godson on the settle.

"Sleep, godson," he said. "You've come a long way."

Next morning Jorgaros brought him a mug of milk, a dry
barley loaf and a large hunk of cheese. The sky was now clear.
The cocks of the village were fluttering on the roofs and crowing.

"Good-bye, godfather," said Vendúsos. "How can I repay your
friendship? Only God can reward you."

"The Almighty pays what is due, don't worry, godson Vendúsos. Good-bye!"

The washed rocks glittered in the morning light, and the rain-
drops on the branches shimmered. Vendúsos strode down the
mountain, whistling gaily. He had found protection for his family,
he was relieved of the nightmare, and he was now in a hurry to
get back to Captain Michales, Kajabés and Furógatos.

The door of a hovel outside the village opened, and a little old
man appeared on the threshold. Vendúsos recognised him—it
was old Zacharias, an uncle of Jorgaros's, a man of skill. He
grafted trees and doctored men and women. Every Saturday he
took a clay bowl, some soap, a pair of clippers and a razor, and
sat down on the small bench by the church, to shear and scrape
as many heads as presented themselves. He had also, close by him,
a small sack, which his customers filled with bread, vegetables
and raisins; next it, too, there stood two jugs, for wine and oil.
And when he had done his barber's work, he heaped up the cut-
off hair and set fire to it, so that the space round about was veiled
in stinking smoke.

"A long life to you, Uncle Zacharias!" Vendúsos called out to
him, and stopped.

"Welcome to the lyre-player!" the old man answered. "What's
happening in the world, my child? Where is it going?"

"Don't ask, uncle! To the Devil!"

"And you?"

"I'm going with it. Can I give it the slip? Last night I slept at
my godfather Jorgaros's. We had a good long chat. Now I'm
off."

The old man raised his hands to Heaven. "At Jorgaros's," he
muttered. "Lord have mercy on me! So that's why the poor man
sent to say that no one was to come to his house to keen for the
dead!"

"What's that, Uncle? What keening would that be?"

"Didn't you notice anything?"

"What should I have noticed?"

"His son was killed, yesterday morning. They had the body in the bedroom."

Vendúsos covered his face and said nothing.

"Hey, Vendúsos," exclaimed the old man, "don't cry! Fare you well! We all have to die!"

At Christ The Lord Monastery too it had rained that night. The faces of the monks, who had been kneeling for three days and nights behind their bulwarks, waiting for the Turks, looked fresh. There were thirty-two of them all told, together with about twenty peasants from round about, who had been ashamed to leave the "Christ The Lord" in the lurch. When they heard the storm-bells, they had fetched their wives and children into a high-lying cave, made by God to be a citadel, and repaired to the monastery with their provisions—a sheep or a goat and a woollen sack full of barley biscuits.

Noon was already near, when Captain Polyxigis with his palikares reached the top of the pass and began to approach the monastery by the ravine. From a long way off they caught the sound of shots and of Turkish trumpets. Some of their comrades made haste to take up positions at the top of the pass, to protect their brothers' rear.

Captain Polyxigis stood up in his stirrups:

"Greetings, brothers," he shouted, and fired a pistol shot. Then he turned to his companions, who were panting after him.

"Let 'em have your greetings, my children! But I don't want a single bullet wasted!"

He pointed at the huge mass of accursed red fezes, swarming about the monastery. Fifteen bullets whistled into the Turks from behind. Some twenty bodies fell to the ground, bellowing.

The monastery echoed back cries of "Welcome, children!" Old Ilarion, the deaf bell-ringer, grasped the bell-rope and began ringing festively.

The Turks became furious. They raised their eyes and through the mist saw that the top of the pass was occupied by Greeks, who were now seeking cover behind cliffs.

"Allah, Allah," they bawled.

The foremost Turkish ranks remained where they were, with a close grip on the monastery; the others stormed upwards towards the crest.

It began to rain heavily. A cloud hid the top of the pass, while the rain beat into the faces of the Turkish soldiers and blinded them.

"God's with us," shouted Captain Polyxigis. "Give 'em another volley."

They reloaded and fired. Shouts and curses rang out. But the clouds now sank lower and protected the Turks too. Only their red fezes and glittering bayonets could still be made out.

The Abbot, who had noticed through a loophole that the Turkish numbers had divided, called out to his people:

"Forward, children! The Turks have divided. Let's attack them and loosen their grip!"

Monks and peasants leapt up, the bell-ringer again siezed his rope and rang the signal for attack. They gathered in the courtyard. The Abbot ran ahead, opened the big door, and they all rushed out, shouting.

For a moment the Turks were bewildered by the two attacks. Some of them tried by a counter-attack to drive the monks back into the monastery, but in the middle they received the order to withdraw deeper into the ravine. They were pursued by the monks.

Suddenly a trumpet call rang out. The Turks stopped. Immediately afterwards other trumpets sounded, behind the monks.

"The Turks have encircled us," shouted a monk. "We're in a trap! Back, reverend Abbot!"

"They've broken into the monastery!" yelled another.

The Abbot stuck his pistols into his belt, drew a knife and without a word hastened back to the gate of the monastery.

Captain Polyxigis had at once recognised the new danger and stormed down with his palikares. The rain had grown heavier, the sun had completely vanished behind clouds. Twilight spread.

Turks and Christians formed a huge knot of fighting men, each of them at once attacking and on the defensive.

"Follow me!" the Abbot now shouted, and Captain Polyxigis also urged his companions on and pressed through to the gate.

A few Turks had already got into the monastery courtyard and were running towards the church. They were flinging burning tow and rags in all directions.

"You damned dogs!" they heard two wild, hoarse voices cry suddenly behind them. The Abbot and Captain Polyxigis had crossed the threshold together and rushed on the intruders. Other Turks who were following were driven against the church wall and massacred by the monks and palikares, who now arrived all at once.

The danger had been just averted. The heavy outer gate of the monastery was double-bolted. Night had come. The fighters broke away from one another, and silence fell.

"Back to the pass!" cried Captain Polyxigis. "God will be with us again tomorrow."

The Christians counted their losses. Of the monks and peasants three had been killed and several wounded. Ilarion the bell-ringer was missing. Of Captain Polyxigis's band two had been killed and many wounded. They buried the dead by night at the top of the pass: two doughty palikares, both from Kasteli, uncle and nephew. Captain Polyxigis took two sticks, made them into a cross and placed it on the mound.

"We'll be back later," he muttered. Then he turned to his comrades.

"Now for some food, children! We're still alive and we're hungry!"

They lit a fire, cooked and ate. The excitement of the battle flickered in their talk. Then sentries were posted for the night. The rest folded their arms and slept, tired out.

Down below, there were lights in the church till midnight. The monks were praising God, Who had stretched out His hand and saved the monastery from fire and death. The aged Photios was mixing balsam, cleaning the wounds and looking after the wounded all night.

And between the two Christian ranks the Turkish soldiers also were burying their dead, caring for their wounded and thinking, as they stared silently into their camp fires, of their wives and children in far-off Anatolia. Who would plough the fields over there, prune the vines, and earn bread for the family? They too were human beings and not, as the Christians called them, dogs.

As the first pallid light appeared in the sky, Christians and Turks sprang to arms. Two dervishes, one with a drum, the other with a flute, ran from group to group of soldiers, to give them courage and fire.

The monks too were taking up their posts. The Abbot's head was bandaged. His wounds were still bleeding, his white beard was full of red drops. Nonetheless he kneeled down before the loophole, and his eagle eye flew over the enemy's position. Wherever he saw a head poke up, his bullet hit it without fail. "It's an evil craft, killing men," he thought. "But it's not our fault, O God! Make us free, O God, then we'll have peace."

Up above, at the top of the pass, Captain Polyxigis was making his round and giving his orders. Each man had already taken up his position behind a boulder and aimed his gun at the red fezes. But Captain Polyxigis was too proud to duck and went upright from man to man.

"Take cover, captain, or you'll get hit!" his palikares called to him.

Bullets were already whistling over their heads. But Captain Polyxigis laughed.

"I'd like to crouch down all right, children. I'm frightened too, God knows. But I'm ashamed. Want to play the captain, Polyxigis? Then you must pay for it."

"You carry a splinter of the Holy Cross about with you," shouted a tall lad with a poison tongue. "That's why you're so fearless."

That angered Captain Polyxigis.

"The holy splinter, you idiot Nikolos," he said, "is the soul of a man. I know no other!"

Down below the battle was flaring afresh. The Turks advanced and the monastery was again in danger.

"Up! Up! Christ will be the victor!" yelled Captain Polyxigis. "Down and at the Turks!"

The palikares leapt out from behind the rocks and rushed down. Stones came rattling behind them—the whole mountain seemed to be in movement.

After the guns had done their work, the short daggers came into play, hand-to-hand. The guns in the monastery also fell silent: it was no longer possible to distinguish the fighters. The Abbot ordered his most daring men to join in the mêlée, while the others stayed behind the bulwarks and guarded the monastery. But the Musulmans were in superior numbers. Against one Christian seven of them were matched. The Abbot and the Captain rushed up and down, putting fire into their men. But wave on wave of Turkish attackers fell upon them, and towards mid-day the Christians began to be tired. The sun seemed to be standing still in the sky, and the rescuing night still infinitely far. The attackers pressed them more and more powerfully. In the midst of the confusion of battle the glances of the Abbot and the Captain crossed. They said nothing, but each saw in the eyes of the other the monastery burning.

Suddenly, however, a salvo thundered in the lower ravine. The Christians saw with amazement a dark banner climbing higher and higher and with it, clambering from boulder to boulder, a bellowing horde. Ahead of them all, on his mare, Captain Michales in his black head-band.

"Hail to you, brothers!" he shouted to them, firing his pistol. And, turning to the enemy: "At last we've got you, you dogs!"

That day and the following day the wounded Turkish soldiers and those Turks who had gone with them as volunteers kept coming in rapid succession back into Megalokastro.

"What's happened about the monastery? Is it still standing? Aren't you ashamed?" shouted the Pacha, tearing his beard.

"It was all going nicely, Pacha Effendi," answered the wounded, "until that cursed Captain Michales fell upon us."

They were hoarse with thirst and demanded sherbet from Barba Jannis. Efendína too emerged and recited verses from the Koran,

which were supposed to allay their pain. From the great plane-tree
hung, like a bell, poor Ilarion, the deaf bell-ringer. The Turks had
taken him alive two days ago. He was still holding in his fist a
piece of the bell-rope, which he had refused to let go, so that the
Turks had had to cut it.

In the Metropolitan's residence, the Metropolitan never put off
his vestments, day and night. He expected every moment that the
Turks would force their way in and haul him off to the gallows.
He did not want to make that journey half naked and bare-footed.
He had sent for Pachumios the ascetic from the Kadumas Monastery by the Libyan Sea, to hear his confession. He took communion
every day, that his soul might be ready at any time. Múrzuflos did
not move from his side and kept him company like a dog. He slept
on the threshold of his bedroom, that he might in no case be
separated from his master, and that their souls might pass together
into the Beyond.

At the monastery night came at last. Christ and Mohammed
separated. The Christians lit fires on the mountainside, the Turks
round about the monastery walls. The monastery remained hidden
in deep darkness. Captain Michales and Polyxigis met and discussed the situation. They settled the place and manner of tomorrow's attack, and parted without having exchanged a friendly
word.

Captain Michales squatted alone by one of the fires, sunk in a
dark colloquy with himself, and rolled a cigarette. His heart was
oppressed. He was fighting, killing and at every moment exposing
himself to death—for Crete. Yet in his mind he was not with
Crete. And when, mounted on his mare, he stormed forward
with the cry: "Follow me, you faithful!", in his secret self he
doubted his own faith. And when night came and he withdrew
into solitude, he was not thinking, as in the past, about the freedom of Crete, but his spirit was wandering elsewhere.

"The shame of it! What have you sunk to, Captain Michales?"
he muttered, and spat into the fire.

In this bitter mood, he suddenly heard light footsteps and a
cough behind him. He turned. It was Vendúsos, who was not

much use in battle and to whom he had given leave to go and put his family in safety. Now here he was back, breathless.

"What's happened, Vendúsos?" Captain Michales asked, and stood up.

Vendúsos, who had long suspected what worm was gnawing at Captain Michales, whispered into his ear:

"Captain, captain, Eminé . . ."

Captain Michales started back. Then he seized Vendúsos by the arm and pulled him nearer.

"Speak softly!"

"The Turks attacked Kasteli this evening and have made off with her."

Captain Michales stretched out his hand to the fire. He wanted the burning pain. . . . After a short silence he wheeled round.

"Where to?"

"Towards Megalokastro."

"When?"

"This evening, as the lights were being lit."

Captain Michales burst out:

"Come with me and keep quiet."

But Vendúsos resisted:

"D'you mean to leave your post? Suppose the Turks made a night attack?"

"Shut up!"

He picked out the ten most hard-boiled palikares:

"Come with me! We're going on a raid."

He turned to the rest of the comrades:

"I'll be back before dawn. Look after yourselves meanwhile."

It was past midnight. Apart from the sentries, the exhausted Christians lay in deep sleep. Inside the monastery the oldest fathers bowed their faces to the flag-stones of the church and implored God to hold His hand in protection over the monastery. The Abbot had bandaged his wounds with oil-cloth, but remained crouching at his post. Through the narrow loophole he could see the soldiers standing round the fires and could catch the clink of their weapons. "The dogs aren't asleep," he thought. "They're planning mischief."

The sky was quiet clear, the stars shone gaily, a sharp breeze came from the mountains and spurred men on. A big star shot in a long sweep. The Abbot crossed himself.

"A great disaster is approaching," he murmured. "O God, grant that it is not the monastery."

And while his eyes were still directed imploringly at the sky, suddenly trumpets and drums sounded and a loud shout of "Allah! Allah!" Dark waves of men struck against the monastery, and at the pass, up above, others rushed upon the sleeping Christians. The soldiers were already beginning to place ladders against the monastery walls.

The Abbot called his monks together:

"Brothers, the monastery is lost. Listen to me. I am the one to blame. It's me they want to take, to avenge their blood. So I'm giving myself up to them. Farewell!"

"Reverend Abbot," said Photios, the healer monk, "they'll kill you."

"What else should they do with me, Father Photios? Of course they'll kill me, but spare the monastery because of it."

"They'll kill you and not spare the monastery. The Turks are treacherous, reverend Abbot!"

"Let me do my duty. Let what will happen, happen. God is above, let Him do as He will."

He took his abbot's staff, tied a white cloth to its tip, went out on to the wall and waved it, shouting loudly. A Cretan Turk shouted up at him:

"What d'you want, Devil's monk?"

"Who is your leader? Go and tell him that the Abbot is giving himself up. He can grind me to powder. But he must give his word that the monastery will be spared."

The resounding voices were heard by both sides. They paused, and in the sudden stillness there rang out from the monastery roofs the crowing of the cocks. Morning was there.

"Lay down your weapons and come out—I shall do the monastery no harm," came the voice of the leader, Hassan Bey.

"Swear," the Abbot cried to him, and he raised his hand towards the heaven, which a rosy glow was already overspreading.

"Yes, I swear by Mohammed."

The Abbot climbed down from the wall. The monks surrounded him, and hugged his shoulders, bidding him good-bye. The rest of the comrades also pressed round him and kissed his hands.

"Farewell, great martyr, farewell!"

He approached the church, fell on his face and kissed the threshold:

"Lord Christ," he whispered, "farewell!"

Then he glanced in a circle over the courtyard, the church, the cells, the storehouses and bulwarks, and with raised hand greeted them:

"Farewell!"

As he stepped over the threshold of the outer gate, the Turks seized him, and he vanished in the crowd. At the same time a horde broke in through the open gate and poured, bellowing, into the monastery.

"They've set it on fire, the perjured dogs!" suddenly shouted Captain Polyxigis, whose head had been wounded by a scimitar-cut and was now bandaged. With an effort he subdued the pain.

"Where's Captain Michales?" he shouted afresh, and put spurs to his mare so that she flew down towards the monastery.

But Captain Michales was not yet back. His standard-bearer, Thodóres, took the lead, and they attacked the Turks from the flank. Flames were already darting from the monastery and through the ravine more and more troops with red fezes came pressing on.

The younger monks swung themselves over the walls and ran with the retreating bands up into the mountain.

"Where had Captain Michales vanished to, Brother Thodóres?" asked Captain Polyxigis, when they had reached the top of the pass. His face, throat and chest were covered with blood.

"I don't know. In the middle of the night he went off on a raid."

"A raid? Where to?"

"I don't know, I tell you."

The Christians looked down from the pass at the monastery. The flames were licking upwards. The edge of the smoke-cloud obscured the sun.

Captain Polyxigis stood there in dark perplexity. He had forgotten his pain: he no longer bothered to wipe the blood away:
his eyes were wet.

"Let's withdraw, captain," said one of the palikares. "You're
wounded. Don't stay looking at the monastery. It's done for.
God willed it so. We've done our duty."

"If only Captain Michales had been with us," he sighed.

They dragged him away by force and started off with him towards Kasteli. The other band with Captain Michales's flag made
for Petrokéfalo. The bitter tidings hurried on before them, and
as they arrived they could hear the wailing for the dead.

A scout, who had been left on the pass to observe what the
Turkish troops down below would do, came up with Captain
Polyxigis's band at about midday. He lay stretched out in a dried-
up river bed under some plane-trees, resting in the shade while
Photios, the healer monk, cleaned his wounds.

He gazed at the scout. "What's the news, Jakumes?" he
cried.

Jakumus, a sun-burned pigmy with grasshopper legs and lynx
eyes came forward. Those eyes had seen so many violent deaths
and enjoyed so many feasts and so often watched the world stand
on its head, that nothing any more could make them shrink or
make them shine. "The world's a wheel," he was in the habit of
saying, "a revolving wheel."—"And who turns it, Jakumes?"
people would ask him.—"Sometimes God, sometimes the Devil,"
he would answer. "The two are in league. One destroys, the other
builds up. They're neither of them ever out of work."

"May your wounds heal quickly," said Jakumes. "Don't be
depressed. We've come down—another time we shall go up.
Don't worry. The wheel turns."

"What's happened to the monastery?"

"What do you expect, captain? The Devil's got it . . ."

"Wither that tongue of yours, you blasphemer," cried Father
Photios, crossing himself.

"I only meant that it's become what it was before it was built.
Dust."

"And the dogs?"

"Have taken the Abbot off with them. You mark my words. They'll make tobacco-boxes of his head. A whole crowd—the poor sinner's made a good start."

And in fact, while the scout was talking so bluntly, the Turkish soldiers were driving the Abbot of Christ the Lord with their bayonets towards Megalokastro. They formed a ring round him so as to prevent the native Musulmans from killing him in their rage for vengeance. The order had gone out that they were to bring him alive to the Pacha.

The sun was still high as they entered Megalokastro with trumpets and drums. Beaming with joy, the Pacha emerged onto the balcony to greet them. The Abbot was placed before him.

"Bow, you *giaour* priest!" shouted the Pacha. Dark, thick blood was dripping from the Abbot's beard. But his eyes were un-dimmed.

He gazed at the Pacha, at the howling Turks all round him, and the sky above them with the slowly setting sun. He felt a strange light-heartedness, and his shoulders were prickling as if wings were trying to break out of them for the crossing to the Beyond.

"Have you no fear?" shouted the Pacha again. "Why is your face all shining? What are you thinking? Where are you in your thoughts?"

"In Paradise," the Abbot answered.

The Pacha was furious. It was not the first time that he had struck a Cretan rock and his knife glanced off it.

"You're not in Paradise, you Devil's monk," he roared, "but facing the plane-tree!"

"It's the same thing," said the Abbot.

"To the plane-tree with the *giaour*," ordered the Pacha, foaming at the mouth.

The Arab and some of the soldiers seized the Abbot and dragged him out of the courtyard. Outside in the streets a thick mob was howling. The plane-tree was only a little way from the Pacha's *porte*, hard by the Venetian fountain with the marble lion.

As always just before sundown, there was a swarming of birds in the plane-tree. They had settled here for the night's slumber and were twittering gaily.

A bench was brought and the Abbot placed on it. Then they called for a Turkish barber. He appeared, with razor and scissors and bronze basin. When he saw the Abbot, he laughed:

"You're a brave palikare," he said, "I'll shave you without lather."

He grasped him by the hair and began to shear off his beard. The Abbot bit his lips, not to cry out with pain. The Turks crowding round shouted with laughter. Suleiman had meanwhile fetched the rope and was greasing it. Several Christians, hidden behind shutters on the opposite side, were following everything with held breath. And now the Pacha too sank into a chair within view of the Abbot.

When the barber had done his work, the scars from the scimitar wounds on the Abbot's furrowed head came into view. The Turk now took the scissors and cut off his hair near the roots.

"Hey, you *giaour* priest," the Pacha shouted at him, "the rope's ready greased, the Arab's standing over you. Acknowledge Mohammed, and you'll save your life."

The Abbott stepped off the bench, seized the rope from the Arab's hands, made a noose and slipped it over his neck.

"Won't you answer?" bellowed the Pacha, jumping up.

"I have answered," said the Abbot, pointing at the noose round his neck.

"Curses on you Cretans!" shouted the Pacha, blue with rage. "Hang him!"

The Abbot stepped up on to the bench himself. The Arab made the rope fast to a thick bough of the plane-tree.

The Abbot crossed himself, looked about him and saw in the air a troop of ancient popes, grey-headed fallen warriors who, like Christ, had worn a crown of thorns and now greeted him with open eyes.

The Abbot uttered a cry of joy: "I'm coming!" He kicked the bench away and hung in the air.

When Captain Michales came back to the monastery towards

noon, to resume the fight beside his companions, he found neither monastery nor companions.

The "Christ The Lord" was ablaze, the cupola of the church had fallen in, the ancient, decorated ikonostasis was smouldering, the vestments, psalters, ikons lay already in ashes. In thick clouds the smoke rose into the still air and remained hanging over the ravine.

Captain Michales tugged at his beard and stared. He could not turn his eyes away from the devouring flames.

"How could I go away? How could I go away?" he groaned, and tore out hairs from his beard.

Last night passed through his mind. The breathless chase, his comrades panting after him on foot, then later, at grey of dawn, the wide, dry river-bed and above it, between the white chalk cliffs, the twenty Turks driving before them a mare, on which there sat a muffled woman. . . .

They closed, they went for one another with knives, they bellowed—for how long? An hour? Two hours? It seemed to him to pass as quickly as a flash. The valley whirled about him, became a threshing-floor. In the middle of the threshing-floor stood an acacia; and under it was the muffled woman. With head erect, sitting motionless on the mare, she waited for the victor, to go with him. She had her face turned away from the men. . . .

And suddenly the beaten Turks were running with cries away from the threshing-floor, throwing down their pistols and knives and making for Megalokastro. Captain Michales turned his head away, so as not to see the musk-fragrant woman, and beckoned Vendúsos to him.

"Take this woman and bring her to my old aunt Kalió, at Korakiés. Tell her she's to give her food and drink till we see what happens."

"Shouldn't I take her back to Kasteli?" asked Vendúsos, with a crafty wink. "Poor Captain Polyxigis will kill himself."

"Let him kill himself."

Now, as he gripped the reins, for a moment, his soul staggered. Whither was he to turn? He would not, could not decide. But suddenly he ground his teeth—the decision was made, he spurred

the mare and stormed down to Christ The Lord Monastery once
once more. And now there he was, staring at the flames.

"I ought not to have gone away," he groaned again, and tore
hair after hair from his beard.

He dismounted, and picked up a handful of hot ashes. His impulse was to smear his beard and hair with those ashes and rub
them into his face. But he controlled himself. He opened his fist,
and the ashes trickled slowly down.

"Let the one who's to blame burn and perish like that!" he
muttered, and leapt on to the mare. He gave her the spurs, so
that her belly bled.

Now Crete was afire from end to end. The mountains, the
ravines, the crossroads rang once more with shots and hoarse
voices, and the men had once more turned into bellowing, biting,
murdering beasts. The grizzled champions thought of their youth
and took to the mountains likewise, some armed, taking part in
the fighting, others, because their years and their old wounds
had weakened them, imparting advice to the new captains in
secret recesses. They taught them the tricks and stratagems of the
earlier leaders of bands—how to send out spies, delude and en-
circle the Turks, break into the Turkish villages by night. . . .

Captain Eliás too came riding out on his old mule. He rode
from mountain to mountain and hid in the various captains' nests
in turn. "Old age is crippling, children," he sighed. "I can't fight
any longer with weapons—I shall make war with my head, until
that too drops to the earth and turns into earth!"

To-day he had reached Vrisses, the juicily green village rich in
springs, and was sitting under an ancient, hollow plane-tree.
Children, women and old men were sitting around him, listening
open-mouthed.

"How often," he said, brushing the darkly luminous foliage
with his inactive arms, "this plane-tree has sheltered doughty
captains in its shade. Whoever saw them thought they must be
immortal. And yet they too died. Who would have believed it?
They have turned into the soil of Crete, and we tread on it."

He sighed. His heart was oppressed to-day. The evil news of

the burning of the "Christ The Lord" was flying like a raven, croaking, from village to village. It had reached Vrisses shortly before noon. Round about Captain Eliás there sat many old men, wagging their heads and muttering, and many weeping women.

Captain Eliás pretended not to see or hear: he was trying to deflect their thoughts from the great misfortune by reminding them of worse disasters in the past.

Suddenly swift hoofbeats were heard, and all turned to look. Between the olives and plane-trees they made out—sometimes obscured, sometimes appearing in the sunlight—a horseman with a black head-band: Captain Michales.

"Captain Michales," they all cried, in violent agitation. Captain Eliás bent his head well down and scratched the ground with the end of his stick.

"He's coming back alone," screamed one woman, who had just given her child suck and was hastily buttoning up her bodice. "Where are our husbands? Where's my husband? The wild boar took them off on his neck!"

"He left the monastery when it was in danger, they say. He ought to be burnt!" cried another, and turned to go away so that she might not see him.

"Don't spare him, Captain Eliás," said an old man. "Nobody leaves his post like that. Rub his nose in it! You're the eldest and the most respected. We're under his orders and can't show him our tongues. You can!"

Captain Eliás raised his stick.

"Enough!" he cried angrily. "I don't need your advice."

"Here he is!" they all whispered, and bunched together, in order to open the circle which they had formed around Captain Eliás.

Captain Michales appeared, sweat-soaked and with his most sombre expression. His eyebrows hid his eyes. Mare and rider were steaming in the early afternoon sun.

As he recognised Captain Eliás under the plane-tree, he wanted to turn. But it was too late. He would have to bite the bitter apple. He dismounted.

"Good-day, Captain Eliás," he said, stretching out his hand.

The grizzled captain pretended not to see the outstretched hand, and scratched the ground again.

"Let's call it a good day, Captain Michales, even if it isn't one." he replied.

Captain Michales's blood boiled. He gripped the mare's reins and looked as if he meant to mount again and ride away. He was not used to having stones thrown in front of his feet by anybody. He observed the faces around him. "They know already," he thought, and his face grew yet more savage.

He tore off some leaves from the plane-tree and threw them down.

"It's the way things happen in war, Captain Eliás," he said. "You know that well. How often in your time Christians were smoked out. Think of Arkadi."

"Don't dare speak of Arkadi!" shouted the old captain, and both his eyes—the glass one as well as the other—sent out sparks. "Were we, at Arkadi, smoked out, or turned into gods? But at the 'Christ The Lord'—forgive me for saying so——"

He broke off and turned to the women and old men: "Leave us alone. Go to your homes."

All stood up, sullenly. The old men, as they went past him, threw oblique glances at Captain Michales, the women cursed softly and gave him a wide berth. Only the young mother who had just given suck to her child, stopped fearlessly in front of him:

"What's become of our husbands?" she asked, looking him straight in the eyes. "Answer for them before God!"

"Get away from here!" shouted Captain Eliás. "Silence!"

When they were alone, he leaned on his stick, gave a heave and stood up.

"Captain," he said, "when you arrived, you offered me your hand. I refused it. You have disgraced your name, Captain Michales."

"Even if you are older than me," Captain Michales retorted, "even if you are a fighter from the 1821, I've something to say to you. And you mark what I say! Whoever speaks to me must weigh his words, Captain Eliás!"

"I too have something to say to you. To-day you have disgraced your name, Captain Michales!"

The gall rose into Captain Michales's eyes. But this man there before him was an old man, old as the hills, a relic of 1821, a fragment from the ruins of Arkadi—he could not touch him. . . . He turned away and walked under the plane-tree.

"Why did you ride away in the night and leave the monastery in the lurch?—You don't answer? Where did you go? Didn't you know that the Turks were frightened of you and would attack as soon as they found out that you were leaving your post? And they did find out, the dogs. I don't know who betrayed it to them. That's how the monastery was lost. And you're the one who's to blame!"

Captain Michales felt his temples bursting. He lowered his head.

"I'm not the one to blame," he said in a whisper.

"Then who is?" asked Captain Eliás, leaning against the tall trunk of the plane-tree. "Who is?"

Captain Michales was silent.

"Where were you? Why did you go away? You're not the one to blame, you say. Then who is?" asked the old man relentlessly.

"Don't ask, old Captain Eliás," said Captain Michales dully. "It's my business. I owe no explanations to anybody."

"You owe explanations to your forefathers, to my forefathers, to all our forefathers who have turned into the earth of Crete, on which we tread. Aren't you a Cretan? Aren't you one with the soil of Crete? What do you mean, then, by propping yourself up with the words: 'I owe no explanations'? Aren't you ashamed of yourself?"

Captain Michales drove his nails into the trunk of the plane-tree. It was the first time he had heard a human being speak to him so boldly and contemptuously. Was the old man perhaps right? But Captain Michales would not give ground.

"I owe no explanations to anybody," he repeated defiantly. "Only to myself. Goodbye, Captain Eliás. I want to be alone, to arrive at a judgement."

"From the judgement that you pass we shall see how much

soul, and what sort of soul, has remained to you, Captain Michales. Go with the blessing and the curse of the Lord Christ. One thing I've still got to say to you—and make what I say fast in your mind: Captain Michales, Crete still needs you! You understand what I mean."

Captain Eliás had suddenly been afraid that the other might kill himself and that Crete would lose that pillar.

"I understand," Captain Michales answered, and was on his mare without having touched the stirrups.

Instead of turning right, towards Petrokéfalo, as he had planned, he took the road to the left, for Selena. The sun had set. Night rose up from the soil. A fresh wind was blowing from the heights. Captain Michales bared his fevered chest to cool it down.

"She's the one to blame, she, the shameful woman!" he muttered suddenly, and halted. He took off his head-band and dried the sweat. He breathed deeply. His brain grew suddenly clear—he understood. He knew now where he was going and what he was seeking. Why, instead of making for Petrokéfalo he had taken the road towards Selena. Captain Eliás was right. The desire came over him to turn back, to seize the old man's hands—those brave banes of the Turks—and kiss them. That was how a man should speak to a man. Mercilessly, like that!

A sturdy old man with a sack on his back and a long shepherd's staff passed him. He did not recognise Captain Michales in the dusk.

"Have you heard the news, godson?" he called out to him. "The 'Lord Christ' has been burned down."

"Yes, burned down," Captain Michales answered, and drove his horse on to avoid a conversation.

"Damnation take the one who's to blame," cried the old man, shaking his staff at the sky.

"Damnation," echoed Captain Michales's voice in the darkness.

The slender half-moon set, and the stars in herds circled round the unmoving Pole-star which drove them on like a shepherd.

But Captain Michales did not raise his eyes to heaven. He kept them fixed on the base of the mountain, where a few weak little lights twinkled. He was nearing the small village of Korakiés.

The house of his aunt Kalió stood at the entrance to the village. At this hour the old woman was certainly asleep. All her life she had got up with the cock and gone to bed when the hens went. She had married, borne children, acquired grandchildren and great-grandchildren, and was now crinkled like a currant, hunchbacked and deaf as well, yet her eyes still had a light in them. Charos had forgotten her.

Captain Michales dismounted and sat down on a stone at the curb. He pressed his head down hard between his two fists. Captain Eliás's words were sticking like knives into his heart. "You have disgraced your name, Captain Michales!" he repeated to himself again and again, to give himself the courage for the carrying out of his decision. In the village a dog could be heard howling long and mournfully, as though it scented Charos near.

"My aunt has no dog in her yard. No one will hear me . . . no one . . . no one," he muttered, but his mind was not on his aunt nor on the dog. He sighed.

He stood up and peered towards the village. A few lamps were still lit, but soon went out, one after another. Houses and human beings sank into sleep. He sprang on to the mare and crossed himself.

"In God's name," he muttered, and rode up towards Korakiés.

In deep night he tied the mare to the ring on the tottering door and entered the yard. He knew the lie of the place well. On the right the winepress, the vats, the casks. On the left the stall for his late uncle's mule and ass, also the compartment for the two oxen. Now the animals were dead and the vineyards divided up aming the sons and daughters. In the darkness Captain Michales could feel the decay.

He glided forwards. His hand groped through the hatch in the top half of the central door and softly pushed back the bolt. The door opened. He listened, holding his breath. Over there, from the small settle, he could catch a sound of quiet breathing, then a slight rustling. Someone was lying asleep at that side of the room. Captain Michales's heart throbbed. Who might it be?

He drew near the settle with a thief's tread. His hand lay on his

M

belt, and clutched the hilt of his dagger. His nostrils quivered. No
scent of musk. "It must be the old woman," he thought, and his
heart beat more calmly. He bent forward and made out white hair
on the pillow and a shrivelled limp cheek. He drew back.

"She's in the middle room, the good one with the ikon shrine,"
he thought, and his heart began again to swell like the sea.

He stretched out his hand and pushed open the small door. The
middle room was faintly lit by a lamp which stood in front of an
ancient ikon of All Saints. Two other pictures were visible to
either side of it: the Archangel Michael and the Martyrdom of
Saint Catherine.

He leaned against the doorpost. Opposite , on his aunt's old
iron bed, he distinguished a body lying under the coverlet. He
could see raven-black hair spread out over the pillow, and the air
smelled of musk.

His eyes grew dim. He breathed hard. He could not control his
heart. With one bound he was into the room, clutching the black-
hilted dagger. He held his breath, glided forward on tip-toe and
pulled away the coverlet with his left hand. Her bosom gleamed.
It made his eyes sparkle for an instant, but his brain remained
black. Blood only was there, in waves.

The sleeping woman stirred and sighed. Her lips whispered a
secret word, and smiled.

Captain Michales bent down. The light from the little lamp
flashed on the dagger. It swooped through the air and with abrupt
violence plunged to the hilt into the white bosom.

Eminé screamed. She opened her eyes, and they were able to
recognise Captain Michales. Surprise, joy, pain, accusation—all
were whirled together in that last look.

"Oh," groaned the man. His body was shaken with pain. He
wrenched the dagger out, to avert death. But it was too late.
Eminé's eyes were already glazed.

XI

THE grandfather sat in his yard under the old lemon-tree, with a slate and a chalk on his knees. Through the open door he looked out thoughtfully at the mountain. It glimmered softly in a misty dusk. A moist south wind was announcing rain to the earth. It was cool.

"Winter's coming," he sighed.

He thought of the women and children who had been hunted from their homes by the Turks and had crept into the caves without bread, without sufficient clothing, without men to protect them. He thought of Crete, once more rattling its chains of slavery and not knowing where to stretch out its hands for help. The Franks—those dogs—had no heart; Greece, a beggar mother, had no strength; the rebel Cretans were still small in numbers, and their stocks of arms and food were even smaller. How were they to hold out? And now, on top of that, God was sending them winter and so was taking the side of the Turks.

"Thou art a Cretan and thou shalt be tried," murmured the old man, and closed his eyes. The whole island with its mountains, fruits and people was conjured up in the space between his two temples. How many risings had he lived through? How often had the houses been burned, trees felled, women dishonoured, men killed! And always God had refused to turn His eyes upon Crete.

"It there, anywhere in the world, justice and pity—a God?" he cried, and struck the slate with his fist. "Or is He deaf and merciless?"

But at that moment his grandson Thrasáki came out of the house, and the old man's features lit up. That was God's answer! All would still end well. Keep calm, old man: think of your grandson!

Thrasáki was sunburnt and in his few months among the mountains had grown into a wild animal. He was becoming more and more like his father in eyes, eyebrows, lips—and self-will. He now went over to his grandfather, took the slate from his hand and looked at it, frowning.

"You've still not written out the alphabet," he said severely.

For a month he had been trying to teach his grandfather the alphabet. By dint of strong desire the old man had managed, in spite of his years, to learn a wretched letter or two, in order—so he said—to be able at least to write his name. To be sure, he had in mind a higher aim, but he betrayed nothing of it to his grandson. But the old brain refused to take in those letters, and the heavy hand, used to mattock and gun, adapted itself badly to the brittle chalk. And so sometimes the chalk, sometimes the slate, would break in pieces, at which Thrasáki would grind his teeth in rage.

His grandfather beat his head: "I had things to do, my child. I wasn't able. Don't scold me."

"What had you got to do? You were sitting on the threshold all day. I saw you! If anyone came by, you struck up a conversation with him. I know you kept the slate on your knee, but where are the strokes and the curves? At that rate you'll never learn!"

"Don't scold me, Thrasáki, my child. It's hard for me. My hand doesn't obey me. How'm I to explain it? I want it to go to the right and it jerks to the left. I press just a little, and at once the chalk breaks. Do you see?"

"All I see is that you'll never learn the letters," answered Thrasáki, shaking his head. "Give me your hand, let me guide it."

But at that moment they heard footsteps. The grandfather looked up, full of pleasure at being released from strokes and curves. A pale, tired stranger came in sight. He wore Frankish clothes, which hung loose about him. In his hand he held an old umbrella, tied up with string.

"Good-day, countryman," the grandfather called out to him, "where are you bound for? Sit down and have a rest. And have a drink of raki."

The stranger stopped and leaned on his umbrella. He said nothing.

"Where are you going?" asked the grandfather again.

"For a walk," he answered.

"A walk?" cried the old man, surprised. "Haven't you heard the shooting, dear Christ? The world is breaking to bits, and you're going for a walk? Put down your umbrella and pick up a weapon, I tell you. Aren't you a Cretan?"

"Yes."

"What are you waiting for? Throw that umbrella away!"

The traveller looked at the cloudy sky.

"It's going to rain," he said, clasping the umbrella tightly to him.

Thrasáki meanwhile was examining the traveller's face. Suddenly he shouted:

"Aren't you Mr. Demetrós? Mr. Demetrós Leanbottom, our neighbour? Your poor wife, Penelope, was quite beside herself, because she didn't know where you had got to."

"And where is she?" asked the other, in agitation.

"How should I know? Probably running round all the villages to find you."

Big drops began to fall. Demetrós opened his umbrella and moved off on his way.

"Do stop, in Christ's name, and let me give you a raki!" cried the grandfather. "Where are you going? It's raining."

"I've got an umbrella," answered Demetrós. Without turning he went on out of sight.

"What's the matter with him? Who's driving him out, granddad?" asked Thrasáki.

"His wife," answered the centenarian, laughing. "The poor man's had enough of her and has made off."

Bertódulos in his little cloak, with his guitar slung over his shoulder, came out of the house. For breakfast he had eaten a barley biscuit soaked in vinegar and oil, plus a large chunk of cheese, and drunk a tankard of wine. So he felt gay and now came with dancing eyes into the yard, to snuff up some air.

He was tired of being all the time cooped up with women and children in the house. He played to them on the guitar, to divert their thoughts from the men fighting in the mountains. When the wind was favourable you could hear ragged firing in the distance. Then the women would step out on to the roof and listen. And their souls would fly into the mountains, to their men. Their only comfort then was Bertódulos. He played the guitar and sang pretty *canzone* from Zante, till they grew a little calmer.

"May God guard you, my little Bertódulos," a newly married girl, the pope's daughter Christiniá, had said to him the day before yesterday. "A song is like a man. It comforts a poor woman."

The good-hearted old man drew himself up proudly. Is song like a man? And all these years, like a fool, I never knew. I too might have had a wife and children and lived like a human being. . . . "What do you mean?" he asked the young woman.

"How could I explain, my little Bertódulos?" she answered, laughing mischievously. "Only we women understand things like that. I shouldn't try prying into them, if I were you."

Now he approached the grandfather and his sharp little mouth had a mocking smile.

"Have we already got past Alpha, little grandad?" he asked. "Have we reached Beta? What sunken rocks have we still got to sail round?"

"If you want my blessing," said the grandfather, turning to his grandson, "don't let this gentleman make a laughing-stock of you by taking guitar lessons from him. That's a thing only good for prima donnas!"

Bertódulos cleared his throat, but said nothing. How should he dare? A few days ago he had answered the old man back, and the old man had at once seized him under the shoulders and with one arm hoisted him on to a high ledge in the wall. He had shouted, while the women cackled with pleasure, until they got him down with a ladder. So he merely cleared his throat, squatted down behind the grandfather and hid the guitar behind his back.

"Come, I'll teach you to aim properly, little Thrasáki," said the old man. "That's a game for men. Bring me the muzzle-loader."

But Thrasáki had already fetched it and stood it behind the door.

"There is it," he said. "I spent all yesterday cleaning it."

"You have my blessing. You'll be even better than your father. Why are you goggling at me? That's what's wanted. Woe to us, if the son doesn't do better than his sire! The world would go to pieces."

He laid his hand on his grandson's head and said:

"You must outdo us all, grandson. We Cretans are not like other people. We have twice as much work to do. In the rest of the world you're a shepherd. You think of nothing but the sheep. You're a ploughman and you think of the oxen, the rain and the crops. Or of your goods, if you're a merchant. But a Cretan thinks of Crete as well. And Crete is a great plague! It takes all you have and is always right! It demands of you even your life, and you give it, and are glad to. A great plague it is, you mark my words!"

He laid the weapon across his lap and stroked it, like a living, beloved being.

"This is my life," he said, and applied himself with great attention to the loading.

"Now find yourself a target! There, that raven on the top of the acacia—have you spotted him? Hey! Put the old girl to your shoulders! Take aim! . . ."

Bertódulos shut his eyes and stopped his ears. A hollow thunder roared out. Smoke rolled from the muzzle, and the raven fell between the leaves of the tree to the ground.

Thrasáki leapt with joy and ran to pick up the dead bird. He threw it at Bertódulos' feet, to frighten him. The poor count drew back, grabbed his guitar and with trembling lips went back to the women.

All the grandfather's daughters-in-law and grand-daughters had gathered in those rambling buildings. In addition, the day before yesterday, Captain Michales's two neighbours, Mastrapas the bell-founder and fat Krasojórgis, with their families had joined them. The Turks had occupied their villages of refuge. They had just escaped on their beasts of burden. Where were they now to find a resting-place? Then they thought of Captain Michales's father. His house was accounted an impregnable fortress, he himself a generous man, who turned nobody away. As they appeared before the outer door, Krasojórgis, practised in flattery, had raised his hand to his breast and greeted the grandfather, who stood welcoming them.

"Hoary royal eagle, I and Mastrapas the bell-founder, neighbours of your son Captain Michales, hunted by the Turks, are
come to shelter beneath your wings. Hoary royal eagle, do not
drive us forth!"

And the grandfather, who had no taste for flattery, but liked
being flattered, answered smiling:

"My wings are broad. Come in!"

Bertódulos too appeared in the yard and greeted the newcomers
with superfluous ceremony.

"Greetings, Captain Séfakas," said Mastrapas. "They are right
when they say your house is a monastery."

But the old man held up his hand:

"Welcome," he said harshly, "but on one condition: both of
you are here to bear arms! So take a weapon each of you, and go
where the men are. I give fodder to no shirkers or cowards! The
women and children I will take care of, don't worry about that."
And with a laugh he added: "Don't point at Signor Bertódulos.
He's a woman and a child, both together."

Everyone laughed. But Krasójorgis and Mastrapas made wry
faces.

"We've no experience at all in warfare, old Séfakas," Krasojórgis made bold to say. "If it comes to fighting, we're lost."

"Well? If you don't go, won't you be lost in any case one day?"

"The later the better, Captain!"

"Bad luck to you!"

Krasojórgis jumped.

"All right, don't be angry, old Séfakas. We'll go. God help us."

They unloaded the beasts. The women got down, and the other
women came to help them. They were taken into the great
entrance-hall, and in a covered corner of the yard they made
themselves a hearth. In the evening all sat together at the big
table. But next morning the grandfather took two guns from a
cupboard, gave them to Krasojórgis and Mastrapas and accompanied them as far as the end of the village. There he handed them
over to his old shepherd, Charidemos.

"Good morning, Charidemos! Take them at once by the path
up the pass, to where Captain Michales has his hide-out. Be

careful, the poor fellows are new to the game. Don't go and lead them into a village full of Turks."

He turned to the two recruits and gave them his hand.

"Go with God's blessing. Do your duty! Be men. I take charge of your families. Good luck! Greet the mountains from me!"

As grandfather and grandson were chatting together again a few days later and the old man was giving the lad some of the fruit of his experience, hoofbeats rang out from the mountain path and about ten men on beasts of burden came rapidly down the slope. The grandfather stood up and looked out, shielding his eyes with his hand. But in the misty air he could make out nothing clearly. Old Mavrudés, the village crier, came by.

"What's the news, Captain Decoybird?"—for that was what the grandfather called him; "Who's this, riding in over there?"

"They say Captain Stefanés' ship has arrived in Aja Pelaja harbour. It's bringing ammunition and food. . . ."

The grandfather crossed himself.

"Poor Motherland," he muttered, "you deprive your own mouth of the best morsels and send them to us. And so?"

"And so your son's men are on their way with animals to fetch the treasure. Here they are. Give them a good reception!"

"They are welcome!" said the grandfather, opening both wings of the gate.

At the head rode Vendúsos as guide. "You're no use in a fight," Captain Michales had told him, "but you have knocked about the countryside and you're cunning and also sound on your pins. So I'll make you our runner."

"Greetings, Captain Séfakas," shouted Vendúsos, jumping down. "If it's no bother to you, we'll doss down to-day in your house and so, if God wills, ride to the coast tomorrow at crack of dawn."

"Welcome, children! First have a drink. You're tough workers!" said the old man, stretching out his hand to the newcomers.

Blackened with powder and emaciated, the palikares came into the yard. The women hurried to them and asked eagerly after their menfolk. A fire was lit. The cauldron was put on and the table laid. As it was getting dark, lamps were lit, and by their

M*

light the bony, serious faces gathered round the copious meal. They ate like beasts of prey, drank like buffaloes, their jaws crunched and their harsh manly smell spread through the whole house. The women stood at a breath's distance round them, and joyfully served the rugged guests. The grandfather too stood near them and marvelled at them without a word.

When they had eaten, drunk and crossed themselves, he said to them: "Now lie down and sleep. Stretch out those tired bodies of yours on the beds. Ah! If only I were young enough to bear all the fatigues with you. What a wretched thing I've become. I sleep in a bed every night, eat and drink morning, noon and evening, am a useless guzzler, no longer carry a gun, and nobody shoots at me. I don't wish even my enemies such wretchedness."

"God grant us we may live to reach your wretchedness, Captain Séfakas!" said Vendúsos with a laugh.

"You're the guide," replied the old man, "you'll go to sleep last, Captain Vendúsos, however tired you may be. We two must have a word together."

"At your service, Captain Séfakas," answered Vendúsos, with an effort suppressing a yawn. "It's not for nothing that I was promoted guide."

The palikares stretched themselves out side by side in their clothes and with their weapons, and even before the women had cleared the table the house was shuddering with the din of the snorers.

Since it was cool, the women heaped wood on the hearth and kindled it. The grandfather sat down in front of it with the lyre-player by his side, and the two warmed themselves. The old man stared silently into the flames. His brows, twitching with wild eagerness, moved up and down. Finally he could no longer restrain himself.

"One thing I must talk over with you, Vendúsos," he said in a whisper. "One thing that makes my heart bleed. But tell me, like a man, what you know. I'm a hundred years old and can't stand lies."

Vendúsos guessed the question in advance. He became thoughtful. At length he said:

"I will tell you the truth, the whole truth."

The grandfather lowered his voice still more:

"Why did Captain Michales go out that night, when the Christ the Lord was destroyed?"

Vendúsos poked the fire. Then he crouched back on the bench.

"Leave the fire alone," said the old man and grasped him by the arm. "Where did he go?"

Vendúsos gulped. If he now gave his tongue a free run, he would betray all. He was afraid of that.

"Captain Séfakas, it's, it's not my business!"

"Speak!" commanded the old man, and shook him by the arm.

"Speak out, don't try deceiving me. Why did he go out? Where? He's brought shame upon me. And that's why he's ashamed to look me in the face. He's afraid I shall ask him questions. But by my soul, I've a good mind to go one day—yes, to-morrow!—and seek him out in his hiding-place, call his palikares together and accuse him in front of them all. And if you don't answer me now, Vendúsos, I shall certainly do it, by this fire! And if he still has the impudence after that, let him go on playing the captain!"

This hoary lion is capable of anything, thought Vendúsos, and shuddered. Then he said:

'Don't get savage, old Séfakas. I'll tell you the whole thing from the beginning. Be patient."

"I'm patient. I'm listening."

"You know that Nuri Bey had a Circassian girl. . . ."

"Oh," the old man groaned, and beat his breast with his fist. "The shame of it! So there's a woman in the game!"

"To be sure there's a woman," said Vendúsos, now determined to reveal all. "Oh, you wanted the truth, there it is!"

"I want the truth. Be sure of that. Only speak softly. Sleep too has ears. Don't let 'em hear us. Well?"

"She's called Eminé. Captain Michales saw her one evening at Nuri's *konak* and became mad for her. A little later, on the day of the earthquake, Captain Polyxigis also saw her, and it was just

the same with him. He kept hanging about her neighbourhood.
He had completely lost his wits. Finally he stormed into her
house, sighed something to her, got into her bed and made up
his mind to marry her, the folo! She was to become Christian.
Baptism and wedding were to be celebrated together, the day
after tomorrow, Holy Cross Day."

"Go on . . . go on . . . . What has that to do with my son?"

"You'll soon understand. God forgive me, but I believe Captain Michales was even more bewitched by the Circassian's beauty
than Polyxigis. On the night when he was fighting before the
'Christ The Lord', I brought him news: Nuri's relations have
broken into Kasteli and seized the Circassian girl! At once he
sprang on to his mare and took ten of us with him. We
couldn't let him go alone. In the early morning we came upon
the robbers near Cruel Mountain. Your son fell upon them all
alone, like a raging lion. Never yet have I seen such a heroic
deed done, Captain Séfakas! All praise to you, who have
begotten such a son! The Turks left the woman and made themselves scarce."

"Oh," the old man groaned afresh, burying his face in his hands.
"So that was it: for a woman's sake he left his post, like a man of
no honour! The shame of it! Call that a heroic deed?"

"Don't curse him, Captain Séfakas! By my father's loins, your
son never once raised his head to look at the Circassian girl!
'Vendúsos,' he said to me, 'take this woman and bring her to my
aunt at Korakjes. She is to give her food and drink until we see
what happens next.' "

He fell silent and gazed into the fire. After a short pause he said:
"What happened next you will have to know, old Séfakas."

But the old man did not answer. His face had turned to wax.
All of a sudden his head looked like a skull.

"One morning she was found dead. . . . A knife in her heart,"
whispered Vendúsos.

The grandfather stretched out his hand, groped for a wine-
bottle and drank. His heart became calmer.

"Who killed her?" he asked, softly as though his voice came
from a cave.

Vendúsos bowed his head. Should he tell that too? His opinion about this business had been fixed for some time.

"She must have killed herself. . . . She herself had hold of the knife. . . . That's what people say."

"Let people say what they like. Who killed her?"

Vendúsos raised his head. Now, he thought, if you will put the pistol to my breast, old Séfakas, you shall hear it:

"Your son, Captain Séfakas."

"Why?"

Vendúsos had got it over. He felt his heart lightened. He had no need to take a run before the next bit. He replied at once:

"From jealousy."

The old man lifted a piece of wood from the ground to feed the fire, and fell into thought.

"He did the right thing," he said at last. "A bad beginning, a good ending. The worm was gnawing him. He was right."

"You don't blame him, Captain Séfakas?"

"He was only to blame for one thing: that he left his post. But he has paid for it and is still paying, and one day he will free. I have confidence in my blood."

"What has the woman done to him?"

"Do you think the woman matters? Only Crete matters, lyre-player. But go now and sleep. And keep your mouth shut! Let no breath of this escape you! If it were to get out, the two captains would kill each other. And that would not be in the interest of Crete. Good-night! Go! I shall sit up by the fire."

The morning twilight found the grandfather still in front of the hearth. The fire had gone out. He had let his head drop on his breast and fallen asleep. Vendúsos and his wolf-pack had already consumed their barley biscuits and drunk several jugs of wine. They had moved on. When the grandfather opened his eyes, there was only the smell of their cigarettes, their boots and their wine-laden breath still hanging in the air.

Towards midday, when the women in the yard had finished the baking and the grandfather had at last formed the first letters,

Alpha, Beta and Gamma, on the slate and was longing to show
them proudly to his grandson, there appeared at the outer door a
young fighter from abroad. He was wearing the *fustanella*,[1] jacket,
pointed shoes and a high fez with a thick tassel. Over his shoulder
hung his gun, and his cartridge pouches were slung across his
broad chest. He swept over the threshold a glance like an eagle's.

"A *Liape*,[2] a *Liape*!" shrieked the women, half scared, half joyful. The grandfather raised his head from the slate.

"Welcome, Hellene!" he cried. "Come in, young eagle!"

The man with the *fustanella* raised a slender leg and stepped over
the threshold. The women took courage, came closer and admired
his supple body. "Oh, what a joy for the eyes of the mother
whose son he is!" whispered one of them. "He's like a Cretan."

The young hero took his stand before the grandfather and
greeted him:

"Are you, sir, the man they call old Captain Séfakas?"

"From head to foot. Only I used to be Captain, once upon a
time. Now I'm only old Séfakas. And what good wind has blown
you to my house?"

"I come from Captain Stefanés' ship. My name's Mitros and
I'm from Rumelia. I've heard that Crete is fighting, and I've come
to fight too. In Syra a man in Frankish clothes, who calls himself
your grandson, gave me this letter for you. Stretch out your hand
that I may give it you. This was my introduction."

The grandfather stretched out his hand and took the letter.
He examined it and passed his hand over it with great joy. It came
from his favourite grandson: the first-born son of his eldest son,
Kostaros. He was the first one he had dandled on his knees, and
the first to call him "Grandpa".

"Thanks, my young hero, for the trouble you've taken," he
said, stuffing the letter into his shirt.

With a laugh he glanced at Thrasáki:

"I shall give it to another grandson of mine, a learned one, so
that he can read it out to me. But later. Now lay the table, women,
we've got a guest of noble lineage, a true Greek. Bring him the
good chair to sit on."

[1] Long coat.
[2] A Greek from the mainland.

They bought an old chair on whose back was carved the two-headed eagle. The grandfather stood with beaming face in the middle of the yard, and at the sight the Rumeliot was reluctant to sit down. He stood in admiration before the strong, snow-white ancient. The old man's like a God, he thought, an Immortal.

"Grandfather," he said, seizing the old man's hands, "I've heard that you have lived like a great oak tree. You have breathed up storms, suffered, triumphed, struggled, laboured a hundred years long. How has life seemed to you during those hundred years, grandfather?"

"Like a glass of cool water, my child," replied the old man.

"And are you still thirsty, grandfather?"

The greybeard raised his hand, so that the wide sleeve of his shirt fell back and revealed the bony, furrowed arm as far as the shoulder.

"Woe to him," he cried in a loud voice, as though he were cursing, "woe to him who has slaked his thirst!"

They were silent for a moment, the young man and the ancient, in mutual wonder. Between the two stood Thrasáki, gazing full of pride at the old man and the young man. And in a circle the women, arms akimbo.

At length the old man opened his mouth to ask a question, at the same time pointing at the sky to the north:

"And what have you brought us by way of news, young warrior, from over there, from Greece? You've no more Turks in your land, you lucky beggars!"

He sat down on the bench with a sigh, and the Rumeliot sat on the carved chair and Thrasáki near his grandfather, gazing insatiably at the man with the *fustanella*.

"We have no Turks, certainly," answered Mitros, "but we have big land-owners, police and politicians. Don't ask me about them, old man."

In the yard there was a smell of hot bread, and the Rumeliot felt faint. He had been fasting since morning. He cast an eager glance at the hot barley cakes. The old man caught the glance and laughed.

"Quick, you women, we'll soon have no strength left," he called. "Bring us some warm bread and some cheese and a jug of wine to put power into the heart."

He let his eyes range over the yard, the barns, the horse-pond, the outer door and the wine-presses. He brought them to rest on the Rumeliot, and laughed again.

"Do you know why I'm laughing, youngster?" he asked. "By my soul, a man's memory, when it grows old, becomes a cemetery. Sometimes, though, the gravestones suddenly tilt up and the dead climb out. Yes, at this moment, when I see a *fustanella* in my yard once more, I suddenly remember 1866, and how in this very yard, in the chair in which you are sitting, Captain Liápes (God rest his soul!) a Greek, sat. And my wife and mother-in-law, old Malámo (God rest their souls!), pulled the bread out of the oven. It was autumn, like now, on Saint Drunkard Jorgis' day. In the village they were settling the wine, opening the casks, and tasting the new vintage. And at that moment there appeared Kastanías (God rest him!) a fellow like from the old days, who could overtake a horse running. With him came Surmelés ('rest him!), the famous captain of the steamer 'Devil Pandelés' ('rest her!). And I said to my eldest son, Kostaros ('rest him!): 'Bless that youth of yours, Kostaros, bring us a small cask of wine and let's empty it.' And while I was still speaking, who should appear also from the mountain but Pig-Jorgis ('rest him!)—his name suited him—my god-father, a rich owner of herds, with a slaughtered ram over his shoulders and behind him his wife, the black-eyed Angeliko ('rest her!), with a soft cheese in each hand? 'Hey, now we've got some good things to eat!' they all shouted ('rest their souls!) and burst out laughing. From the street the schoolmaster (God forgive him!) Manelaos, the sweet tooth, who was passing by, heard the laughter, barged open the door and came in. 'Welcome, schoolmaster,' they cried (God rest them!), 'sit down and do your paper work while we eat and drink.'—'Devil take schoolmastering,' he answered. 'I'm going to eat and drink with you too, and I'll call old Maliarió the rhymesmith over, so that he can amuse us with his verses.' With one bound he was outside and fetched Maliarió ('rest his soul!) with his lyre. He brought, as well, Andrulés from

Sfakia ('rest him!) with his bagpipes, and Purnáras (God rest him too!—when he opened his mouth to sing, the stones shook). Ah, God rest them all, what's become of their lips and throats and hands?

"I jumped up, took the pipe which I used for filling casks, and made it fast to the bung-hole of the cask. 'You wild beasts,' I called out, 'what d'you want glasses for? Do bull-calves drink out of glasses? We'll drink straight from the cask—you take a pull, then I take a pull. You start, Captain Liápes, you're the eldest!' I hardly finished saying it when he'd grasped the pipe and begun gulping the stuff down, so that there was a gurgling from the cask like from a nargile. God rest him, he drank and drank—we began to think he'd drink the cask dry. Finally we took the pipe away from him, all the others (God rest them!) had a swill in turn. I wasn't left out either, God be thanked!

"Yes, by God, what a feast that was! Ah, God rest them, how they ate and drank, how they filled their hands with cheese! While we were at it, the ram was roasted, and Liápes, God rest him, got hold of the pipe again. 'You seem to be doing nicely, old chaps,' came a voice from the door. It was Nechtaris the pope (God rest him!), with the Abbot of Our Lady with the Myrtle ('rest *him*!). Both of them were as full as sponges with drink and began dancing in the yard, kicking their legs up high, and singing the funeral hymn: 'To the last greeting come'. And every time they came to the words 'last greeting' they kissed the pipe and took a pull, and from inside the cask there was already the gurgle of the last drops among the lees! Ah, God rest them! what a laughing and singing and mocking of Charos that was! 'Stamp on the earth that's going to eat us,' they cried, and planted their wide soles firmly—some in boots, others bare-foot. They had hitched their breeches well up. What bones were those, and what calves, and the hairs on them—real bristles!"

The grandfather fell silent. He took hold of his beard and sank into thought. His clear eyes stared into the air and saw all those forms. Dread had seized the young man in the *fustanella* as he listened to the grizzled Cretan peopling his yard with the departed. He could hear the soles of the dead men's feet stamping on the ground, he could see their bristly manly calves. The women stood some way off, smiling, and Thrasáki was striking the ground happily with his small feet and laughingly challenging Charos. Only poor Bertódulos, who joined them in order to admire the *fustanella*, shrank back into the house as soon as he saw the apparition of the departed.

The grandfather opened his mouth again. His eyes were moist: "I started by laughing," he said, "but now that I've reminded myself of all those people gone underground, I have to be sad. No, not sad, but angry. Yes, angry. There's something here that's not right at all! Let God do anything else He likes, but He's done this wrong—may He forgive me! There are men who ought not to die. Why don't the mountains die? These men shouldn't die either. They should remain where they are on earth like pillars and support the heavens. There, there, I'm stamping on you, earth, damn you! Gobble up the fools, the cripples, the crooked mouths! Gobble 'em up! Get rid of them! But not of Captain Liápes and Kastanías and the Abbot of Our Lady with the Myrtle and my eldest son Kostaros!"

The grandfather stamped on the ground, and two fat tears welled from his eyes.

"Hey, grandfather," said Thrasáki, catching him by the hand. "The table's laid. The *Liápe's* hungry."

The old man looked at his grandson, felt the cool little hand on his bony, burning fingers and once more made his peace with God.

"Forgive me, children. I was remembering the ones that have gone and I lost my bearings. But we're still alive. So forward! To table, all the living!"

With these words he sat down on the ground and pulled the table between him and the Rumeliot. He made Thrasáki too sit near him.

"Welcome, countryman! God bless us and keep us always close together!" he said, piling his guest's plate with food.

Meanwhile Vendúsos and his wolf-pack were approaching the coast. The sea-breeze was in their faces, making the tassels on their head-bands flutter. Joy gave them wings: they were going to land

weapons and load their mules with provisions and give the revolt
fresh nourishment. It was all theirs. Greece had sent it for them.
And yet—is there any fun in receiving something peacefully and
sharing it out justly and reasonably? What did they do over the
wives? When the parents had come to an agreement, the bride was
combed and adorned and the tables were laid; but did meat one
had not stolen taste good? So the bridegroom would storm in on
horseback and seize the bride. She would pretend to resist. He
would lift her on to his saddle and make off with her like lightning,
shooting in all directions and yelling, to his home.

Captain Stefanés's corsair ship, the *Miaulis*, had managed in the
darkness to elude the Turkish patrol vessels. She had run the
blockade and made land in the small remote harbour of Aja Pelaja,
under its mighty cliffs. The sea was gentle as milk. The neighbouring villages had not yet noticed that a laden ship was anchored off
their beach. And so Captain Stefanés had had time to unload his
freight undisturbed and to spread it out on the cliffs.

The sun to-day was mild, autumnal; the sea-mews circled over
the ship or squatted on the rocks and watched. Captain Stefanés
had come ashore and was hobbling up and down over the thick-
strewn flints. He had also brought Saint Nicolas ashore and made
him fast to a rock so that his face was turned to the ship. He was
to sun himself, but also to keep watch.

"Hurry up, children!" he called out to his sailors, "don't let
the Turks catch us. Don't give the Christians time, either, to find
us and start plundering. They're the ones I'm most afraid of. Be
quick, children! Captain Michales's palikares will turn up, where-
ever he may be."

"There they are already!" shouted the ship's boy, who had
climbed to the top of the mast. He was pointing at the ten palikares, who came riding down on their mules.

Captain Stefanés turned round and recognised Vendúsos at
their head. With a laugh he called out to him:

"Have you too joined the warriors?"

"That's what I've been condemned to," answered the other,
jumping off his mule and embracing the captain. "You've come
in the nick of time. We'd no powder left, and hunger was begin-

ning to worry us. A thousand times welcome, Captain Stefanés!"

But the seaman was in a hurry.

"Help us unload," he said, "so that I can sail away promptly, as soon as it's night. I've been caught once, and that's enough. Go at it, get going! Pretend you're robbing us, to make it more fun."

Vendúsos took him by the arm and led him aside. "Greetings from Captain Michales," he said to him in a low voice. "And if you've any message . . ."

"What message?" said Captain Stefanés, scratching his head.

"Entrust it to me. No one except Captain Michales shall know of it."

Captain Stefanés bent down, picked up a big pebble, and threw it into the sea. He threw another and still said nothing. At last he plucked up courage and said:

"Vendúsos, you're a good lyre-player, I know. But, forgive my saying so, I've no trust in that little tongue of yours. As soon as you've had a drop too much . . ."

Vendúsos sighed:

"Where am I to get a drop too much? Don't worry. . . ."

Captain Stefanés looked at Vendúsos searchingly. The sun had browned him. His body was taut, the fat had vanished from his neck and cheeks, and his eyes now shone with something other than wine.

"Unbar your ears then, Vendúsos," he said, in a muffled voice. "Report to Captain Michales my exact words—do you understand? Don't soften them down, and don't blow them up."

"You needn't worry, Captain. Speak out."

"I've no good news to send him. I've knocked at some important doors, spoken with leading men and urged them to tell me the truth: whether they had any hope that Crete would be freed, or thought that all our pains would again be thrown to the winds. Some of them beat about the bush, others talked a lot of high-sounding nonsense, and only one man spoke out honestly. And who was he? Captain Michales's nephew Kosmas, who had just landed in Syra—he'd come from the Franks' country. 'You must be brave, Captain Stefanés,' he said to me. 'Crete will not see freedom this time either.'—'Will our blood be shed in vain, then?'

I asked.—'Blood is never shed in vain,' he answered. 'Don't you know that freedom is a grain of seed? But it doesn't sprout if you give it water. It has to be blood. So we're sprinkling the seed now in the right way, and it's certain that one day the plant will come up, but that day hasn't arrived yet.' Then he pulled a letter out of his pocket and gave it to me. 'Send it,' he said to me, 'by a trustworthy man to my grandfather, old Séfakas.' It's been sent to him already, by a *Liápe* who was on board our ship. Captain Michales can learn the rest from that letter."

Vendúsos listened with bent head, while his feet kicked the pebbles about violently. When Captain Stefanés had finished speaking he burst out:

"Is there no God, then? What do you think, Captain Stefanés?"

"What's a poor wretch like me to think? I don't even know if there's a Saint Nicolas, and are you asking me about God? And Saint Nicolas is sometimes there when he's wanted, and sometimes he's not there when he's wanted. I've learned that all right, in the many years I've been beating up and down the sea. So let's not talk about God, but see what happens."

The sea was growing dim as the sun sank. The whole belly of the ship had been emptied, and guns, cartridges, leather equipment, flour and salted fish were now on the backs of the mules— sheer gifts of God to the Cretans.

"I'll bring you more powder and food yet," cried Captain Stefanés to the ten corsairs by way of good-bye. But as he was about to jump on board, he remembered the ikon.

"O mercy, I've forgotten Saint Nicolas!" he said, and limped up the cliff as fast as he could. He carried the picture down and dipped it in the sea to refresh it. Then he kissed the hands of the Saint, still dripping with salt water.

"On the journey here you managed well, Nicolas, my captain!" he said to the ikon. "Good luck to you, and now mind you don't disgrace us on the return journey. And I vow, by the sea, that I'll order a picture of you from the holy Mount Athos: with short breeches and a black fez and a telescope in your hand, like the sea-hero Miaulis. Miaulis and Ai-Nicolas in one—that would be safest. . . ."

He leapt aboard. Clouds were now gathering in the sky: the
world grew dark. A light breeze was blowing from the land, and
a swell was beginning. Captain Stefanés picked up his telescope.
The sea seemed dead. He crossed himself.

"In God's name, he said. "Weigh anchor, children! Saint
Nicolas, we're casting off!"

After he had eaten and drunk and the table had been cleared
away, the *Liápe* leaned against a doorpost and went to sleep. The
rude sea had turned his inside upside-down. It was the first time
he had come down from the Pindus mountains and gone on board
a ship. His hero's courage had melted away when he had soiled
his *fustanella*. Even now it seemed to him as if the earth were
swaying under his feet like the ship's deck. It was only when he
had smelled horse-dung that he had felt better. Tomorrow morning, early, Charidemos, the old shepherd, was to take him to
Captain Michales's citadel. He gave himself up to sleep with a
feeling of security.

When the grandfather heard the man in the *fustanella* snoring,
he beckoned Thrasáki, and sat down with him under the old
lemon-tree in the middle of the yard. The women were no longer
working at the oven and had gone indoors. Silence reigned over
the yard. It was a good opportunity for the reading-out of the
letter. The grandfather expected bad news, for his grandson
Kosmas was only in the habit of writing to him if there was something important. The old man pulled out the letter and tore open
the envelope.

"Come, Thrasáki," he said, "read it slowly, word by word, so
that I can understand."

The writing was clear. Thrasáki read, without stumbling:

"Honoured Grandfather, I have returned to the sacred soil.
Perhaps I shall soon come to Crete and kiss your respected
hand . . ."

"He's a flatterer too, muttered the old man, shaking his heavy,
white-haired head. "But what sort of a letter is this? He doesn't
begin by asking after our health. All right! Go on, Thrasáki."

"But before such a pleasure can be vouchsafed to me, I find

myself compelled to write you this letter. As soon as you have read it, sent it by sure hand to my uncle, Captain Michales. I hear he has raised his banner and is once more fighting in the mountains against the Turks. It is good that he should know how things are, and not grope forwards blindly. Afterwards let him do as God enlightens him."

"A long yarn. Still, read on. But slowly, Thrasáki, there's a good lad."

"So then: from Greece no hope is to be looked for. She is too weak. A poor beggar of a country without a fleet and, what is worst, without the slightest support from the Franks. Crete is a good morsel. And the mighty of the earth are interested in its remaining on the Sultan's plate. If he comes to grief and the heritage has to be divided up, each of the Great Powers hopes that Crete will fall to it. If, on the contrary, Crete became united with Greece, neither God nor the Devil could separate them again."

"Oh," groaned the old man, "this grandchild of mine has learnt a lot. Go on!"

"Realise, then: Crete is condemned to failure this time too. We can have success only in one way: by starting negotiations, to get the Sultan to enlarge our rights. This, I know, is merely a bone, but it has some meat on it. Let's gnaw it till the good moment comes."

"We're reduced to dogs, mangy dogs. People throw bones to us! Go on."

"I have spoken with many official personages among the Franks and in Greece. Tomorrow I am going to Athens, to see some men who are very highly placed. If necessary, I shall come to Crete, to help save what can be saved. This time again, unfortunately, the pen will be mightier than the sword. The sword-bearers have done their duty and prepared the way. But they could not reach the goal. Now the pen-bearers are going into action—don't be angry with me, Grandfather. . . ."

"These quill-drivers!" the grandfather shouted, and spat; "glasses, tight breeches, hats, swallow-tails and stockings! Ugh!" —and again he spat.

He turned to Thrasáki:

"Finished? Is there any more?"

"One sentence, granddad: 'I kiss your hand with deep respect, Grandfather. Give me your blessing! Your grandson, Kosmas.' "

The grandfather let his head sink forward. There was rage in his breast. He closed his eyes and saw, standing before him in the middle of the yard, bewildered, bloodstained Crete. Was it Crete? Or was it the Virgin, coming from her Son's cross? Some large drops of rain fell.

"My little Thrasáki," said the grandfather at last. "You have learned a secret. You're a man. Don't betray it!"

"Don't worry, granddad. Not a soul shall know. Only we two, and a third—my father."

"And a fourth—God. That's enough."

While grandfather and grandson were still talking, Tityros appeared on the threshold with his staff, with his sack on his back, and with red cheeks. The grandfather was sitting on the roots of the lemon-tree, now wet with rain, and raindrops glittered in his beard. He himself was like an old tree-trunk and let himself be sprinkled without stirring. The old man's leathery hand gleamed. For a moment he did not recognise his son, who looked stouter and more sunburned and had no stoop.

"Is it you, Janakos?" he called out, and raised his head to see better. "You've changed, thank God. Aren't you a teacher any more? Come in."

"Don't you recognise me, Father?" asked the teacher delightedly.

"How should I recognise you? I'd be ready to swear you've given up paper work and fashioned yourself a neck, a pair of shoulders and good, healthy cheeks. Didn't I tell you? Those letters are leeches, twenty-four leeches that suck a man's blood. I too have been trying hard to learn that damned alphabet. A stony road! A torment! I stumble from one letter to another. But I've got a definite aim. What about you?"

Tityros laughed, and seized his father's hand and kissed it. "Father," he said teasingly, "it was your fault that I became a teacher. Do you remember?"

"Of course I remember. Do you think I've grown feeble? You were no good for anything else. But really, I was wrong."

The old man looked at Tityros right and left, pinched him in the arm, squeezed his hand and pulled up his lip, as they do with cattle, to examine the teeth. He was satisfied.

"By my faith," he said, "this one's beginning to be a pleasure to me. Of course, you were my child, I was fond of you . . . but how am I to put it? You were no pleasure to me. You seemed to me like the lather from soap, with your book-learning and your stoop. You didn't fit into our family. All our forefathers had worn full breeches and high boots, and carried a gun. But you dressed in the Frankish style, wore glasses and carried a pen. 'That's that,' I thought, 'the blood's exhausted and is going to the devil. . . .' But now here you are, coming back to the natural way of men, thank God! And my name shan't be Séfakas if I don't give you some full breeches and high boots and hang a gun over your back! Did you hear what I said? Why are you laughing?"

"Are you a prophet, Father? Can you read behind my forehead? That's just what I've come to the house of my fathers for, to-day, I swear! You're bound to have an old suit, that you or one of your sons who was killed used to wear. And in your store-room there's surely a gun left. Here in the yard we'll burn my Frankish clothes together, as they burn Judas, and I'll dress up like a Cretan. Then I'll take a gun on my shoulder and go into the mountains. I've got a special aim too."

The old man grasped his son's head and pulled him against his breast.

"Take my blessing," he said. "I'm going to kill a goat in your honour, and this evening we'll celebrate. I thought of you as lost. Welcome, Janakos!"

The old man forgot his grief over his grandson's letter, began opening old chests, and brought out the finest suit there was: an embroidered jacket, full breeches of thick wool, a silken linen belt and a fez from Tunis. He chose boots of the smallest size, and fetched a gun, from the store-room. All this he placed on top of a chest, to deck out his youngest son on the morrow like a bridegroom.

There was great rejoicing in the house. For the rumour had gone about that the schoolteacher had had a trap set for him by the Turks in the course of his wanderings through the villages and that they had taken him prisoner and spitted him like an Easter lamb. And now here he was, in full health, devouring with his father the whole of a small kid and drinking wine out of the jug. Beside the two of them Thrasáki felt quite small! He could hardly bring himself to eat. He simply stared in bewilderment at the schoolmaster. Was this the same man under whose feet they had strewed shot so that he fell full length and broke his glasses? And against whom they had let loose mice and made him tremble?

"Off with you, Thrasáki, to bed with you," said the grandfather. "I've still some things to say to your uncle. And never call him schoolmaster again, do you hear? Always Uncle Janakos now!"

"What was the truth of that business with your wife?" he asked, when they were alone and seated on the low sofa. "Why did she hang herself? Can you explain it? I've asked the others, but they all put me off with talk."

"God forgive her. The poor thing was sick with fear and ran away."

"She did right," said the grandfather. "There was strength in the woman. It takes courage to kill oneself. She was running away from you as well, that's sure. . . . And now what do you mean to do? Won't you marry again? Won't you beget me a little grandson? My last? You must hurry up. My days are numbered."

The schoolmaster's face beamed as he said:

"What a miracle, Father! The nearer you come to death, the more you resemble an immortal. Yes, you've discovered my second aim that brought me here."

"Well tell me, Janakos! Has some girl dazzled your eyes?"

"Yes, she's dazzled me, and I ask for your blessing."

"Who is she by Saint Onufrios? Is she all right? Strong bones, broad hips, a good family with lots of vineyards and fields? Has she her thirty-two teeth?"

"She's all right," the man bent on marriage answered. "She's got all her teeth—thirty-two and more."

"No, not more! That would not be good. Then she could ride you. A thing that's unnatural is against God's will. Thirty-two are enough. But let's hear who she is. Who are her parents?"

"She's a grandchild of Captain Eliás. Her name's Pelaja. And I've come to ask for your blessing."

"Ah, bravo, Janakos! You have my blessing! That's a fruitful stock with sons, grandsons, vineyards and fields. And will she have you?"

"She'll have me and has spoken to her father. He answered: 'We'll ask the old man—he's head of our race!' They told him. At first Captain Eliás looked sourly. 'A schoolmaster,' he said, 'I know him. A lean-bottomed weakling. All the same, his family's all right. Fruitful, with sons and grandsons and vineyards and fields.' —'It's true, what you say about the family'.—'Wait till I've had time to think it over.' But the girl was in a hurry, and she talked to him and was nice to him and won the grandfather over to our side. 'Good,' he said. 'I give my blessing. But on.one condition. On this I insist: he's to put off that Frankish suit of his and dress like a man.' "

Old Séfakas clapped his hands:

"God protect you, old Eliás! It was a great worry to me too, but I said nothing. And now, into the fire with that suit, tomorrow, first thing!"

The schoolmaster slept well, close to the chest with his bridegroom outfit. Pelaja came into his dreams and he had no wish to wake up. But the grandfather did not close an eye. He watched the window impatiently for the dawn twilight. God let the twilight come, and the black cock crowed. Soon afterwards the white one too, and the bright day was there. The old man sprang up and gave Tityros a kick. "Wake up," he called out to him, "the clothes are lying on the chest. May they bring you happiness! And fetch that Frankish suit into the yard. I'm going to light a fire."

He had always disliked the Franks. Now, after his grandson's letter, they made him furious. He went downstairs. The women were not yet up. He lit the fire. Then he went to wake Thrasáki. He had been given one of the big vats to sleep in, like a cradle. He shook him awake.

"Get up, Thrasáki! Come into the yard with me. We mean to burn Judas!"

The schoolmaster appeared: from head to foot a Cretan. He laid breeches, waistcoat, jacket, hat and shoes together in a pile in the middle of the yard. They poured petroleum over them, so that the Devil might receive them an hour earlier. The grandfather handed a piece of burning wood to his grandson and said:

"Come, my child, send 'em to the Devil! The Franks have burned us, now we're burning them. Fire for fire! Wind for wind!"

Thrasáki grasped the burning wood and threw it on to the oil-soaked clothes.

They flared up at once and lit up the three faces. The grandfather's soles tickled him, and he wanted to dance. When the fire had done its work, he took a handful of ashes, opened the outer door, stood in the middle of the street, raised his hand and strewed the ashes in the air.

"You Franks," he cried with passionate scorn, "may the eyes of my children, or of my children's children, live to see the day when your houses and factories and kings' palaces burn and dwindle into the air as ashes. As you have burned us, you Franks, may you too burn!"

Towards noon Mitros, the man in the *fustanella*, sweating from the climb, arrived at the headquarters of Captain Michales. On the highest of the mountian plateaux about a hundred palikares were quartered in a dozen stone huts. Far below them stretched an upland plain ringed by mountains, on which the villages showed like white flocks. Two of them were burning, and in the stillness their smoke stood calm above them like some friendly, protecting cloud.

Captain Michales was standing high up on his look-out post, holding a pair of field-glasses. This was a present from a Frank, a philhellene, who had climbed up to the mountain camp a month before and had not had the heart to leave it. "Where should I go?" he had said to Captain Michales. "Why should I go down to the towns again? I like it here. Nowhere have I eaten more delicious bread, nowhere have I drunk such immortal water, nowhere have I seen men more like the Greeks of old! I shan't call you Captain

Michales, but Captain Achilles. My name's Erikos." He wore a domed hat, which resembled an ancient helmet. His pockets were full of papers and pencils. In his modern Greek gibberish he carried on conversations with the Cretans and eagerly made notes all the time. The Cretans laughed. "He's cracked," said one of them. "He writes for the papers," was another's opinion. "Hey, countryman, what do you think you're doing in Crete without a weapon?" they asked him. "Where's your gun?"—"Here!" he replied, pointing to his pencil.

He had a fair, pointed beard, two of his front teeth were gold, and his cheeks were rosy. On his head a thick tuft of hair stood up, and when the Cretans heard that his name was Erikos the tuft made them twist it into "Kukurikos".

One day when Captain Michales's palikares gave battle to some Turkish soldiers, he had run down with them to that upland plain. He had no weapon, yet he yelled out: "Forward, Captain Achilles!" He stood up all the time and took notes furiously. A wild Cretan who was very fond of Kukurikos ran up and brought him as a present a Turk's head, which he carried by the hair, while the blood dripped from it. Hardly had Kukurikos seen the head when he gave a cry and fell down in a faint. The Cretans laughed: "What a cotton-wool bottom the man is!" they said, and flung a jugful of water over him to bring him to himself. When Captain Michales came on the scene, he shouted at them: "Do you think all men are Cretans? Stop playing the fool!" He turned to Furógatos: "Take the poor fellow under the arms carefully and help him through the climb."

From that day Kukurikos had lain in a fever. He had grown pale and could not bring himself to eat any meat. He had bad dreams. Life with ancient Greeks now seemed to him hard, and he decided to go. One grey, rainy morning he took leave of Captain Michales.

"The ancient Greeks are wonderful, Captain Achilles, but it's difficult to live their life. I'm a professor—that's to say, a schoolmaster—a good man but made of paper. You're made of flesh and blood. I can't stand up to you. Good-bye, and take this to remember me by!"

He took from his neck the cord with the field-glasses, and hung it round the neck of Captain Michales.

"You're a captain, so you must see further than your palikares."

And now Captain Michales was holding these field-glasses to his eyes and examining the plain. Behind the clouds of smoke over the burning villages he thought he could see the movement of red fezes. Fresh troops had come from Megalokastro and were forming up to attack the heights. "The dogs are short of nothing," he muttered. "Our position's small, and there are only a few of us. And Captain Polyxigis keeps us waiting. I must send him a fresh message."

And as he lowered the field-glasses and was about to ask whether Vendúsos was back from the coast, behold, there in front of him was Mitros in his *fustanella*.

"Greetings, captain. I'm from Captain Stefanés's ship," he said, producing the letter and holding it out.

"Welcome, countryman," said Captain Michales, shaking hands with him. "Go and join the other palikares, while I read the letter."

Hastily he tore open the envelope. Inside he found an opened letter and a small piece of paper. On this he recognised his son's handwriting, and his sombre face lightened for a moment. "I, Thrasáki, send you greetings, and here is a message from Grandad: 'read the letter, and do as God enlightens you. There is no hope for us, and this time too we are threshing empty straw. So take council with your heart and weigh your decision.'"

He frowned, and drew his upper lip back so that the boar's fangs were bared. "God forbid," he growled, "I should take council with my heart. The world would be blown sky-high."

He unfolded his nephew's letter. Syllable by syllable he moved forwards, jumped from word to word as though he were climbing up a mountain. Sometimes he paused, and groaned. And then he gave a fresh heave. When he had reached the end, he tore the letter into a thousand pieces and put a match to it.

"I alone must know this, nobody else," he said, stamping on the ashes.

No hope then! The motherland weak, the Franks treacherous, the Cretans too few. . . . No, in spite of everything, I'm not stirring from my post. I'm not giving up the eyrie I've withdrawn to! It's not enough for God to desert me and to order me: "Give it up!" I'm not giving it up!

He grasped the field-glasses again and looked down. Still more red dots showed on the plain, and from the ravines more and more troops were emerging. The Pacha had sworn to thrust Captain Michales's band from the eagle's nest where it had dug in its claws, into the abyss. Exhausted, wounded Crete was gradually returning to peace: only isolated shots were now to be heard, and only isolated blockheads still held their refuges above the precipices and refused obedience. The Sultan was angry: he sent the Pacha a shipload of chains and ordered him to capture these Cretans and send them in chains to Constantinople. If not, he might tackle them himself and come in person.

This command made the Pacha's blood race. He saw that his head was no longer firm on his shoulders, and decided to give up his agreeable life in Megalokastro and take to the field at the head of his soldiers against Captain Michales. The Metropolitan heard, and sent a secret message to the captain: "Escape! Take ship and escape! The Pacha has sworn your downfall." But Captain Michales stiffened in his defiance. "I'm not escaping. There's a heavy guilt weighing in my neck. There'a a monastery burning day and night in my heart. I must pay for my guilt. Even if all the others leave, I'm staying here on the cliffs, and I'd rather pour petrol over my clothes and hair, so as to burn as you did, 'Christ The Lord'!"

He swept the plain with his field-glasses. On the slopes more Christian villages were beginning to burn.

"Captain Polyxigis is late," he muttered anew, examining one mountain-path after another. "He'll come, all the same. He's given his word. This is war. In war I trust him."

Since the terrible moment when he had plunged his knife into the Circassian woman's heart, Captain Michales had felt the old friendship returning. He now thought of Captain Polyxigis without hostility—indeed, with compassion. The villages had echoed with the funeral, and his friends had had to prevent him from killing himself. He went dressed from head to foot in black. Wherever there was fighting, he flung himself on the Turks blindly, seeking death. He was convinced that the Turks had killed her to prevent her baptism. And so he had sworn to build a tower of Turkish corpses upon her grave.

With joy Captain Michales heard voices and the hoofbeats of mules. He bounded from rock to rock down to the plateau, and reached it just as Vendúsos and his ten booty-laden palikares arrived. Everyone fell on the mules and unloaded them. Some lit a fire at once. For days they had lived on dry bread, and they were longing for a hot meal. Others stowed the stores away safely in their chief's stone hut. "Thank our Mother," cried Vendúsos, firing a pistol shot into the air, "thank our beggar Mother, who's hungry herself and sends us food!"

"Vendúsos," shouted the captain, "don't waste your bullets. Come here. I want you to do something."

The lyre-player went over to him and listened intently to what he said. Then he balanced on tip-toe, ready to run off.

"D'you understand, Vendúsos? It's very urgent! And take care they don't kill you on the way there! On the way back it doesn't matter so much."

"I shan't give you that pleasure," said Vendúsos with a laugh. "Not even on the way back. By the Virgin with the bunch of grapes, I've still got a lot of casks to drink dry. And drink them dry I will."

He started off down towards the valley. But Furógatos caught hold of him by the breeches as he came by.

"Brother Vendúsos, did you see my friend Bertódulos? What's the poor chap doing? Do you know, I think more about him than about my wife? Extraordinary, isn't it?"

"He's all right. Hasn't any worries. I saw him at old Séfakas's. He keeps with the women, and will soon be wearing a skirt."

"What's become of our drinking parties in Captain Michales's cellar, Vendúsos? Did I only dream them?"

But Vendúsos had already hurried on and could no longer hear him.

Bent over the slate, old Séfakas held the chalk as loosely as he could, so as not to break it, and anxiously wrote the letters, one after the other. In the last few days he had felt a strange weakness, as if his strength were failing and flowing back to the earth. He had grown pale, could not sleep, and his knees trembled.

"I must hurry if I want to learn in time," he thought. And now he used all his force to make the reluctant hand move. In spite of the difficulties he formed fine, clear capitals.

"I don't need the small letters," he told his master Thrasáki, who wanted to push him on to fresh efforts. "My work can be done with the capitals."

Grandfather and grandson sat down on the threshold.

"To-day, Thrasáki," said the old man, "you're not going to scold me: I've got my lesson at my fingers' ends. Look here!"

With pride he displayed the slate full of capitals.

"The whole alphabet," boasted the grandfather, "from alpha to omega."

"Bravo, granddad! You get full marks to-day! How did you manage to learn it all so suddenly?"

"I haven't much time now, Thrasáki, so I took myself in hand. And now the time has come. Listen, and I'll tell you my secret. Do you think I wanted to learn to read at my age? Why should I? With my hundred years, I know everything and I know nothing."

"What did you want then, granddad?"

"I simply wanted to learn to write one thing, before I die."

"What?"

"A Cretan saying. Put your little hand on my hand and guide it. Only three words." And now he whispered: "Freedom or death."

"O," cried Thrasáki, "that's it! Now I understand."

"You don't understand yet, my Thrasáki. Don't be in too much of a hurry for that. . . . Now guide my chalk."

The child grasped with both his hands the grandfather's hard, calloused hand and guided it slowly and patiently, until on the slate in wide initials there stood the words:

FREEDOM or DEATH

N

XII

ICY winds were blowing from the snow-covered peaks. Crete froze. On the slope of Selena, below Captain Michales's camp, there was a large cave, filled to overflowing with women and children. It was here that the Christian women had taken refuge in all the risings, to escape the knives of the Turks. In the 1821 rising the Turkish soldiers had flung burning branches into it and suffocated those who were crowded inside. Their bones still glimmered in the damp and frosty air of the cave; and now, once more, women and children stretched themselves out upon the old bones, shivering with hunger and cold and at the danger of being killed by the Turks and of leaving their bones too to whiten here. By day they would go out to gather a handful of grasses, roots and acorns and live on this like cattle. To give themselves courage, they kept glancing up at the cliffs where Captain Michales had nested. As long as he held out, they were not afraid.

Yet now Turkish soldiers had climbed up and were nearing the narrow ravine which led to the cave. But alerted by the shrieks, Captain Michales had come down from his eyrie. The battle was waged with the utmost bitterness. Some of the women even had the courage to rush to the help of the men with knives and clubs. The rest kneeled wailing in the cave and cried out to God.

The Christians were outnumbered and starving, while more and more Turkish soldiers kept coming up from the plain, driven on by the raging Pacha. He had sworn to send the head of Captain Michales, embalmed and wrapped in a turban, to Constantinople as a present to the Sultan.

Towards two in the afternoon the Christians began to waver. The Turks gave a howl of delight, which drowned the wailing of the women.

But suddenly God intervened: to the rear of the Turks appeared Captain Polyxigis with his men, and spread confusion among the red-hats. Already some of these were fleeing down to the plain.

The two leaders hunted the enemy together on their mares. Both were wounded—but did not notice it in the heat of the slaughter. In the evening they went back to their citadel and had their wounds bandaged. They were only slightly hurt and felt their hunger more violently than their wounds. The palikares opened the newly-received treasure, God's alms: bread, olives, onions, cheeses.

In the stone hut over which Captain Michales's banner with the red lettering waved, the two captains squatted side by side on the ground, feasting. Through the holes in the rude walls a cutting wind whistled its way in. Snow was whirling outside. Thodóres entered with an armful of brushwood. He felt sorry for the two wounded and freezing men. He lit a fire for them. Then he went out again, to leave them alone. His ear had caught some words full of meaning. At present they certainly wanted no one near by.

"Blessings on you, Captain Polyxigis," said Captain Michales. "God sent you. The dogs already had us by the throat."

As he spoke he gazed at his comrade with pity and affection. Captain Polyxigis, dressed in black and with a black cloth wound round his head, appeared suddenly aged and pale. He ate, but his thoughts were elsewhere.

"Your health, Captain Polyxigis," said Captain Michales, raising the bottle to his mouth.

"Yours, Captain Michales. Mine's gone. . . ."

Captain Michales's heart contracted. Not for the sake of the woman whom he had killed. She had had to be killed, so as not to divide the two men. Since the night of the murder his heart had been lightened. He was no longer ashamed when he was alone. His spirit had shaken free from the Circassian, and he fought for Crete single-mindedly. He was only sorry for the good palikare, who was pining away because of the loss of a woman.

"Captain Polyxigis," he began, "I have something to say to you. Forgive me, but it is shameful to be thinking of a woman when Crete is swimming in blood. I tell you, by my honour, if a woman stood in the way of my fulfilling my duty, I would kill her with my own hand."

So saying, he raised the hand with which he had killed the Circassian.

"Captain Michales, you're a wild beast. I'm a man," answered Captain Polyxigis, and threw away the piece of bread he had been holding in his hand. He felt as if his throat were noosed. He turned to look at his friend. Suddenly he felt ice-cold.

Captain Michales too huddled over the fire. For a while the two gazed silently into the flames. Thodóres came in again, added some brushwood and, since he saw the two captains sunk in thought, went out on tip-toe.

And suddenly the voice of Captain Michales sounded, hollow, choking, asking the question as if from a long way away:

"Do you know who killed her?"

He was overcome by the desire to stake all on one throw: heads or tails.

Captain Polyxigis started and stared at him. He had not the strength to ask: "Who?" He waited.

"Do you know who?" asked the voice again.

"Do *you* know?"

"Yes."

Captain Polyxigis seized Captain Michales by the arm.

"Who?"

"Not so fast. Don't go wild! You can't hurt a hair of his! He is beyond death."

"Who?"

"Wait, I tell you. First I must reveal to you a secret—a very bitter one. Listen quietly. And when you've heard it, you'll be ashamed, I swear, and not think of women any more, or of their murderers, or of yourself either."

"Who?" asked the other again, with burning eyes.

"I've received a letter—which I've torn up and burnt—from my nephew Kosmas. Captain Polyxigis, our labour is once more in vain, our blood will have been shed senselessly. This time too Crete will not see freedom. Greece is weak, the Franks have no honour, the Sultan has the power."

But Captain Polyxigis was not listening: leaping up, he hit his head with a dull thud against the stone wall.

"Who killed her? Who? Everything else later!"

"I did," answered Captain Michales, standing up too, and calmly and firmly gazing into the other's eyes. "I did, Captain Polyxigis."

Captain Polyxigis leant against the stones, and his brow darkened.

"No, no!" he shouted at last. "That's impossible! You? You!"

"I had to kill her or you. I thought of Crete. You are a good fighter. Crete needs you. So I killed her. It lightened my heart. Yours too will grow light again. Don't fumble for your knife. If you like we can bar the door, put out the lamp and fight it out here and kill each other. But think of the women and children in the cave. Their lives depend on us. Think of our forefathers. Think of Crete. Then decide."

Captain Polyxigis reeled and fell. He buried his face in his hands. His chest was heaving. He could no longer control his sobs.

"As I read that there is no more hope," Captain Michales went on, without paying any attention to his friend's tears, "I don't know what demon it was rose up in me, Polyxigis. Instead of letting it press me down, I felt a new, savage courage. So that's how it is with you, Great Powers—you refuse to give Crete freedom. Shame upon you! I, Captain Michales, I, a little Cretan porcupine, don't need you! And let God leave Crete in the lurch if He pleases, I'm not leaving her in the lurch!"

He touched Captain Polyxigis lightly on the shoulder.

"Captain," he said gently, "aren't you ashamed of yourself?"

The other had mastered his tears. The murderer's words bored into his head.

"Since the hour when I lost all hope, Captain Polyxigis," Captain Michales went on, "I've had the feeling, by the soil on which we tread, that I'm immortal. Who can do anything to me now? What can death do against me? Even if all the Turks come storming at me, my ear-lobes won't twitch. I picture myself like Arkadi: my clothes, hair and guts are full of powder, and when I see that there's nothing else for it, I blow myself sky-high. Do you understand?"

And it was true—only defiance and pride now found room in

him. Was it a demon, a God or some wild idea from before history? He himself did not know. He knew only one thing clearly: whatever might happen, he would not stoop to curse his destiny or to bewail it. He would come to terms neither with the Devil nor with God nor with the Sultan. He would blow himself sky-high like Arkadi.

Captain Polyxigis stood up. Violently he tugged the heavy cloth round his head straight.

"I cannot sleep in the same house with you, Captain Michales," he said, gazing into the distance, "nor do I want us to kill each other as long as our country is at war, nor will I desert you in danger. But we two will have our reckoning as soon as Crete is at peace again. For you have turned my heart to ashes, Captain Michales."

So saying, without a glance at the murderer, he went to the door and out.

'What can be happening to the Christians up there?" The women had climbed up on to the flat roof, to scour down its dangerous burden of snow. With sighs they gazed out at the mountain. What, O God, would be happening up there, to the Christians? Katerina, too, raised her eyes to the snow-covered peaks and thought of her fear-inspiring husband.

But to-day the sun was shining brightly, the sky was deep blue, the air icy. The grandfather sat indoors by the hearth and stared into the flames without a word. For some days, he had not spoken: he grew more and more pale and remained sunk in dark thoughts.

As Thrasáki entered, the grandfather stood up. By his command a tin of red paint and a brush had been brought him from Kasteli. He beckoned to Thrasáki.

"Take the paint, little Thrasáki. Let's go. And give me the brush."

"Where are we going, granddad?"

"You'll soon see. Be quick, while it isn't snowing."

They reached the street door. Grandfather and grandson stood still and gazed at the village, which lay as though dead, swathed in snow. The gleaming, intact snow made everything beautiful. Thrasáki could not have enough of marvelling at this overnight transfiguration of the village.

The grandfather pulled a large, many-coloured handkerchief out of his belt and began to clean the snow off the door. Then he took the lid off the tin and dipped the brush into it.

"In God's name!" he murmured.

"What are you doing, grandfather?"

"You'll soon see."

He raised the brush and began, slowly and carefully, to paint the first letters in red on the door. There was an F, then an R, then an E . . .

"Ah," said Thrasáki, "I understand!"

The grandfather laughed.

"Now you see why I took the trouble to learn to write. I had my purpose. In the whole village I'm not going to leave a wall— I shall even climb up the bell-tower, I shall go into the mosque, and before I die it'll be written everywhere: 'Freedom or death!' "

After each letter he put his head back and admired his work. His mind could not grasp the mystery of how one could put together little strokes and curves and raise up out of them a voice —a choir of voices. How could those signs speak? Great art Thou, O Lord!

So now his street door spoke. He marvelled at it for a while.

"Have I written it well, Thrasáki?" he asked anxiously. "No mistake?"

"I give you full marks, granddad. Excellent," said his grand-child with a laugh.

"Then let's go on!"

At the street corner there was a piece of wall free from snow. The grandfather again dipped his brush and wrote and wrote. Then he moved on. The paint splashed over his beard and boots, it spotted his waistcoat, but he did not notice. A sacred flame had laid hold of him. Wherever he found a flat, clean wall or a large door, he stopped and painted on it the magic signs. And a wall, which before had stood dumb and forlorn, now loudly announced its longing, palikare-like.

His hand had now acquired the knack of writing and flew along.
He reached the village square. That was where the school, the
church and the mosque were. A little father on, the coffee-house.
He dipped the brush into the paint and set to work on the school
door. Freedom or death! Two old men came out of the coffee-
house.

"Hey, Captain Séfakas, since when have you known your
alphabet? What are you painting there? What's come over you?"

"It's my farewell greeting," replied the grandfather, undisturbed. "Take it, to remember me by."

The old men shook their heads and moved on.

"An angel has visited old Séfakas," they muttered. "Charos is
near."

The grandfather now stood before the mosque. The walls had
been freshly whitewashed, the door was painted yellow.

"Here's where I'll do my best work," said the ancient, "and
adorn each letter with a flourish. Just look!" He moved the
brush powerfully and with mastery up and down on the yellow
door.

"Now let's go home. I'm tired. The church another day. I'll
climb up the bell-tower then on a ladder."

"I can't have you falling down, granddad. I'll do the climbing."

All over Crete the captains had put water in their wine, taken
counsel, debated this way and that. The *fustanella* State and the
Franks and the Muscovites—all were holding aloof. Only a few
of the captains still hesitated, but they too seemed ever more
ready to bow the neck.

"I have subdued Crete," proclaimed the Sultan, "not a gun is
now to be heard on the island. The privileges which in my goodness of heart I had extended to the Cretans, I withdraw, because
they have showed themselves treacherous and rebellious."

Yet still the guns were not silent on the crest of Selena. Captain
Michales did not surrender. His shots sounded in Constantinople
and the Sultan was enraged. He sent an order to the Pacha of
Crete: "Rake in Captain Michales's head and send it me. If not,
your own!"

And the Pacha jumped up and swore: "Yes, by my faith, I'm going to crush the *giaour*."

He girded on his scimitar and, going over to the window, looked out towards those accursed Lasíthi mountains. The *giaour* was fully determined to throttle the supply of food, water and ammunition. So the Pacha had sent a message to Captain Michales: "Go, Captain Michales, take your palikares and leave, with your weapons and with your flags flying. By Mohammed, I will not hurt a hair of any of your heads!" By the same messenger Captain Michales had answered him: "As long as any breath comes out of my nose, I am not going. Let all Crete submit if it will, I am not submitting. I sh—— on the beard of your Prophet!"

"Damn Crete, damn all Cretans, damn my lot!" muttered the Pacha, and unbuckled his scimitar again. "How am I to clamber up the mountains in the snow and hunt after this Devil's own fellow! I shall send still more soldiers."

He clapped his hands. The Arab appeared.

"Bring me some chestnuts and a raki. I'm very worried again to-day. Do you see what the Sultan has sent me?"

Without a word the Arab brought a glass of raki, then knelt down and laid a row of chestnuts on the glowing cinders in the brazier. The Pacha stretched himself out on the divan.

"Tell me, Suleiman, some pretty tale, even if it's untrue. By Mohammed, I don't care!"

The Arab's teeth showed in all their width and whiteness.

"To-day as it happens, Pacha Effendi, I'm able to bring you a piece of good news that will turn your heart into a garden."

"Tell it, you liar, with my blessing! Has Captain Michales laid down his arms?"

"That's not the news, Pacha Effendi, but something better! You've heard of Hamidé Mula, the sorceress, who has the saint in her yard. I made her cast the beans to-day and foretell your fortune. She squatted down in the middle of the yard, took a sieve and brought out her little bag with her beans and shells and pebbles and bats' knuckles. She shook them into the sieve, rattled it and bent over it. Then she muttered the charm. Suddenly she gave a cry, threw off her shawl and began to dance. 'What can you see,

Hamidé Mula?' I shouted to her, 'what have the beans got to say?'
She became calm, sat down again and stirred the beans with her
fingers. 'I see a red fez clapped down over the whole of Crete
from Garbusa to Topla Monastery! I see the Pacha—that small,
dead snail—receiving a firman from Constantinople, with a gold
seal, gold lettering and golden cord. The Sultan is sending him
gold pounds and gold braid. Yes, isn't he also sending him his
daughter, to make him his son-in-law? By the Saint, who is
listening to us, I can't quite make it out.' 'Tell me exactly, Hamidé
Mula,' I said to her, 'When are all your deeds and wonders going
to happen? That I may go and announce them to the Pacha and
receive a small baksheesh, and you too, my poor woman.' She
bent again over the beans, mixed them and threw them this way
and that. 'In three periods of time,' she answered, 'Tell the Pacha
that. He's not to worry.' And just as you clapped your hands, I was
coming in from Hamidé Mula's yard to bring you the news."

The Pacha had been playing with his amber necklace all the
time and listening open-mouthed. His face had become gentle and
peaceful; his eyes were closed and saw the Sultan's messenger
entering Megalokastro. He was followed by caravans of camels
with the dowry from his father-in-law: sacks full of gold pounds,
emeralds and opals, and others full of musk, almonds and cinnamon. And a little hanum, the Sultan's daughter, dressed in silk,
climbing down from a white camel and with supple movements
sweeping up the marble steps of his seraglio.

Suleiman at length fell silent, and suddenly the Pacha started,
as though awakening. He yawned.

"Have you finished, silly Suleiman?"

"I've finished, Pacha Effendi."

"Now stick the pot into the fire and make me a coffee, a foamy
one, to wake me up. Are the chestnuts roasted?"

"Aren't we going to send any baksheesh to poor Hamidé
Mula?"

But the Pacha laughed:

"Silly Suleiman, we're going to take care and not let our mind
be puffed up with wind! We're going to let two 'periods of time'
go by first!"

"He's not such a fool as I took him for," muttered the Arab, with a sour look, as he stuck the pot into the fire.

As the day was nearing its end, the Metropolitan in his Residence kept pointing his telescope fearfully at the restless surface of the sea over against Crete. He was expecting to-day, with the steamer that touched at Megalokastro every week, the secret messenger who was being sent to him with instructions from Greece. In the mountains the captains were still negotiating with the Turks. They had made up their minds to this, but had not yet laid down their arms. "In God's name," cried the more reasonable ones, "let's harden our hearts to stone, bury our weapons yet again, and collect our strength until even the mourning mothers once more gain strength. And then, after some years, we can raise the banner again. Pretend to kiss the hand you cannot hack off." Yet still the more fiery ones retorted: "Freedom or death!"

Greece too was undecided: sometimes she uttered vague threats against the Turks, sometimes she fell at the feet of the Franks. The Metropolitan did not know to which opinion he should give his allegiance. His understanding advised him: "be measured, patient, and yield"; but his heart, with its crazy courage, shouted: "freedom or death!" To-day, thank God, the secret messenger would arrive from Greece and show him the right course. But darkness was falling already, and there was no sign of the ship.

"I must be patient. God will let tomorrow too be a day. Then the news will come. To-day is over."

He went downstairs and into the church, to pray God to calm the sea.

The night passed, the sea grew smooth. At daybreak a soft fragrance of thyme from the mountains came flying by, and Kosmas, the eldest grandson of old Séfakas, standing in the bows of the old steamer, breathed in deeply the fragrance of his native land. Crete lay before him. Wild cliffs, mournful trees here and there, distant rose-coloured mountain-peaks. It was a spring day in the heart of winter. God was sorry for birds and men and spread out over them the sun. Kosmas craned his neck till it was nearly off—he could not have enough of gazing at the flesh and bones of

his country. How had he set out, twenty years ago, a child with
downy cheeks and downy soul? And how was he now coming
home? He turned. A young woman, small and pale, came up to
him and likewise gazed—with large, terrified eyes—at Crete.

"Crete," said the young man with a laugh, gently touching her
shoulder.

The woman shuddered.

"Yes," she said, and was silent.

"This is where you'll bring our son into the world," he said
softly. "This is now your country. Forget the other . . .", he added
tenderly.

"Yes, Kosmas, dear," said the woman, and fell silent again.
And suddenly she gripped his arm and pressed it fearfully, as
though to make sure that it was there. She became a little
calmer.

Crete's mountains, olive-groves and vineyards drew nearer.
Megalokastro appeared in the white scintillation of the early
morning. The scent of thyme grew stronger. The full light had
now glided from the peaks over the slopes down to the plains.
The trees began to show separately, the cocks were audible in the
sweet morning moment, the world was awakening.

The man bent over towards his wife.

"Please," he said softly, "now that you are entering my father's
house, keep your heart firm and don't be afraid. Remember that
I'm always with you. Remember that you're carrying our son,
you mustn't be afraid. My mother is a god-fearing woman, she
will take you to her heart. My sister, I must tell you . . ."

He stopped, frowning.

"What?" she asked, looking at her husband anxiously.

"When she was twelve, her father gave her this order: 'You are
not to cross the threshold of the street door any more, and you are
not to appear before me any more. Go!' And from then on, the
poor thing remained shut away from the outside world and from
her father. She sat all day weaving and knitting for her trousseau.
When the old man came home in the evening, she fled to the inner
part of the house, to hide. When she was twenty, he noticed that
day after day a young man passed by and kept watch for my sister.

One evening a woman of the neighbourhood brought her a note from the young man. And later several more. He was in love with her, and he wanted her to come one night and talk with him, that they might get to know each other, with a view to marrying later. After many letters the girl was moved by sympathy and one evening told the neighbour to say to him: 'At midnight I'll be standing at the door!' "

Kosmas pulled up short. The veins on his brow were swollen. In him hatred, fear and admiration of his father reigned once more. Crete had vanished: instead, the terrifying shade of his father swept through the air.

"Be quiet!" whispered the young woman. "That's enough." And she raised her hand to close his mouth.

"No, you must hear it all," he replied. "At midnight she went down with bare feet, to make no noise on the stairs. But the old man was on the watch. He glided behind her without a sound. The poor girl went out into the yard, and at the moment when she stretched out her hand to open the door, the old man rushed upon her, seized her by the hair, bored his nails into her and flung her, fainting, into her room, which he locked. Year after year my sister never once dared to go to the window. The old man was killed at Arkadi. Since then twenty years have gone by. But my sister's brain is still shattered. She works all day in the house, washing, cooking, and still weaving and sewing, poor thing, at her trousseau. In the evening she doesn't got to bed. When midnight draws near, she opens her window, leans out, and if some nocturnal wanderer comes by, calls out to him timidly: 'Is it nearly midnight?' "

Kosmas fell silent. The fair hair, the blue eyes, the charm of his sister, her laughter when she was young. . . .

He took several steps along the deck and looked down into the hold, where Turkish soldiers lay stretched out. "Unlucky Crete," he murmured, and felt with his hand the lining of his coat, where he kept the letter with the secret information hidden.

After a while he said to his wife:

"Please don't be frightened."

Kosmas could now clearly distinguish, behind Megalokastro,

the celebrated mountain Iuchta with its human shape: a gigantic head lying on the ground among olives and vineyards, with a high, bold forehead, a bony nose, a wide mouth and a beard of bluffs and boulders. It lay there, a dead, pale-blue, marble god.

"The giant is not dead," Kosmas thought, and suddenly fixed his gaze on the reassuring mountain. "As long as he's alive and rumbling inside me, he hasn't died. As long as I'm alive and thinking of him, he won't die. . . . The others may have forgotten him. His life depends on me. He holds me, but I hold him too."

He could feel how his father had struck roots in him and would not break away. Abroad, he had often remembered him, and a trembling had come over him. But never had he felt the dead man so near to him as at this moment. Or so menacing. "He knows," he thought, "why I'm coming back to Crete and what my secret mission is. Relentless fighter that he is, he'd like to stop my mouth."

Kosmas turned again to his wife. He could feel his father casting an eye full of hatred at the foreign woman. But the young man's love for this woman grew still stronger and bolder in the presence of his father. He pressed her to him and defended her and would not give her up to the dead man.

They entered the harbour. On the right gleamed the stone lion of Venice with the open Gospel in its claws. The harbour was once more ringing with din and reeking of rotten lemons, oil and turnips. Kosmas jumped on to the mole and grasped his wife's hand:

"Step on to it with the right foot first," he said softly; "it's a jungle you're coming into! In God's name!"

She stepped on land with her right foot and hung exhausted on her husband's arm.

"I'm tired," she said, as cold sweat broke out on her temples.

"The house is close by. Be brave. We've arrived."

They advanced. Kosmas gazed insatiably at the houses, the people, the streets. All had grown old. The black hair white, the cheeks shrivelled, the colours washed out, the walls flaky—many of them crumbling. Weeds grew on many thresholds. He squeezed his wife's hand.

"This is my country," he said. "The earth we are treading on gave me birth."

The woman bent down and picked up some earth, which trickled away between her fingers.

"It's warm," she said. "I like that." She thought of her own distant, cold country.

They lost themselves in the narrow alleys. Kosmas, who had let go his wife's arm, strode hastily forwards. His heart was beating violently. He turned to the right into a small street. From afar he made out the parental door. It was shut. The window above it was also shut. No-one in the street, no voice. It was as in a dream. He approached the old, arched doorway with the thick iron ring. His knees were trembling. Then he plucked up courage and knocked.

In the yard, steps became audible. Someone sighed. The steps stopped. He knocked again. The door opened. A short, lean old woman, quite white and clothed all in black, appeared. As she looked at the newcomer, she cried out: "My child!" and leaned against the doorpost to prevent herself from falling.

Now came the sister too, short and lean likewise, with grey hair and eyes dimmed by dark anger and bitterness.

Joy, tears. Hands grasped eagerly at the beloved body. And suddenly, as the mother was pressing her big son, now back from abroad, yet again to her bosom and was speaking to him as if he was still a child, she noticed the young woman on the threshold.

"Is that . . . ?" asked the mother softly.

"Yes, my wife."

The sister turned curiously to look at her. The mother bent over her son:

"Why did you marry her? A foreigner!"

"Mother," said the son softly, kissing the shrivelled hand, "I must ask you for a favour."

"You're my one and only son, and are you asking me for a favour? I'm hanging on your lips, command me!"

"I entrust my wife to you, Mother. . . . Love her. And my son," he added, yet more softly.

The mother started. She gazed at her son speechlessly, asking, imploring.

"Yes," he answered, "she is carrying your grandson."

A delicious warmth rose to her throat and cheeks. But suddenly a shudder overcame her.

"Have you asked permission of your father?" she said, muffling her voice. "Does he know? He decides. You must ask him. I'm afraid of him." She was whispering, so that the dead man might not hear.

"What can he do to us?" asked the son, while his heart nonetheless suddenly faltered.

"How should I know, my child? Has he still a body, so that one can know where he is? Perhaps he's at this moment in the yard and forbidding her to cross the threshold."

The son cried furiously:

"He's no right to do that! He's no longer in command here. I'll bring her in!" He ran across the yard with his heart beating angrily and fearfully. His voice was suddenly rough as he said:

"Chrysula, come!"

He took her by the hand and led her to his mother.

"Mother, your daughter," he said.

The young woman bent down to kiss the mother's hand. Then she stood there and waited.

The mother looked at her closely. She caught sight of the little golden chain around her neck.

"You're baptised?" the old woman asked, without stretching out her hand to her.

"She is baptised," answered the son. "Here is the cross. She bears your name, Mother. She was called Noëmi, now she's called Chrysula."

He took the chain and pulled from her bosom a small golden cross.

"She is welcome," said the mother and touched her head, hesitating slightly. They went into the house.

Kosmas walked about with heavy heart, paced up and down, silently caressed the doors, the old furniture, the heavy clock and the silver pistols of his ancestors, next to the ikons.

"And how's Grandfather?" he asked.

"In his village. A hundred years old, but full of vigour. Charos doesn't touch him. He was always asking after you."

The two women sat down on the very old, wide divan. The mother looked at her son, noticing how he had ripened into a man. He was like his grandfather, Captain Séfakas. The same eyes, which looked at things with warmth and tenderness, the same attractive, eloquent mouth. Sometimes she cast a sidelong glance at his wife. "What am I to say to her?" she thought. "Another race. Another God created her. I don't like her." And the young woman saw the stony yard, the pots of basil, the wintry bare vine-trellis above the trough. . . . And beyond the yard, behind the tendrils, limitless plains under snow and forests under ice and dark towns and cossacks with naked sabres breaking doors in and falling upon the Jews. . . . The snow was melted by hot blood and changed to a red stain. Men, women and children were shrieking and fleeing.

She turned round. She saw the old woman observing her. She tried to smile and could not manage it. Her eyes filled with tears. The old woman was touched and asked:

"What are you thinking of? Your country? Where were you born?"

"A long, long way from here. . . . In a dark town full of factories."

"What sort of factories? What did they make?"

"Cannons, rifles, machinery. But my father——"

She wanted to say: "he didn't soil his hands with these things, he was a rabbi." But she kept it to herself.

"What was your father?" the old woman asked.

"He was a good man," answered the young woman, with a sigh.

The old woman stood up, went out into the yard, broke off a sprig of basil and brought it to the young woman.

"Do you have basil there?" she asked.

"No."

"It grew on the grave of Christ," said the old woman, and fell silent.

Meanwhile the good news had spread. Chattering contentedly the women of the neighbourhood came running. The house filled. They examined the Jewish girl from head to toes like some extraordinary animal. They snuffed her up and down.

Kosmas watched his wife, full of sympathy. She seemed to him like a wounded swan in a troop of geese and ducks.

Maria brought the salver with dainties and coffee. She was thin and shrivelled, and wore a broad black band round her throat to hide the wrinkles. She eyed Chrysula with enmity, for this girl was younger and prettier and had snatched her brother from her.

Kosmas stood up. The first joy was over. He had no time to lose.

"I'm going on a little round, to greet Kastro again," he said, and hurried off to the Metropolitan's Residence.

The Metropolitan was sitting in the Bishop's Palace, waiting for Kosmas. Early that morning he had heard the steamer whistle as it entered the harbour, and had crossed himself.

"Grant, O God," he had murmured, "that he is bringing good tidings for Christendom."

Kosmas went swiftly through the streets. He looked about him with emotion. The beloved town had aged, crumbled—she was beginning to fall into dust, which the wind would carry away. . . . One day, certainly, a new town would be built on top of her, but it would not be his. "Beloved Crete," he thought tenderly, "we're growing old."

He reached Ai-Menas, strode across the forecourt, and greeted the old lemon-tree, under whose blossoming boughs the Metropolitan every year celebrated the rising Christ. Moved, he gazed about him, but he had no time. He climbed, two stairs at a time, the staircase of the Residence.

The Metropolitan rose, unquiet and impatient:

"Welcome, Kosmas," he said. "God sends you in a heavy hour. What are you bringing us?"

Kosmas kissed the Metropolitan's hand.

"This letter, Mylord," he said, pulling the secret paper out from his breast.

The Metropolitan took it and opened it, leaning against the window, with burning hands.

He read it greedily, then read it again quite slowly. Then he let that lordly head of his sink upon his breast. At last he tore himself away from the window and dropped, exhausted, on to the divan. He buried his face in his hands.

"Unhappy Crete," he murmured.

There was no hope, said the letter. "The Franks are unwilling to fall out with the Sultan; the Sultan, grown bold again, means to withdraw the few privileges he had granted to Crete against his will; the General whom he has sent possesses full powers to root out Christianity from Crete. Therefore bury your weapons afresh, practise patience, and do not plunge Greece into a bloody adventure. The poor thing is willing, but powerless."

The Metropolitan raised his head:

"Do you know what's in the letter, Kosmas?" he asked.

"I know, Mylord."

"I shall send a letter to all the captains, telling them to lay down arms. We can't give ourselves our head. There's only one captain I'm afraid of—your Uncle Michales. An unbridled, rebellious soul. A long time ago I sent him warning—he was to get out, with his weapons and flags. No one would hurt a hair of his head—the Pacha had sworn it. Do you know how he answered me? 'Do I meddle in your office Mylord? Then don't you meddle in mine either. Never will I kneel before the Turks. I'll blow myself sky-high!' You, my Kosmas, must seek him out and speak with him."

"I'll go, Mylord, but without any hope. He's like my father, a wild beast."

Trumpets sounded, and heavy, marching steps and the neighing of horses. The Metropolitan looked at Kosmas anxiously.

"Turkish soldiery," said Kosmas. "They came with me. We took them on at Kanea. They have orders to annihilate everything."

"Unhappy Crete," said the Metropolitan again, raising his hands to Heaven. "How long yet?"

Perplexity overcame them both. They were silent. At length

the Metropolitan, to give their thoughts a new direction, asked:

"You've been for many years in the land of the Franks. What's happening there? What have you seen? We here live in the wilds."

"Many things, good and bad, Mylord! Where am I to begin?"

"Are they believers?"

"They believe in a new godhead, a cruel, Great-Power one, which may some day become all-powerful."

"In what?"

"In Science."

"Mind without soul. In the Devil, that means."

"We have entered into a terrible sign of the zodiac, that of the Scorpion—of the Devil, Mylord."

"The rest of mankind perhaps. Not we Cretans. We have a higher belief than in the individual. The belief in tears and sacrifice. We are still not departed out of the sign of God."

Kosmas said nothing. What would be the object of speaking? The Metropolitan was old and believing. Other support than belief, he had none.

"Not we Cretans, nor the Russians either," the Metropolitan went on. "When I was Archimadrite in Kiev, I understood what believing means. What God means, and how He comes down upon earth and goes about and speaks with men. As long as Russia exists, I have no fear."

Kosmas rose.

"I shall leave you, Mylord, and let you send the letter to the captains. We must not lose a moment."

"My blessing! And come again tomorrow. I'm going to call the elders together. You too must speak with them."

When he returned at nightfall to his parental house and climbed upstairs to the old bedroom of his youth, he found his wife stretched out on the bed, crying. He took her in his arms, stroked her hair, touched her chin and raised her troubled face to his. She smiled at him.

"What's the matter? What have they been doing to you?"

"Nothing, nothing. I'm tired."

She let her face droop upon her arm and was silent. Then she said:

"They all sniffed round me. Then they turned away and whispered among themselves. Only your mother had pity on me. She stood up and said: 'My dears, good-bye, we're tired. See you to-morrow!'—She took me by the hand and led me upstairs into your room. She made a movement as if to kiss me. But she thought better of it. 'Lie down,' she said; 'don't pay any attention to them. Go to sleep!' And so I've been lying here and waiting for you."

Kosmas kissed the curly hair on her neck. She closed her eyes, smiling. The moon rose and shone upon her face. Kosmas was appalled by that pallor. "Go to sleep," he whispered in her ear, "you're tired." She clasped his hand. "I couldn't alone. Lie down by my side."

She put her arms round him, snuggled against his chest and murmured a few tender words in her mother tongue. Then she went to sleep.

The moon climbed further up the sky, huge and dumb, filled with sweetness. It was the moon of his youth, of those honeyed nights when with his friends he had carried on weighty conversations about the great unanswerable questions—whence? whither? why?—as these trouble young men the world over.

The moonlight now laid itself like a white linen sheet over the bed. The honey-golden hair of his wife, spread out on the pillow, gleamed as though it were peopled by glow-worms. Her face shone like marble. Kosmas stretched out his hand to caress her, but drew back for fear of waking her.

"How much I love this woman," he thought, "is beyond telling. How much good she has brought me is beyond telling. She has opened my head and heart; she has taught me to love foreign races, which I hated, to understand foreign ideas, which I fought, and to feel that we human beings are all of one origin. What good fate was it that took her by the hand, that evening, and brought her to me?" Smiling, he shook his head. "There's no such thing as fate. I myself grasped her by the hand that evening, nobody else."

And he remembered how he had been in a bookshop in a

distant town in the north, looking for a book he loved: Chinese poems of the Sung dynasty. He could not find it and as, depressed, he looked out into the street, he saw a girl in an orange silk blouse passing by. For a second she stood as though in the beam of a searchlight—then she had vanished. He was stirred to the depths. The girl seemed to him to have an enigmatic, tragic beauty. And her blouse was of the colour he loved above all others.

Like lightning the thoughts pressed through his head. "If I want, I shall run after her, and she'll become my wife. If I don't want, I shall stay here and let her go. I do what I want. But what do I want?" And immediately he was forced to think of the story of the Cretan shepherd who had never seen Megalokastro, the great city—that was how he pictured it. It had been described to him as Paradise, where the most precious things in the world were displayed: white boots with double soles, guns and sabres, sacks full of beans and salt fish, and musk-scented women. For years his mind had been obsessed with this Paradise, for years he had longed to go down to it. One day he could bear it no longer. He slung his old boots over his shoulder, so as not to wear them out on the rocks, and clambered, springing from stone to stone, down to Megalokastro. He hurried and hurried, seven hours long. Towards evening he reached the big fortress-gate of the town. There he came to a standstill with a sharp jerk. Perhaps he was suddenly ashamed that he had not resisted the temptation. He struck the hard threshold with his shepherd's staff and cried: "If I want, I'll go in. If I want, I won't go in. . . . I won't go in!" And he returned to his mountain.

"But I will go in!" muttered Kosmas, and ran after the girl. In the black throng of human beings the orange blouse gleamed. The girl turned and looked at him with terror. "The moment you went by," he told her, "I thought: 'If I want I shall speak to her and we shall become friends. If I don't want, I shall let her go by.' I've made up my mind that I do want."—"Either you're mad," the girl answered with an anxious glance, "or a poet. But I've no time. . . ."—"Come with me and let's talk. . . ."—"I've no time. I must go."—"Where are you going?"—"I've got to go," she said again, in a voice that trembled. Kosmas took her by the arm

and said tenderly: "Don't go away. Come with me." The ring of
her voice had frightened him. She said, "I've got to go" as if
she were crying "Help!"

The girl's thick, finely-arched eyebrows drew together. At
that moment the whole of her life lay in the balance. "I want,"
"I don't want"—her fate was imprisoned in those short syl-
lables. "Come," repeated Kosmas.—"Where?"—"Anywhere."—
"Where?" She spoke like a child who is afraid of being punished.
"Let's go for a walk. . . . Life is short. Let's talk, while there's still
time. . . ." She had bowed her honey-fair head: "All right, let's
talk, as long as there's time. Life is short. Let's go!"

They had gone into a park. Evening had passed from golden
green to pale violet, and gradually to dark blue. Both spoke
hurriedly, breathing rapidly. Kosmas first, to give her courage.
He spoke of Crete, that fearful, beloved island, of his father, that
dragon, and of his mother, that holy martyr. The girl's bosom
swelled. "Why do you speak to me so trustfully?" she asked
anxiously. "Since I'm going away and you too are going away and
we've no time. . . . In other times people needed years to reach the
point where we've arrived at once bound."

They had sat down on a bench. "What's your name?" asked the
man.—"Noëmi."—"Tell me. Noëmi, I'm sure your life is hard.
Trust me. I'm a Cretan."—"A Cretan? What's that?"—"A man
with a warm heart, Noëmi."

It was the depth of night when they stood up. The young man's
heart was overflowing with indignation and bitterness. This little
girl had drunk up the misery of the whole world. Her words had
revealed to him the horror, the shame, the madness of the world.
He had listened to her with his face hidden in his hands, and had
seen the things she described to him: how the Cossacks had ridden
through the town, stormed the Jewish quarter, splintered the
doors, killed the men and rounded up the old men together with
the women and children. Her father, the old rabbi with the white,
divided beard, had marched in the deep snow at the head of the
prisoners. Days and nights in deep snow. They had grown fewer
and fewer. To right and left of the road, women and children
were left lying in the snow. Noëmi began to cry. Kosmas put his

arm round her: "How did you escape?"—"I don't know. It was
like a dream. . . . Don't ask!" she cried, suddenly. Kosmas
stroked her hair. "I won't ask. Be calm now." Both had fallen
silent. Then Kosmas had asked: "Where did you mean to go this
evening? Why were you in such a hurry?"—Noëmi raised her
head: "I had come to a decision," she whispered.—"What decision?"—"A friend gave me this orange blouse. I washed and did
my hair properly and was going. . . ." After a short pause she said
quietly: "To kill myself. To be out of it all."

Kosmas had kissed her hands. "Let's go," he said.—"Where?"
—"Come with me, Noëmi"—"Where?"—"Why do you ask?
Have you no trust? I don't know if I love you, but I won't desert
you. Everybody's deserted you, I won't desert you."

The girl had bent her head. In the darkness of the park Kosmas
could not make out her face. He stood still, without a word. He
could feel that the orphaned girl was questioning her thoughts and
waiting for an answer. Suddenly Noëmi had raised her head and
said, quietly and with decision: "Let's go." She had given him
her hand.

The moon vanished, the bed lay in darkness. Mother and sister
were still chatting softly downstairs, and Kosmas listened to his
mother's monotonous voice. It was like running water at night.
A dog howled and was silent again. From the yard rose the scent
of basil, which had accompanied all his youth. Basil, marjoram,
gilliflower and jasmine were old and dear companions, and Kosmas took a deep breath.

"That's my country," he thought, "this is the house where I
was born, this is my wife. . . ."

In the midst of his meditation he heard the window of his
sister's room being opened. It must be near midnight. He listened.
Suddenly footsteps could be heard in the street. A nocturnal
wandered was passing by. And immediately there rang out a
longing, perplexed voice: "Is it already past midnight? Is it already
past midnight?" The footsteps stopped, but at once the window
was violently shut. Kosmas shuddered.

"My God," he murmured. Tears ran down his cheeks.

Now he could not close an eye. With open lids he waited for the twilight. When at last he saw through the window the sky growing light, he slipped from the bed, so as not to wake his wife, dressed, went downstairs, and sat on the settle in the place where his father used to sit. Defiant, he wanted to challenge the dead man, to drive him out from the house and courtyard to which he clung, and to bolt the door behind him so that he might never come back and harm his wife.

Ancient dreads had awakened in him. It was in vain that in the land of the Franks he had tried to free his mind from them. His heart was still a dark cave full of spectres.

The sister appeared, yellow and sullen in the morning light. When she saw her brother sitting in the old man's place, she started back in terror, as though she saw their father. Ever since that midnight when he had seized her by the hair and barred her from all men, a hatred had been raging in her, that had followed her father even into the grave. She would have liked him to be still alive there, that she might go on hating him and cursing him. Every night she opened her trunks and examined the trousseau which she had made with her own hands: the nightdresses with the wide lace sleeves, the embroidered kerchiefs, the silken sheets. Sometimes the impulse came over her to throw the whole lot into the yard and burn it there. "My winding-sheets! Curse him!" She would also open the cupboard containing his suits and would whimper like a bitch that has suddenly scented a wolf-skin. She never touched those clothes. She reproached her mother for never having resisted him. She had loved her brother until yesterday, when she had understood that he was married. She loathed his wife, like her father's clothes. "Maria," her mother had said to her, "be patient."—"Damn patience," she had replied. "I'd rather kill myself than go on seeing her."

As her brother now greeted her, she could not control herself and burst into tears. Kosmas put his arms round her:

"Keep calm, sister," he said. "Life's going to be different, you too will have joy."

She shook her grey head.

"I'm marrying Charos for my joy," she said, pushed her brother away and left the room.

Kosmas went out into the yard for a breath of air. But suddenly disquiet took hold of him. Had someone sighed in the room upstairs? He ran upstairs to see if his wife was all right.

She was asleep. Her slender foot was sticking out from under the sheet: he bent down and kissed it. He stroked her hair softly. A warm breath smelling of carnations came from her slightly open mouth.

But suddenly, as he was bringing his lips close to her mouth, he thought he heard the stairs creak. Slow footsteps were coming up. It was the old man, the dead man! He recognised the tread. As though turned to stone he sat up on the bed. He held his breath and listened. The stairs creaked again, the heavy footsteps were coming nearer. They had reached the landing, and sounded on the narrow piece of floor in front of the door.

"The old man," murmured Kosmas, terrified, and spread his hands above his wife to protect her.

The footsteps halted before the door. The son's heart beat wildly. The whole house seemed to him to be shaking. "Who's there?" he wanted to cry out, but his throat was as though blocked.

At that moment, Noëmi started up with a shriek. She gazed towards the door, and the sweat poured over her. Kosmas put his arms round her.

"What's the matter?" he said softly. "Did you hear something?'

"Someone came up the stairs. . . . Someone's standing behind the door." She was trembling.

"Keep quiet. Don't be afraid. You've had a dream. Look, and you'll see it's nothing."

He jumped up. He too was trembling, but he was ashamed of it. He tore the door open. Nobody. He laughed carelessly, to give her courage. He returned to her, covered her up, and kissed her trembling knees.

"Don't be afraid," he said. "This is your home, Noëmi."

The young woman looked about her, at the table, the chest, the window and the ikon-shrine with the three ikons: the Creation, the Crucifixion, and Saint Michael.

"Yes," she said, "here is my home. I shall get used to it." Her eyes were full of tears.

Kosmas saw her weeping, and at once felt a limitless, longing love. Never had he been so strongly moved. Not even on that first night, there abroad, when he had taken her. He left the door open, to show he had no fear of the dead, took her in his arms and caressed her from her toes to the top of her head.

A day went by; two went by, three. Kosmas saw his mother and sister. They said to each other what they had to say. They talked of the house, of their relatives and neighbours, of the dead man who still walked in the house and oppressed them, of Crete. . . . There was nothing more to say. Only deep affection united them still, so they were silent.

He ranged about the narrow alleys, following the old paths of his youth. Here, in this square, at the Three Vaults, his heart had leapt for love for the first time. It was here that he had seen the first girl he had loved—in a golden evening cloud, holding a yellow rose in her hand and clasping sprigs of jasmine. The world smelled of musk. It was a summer evening, and the unmarried girls in red, green and blue dresses were walking up and down, with firm breasts and quick steps. Their hair hung down, ribbons fluttered behind them and they made stealthy signs. . . . They were like corvettes flying all their flags and standing out to sea to conquer the world. And the lads trotted, pale and shy, behind them. They pretended they meant to tease and make fun of the girls. But their hearts were trembling. Kosmas too was among them, aged sixteen.

Now he hurried across the square and kept his eyes fixed on the ground, in case he should meet and recognise some fat matron whose eyes might remind him of the pennant-bedecked girl of that youthful summer evening.

Up above, in Petrokéfalo, the grandfather sat to-day—it was Sunday—in front of the blazing hearth, and froze. His cheeks had fallen in, his knees shook. He stared into the fire and brooded over his life.

In came a drover and greeted him.

"Good news for you, old Séfakas. Your eldest grandson, Kosmas, has arrived in Megalokastro from the Franks' country. They say he's got pen and paper, and writes."

The grandfather started, and raised his staff. "What does he write?" But the drover had already gone.

The grandfather said not a word more. He took the coming of his grandson as a secret annunciation of death. "My hour has come," he thought, and stood up.

"Take the big ladder on your shoulder, Charidemos," he said, "and come with me."

"Where to, old Séfakas?"

"I've told you a thousand times, you're not to ask me questions. Be quick about it!"

Charidemos loaded the ladder on to his shoulder. The grandfather led the way, with the paint-pot and brush. Hastily he hobbled over the cobbles. Reaching the village square, he pointed at the small, white-washed bell-tower of the church.

"Lean it against the wall there. Hold it firmly so that I don't fall. Where's Thrasáki?"

"He's gone out with his crew and the old gun, old Séfakas."

"That's right. He has my blessing."

The shepherd leaned the ladder against the bell-tower, shoved a couple of stones under it and held it firmly with both hands. The old man gasped as he climbed up. Charidemos was terrified. "Lord, have mercy on me," he muttered, crossing himself.

The greybeard had now clambered to the top of the ladder and had reached the smooth corner-stone just under the belfry. He dipped the brush into the paint, stretched out his arm and began, one after another, to make huge letters. F R E. . . . His heart beat joyfully. "Who would have foretold me," he thought, "that my life would end like this? With a brush, a paint-pot and letters on the wall!" When he had finished his work and was still holding the paint-brush in his hand, he forgot that he was on the ladder and bent backwards to admire what he had written. He lost his balance and, with his arms outstretched, fell.

Charidemos yelled; neighbours came running, and picked the old man up. His head was all bloody. But his mouth was sealed. He did not utter a sound.

"His eldest grandson has come back to Crete," Charidemos explained to the neighbours. "The joy at the news went to his head. . . ."

The village was convulsed as though an earthquake had broken its main pillar. All the women with any art of healing hurried to the scene and plied him with ointments. A messenger was sent on muleback to Megalokastro to fetch Mustafa Baba, who knew all herbs and was also a good man who doctored Turks, Christians and Jews without distinction. "They all fall ill, poor things," he used to say, "even if they're Greeks or Jews."

Next morning Mustafa Baba arrived, riding the mule, brought out his small case, opened his little bottles and took the split grey head in his hard hands.

On the third day the grandfather opened his eyes. He looked about him and caught sight of his daughter-in-law, Katerina. He beckoned to her.

"What's happening up the mountain? What have you heard from your husband?"

"He's not submitting," the wife answered.

"He's right," said the old man. "Put a cushion in my back, so that I can sit up. I'm tired of lying flat. Send for Kostandes from the pen, I want him." Then he shut his eyes again.

An hour later a fellow appeared, half man, half goat, and took up position in front of the small sofa on which the old man lay. He waited, his chin supported on his staff. The grandfather's eyes were closed. He saw nothing. In his ears there was a humming. He heard nothing. Kostandes waited patiently. "Some day he'll open his eyes and see me and tell me what he wants of me," he said.

The grand-children and daughters-in-law stood in a ring round the old man. Thrasáki too came in, with the old gun on his shoulder. He had been up the mountain again, playing at war with his friends. He was waiting to know what would happen with his grandfather, and then—all was prepared—he would lead his band in an attack on a Turkish village and challenge the Turkish youths.

"You wake him, Thrasáki. You're not afraid of him," said Kostandes.

"I'm not afraid of him, that's true," replied Thrasáki, "but I'm sorry for him. He's asleep."

The grandfather heard the whispering and opened his eyes. Kostandes set his huge feet in motion and went over to him. The old man blinked at the circle about him and became aware of the throng. He flew into a fury.

"I'm not dying yet, you half-witted heirs of mine," he said. "Out with the lot of you! Come here, Kostandes. Bend down!"

The hairy fellow bent over and took in the instructions of old Séfakas, who spoke slowly, breathing irregularly and sometimes interrupted by pain. At the end he asked:

"Understand, Kostandes?"

"I understand, old Séfakas."

"And afterwards, when you've made it known in the villages, hurry down to Megalokastro. Run to my eldest son's house, you know the one, to my daughter-in-law Chrysula. Take two whole cheeses and a nice lamb with you as a present for her. My first grandson, Kosmas, has arrived, so they say. See him with your own eyes, touch him with your hands, do you hear? And say to him: 'Come up, your grandfather's dying. He wants to give you his blessing.' Understand, you idiot Kostandes?"

"I understand, old Séfakas."

"Well, be off with you! Run!"

As the old man turned towards him, he was already away. The clattering nails of his boots were all that could he heard.

Next morning both wings of old Chrysula's street door flew open at one kick, and a hairy fellow carrying two whole cheeses in a sack and a slaughtered lamb under his arm strode over the threshold. He walked into the middle of the yard, with his furry chest bare and reeking of garlic and onions. He laid the presents

on the ground and leaned on his long shepherd's staff. The three
women were sitting, drinking coffee, on the sofa. Upstairs Kosmas
was getting ready for a visit to the Metropolitan. They had already
composed the letter and sent it into the mountains. With sighs the
captains bowed their heads. 'Since the Mother Country wills it so,"
they answered, "we obey her command!" But Captain Michales's
answer was still lacking. When he received the Metropolitan's
letter, he had sent for the second captain on Selena, Polyxigis.
The two had shut themselves up in the stone hut, and bolted the
door.

"I'm not submitting," Captain Michales stated.

"The Mother Country's demanding it," retorted Captain
Polyxigis. "Let's not pull against her."

"What Mother Country? I've no confidence in the heads that
govern there."

"You've more confidence in your own head?"

"What's the good of joking? No, not in my head, but in my
heart. It tells me: don't submit. And I'm not submitting. Do what
your heart tells you."

"I'm doing what I've decided. I'm obeying."

"Then go, and all the best! Leave me, you too. Other comrades
have already left me. I need no one. Good luck to you and a fair
wind in your sails, my palikare!"

Captain Polyxigis hesitated. His heart rebelled against the re-
treat and was unwilling to leave this man to his death.

"You're perishing to no purpose, Captain Michales," he said.

"In war no one perishes to no purpose," Captain Michales
shouted. "Are you feeling sorry for me?"

"There was one human being I loved in the world. You killed
her for me. No, I'm not fond of you, Captain Michales. But I don't
like to see you perish. Crete—Devil take it—still needs you!"

"I don't need Crete any more," groaned the other. "Go, I tell
you."

"Haven't you any thought for your wife? Haven't you any
thought for Thrasáki?"

"If you value your life, go!" roared Captain Michales, and the
veins in his neck swelled. He kicked aside the baulks that barred

the entrance of the stone hut and pushed Captain Polyxigis out. Then from the threshold he shouted for Vendúsos.

"Off with you, Vendúsos, take what legs you've got and rund own to Megalokastro, to the Metropolitan's Residence. Greet the Bishop and tell him that I've received his letter, and have set fire to its four corners. I'm sending it back to him. I'm not submitting!"

"At your orders, Captain Michales," said Vendúsos, and stuffed the letter into his bosom.

"Run fast. And if you value your life, don't come back, Vendúsos. Here it's death."

"I've children, Captain Michales," said Vendúsos with a sigh, "I've my daughter to find a husband for, and my wife and the tavern. . . ."

"Then don't come back. You're Vendúsos, I'm not asking for anything. Behave like a Vendúsos! Take Kajabés and Furógatos with you, too, and look for Bertódulos down there, and Efendína!" Captain Michales growled, and turned his back on him.

Vendúsos clambered swiftly down the hidden path to the upland plain, sighing and cursing. "You're Vendúsos, behave like a Vendúsos." The words lashed his back as he ran. He reached the town and climbed the staircase of the Residence.

It was at that moment that Kostandes had entered the parental house of Kosmas and was standing in the middle of the yard, pressing his paws against his sweating chest. "Long life to you," he cried, in a voice that was hoarse from his having spent his whole life among goats and rams. "Long life to you, women. May you enjoy it! All the best!"

"Welcome, Kostandes," said the mother. "Come in. Sit down and drink some wine. What news have you got for us from the village?"

"Your father-in-law, Captain Séfakas, is dying, Madame Chrysula. Nothing's any use to him now. Even the Devil's no use to him now," said Kostandes, with a loud laugh. "And I'm to give you, he says, these presents from him." He squatted down and laid his staff across his bony knees.

"By God, he's led a good life: eaten, drunk, killed Turks, filled his yard with children and asses and mares and oxen, turned wild land into ploughland, planted vineyards and olives and built a church for his soul, too. He's insured himself for up there, too. What more could he do with life? He's hoisted the flag for departure too."

Kosmas heard the voices and came down from his room. Kostandes looked him over curiously from head to foot.

"You are the eldest grandson of old Sefakas, sir? Or am I wrong?" He craned his neck to see him properly. And then he got up and touched him with his paw. Grandfather's orders!

"No one else," replied Kosmas.

"Then your grandfather sends to tell you to go to him, but quickly, and close his eyes. Quickly, I tell you, if you want to see him still alive. By the sun that's above us all, I think he's been waiting for you, sir, all these years, so as to be able now to give up his soul to the Archangel. 'Take a mule with you,' he told me, 'so that he can ride! I' he said, 'have held an axe, my son a gun, but my grandson, they now tell me, holds a pen. So he won't be able to run on foot. Take a mule and show him the way.' The mules at the inn, waiting. Let's go!"

To the mistress of the house he said:

"There's the news, Madam Chrysula. And the wine you're offering me—I'll drink it so as not to upset you."

He drank the wine at one gulp, seized a hunk of bread from the table, smacked his lips contentedly and laughed.

"And listen," he said, "to what else I've got to tell you. Captain Séfakas has also sent out an invitation to a feast. As if he was going to the underworld as a bridegroom! It's not yet twenty-four hours since he sent for me. I'm his shepherd, ever since I was born, and his messenger. 'Run, Kostandes,' he said to me, 'take your staff and climb up to the higher mountains and call together the old war-leaders. Stand in the middle of each village and cry: "Children, Captain Séfakas is dying! You who are of his time, who went out bearing arms with him and are still alive—Captain Séfakas is inviting you to his mansion! He doesn't want presents, have no fear! You'll find his tables laid, and you'll sit down in his

o

chairs and eat and drink. And afterwards Captain Séfakas has something to say to you, something important. Pick up your staffs and come!" ' "

"What's he want to say?" asked Kosmas, who had listened greedily. Only the patriarchs of the Old Testament had died with such dignity, he thought, and he felt a mighty pride at being sprung from such a race.

"What's he want to say?" said the shepherd. "How should I know? I wanted to ask him, but I was afraid—he might have hit me on the head with his stick. So I said nothing. With one bound I was outside, running over the mountains and going into the villages. There I cried it. Only three old men from three of the villages came out. Captain Mándakas, Captain Katsirmas, and the old schoolmaster from Embaros, the lame one. 'Tell him,' they said to me, 'hold out, Captain Séfakas, don't give up that soul of yours yet, we're coming.' They put on their fezes with the big tassels and girded on their belts. . . ."

Kostandes laughed again: "Three ruins, poor chaps!" he said. "Their heads sown with scars like a sieve! Their feet couldn't shove them forwards any more. Three hundred years old, the three together. The spittle running out of their mouths, their eyebrows sagging. They picked up their silver pistols as though they were going to war. Then they hobbled forwards, leaning on each other so as not to fall. You don't believe me? When we get to the village, you'll see them."

He stood up and said to Kosmas: "Put on your fez, sir, and come with me. Your grandfather's dying, didn't you hear me say? And he wants you to close his eyes."

The mother crossed herself.

"He'll go to Paradise," she said with certainty, "he was a good man."

"So will Father go to Paradise," said Kosmas. "We shall all reach Paradise, because we've suffered in this world."

His sister shook her head and said with an angry laugh:

"God is just."

"God is merciful," cried the mother. She went to fetch the incense-burner and light the incense.

Kosmas turned to his wife, who had come down and was listening silently on a corner of the sofa:

"You're coming with m , Chrysula,"

But Kostandes struck the ground with his staff:

"What d'you want with women, by God?" he cried, "They're a pest. 'Forward,' you say, and they say: 'Stop!' And sometimes ambition does get hold of them and the poor things do rush forwards, but then they gasp and make you sorry for them. Can you leave them behind on the road? That's wrong! Take them with you? A pest! But you're the master. It's for you to decide. I've said my say."

"Kostandes is right," said the mother, appearing with the incense-burner. "Don't take her with you, my child, she'll get tired."

"Take her," said the sister slyly, "she'll hold out."

Noëmi shuddered at the thought of remaining without protection in such a house. The air was heavy, and she would have liked to become quite small, like an insect, to be able to hide under one of the basil plants in the yard.

"I'm coming with you," she said. "I want to get to know Crete."

"Go and don't come back!" muttered the sister. She could not bear her, she held her breath when she came near her. She had prepared special glasses and plates, knives and forks for her.

"I shall hold out," Noëmi whispered, and rose to go and get ready.

But as she rose, suddenly a giddiness seized her. The house spun round her. She leaned against the wall with her eyes closed. All that day she had felt a heaviness, as if her body were changing and twisting.

Someone touched her softly on the shoulder. She saw her husband standing in front of her with a glass of water. With a smile she out put her hand for it, but faltered and collapsed in a faint. The mother hastily brought rose-vinegar, with which to rub her face and neck.

"She's tired," she said compassionately.

"It's nothing," the sister hissed. "A faint—even I have fainting-fits."

Kosmas supported her up to bed. Noëmi opened her eyes and saw the mother bending over her.

"Forgive me, Mother," she said, "I'm tired."

"Go to sleep," said the mother, and for the first time laid her hand caressingly on her hair.

Kosmas kissed his wife on the neck.

"Go to sleep, Chrysula," said he too. "Don't come with me. Be patient. I shall be back soon."

She shook her head, and shut her eyes.

"Go, and blessings with you," she said.

Kosmas hurried to the Metropolitan, whom he found in the highest agitation.

"This minute I've received the answer from your uncle, that wild barbarian. He's not submitting, he says, and we're not to meddle in his business. Christ will bless you if you go to him. Tell him, Crete is in danger by his fault. Knock some sense into that hard skull of his. Do what you can, my child, it's necessary."

"I'll do what I can, Mylord. I'm going."

Noëmi was sitting up in bed and waiting for him. She was now wearing her yellow night-dress, and her honey-golden hair fell freely in curls over her shoulders. She clasped her knees and propped her chin on them, brooding. What power love had! How had she been led here, to the end of the world, to this bedroom with the ikons, with the crucifixion of Christ—she, the Rabbi's daughter? "Ah, if I had not seen what I saw," she sighed, "and my soul were a white leaf with no writing on it, what happiness there would be here!" She thought of last night, when she had lain stretched out on the old iron bed, shortly before she fell asleep. Through the open window came the night wind, laden with the scent of basil and marjoram. Not a dog barked, not a human step echoed. The world lay there in tender moonlight. Only, from far away, there sounded a soft, unceasing, rhythmical sighing. It was the sea, which, like her, could not get to sleep.

"How sweet night is, how trustfully the man I love sleeps at my side. And inside me. . . ."

Kosmas came in, shut the door and sat down near her. He gazed at her with inexpressible tenderness, with a long look as though of farewell.

"Are you going away?" Noëmi asked, clutching his hand. Her head was burning.

"Noëmi," said her husband anxiously, "you've a fever."

"No, it's not a fever, my dear. I think it's the normal temperature of my race," she answered with a laugh. And immediately afterwards: "You looked at me as if it was a farewell"—she was on the point of adding: "for ever." She trembled and nearly cried out: "How can you leave me alone in this house?" But she controlled herself.

"I shall be back soon, beloved. I want to close my grandfather's eyes. . . ."

He held his wife's hand, and life seemed to him simple. All times gathered into this short moment, during which he clasped warmly in his hand the hand of the being whom he loved. This moment was eternity.

Noëmi gazed at her husband and said nothing.

Now it was Kosmas who cried: "Don't look at me like that, as if you were saying good-bye to me for ever."

He kissed her eyes. A bitter taste came upon his tongue.

"That's how you're looking at me," said Noëmi, dropping her head back upon the pillow.

From below the angry voice of Kostandes rang out:

"Hey, master, your grandfather's dying. Come on! Your mother's filled the sack. Good luck to her. We'll eat and drink on our way, like the wind! But be quick! Evening's there."

Kosmas bent over and kissed his wife's bosom, purely and trustfully as we kiss sacred pictures. "Good-bye," he said to her.

"Good-bye," whispered the woman, taking his head in her hands.

For a long while he remained still, leaning on her breast. Her eyes were full of tenderness, foresakenness and dread. "Good-bye," she said yet again.

Kosmas rose, and would have kissed her on the mouth. But she put her hand over it.

"No," she said, "no, Good-bye."

XIII

THE face of Crete is stern and weathered. Truly Crete has about her something primeval and holy, bitter and proud, to have given birth to all those mothers, so often stricken by Charos, and all those palikares.

When they had left Megalokastro and reached the olive-trees and vineyards, Kosmas rode ahead, while Kostandes trotted behind with his shepherd's staff over his shoulder. Evening was approaching. The landscape round about was speckled yellowish and purple, like a leopard-skin. Psilorítis stood there in its mantle of snow, cheerful, strong and kindly like a grandfather. In the foreground lay the Lasíthi mountains: they also looked cheerful under the soft winter sun. Below them spread the newly ploughed fields, some cinnamon-brown, others deep black. Here and there stood a group of olive-trees with silvery branches, a lonely cypress, an unleaved row of vines on which one or two forgotten clusters still hung by shrivelled stalks.

Kosmas gazed about him indefatigably. "This is Crete, this is the earth from which I was born, this is my mother," he said to himself, with his heart beating violently. When he had thought of Crete in far-off countries, a severe, relentless voice had always sounded within him. "What have you been doing, all these years?" it used to ask him. "Aren't you ashamed of yourself? You keep fighting the air and exciting yourself with words. But flesh and blood you leave in the lurch, and nourish yourself on illusions. I don't like you." And now he was roaming over the soil of the island—its scent of thyme was crowding into his lungs. Now he could no longer escape from it, and he owed it an answer. But what answer? He had accomplished nothing, he was nothing. Were these hands, thighs, and a chest, or were they mere lumps of flesh? He was a disgrace to a hard, irrepressible stock.

And where was he bound now? So low had he fallen: to bury one dragon of his race and to persuade another to surrender. His heart faltered. He turned to Kostandes, to hear a man's voice.

"Kostandes," he said, "tell me about my grandfather, old Séfakas. Come here, so that I can hear you."

He gave him a cigarette, which Kostandes stuck behind his ear.

"What am I to say to you, master?" he began. "We're alive, he's dying. What hasn't he eaten, what hasn't he drunk, how many Turks has he not killed, God forgive him! You mark my words: he's filled his life well, very well. Don't you go pitying him! When he used to come up to the pen, he'd swallow a giant of a cheese with two bites. Then he'd kill a hare with his stick and say to me: 'Roast that for me, Kostandes!' I'd roast it for him and he'd make short work of it! Not a bone would be left of it. He ate and drank, the sinner, and on his wedding night, so I've heard tell, he broke three beds. Don't laugh, master, I'm telling you the truth."

He stopped speaking, took off his head-band and wiped the sweat from his dark face. He was laughing now himself.

"Did you hear what happened when he married your grandmother?" he asked.

"No, tell me, Kostandes."

"Her parents didn't want to give her to him. He was poor, they were powerful, respected, wealthy people. He was a wild spark, and wherever there was a row he was there. If there was trouble anywhere, he grabbed for his gun at once and made for the mountains. And they were dish-lickers, an obedient, well-behaved family. He was not their sort. Your grandfather sent to ask for her hand; the Abbot of 'Christ The Lord' also spoke up for him. But 'no! no!' the bride's parents answered, 'we don't want him!'— 'Ah, that's the sort of people you are,' your grandfather replied, 'you cattle, now I'm going to show you!' One night he jumped on his mare and rode to the bride's village. He took nothing with him, except a can full of petrol and a box of matches. And one thing else—a gold betrothal ring tied up in his head-band. He rushed through the village and sprinkled house after house with petrol. 'Hey, peasants,' he shouted, 'I'm setting fire to your houses!' They recognised his voice and jumped out of bed. The bride's parents, too, came running.

" 'In God's name, Captain Séfakas, don't be guilty of such a crime!' "

" 'Give me Lenio!' he shouted.

" 'Have you no fear of God?'

" 'Don't mix God up in my business. Give me Lenio! Here's the wedding ring!'

"He undid it from his head-band. 'Choose,' he cried. 'Fire or the ring!'

" 'God will pay you out for this, you madman!' the bride's father yelled.

" 'Fire or the ring!' he shouted again.

" 'Have pity on the village!'

" 'Fire or the ring?'

"By now the peasants were furious. Was a crazy fellow to order them about? 'To arms, children!' But at this point the pope came up: 'Fear God, brothers, master your anger.' He turned to the girl's father: 'Hey, old Minotes, cross yourself. He's a good son-in-law. Give her to him!' The more cautious ones took the pope's side. 'I'll give her to you, you madman!' yelled the father, 'but clear out of here at once!'—'I want her now. Bring her to me!' —Cursing, the father now brought the girl, followed by her mother, weeping.

"Your grandfather bent down, took the bride under the arms and hoisted her up on to the crupper of the mare. He dug in the spurs. Dust whirled up. The peasants and the pope ran after him, breathless. At grey of dawn they arrived at Petrokéfalo, where the marriage was taking place. 'Back you march now,' cried your grandfather to the peasants. 'Next Sunday the tables will be laid, and you'll be welcome. I'm busy now. . . .' "

Kostandes pulled out the cigarette from behind his ear.

"That's the way men ought to get their wives," he said, and gave himself a light, using a piece of dried mushroom as tinder.

They reached a deep ravine. A thin trickle of water ran over light-coloured rocks.

"Are you thirsty?" Kostandes asked.

"No. Let's get on, Kostandes! It'll soon be evening!"

"I'm thirsty. Stop!"

He lay down on the rocks, thrust his wedge-shaped beard and

his moustaches into the water and began lapping the water with his tongue like a tiger.

"There'll be nothing left of the brook," thought Kosmas, marvelling at the wild man of the mountains. With pride, as if they were his own, he observed the powerful calves, the slender hips, the pitch-black hair soaking up the trickle.

Kostandes leapt to his feet in one movement, wrung out his beard and shouldered his staff.

"Here, on this rock where I lay and drank," he said. "I killed the Albanian, Hussein, the hater of Christians. Pitch cover his bones! I swore, then, that every time I came through this ravine I'd have a drink, whether I was thirsty or not!"

"You killed him, Kostandes! All alone?" asked Kosmas, who had heard about the appalling deed from the Metropolitan the day before. It had been one of the causes of the massacre of the Christians in Megalokastro.

"Of course alone!" Kostandes replied. "What else? Man against man, as things are done between men. I'd heard that the dog meant to come this way, after he'd set fire to one of the villages. You'll see it. We get to it soon. He'd killed all the men of the village. So I swore to kill him. I lay in wait for him and cut his throat."

He strode forward again and began to whistle.

The shadows were lengthening over the face of the land. The two men reached the devastated village. Two or three houses had walls still standing. Out of the ruins came women in rags; a girl fetched a sprig from a pot of basil which had remained still intact, and threw it to Kosmas. "Welcome," she called out.

They gained the village square. Grey-beards gathered round them. There were also a few women among them, but they held back. A huge, bony old man, the spokesman of the commune, came forward and took off his cap. "We've no chair to offer you to sit down on, we've no glass to bring you water in, if you're thirsty, we've no bread if you're hungry. The dogs have burnt up everything—may God burn them!"

"We've no proper man, either, to talk with you," said an old

o*

woman, and began the keening, in which a couple of women joined.

"Courage, you women!" said the old man. "Didn't the same thing happen to us in the 1866? And yet there were a few little children left over, and out of them the whole village was renewed. As long as there are still a man and a woman, Crete doesn't die!"

The old man turned to Kostandes. "God bless that hand of yours, my Palikare," he said, "and may you enter Paradise with the knife which slew Hussein."

"Come," said Kosmas, who could bear the horror no more, "good-bye!"

In silence the grey-beards propped their chins on their staffs and watched the two press on. The old women wiped their eyes. A girl stood in front of the ruins of her house and gazed proudly after Kostandes, as with youthful vigour he strode from stone to stone.

The sun was already saying farewell as they came to a shut-in, desert plain on which a dark group of oak trees stood in mourning.

"We must hurry," said Kostandes, hitting the mule with his staff, "if we want to get to the next village before night-fall. We'll stop there, with old Kubelina. She's my aunt, my mother's sister. She's got no house, but she has a heart, and that'll be enough for us. You won't find a house standing in this village either. The bandits have raged there too. Curse them!"

A barefooted, half-blind old woman, laden with wood, rose up before them.

"How are things with you, little woman?" asked Kosmas.

"As they are with dogs, my child," she answered, "if God would only stop loading Man with as much as he can carry!"

"Have the Turks ruined you too?"

But Kostandes made violent signs to Kosmas to be quiet.

"What did you say, my child? I'm hard of hearing. God be praised!"

"Goodbye! We must go on."

"Are you a Cretan?"

"Yes."

"Take my blessing! Beget children! Crete has grown empty. Beget children, so the Cretans mayn't vanish from the world. They'll be needed, too."

"Come," said Kostandes. "It's late." He hit the mule. They hurried on.

"A good thing she didn't throw stones at us," he said. "We had a lucky escape, That's old Kostandinia, 'the pilgrim's widow', as she's called. When the poor thing sees a man, she loses her wits. She picks up stones and throws them at him. She takes every man for a Turk."

He gathered some acorns off the ground, shelled them and ate them. As Kosmas looked at him with surprise, he said:

"Those aren't acorns, they're chestnuts. At least we call them chestnuts when evening comes and we've had nothing to eat and can't make things out clearly any longer."

At last they left the plain: the mountain in front of them opened a pass.

"There's the village," said Kostandes, raising his hand. Kosmas could discern only heaps of ruins on the slope of the mountain.

"Where?" he asked. "I can't see anything."

"In front of you, those stones," said Kostandes. "Soon the people too will come into sight. There, the dogs have got wind of us."

Some dogs rushed barking out of the ruins. Their ribs gleamed from hunger.

"I don't see a light anywhere," said Kosmas.

"Where would they get oil, master? Or petrol? At sundown they huddle into the ruins, like owls."

"Welcome," cried voices, and five or six heads peered out from behind the raw stones. "Where are you going?"

"To old Kubelina," Kostandes answered. "She'll make up a bed for us in her lordly mansion."

Laughter came in answer.

"Have you a bite of something with you?" one of them asked.

"Yes, we've got something."

"Then old Kubelina too will have something to eat. Have you got some bits of stuff to keep warm in, too?"

"We've got that too."

"Then old Kubelina too will be able to keep warm," said the voices, and fresh laughter rang out behind the stones.

"They can laugh!" said Kosmas, overcome.

Kostandes stopped and began counting the heaps of ruins. "Four, five, six—ah, here's my aunt's house!" he said. "We needn't knock, it hasn't got a door. Hey, Kubelina, come out on the balcony!"

A frail old woman in rags, leaning on a bent stick, came out between the stones.

"Is that Kostandes?" she asked. "When will you learn reason? And who's with you?"

"Throw open the doors, I tell you!" answered Kostandes. "Kill two hens. Give 'em to the girl to prepare. We'll have one boiled, the other roast, with potatoes. Open the chests too, get out the silken sheets and make up beds for us. We're glad we've arrived. Be happy in your kingdom!"

"All shall be done, you whirlwind," replied the old woman. And groping her way forward, "Welcome, sir," she said to Kosmas, who had dismounted and was stumbling over debris. "Welcome, my child! Don't listen to that silly Kostandes. I've roofed a corner with rushes—that's the best room in the house. Come in."

They squatted on the stones. Kostandes collected some brush-wood and made a fire. Kosmas opened the sack and took out the plentiful provisions his mother had packed for him. The old woman squatted down beside them, and they began to eat. The old woman crossed herself and fell upon the food.

"Come every evening, my children, every evening, and then I too, poor thing, will have something to eat. Have you got some wine as well with you?"

Kostandes pulled out a bottle, which passed from mouth to mouth. The old woman drank and drank, and her eyes grew bright. In her youth she had certainly been beautiful; now all she had left was those huge, gleaming, dark-brown eyes.

"Hey, aunt," said Kostandes, whom the drink had made gay, "may I be allowed to sing something?"

"You have my permission," replied the victim of Charos. "You're still alive, so sing, you idiot!"

The lusty fellow sang, with long-draw-out notes, while his aunt listened and giggled, with her toothless mouth half-open:

> *I took my Aunt Thodora down*
> *One summer evening to the town.*
>
> *Your beauty's set me in a whirl.*
> *Ah, if you were some other girl!*
>
> *Child, be a man, and have your way.*
> *I'll be your aunt again, some day.*

New life came into the spellbound woman. She clapped her hands and blushed. Kosmas gazed at her thoughtfully. . . . "What strength these souls have in them!" he thought. "That is Crete."

"Poverty must have its pleasures, my child," said the old woman, laughing. "Suffering needs singing and drinking, otherwise it feeds on us. But this rough customer isn't going to make a meal of us. We'll eat him up."

In the morning, as they took leave of her, the old woman picked up from the paving of the yard a stone covered with red stains, and gave it to Kosmas.

"It's the only present I can give you," she said. "Keep this stone in remembrance of Crete." She pointed to the dark red spots: "My son's blood."

In the street Kostandes strode forward again with his staff on his shoulder and sang without ceasing. Kosmas looked about him speechlessly. Round him spread his native country, whose lost meaning he was now experiencing for the first time. Hard of approach, rebellious, harsh was this land. She allowed not a moment of comfort, of gentleness, of repose. Crete had something inhuman about her. One could not tell whether she loved her children or hated them. One thing was certain: she scourged them till the blood flowed.

He turned and looked at the stone heaps which were the village, between which a few women and children were visible. He heard voices and laughter. "What strength there is there," he thought, "what souls! For thousands of years they have struggled in this wilderness of rocks, with hunger, thirst, discord and death. And they don't bow down. They don't even complain. In the deepest hopelessness the Cretan finds redemption."

As they came in sight of the grandfather's village, the sun was at its noon height. A hot south wind was blowing from Arabia, and the sea began to rise into view beyond the mountain.

Old Séfakas's big house stood out at the highest point of the village. It had a stately air, with its wine-presses, oil-presses, stables and storehouses, where casks and jars lay in rows. It had wide verandas, where in summer the rugs and pillows were stacked in heaps up to the roof, and high bedrooms on the first floor. The doors now were open; the people were going in and out to see how things were with the captain, who had been striving for so many days against Charos. The old man's daughter's-in-law and grandchildren were running busily up and down, counting the jars, valuing the store of flour and oil, verifying the casks in the wine-cellar. How many fleeces were hanging from the rafters? How many cheeses were there in the cheese-larder? They reckoned out loud what inheritance fell to each one. They were carving up the grandfather alive. Angrily he called out to them:

"Put me in the yard, so that I can't hear you!"

The daughters-in-law and grandchildren prepared him his bed in the yard.

"Put me on the ground under the lemon-tree. Here's where I want to draw my last breath—where the earth touches my flesh and I can touch it. Prop me a bit higher, so that I can see about me!"

They stuffed a cushion against his back to support him. They placed near him his stick and a cup of water to drink from.

"Now leave me alone. Away with you!" he ordered. "Only Thrasáki's to come and sit by me."

He now took a good look round him at the stables, the presses, the fountain, the troughs, the two cypresses to right and left by the door, and he snuffed the air, which smelled of lemon-leaves and dung. The smell delighted him and he stroked his beard in contentment. He heard a sigh close by and, looking to one side, became aware of a sturdy, curly-haired youth who stood waiting.

"Well, who are you?"

"Kostantes."

"Whose son?"

"Your son Nikolis's."

"And why are you standing here, so close to me?"

"You're a long time dying, grandad, and I'm in a hurry to be back at my sheep-pen. I want to be off."

"Off with you then, don't wait about uselessly. I shall be some time. And look after the beasts well."

The curly-headed young palikare bent down, grasped his grandfather's hand and kissed it.

"I shan't go," he said, "if you don't give me your blessing. That's what I've been waiting for since early this morning."

"Take my blessing, then, and go. And listen—go indoors and tell them they're to lay the tables in the yard in front of me, so that the three captains can eat here and I can see them. Are they still eating?"

"Yes, still. . . . Since yesterday evening, when they arrived, by my faith, grandad, their jaws haven't had a rest. From time to time they dropped off to sleep on each other's shoulders, and then they woke up again and the chewing went on. And the school-master's brought his lyre with him and plays an accompaniment. And they keep bothering the women."

"What's come over you, you clucking hen? Shut up! Do as I tell you. The tables are to be laid here, so that I can see. And if they can't move, help them, Kostantes! And don't laugh. They're captains. They deserve respect! Go!"

Now there appeared, panting, Charidemos. He had been sent by the grandfather to Captain Michales with the news that he was dying. He was to come down for the leave-taking. The ancient raised his eyes and recognised Charidemos:

"What answer have you brought me? Will he come?"

" 'I can't leave my post, Father,' he told me to say to you. 'Forgive me, but I can't leave my post. Give me your blessing from afar. Farewell! And may we meet again soon!' "

"He's right. He made one mistake. Now he's learned prudence

Let him have my blessing from afar," said the old man, raising his hand and blessing the air.

He turned to Thrasáki: "My little Thrasáki, do you understand what's going on?"

"I understand, grandad."

"Keep your eyes open, Thrasáki, and see clearly. Keep your ears open, and hear clearly. Let nothing escape you. Now three mountains will be coming into view—the three captains."

While he was still speaking, Stavrulios, the village carpenter, appeared at the door. The grandsons had sent for him, to take the measurements for the coffin. He came in stealthily and fearfully. The grandfather had half shut his eyes, and pretended not to see him. The man bent down, stretched out both his arms cautiously to begin measuring, and asked, to appease the old man:

"How are you feeling, Captain Séfakas? You're all right to-day, God be thanked. You'll have Charos beaten yet!"

The old man saw how the carpenter was trying to measure him tremblingly and unobtrusively, and he smiled under his lusty, flowing beard. At length he took pity on him and said:

"Don't be afraid, Stavrulios, you idiot, just bring that rule of yours into the open and measure me!"

The carpenter started: "What did you say, captain?"

"Blockhead, get on with your work and measure me!"

The carpenter thought that the old man was feeling for his stick and was alarmed. He pulled the tape-measure out of his belt and placed it against the massive body.

"How long?" asked the old man.

"Six foot exactly, captain."

"I've shrunk," he said with a sigh. "Measure my breadth too."

Stavrulios measured his breadth as well, and then stood still.

"Run along with you, poor fellow! I want it of good timber! Have you got walnut?"

"Of course, captain."

The old man turned to Thrasáki:

"Can you tell walnut-wood, Thrasáki?"

"That I can, grandad!"

"Good! Well, make sure that Stavrulios doesn't swindle us. I want it made of walnut. Go!"

Meanwhile the women were laying the tables in the yard. They brought roast meat and dainties, jugs of wine and copper drinking-cups. The grey-beard, propped up on his pillow, watched. Two bees hummed about his huge head of thick hair, and some ants had got wind of him and were crawling over his naked, furry calves. Their scurrying amused him.

"Where are the captains?" he asked.

"There they come, granddad."

With their faces set askew, with their moustaches drooping, with their broad red belts riding loose, with baggy breeches of thick wool, with boots trodden down and with each a camomile flower behind the ear, the three hobbled slowly out, supporting one another.

"Let's step out firmly, brothers! If not, we shall disgrace ourselves," they whispered to each other.

"Hold me fast, so that I don't fall," croaked the lame school-master, whom they had placed in the middle. The lean, proud little man was half-seas over. His hefty lyre was slung from his shoulder, like a cartridge-belt.

On his right Captain Mándakas towered above him, with short hair and beard, strong neck, solid bones and gigantic ears. At his waist flashed the silver pistols. On the left went Captain Katsirmas, the corsair, weathered by the salt air, with his savage face and squinting eyes.

When they saw the old man, they stopped.

"Are you still living, brother Séfakas?" cried Captain Mándakas, roaring with laughter. "And we've been eating and drinking and saying: 'God be merciful to him.' "

"Won't you eat and drink some more, captains?" the old man invited them. "Since yesterday, I hear, your jaws haven't rested. When will you have had your fill, so that you can forget the miserable belly and we can talk together like men?"

The schoolmaster made to speak, but the words rolled about in his mouth and tasted to him like flints.

"Be quiet, schoolmaster!" said Katsirmas and covered his whole

face with the palm of his hand. "Or they'll see how it is with us."
Then he addressed old Séfakas in a dignified voice, placing his
hand on his breast:

"Many years to you, Captain Séfakas! We're happy to visit you
in your mansion. We've eaten and drunk. We'll eat and drink
some more to your health. And then, as you say, we'll talk together like men. Don't be in a hurry."

"I'm not in a hurry," the old man replied. "Someone here is in
a hurry."

"Who?"

"Charos."

"We're three leaders," said Captain Mándakas, twirling his
moustache. "With you, that makes four. He must wait!"

The three swayed in unison like a three-headed, six-footed
monster. They held the schoolmaster fast by the neck, so that he
should not fall. The grandsons and daughters-in-law had come
out and were laughing out loud at the spectacle of the drunken
heroes. But old Séfakas called out angrily:

"What are you laughing at, there? They're captains, strong
men! Hold them up. so they don't fall!"

"If anyone comes near me, I'll split his skull!" bellowed Captain Katsirmas. "I can walk without help."

He cast loose from his companions and with big strides reached
the tables.

At last all three reached their thrones and filled the cups. The
schoolmaster took the lyre from his shoulder and placed it up
right on his lap. He grabbed for a piece of meat, to fortify himself before striking up on his instrument.

Just as he took up the bow, Kosmas arrived on the threshold.
The grandfather noticed him and drew his brows together to see
more clearly who it was.

"Who's that lean-bottom, standing there on the threshold of
my door?"

"Your grandson, granddad," answered Kosmas, going over to
the old man.

"Which one?"

"The son of Captain Kostaros, your first."

"O welcome," cried the grandfather, stretching out his hand. "Come, let me give you my blessing. . . . Where have you been knocking about, all these years? What were you after in the Franks' country. What have you learned? Yes, if I'd only time to ask you questions, and for you to answer. But the oil in my lamp's coming to an end. The world's growing dark."

Kosmas bent down, to receive the blessing. The old man kept hold of his head and would not let him rise:

"You write, they say. What do you write, by the God you worship? You'll come down to being like Kriaras the rhyme-smith, who wanders through the villages and passes a plate round for money!"

With his small, piercing eyes the grandfather searched him and weighed him up. What sort of a grandson is that? Has he any value, or not? How could his seed have produced a quill-driver?

"Married?" he asked.

"Yes."

"They say you've chosen a Jewess."

"Yes," said Kosmas, looking hesitantly at the old man.

"Nothing wrong with that, you fool. They too have souls. One God made us all. You did right. You liked her, you took her like a palikare! Provided she's honourable and a good housewife, that she's good-looking and bears sons—ask nothing else of a woman."

"She's had herself baptised, grandad. She's a great soul. You'll like her."

"Has she some flesh on her bones? Tell me that! What should a woman do with a soul? Flesh is what the seed requires to grow. How long have you been married?"

"Two years, granddad."

"And children?"

"None yet. . . ."

"You're taking your time! What do you do every evening, you pair of idiots? I want strong great-grandsons, made of steel. She's to bear Cretans, I tell you, not Jews. And listen to me: beware of book-learning!"

"She's got a son on the way, granddad!"

"My blessing! Call him Séfakas, d'you hear? That's how the dead rise again! And now go, move aside!"

He beckoned to his daughter-in-law, Katerina, who was standing behind him with her arms folded.

"Stick another cushion in my back," he said to her. "I want to sit quite upright, so I can speak. Pick me some lemon-blossom. I want to smell it. And while we captains are talking, not a sound from any of you! Make room! I want to speak to the old ones!"

The old ones had meanwhile fallen to eating and drinking again. The schoolmaster had propped his dark head against the trunk of one of the cypresses and kept singing over and over, to the accompaniment of his lyre, the same *mantinade*, with tears in his eyes:

> *At larks all day I've blazed away,*
> *Used every cartridge.*
>
> *At last a sight—and my heart's alight!—*
> *Of you, my partridge!*

The grandfather clapped his hands, and cried:

"Hey, captains, are your miserable stomachs still not full? That's enough! Wipe those beards, wash those hands, tighten up your belts and come over here. I've a word to say to you. That's why I invited you. And you, schoolmaster, sling that lyre over your shoulder and leave the larks—powder and shot and all. We've had enough of them! Hey! Children!"—he turned to the women and his grandsons—"bring them some water to wash in. Bring them some scent, to stop them stinking so. Wash them and tidy them up, children, before they come over to me!"

The girls brought scent and splashed it over the old men. They brought rose-vinegar for them to sniff, to sober them up. They supported them and brought them over to the grandfather, till the two captains were on his right and left and the schoolmaster was crouched in front of him, cross-legged.

Old Séfakas opened his arms and masterfully greeted the leaders, as if he were seeing them for the first time:

"Captain Mándakas, renowned leader in fighting on dry land; Captain Katsirmas, relentless corsair on the high seas; and you,

Captain Schoolmaster, who also have battled among our shadows and composed the papers of the revolt and written what had to be written to Turks and Franks—a thousand times welcome to my poor house!"

"Our greetings to you, Captain Séfakas," answered the three, laying their hands upon their breasts.

This had tired old Séfakas. He drew breath and drank a gulp of water from the cup. Then he opened his mouth again:

"Brothers, do you still remember how, at every rising, we captains gathered under an oak-tree or in some monastery, and took oaths and kissed one another, because we were going out to meet death? Such a gathering is this, now, under old Séfakas's lemon-tree! Know that I have been for days and days on the point of taking leave, but still I don't go. I've made confession and communion, but I don't go. I'm not going, captains, before we four old ones have talked together. This too is a sort of rising. Brothers, what are we going to decide? . . . Do you hear what I say? Is your mind clear? Can you hear and speak? Or am I wasting my words?"

"We can hear and speak!" said the three, laying their hands on their breasts as though for an oath.

"Then hear me! I am a hundred years old. You all of you know my life, I've no need to make a written paper of it for you. That I've fought and worked, that I've had joy and sorrow, that I've done my duty as a man, you can all bear witness. Now my hour has come. The earth is opening, she wants, it seems, to swallow me. Let her swallow me, let her take her revenge! But she's not swallowing all of me! Look what I'm leaving behind!"

He pointed to his daughters, grandsons, grand-daughters, and great-grandchildren.

"A whole people! So I'm not worried about death. I've beaten him. The Devil's got the best of him. Different anxieties are devouring me. . . ."

With a sigh he paused. Then, in a voice that for the first time trembled, he said:

"For a long time now I've been unable to sleep, captains. A worm is gnawing at me."

He looked at the captains one after another. He bent his head
and in a loud voice asked:

"Do you hear what I'm saying? Pay attention! Your eyes have
gone dim, schoolmaster!"

"We're listening," retorted the schoolmaster harshly. "What
worm?"

"A worm is gnawing at me, brothers! I look back at my life.
I look forward at my death. And I think and think: 'Where do
we come from, children, and where are we going to?' That is the
worm that's gnawing at me!"

He was silent, and his lips were trembling. The three captains
were agitated. The schoolmaster scratched his pointed, bald head
and opened his mouth. But he thought better of it. He did not
very well see what he should say.

"Has this thing never come into your minds?" asked the grey-
beard. "Has this worm never bitten you?"

"Never," answered the three.

"Nor me either, all my life, God is my witness. But lately I've
not been able to sleep at nights. To whom was I to tell what I was
suffering? My grandchildren are young—fifteen, sixteen years old.
Their brain's not firm enough. What would they be able to understand? Kostaros, my first-born son—he'd be now over seventy
and would begin to understand. But he was turned to ashes at
Arkadi. So I decided: 'Call a meeting, send for the companions
of your youth and have a word with them.' Like ears of corn at
harvest-time are your hands, captains—full of seed. You have
surely scented something. Speak! Open your hearts. You've been
drinking wine, so they'll open easily. Forward! Let us consult
together, children! I don't want to die a blind man. You speak
first, Captain Mándakas. Next to me you're the eldest. How old
were you in 1821?"

"Twenty-two, brother Séfakas. Have you forgotten?"

"I was thirty, just over. I'm eight years ahead of you. You open
your mouth first. Speak. You've lived and worn a belt for so
many years now. What have you learned?"

Captain Mándakas raised his hand to his mouth and slowly
stroked his thick beard. He fell into deep thought.

"Is it for that that you've called us, Captain Séfakas?" he said
at length. "It will mean a deal of trouble for us. You're making
us pay very heavily for the wine and meat you've set before us.
What do you think, schoolmaster?"

"Let the schoolmaster alone!" shouted the old man, "and speak
to me. Have you come to understand anything in all the years
you've lived? Don't turn and twist about! Speak out boldly, like
a man!"

Captain Mándakas pulled a tobacco-box from his belt and rolled
himself a cigarette.

"You put the knife to my throat, old Séfakas." he said after a
while. "What am I to say to you? How am I to begin? I've lived
the whole of my life as a blind man, just as you say about yourself,
and I don't regret it. Blindly I've gone to war, and hurled myself
upon the Turks. I married blindly, I begot children blindly, and
went to church and lit candles and kneeled before the ikons.
Blindly I've sowed, harvested, threshed and eaten my bread. I
never asked myself why I ate, why I prayed, why I killed. And
now, since you ask me—stop, Captain Séfakas, if you believe in
God! Give me a chance to squeeze my brain until a drop comes
out. Are you in such a hurry?"

"All right, I'll be patient. Squeeze your brain, Captain Mándakas," said the grandfather, folding his arms.

Captain Mándakas called to his foster-son, who was standing
behind him:

"Hey, Janakos, bring me my sack!"

All waited in silence. The grandfather beckoned to Kosmas:

"Get a stool and sit down, so you don't get tired. Listen. Do
you understand what we're saying?"

"I understand, granddad," answered Kosmas as he squatted
down.

Janakos brought the sack and laid it down in front of his
foster-father. Old Mándakas fumbled in it and brought out a wide-
mouthed glass jar sheathed in leather.

"What have you got in the jar?" asked the grandfather, craning
his neck.

Captain Mándakas laughed.

"Is that your answer?" asked the other furiously. "What sort of bottle is that?"

"Other people," Captain Mándakas replied, "take bread, wine and meat in their sack with them when they go on a journey. I too take them, but I take the jar, which you see, as well."

"What's inside? I can't make it out."

Captain Mándakas raised up the glinting thing close under the eyes of old Séfakas. The last light of day fell on it, and it gleamed red.

"Can you still see nothing?" asked Captain Mándakas, turning the bottle round.

"Bits of meat," answered the grandfather, "swimming in water."

"Those aren't bits of meat, old Séfakas, they're ears. It isn't water, it's spirits. On the day—in the year 1821—when a Turk bore me down and bit off one of my ears, I took an oath: every Turk I slew, I'd cut off one of his ears and keep it in a bottle. To tell you the story of my life, Captain Séfakas, all I need is to look at one ear after another preserved in spirits and to tell you whose it was. This one here at the bottom of the jar—the hairy one—belonged to that terrible hunter of Christians, Ali Bey. He had killed my brother Panajis and then retired to his estate at Rethymno to hold a feast of celebration with his harem. For the same reason he had had the lamps on his tower lit. That evening I went and sat in the Turkish coffee-house and smoked my *nargile*. "Bring me a bit of charcoal," I said to the Turk who made the coffee, "my *nargile*'s going out." I quickly folded up the mouthpiece of the *nargile* and ran out. With wings on my feet I dashed over the fields to Ali Bey's estate. I ran upstairs to his bedchamber, where he lay in bed with his hanum, fell upon him, cut off his head, took the ear with me and wrapped it in my kerchief. And so I got back to the coffee-house just as the waiter was bringing me the charcoal. I unrolled the mouthpiece and went on smoking. No one had noticed my absence. Next day, when the news of Ali Bey's death spread, the Pacha yelled: 'It was Mándakas!' But the Turks from the coffee-house swore: 'Captain

Mándakas was smoking his *nargile* in Hassan's coffee-house the whole evening.' "

He pointed to another ear:

"This thick, dark one with the ring in it comes off a Moor. Remadan, his name was. Another gobbler of Christians, may his bones soak in pitch! I ran into him one evening alone on the beach at Trypiti, outside Megalokastro. 'Remadan,' I asked him, 'have you no fear of God?' 'He's afraid of me,' the dog answered, 'for I'm Remadan!'—'And I'm Mándakas,' I said, drawing my knife. 'Draw your knife, you too!'—'I haven't got it with me. You've come upon me unarmed, *giaour*.'—'I've got two. Choose!' I threw him the one he chose, and he brandished it in the air. The fight on the pebbles of the seashore began. We fought and fought, until night broke in on us. Blood was streaming over us, the sweat was flowing, we were boiling. We went into the sea, to cool ourselves. It turned red. We didn't speak, we bellowed. A friend of the Moor's came by. The blackguard wanted to help him. 'I'll spit you like a sardine,' the Moor shouted at him. 'You let us alone and clear out!'—'Hey, Remadan,' I said, 'you're a palikare.' —'So are you,' he answered. 'We're two wild beasts.'—'Then one of us has got to be killed!' I yelled and went for him again. He flagged. I sprang astride his neck and plunged my knife through his windpipe, as you slaughter a sucking-pig. I took his ear with its ring, too. Here it is!"

Again he stretched out his finger. The memory of his heroic deeds was warming him up, and he went on:

"This ear, that's beginning to turn green, belonged to that butcher Mustafa. This one, here in the middle, to an Albanian. The torn one, there, to an imam. Damn him, he had a voice like a bell. Pity! I ought to have cut out his tongue and preserved that in spirits. Next to it, this little one, rounded like a sea-shell, comes off Pertef Effendi. The shameless fellow, handsome as a picture, looked like Saint George! How could I help it? He used to ride through the Christian quarter and seduce our women. None of them could resist the dog. I was sorry for them, and one night I forced my way into his house. We fought in his bedroom. But he was very delicately built and used to women, and didn't put up much resistance. So I cut through that delicate neck of his and took this rounded ear.

"This glass jar contains all the risings of Crete! I couldn't collect the ears of the ones I killed in battle. But here are the risings of 1821, '34, '41, '54, '78. Now I've grown old. The last rising has brought in no ear! . . . Truly I was a wild beast, I did terrible things, God forgive me. Whenever a rising broke out, I left my house, my children, my unpruned vines, my unploughed fields, and rode to join my leader, Captain Korax.[1]"

As he remembered that famous name, he suddenly sighed:

"Never has so mighty a man arisen in the world again. What are we, compared to him? Figures of fun! No one ever joked in front of him, or heard him laugh. His eyes were round, dark and wild, like eagle's eyes. He had no faults. He didn't drink, didn't curse, didn't run after women. When he went out to battle he ploughed his mare with his heels and swooped plumb upon the Turks. He never looked round to see if anyone was following him. He never looked in front to count the Turkish fezes. No bullet touched him. That was not a man. No, God forgive me, that was an archangel."

He sighed again:

"Only the wings were missing!"

Old Séfakas listened and fidgeted nervously on his cushions. But he showed patience and sniffed the lemon-leaves. At last he could bear it no longer and cried, angrily:

"Put that jar in your sack, Captain Mándakas! There's no limit to the wild-beast ways of men. Answer my question: What have you learned with all these ears? Where have you arrived? Since you can see your life now in that glass jar, tell me: has your course been the right one, or do you regret what you've done?"

"Regret it!" bawled Captain Mándakas, incensed. "No! If I had to begin all over again, old Séfakas, I'd marry the same wife, beget the same children, kill the same Turks—perhaps even more! —wear the same breeches, the same belt, the same boots! Not a hair would I change. And if I go before God tomorrow, I shall

[1] Raven (translator's note).

take my jar under my arm and say to Him: 'Either You let me into Paradise with this jar, or I'm not going in at all!' "

"Was that what you were born for?" old Séfakas shouted, "to kill? Was that why God sent you into the world?"

"No, don't twist my words, old Séfakas. I'm not blood-thirsty. No, I don't kill for the sake of killing. But . . ."

He scratched the top of his skull reflectively. Then suddenly he shouted:

"But I was fighting for freedom!"

And now Captain Mándakas had got going. His brow had lightened:

"Yes," he said, "you ask me where we come from and where we're going to. When I began speaking, I didn't know yet—by the night which will fall and cover us—what answer I should give you. But while we've been talking this way and that, my brain's become clear. We're coming out from slavery, Captain Séfakas, and going into freedom. As slaves we were born, and have fought all our lives to become free. And we Cretans can only become free through killing. That's why I killed those Turks. That's it! You asked, I've answered you. Now I'm old: I've put away my dagger and folded my arms. Charos can come!"

He called to his foster-son:

"Janakos, put the sack where it belongs."

"Those were sound words," cried the grandfather. "Blessings on that mouth of yours, blessings on those hands of yours, Captain Mándakas! You were a long time about it, but you've understood. That is your way that you have taken. You've reached the end and done your duty. But do you believe there's only one way? Others are possible, as you'll see. You speak now, Captain Katsirmas, you corsair—it's your turn!"

The sea-wolf clenched his fists; his squinting eyes grew red:

"I don't like the way you're treating us, old Séfakas, at all," he said. "You've made us come here, into your yard, and just because you're a few years older than we are you play the leader and demand a reckoning from us. No, I'm not saying anything!"

"Don't flare up, you stubborn idiot," cried the grandfather. "No, I'm not taking the lead over you because I'm older than you, but I'm going under the earth first and I've no time to lose. That's why I'm asking. I don't want to die blind. I'm asking for help, children, for light! Don't you understand, Captain Katsirmas?"

"Yes," he answered. "You needn't yell. But you're not a ship in danger, which I can come and rescue in my boat. All my life I've struggled with the sea. That's the only place where I know my way about. I can't help anywhere else. So what do you expect from me?"

"I'm drowning, old corsair," roared the grandfather. "And a drowning man has to be caught by the hair!"

"Your hair, old Séfakas, not ours! You are standing on the threshold of Hades, and fear comes over you. You call it a worm, I call it fear. So you summon your old comrades: 'What is this, children? Where am I going? Where am I being taken?' How should we know anything that could comfort you? We live haphazard, we die haphazard, rudderless, with sails bellying. A wind blows. Where it blows, there we go. Water rushes into our ship, we work at the pumps day and night. But the water keeps rising and the pumps are rusty. The wretched things won't work any more, and we go to the bottom. That's human life, and you can yell as loud as you like. What's our duty? To serve the pumps day and night, not to fold our arms, not to complain, not to moan. We ought not to give up shamefully, but to work at the pumps day and night. That much I've learned from life, and you can take it or leave it!"

He turned his savage fage to Captain Mándakas:

"I wasn't like you, sir, nailed to the land, with blinkers before your eyes, so as not to see anything but Turks and Christians. And to kill Turks and cut off their ears and lay them up in spirits. And I can't bring a glass jar out of my sack and show it around and say: 'That is my life.' I've made voyages, Captain Mándakas, I've seen the whole world. I've slept with women of all kinds, I've pushed far down into Africa, where the bread is toasted by the sun. I've made great harbours and little ones, I've seen millions of black men, millions of yellow men—my eyes brimmed over with them! At first I thought they all stank. I said: 'Only Cretans smell good. And of the Cretans only the Christians.' But slowly,

slowly, I got used to their stink. I found—I found that we all smell good and stink in the same way. Curse us all!

"And then I threw myself into piracy. I found out that the world is made up of copper kettles and clay jugs, banging against each other. Be of copper, Katsirmas, you wretch, or else you'll go to pieces! And if you get broken, you'll never be stuck together again: it's finished. So I made friends with some Algerians; we hoisted black flags, lay in wait at corners of the sea, fell upon trading ships, killed, plundered, fled and hid our booty on deserted islands. And once—you all remember it—I unloaded at Grabusa a shipload of cinnamon, cloves and musk-nuts, so that the whole of Crete had a sweet scent. Have you forgotten, old Séfakas? I even sent a sackful of cloves and cinnamon to Your Grace."

"Go on," said the ancient. "Come to some conclusion. What does all that amount to?"

"It's to show you what you've got to understand. We feared neither God nor man. I was a Christian, they were Musulmans. But we let no ship through, whether she was bound for Mecca or for Jerusalem. We set upon her and killed the pilgrims. I was a wild beast among wild beasts. Like the Algerians I grew a pigtail and had the rest of my head shorn. I collected a mass of thaler, ducats and Turkish money. I robbed each ship of two or three women—enjoyed them and threw them into the sea. I was a beast, I tell you—worse than you, Captain Mándakas! And if you ask me, Captain Séfakas, whether I regret it, then here's my answer: I've lived my life well and soundly and like a palikare, I don't regret it. God made me a wolf and I eat lambs. If He'd made me a lamb, the wolf would have eaten me, and rightly! That's how the order of things will have it. Is it my fault? It's the fault of Him Who made wolves and lambs."

For a moment he squinted at his companions in silence. He seemed to expect some retort. But not a sound was to be heard. So he went on:

"And now, captains, I'm old. The timbers have sprung, the hold's splitting apart, water's rushing in, the pumps are working badly. And so I've slunk on to dry land, and adopted good manners. I play the human being. Why? I can't do anything else now.

My strength's gone. Hair and teeth have fallen out. The wolf's grown mangy and lousy. I play the human being. I've sunk to that. I don't kill any more, I don't howl, I bleat like a lamb. When I sit at the village fountain and see the girls the way they fill their pitchers, my eyes eat the fish, but my belly remains empty. Often tears come upon me. 'Why are you crying, granddad?' the girls ask me, and giggle. 'Because I've got to die, damn you, and leave such beautiful bodies behind on earth.' By God, if I were King or Ali Pacha, I'd collect for myself a band of the loveliest girls and have them slaughtered on my tomb, to take them with me."

"You're a bloodthirsty wild beast, Captain Katsirmas," cried the grandfather. "Be quiet!"

"You asked, and I've answered. I was to open the trap-door, and I've opened it. Has it given you a fright, old Séfakas?"

The mocker with the toothless mouth raised his savage glance to the grandfather. He yelled:

"The trap-door is open, the evil spirits are coming out. You wanted to see and hear them! 'Where do we come from?' you asked. Up out of the earth, Captain Séfakas. 'Where are we going to?' you asked. Under the earth, Captain Séfakas. What is your duty? To eat, if you're a wolf; to be eaten, if you're a lamb. And if you ask me about God: He is the big wolf—He eats both lambs and wolves!"

Don't blaspheme, old pirate!" cried Captain Mándakas, stretching out his arm. "You're drunk, your mind's reeling, you don't know what you're saying. The big wolf is Charos, not God!"

Captain Katsirmas laughed:

"God and Charos are the same thing, cousin! But why should I argue with you? Your brain lives on beans and knows nothing but beans." He turned to Captain Séfakas:

"That's what I had to say to you, old Séfakas. You shouldn't have asked me. Now order them to fill up my cup with wine."

"Fill up his cup with wine," said the ancient to his grandsons. "He's confessed, let him have communion. . . ."

He bent his head in meditation. After a pause he said:

"I'm no judge and I give no judgement. God heard him. Let Him judge him."

He turned to the schoolmaster, who, all the time the captains had been speaking, had been wagging his pointed, bald head to and fro.

"Speak, schoolmaster. Raise that head of yours!"

The schoolmaster took the lyre from his shoulder.

"All my life," he said, "I've talked. Now it bores me. You ask about difficult things, Captain Séfakas. What Devil put that into your mind? They have no place in words."

"Are we to be dumb, then?" asked the ancient, looking at the schoolmaster angrily. "Be dumb, be blind, be castrated, be at peace? Is that what you want? But you fool, that means a man is a head of cattle!"

"A question has its place in words, Captain Séfakas. Don't get angry. Ask questions as long as you're not tired of asking questions. You can shape a question in words, but not the answer. And yet you demand an answer from me."

"I want an answer," said the grey-beard, throwing back his head.

"You want an answer, old Séfakas. You shall have it. I shall answer you with the lyre. It is my real mouth. If you understand what it says, all is well. If not, I can't help you. Then you'll die blind, as you were born blind."

"Play on your lyre, schoolmaster. God be your helper!" said the grandfather, closing his eyes.

The sky had darkened. Fat drops pattered on the leaves of the lemon-tree. Some also fell refreshingly on the cheeks, the closed lids and lips of the grandfather. He licked them up thirstily.

The schoolmaster grasped the bow, bent over the lyre, and became one with it. The bow danced over the three strings, the little bells tinkled, the dark yard filled with bright laughter, as if it were a schoolyard in which the children were playing and chasing one another during break. Or as if birds in a thick-leaved poplar were awakening at dawn and rejoicing in the sunlight.

The fiddle-bow leaped, laughed, danced, and the hearts of the old captains became children, birds, gurgling springs. The grandchildren and daughters-in-law moved nearer, the men and maids

ran up and sat down on the ground together. And in spite of the
falling rain, they craned their necks and listened.

The old grandfather felt as though his heavily-built body were
losing its weight, rising into the air and flying, stretched out above
lemon-tree and cypresses like a cloud. Only in dreams had he so
felt the joy of flying. In dreams and one other time; he had been
on his way back from war, on a Sunday; he had washed off the
blood, put on clean clothes and gone into the church to communion. Then too his body had felt like a lightly flying cloud.
And on the way home it had seemed to him as if his feet did not
touch the earth at all. . . .

But slowly the voice of the lyre altered. It became wild and
furious. The bells on the bow rattled like those on the neck of a
trained hawk as it shoots upwards in search of prey. Those were
men's voices that rang out from the strings. The captains thought
of their youth, of war, of the groaning men who lay dying, of the
women mourning, of the horses whinnying and standing on the
field, bloodstained and riderless. "Give me back my youth or be
still, schoolmaster!" Captain Mándakas was on the point of crying.
But already the lyre had again changed its tune, and soft, lulling
tones sounded, to which the old men listened with happy smiles.

The sound, through the moist air, was like a distant humming
of bees, or the murmur of a deep stream. The sound was like a
woman's love-dirge far beyond the mountains, on the shore of the
foaming sea. Or was it the sea itself, leaning on the shore and
moaning? Or was it a yet more mysterious, more magical voice
from beyond life, from the other bank, sweetly and sadly and
lovingly freeing souls from the flesh? Was it perhaps God Himself, hidden in the moist darkness of the night, Who was calling
and raising up to Him with gentle allurement His eternal beloved,
the soul of Man?

The schoolmaster played as one possessed, so that the fiddle-
bow seemed to strike sparks. More and more he was lost in the
darkness. It was as if the lyre, alone and erect under the lemon-
tree, were intoning a funeral hymn. But its wailing was also a
seductive call.

A deep, broad smile overspread the old grandfather's lips. His flying, light body rose in one sweep from the lemon-tree further into the air, and now lay like a cloud above the house. Soon it would by a soft transformation become a cloud, falling as rain to the ground, to nourish the young shoots.

"That is death," the grandfather felt deep down in himself, "that is Paradise. I am going to Paradise. I am there, already. Greetings, O my God!"

He opened his eyes and saw nothing but darkness. And out of the darkness a soft, tender voice called him by name.

"I'm coming," answered the grandfather.

All night they let him lie stretched out in the yard. He was showered with rain like a great tree-trunk. Kosmas, kneeling down, had closed his eyes for him. Thrasáki squatted beside him and watched him. It was the first time he had seen death from so near. With shuddering he gazed upon the grandfather whom he had loved so much. It was as though his grandfather had acquired some new power, dark and sinister. As though he were only waiting to pounce on men and drag them with him under the earth. Thrasáki had a longing to run away. But he dared not stir. So he remained, spell-bound by fear, where he was.

Round about the corpse his tribe kept watch. The door had been left open. The village had been shaken when it heard that old Séfakas had given up his soul, and all streamed past to take their leave. One after another silently kissed his hand, which lay stretched out upon the stones.

Two old women had washed him with wine and wrapped him in a white shroud of silken linen. It was a relic of his dead wife, Lenio, who had woven it for this hour. Two of his daughters-in-law placed a big lantern near his head and a second near his feet. Under the soft light from the oil flames, the face of the dead man took on a mild expression.

"Shouldn't we take him in?" suggested Katerina. "It isn't right that he should lie here on the ground and be soaked with rain."

But Kosmas opposed her:

"The dead man wants to be here and soaked with rain."

A light, compassionate south wind was blowing. The grand-

P

sons brought logs and brushwood and kindled a fire in the middle of the yard, to warm themselves. The flames lit up the yard and attracted the animals. The mule, the two asses, the mare and the two plough-oxen stuck their heads out from the openings of their stalls and looked with wonder at what was going on in the yard. The three captains had curled themselves up, full of drink and food, against the strong trunk of the lemon-tree, and were snoring.

"Goodbye, old Séfakas. Greet the dead!" cried the women, loosening their head-bands.

"Till we meet again, Captain Séfakas!" cried the old people, pressing his hand. "A happy journey!"

Each woman also threw him a sprig of basil, that he might take it with him into Hades as the scent of the upper world. One mother stricken by Charos laid beside the dead man the chalk and scribbled slate of her little son who was dead. "Take my child his slate, old man!" she cried. "Do me that kindness! His name was Demetrakis, he was your neighbour's child. You'll recognise him. He wore a red woollen cap with a tassel, and went barefoot."

Katerina got up and spread a heavy rug over the snoring captains, to prevent them from catching cold. Then she took Thrasáki by the hand:

"Come to bed, my child. It's nearly midnight."

But Thrasáki refused to obey:

"I'm watching by granddad," he said. "Father hasn't come. I'm watching in his place."

In the light from the flames his eyes flickered hard and decided, like those of his father. The mother drew back and said no more. The rain showed no signs of leaving off. Renió and the other granddaughters brought coffee to keep the guests and members of the household taking part in the death-watch awake. Sometimes silence fell upon the yard. Then the deep, confused voices of the night could be heard: small animals and insects, night birds, restless dogs, groaning cattle. And suddenly the cocks rose up and crowed. Day broke.

When the sun was already above the horizon, the three captains blinked, and saw the dead man stretched out on the stones of the yard. They understood who it was. But they did not move. They were still overcome by sleep.

Towards noon Stavrulios brought the coffin on his shoulder. Thrasáki ran up, to examine the wood. It was walnut.

Two hours after midday the grandsons raised up the coffin, in which the grandfather lay at rest, and bore it to the door and out. Moving slowly, they carried him first round the neighbourhood to take leave of it. Then they stopped at all the cross-roads of the villages, and the girls threw basil and marjoram on to the corpse, as if it were a picture of the Crucified One.

The whole village accompanied him like a single family, bare-headed and serene, as though he really was the God of the village who had died. They paced slowly along, that the grandfather might take leave of his village with his accustomed calm. Suddenly, when they were already outside the village and nearing the graveyard, the sluices of Heaven opened wide for a strong downpour.

The peasants yelled with joy. For months they had longed for rain, for the crops threatened to be dried up. And now, God be thanked, they raised their sunburned faces with eagerness towards the streaming sky.

"The grandfather had turned to rain," murmured one of the old men, "he's coming back to our village."

"He knew what was worrying us," said another. "He's turned to water and is watering us."

Without hastening they reached the cemetery, wet through. Two stalwart grandsons had dug a grave. The red, loamy soil was full of mussel-shells, as if these mountains had once been the bottom of the sea. It rained and rained. The grandfather was lowered peacefully and gently. The mourners each threw a handful of earth upon him. Then they went back to the house.

Now they ran fast. For they were in a hurry to sit down at the loaded tables and to devour the black ram which the grandfather had marked out for his funeral feast, and to drink some wine. And to forgive his soul.

Kosmas sat on the broad settle. His soul was troubled, his body tired. He shut his eyes. He wanted to rest for a little before going up the mountain. He had bidden Charidemos to find a storm-

lantern and to hold himself ready. Before break of day tomorrow
he must be at Captain Michales's headquarters. His sleep only
lasted a moment, but it was enough to let his dead father in.
Kosmas saw him, as clear as could be. He was standing on the
stairs of his house and making to go into the bedroom. He had
already raised his foot to place it on the first step. Kosmas was
terrified. Upstairs his wife was sleeping. The dead man would
now go up and frighten her. He leapt up. "Where are you going,
Father," he called out to him. The dead man with the drooping
moustache and a wart on his right cheek wheeled round and looked
at him savagely. On his head he was wearing a black head-band
with a red, bloodstained tassel. And his mouth was a wound
stopped with cotton wool.

He stared at Kosmas, frowning. He was clearly angry, for be
was grinding his teeth, and a small red flame darted out from his
nostrils and licked over his face. Suddenly he opened his mouth.
The cotton-wool fell out, and the wound lay bare. He gave a wild
moan and moved hastily towards the stairs, to go up.

"Father!" cried Kosmas. "Don't do her any harm. She's my wife!"

The son bravely took a step towards the dead man and called
out to him a second time: "She's my wife. Don't touch her!" He
stretched out his hand, to prevent his father from going up. But
the dead man vanished in smoke, and Kosmas now heard—without seeing anything—heavy steps ascending the stairs. . . .

With a cry he woke up. He opened his eyes and saw the guests
at their funeral meal. A great dish was just being brought in, with
the steaming ram upon it. It lay on its back, with its four legs in
the air, and complete with head and horns, as though alive. The
ravening peasants fell upon it and divided it up. The grandsons
brought some jugs of wine, too, and now the funeral meal turned
into a joyous feast. But it was not only the wine, it was the heavy
rain falling on the thirsty earth; it was also because Charos had
paid a visit and had not touched themselves, but only taken the
old man away with him! So they ate and drank, and the joy waxed.
Their feet were tickling. They wanted to dance. But the wine did
not remain dumb either, and the good singer of the village, Stavrulios the carpenter, so far forgot himself as to strike up a love-

song. But his neighbours rounded on him and stopped his mouth. To smother the scandal, the pope washed his throat with a mighty swig of wine and loudly intoned a hymn.

Kosmas stood and took his aunt Katerina on one side.

"Aunt Katerina," he said, "I'm going this evening to visit my uncle up on the mountain. Haven't you any measage?"

The woman sighed:

"Are messages any good with him, my child? What he's got into his head, that he'll do, and the world may go hang. May God guide his hand."

"Won't he think of his son, Aunt Katerina?"

"To be sure. Thrasáki's the one thing he loves in the world. But he won't turn his head for that. He'll do what he's decided to do. There's no hope, my child, from a man who's never once thought of himself."

She wiped her eyes and said no more.

Kosmas went over to Charidemos, who was taking part in the general gaiety and had the ram's kidneys in his hand, while the grease dripped from his goat-beard.

"Charidemos," Kosmas said to him, "you've eaten and drunk well, you've celebrated granddad's death. Get up now. We're going."

The grizzled servant made a sulky face:

"It's raining. A cloud-burst. I can't see to the end of my nose."

"We're going," said the eldest grandson in a tone of command. "It's got to be done."

"All right, let's go," Charidemos sighed, cursing his fate, which never allowed him to enjoy anything. Just now, as the fun was beginning . . .

"Forward," said Kosmas. "Got the storm-lantern?"

The hymn was over and Stavrulios asked the pope:

"Will you let me sing a robber song?"

And without waiting for the answer, he threw back his neck and made the house hum:

> *When will the starry sky be clear?*
> *When will February be here,*
> *So I can take my gun. . . ?*

XIV

OLD Charidemos threw the light from his storm-lantern on the narrow goat-path which zig-zagged up the mountain. He had not yet recovered from his tipsiness: sometimes he stumbled, and after a time he fell full length. Ashamed, he got up again and pulled himself together. "Damn wine," he muttered, "the Devil take water!"

He turned to Kosmas, for he longed to talk with him. Suddenly, bathed in sweat, he stopped dead.

"Master, won't you open your mouth? I'm nearly dropping. That's why I'm so unsteady on my legs."

"None of your gab, Charidemos! It's pouring. Let's hurry!"

He wanted to be at his destination by dawn without fail—before the Turks could sight them from the plain. The cloudburst continued, the arteries of the land were swelling, the water splashed downwards in the brooks. From time to time a bright flash lit the sky, and the thunder rolled from mountain to mountain. As soon as its echoes had died away, the gurgling of the masses of water could be heard as they streamed down.

"If you believe in God, open your mouth, master, and talk to me!" the old man of the mountains begged afresh. What's happening out there in the world? Are they sick men like us? Or devils?"

But Kosmas had no desire to chatter. Without a word he climbed in the darkness and rain, determined not to profane this holy hour with idle words. A strange, new, more vital emotion had come over him. He endured the rain serenely like a rock, a Cretan rock. To the marrow of his spine he felt the joy of the rocks and of the earth as they drank their fill.

The rain was mercifully putting out the fires started by the Turkish soldiers in the Greek villages and monasteries. It was putting out also the flames in the Turkish villages where Christians had been the beginners of the destruction. Turks and Christians went back into their ruins and set themselves to place stone on stone once more and to build the houses up afresh.

Bleeding from many wounds and gnashing her teeth, Crete bowed again under the yoke. In caves and monasteries the captains had meanwhile been debating. They had read the Metropolitan's circular again and again, until they had at last understood: it was the voice of Greece. They became furious and cursed, they cast threatening glances at the sky and clenched their fists. But at length they bowed their heads. They stuck their daggers into their sheaths, buried their weapons and went home to their work.

Sulkily and taciturnly the Kastrians opened their shops and the peasants ploughed and sowed. The heavy wheel of the everyday began to turn again. Captain Polyxigis too came back from the mountains, with a new black band round his fez. He went to Saint Menas, the captain of the town, lit a candle before him and remained standing for a moment in front of his ikon, reproachfully. Then he opened his shop. He retired into the back of it, so as not to see or be seen. He ordered a *nargile* and smoked, sunk in thought. He paid no attention to the farmers as they came in through the Kanea gate, bringing with them what they had saved by way of lemons and oranges, wine and oil. He did not want to see. His lips no longer smiled, nothing but venom trickled from them now. He was already sorry for his weakness in leaving the mountain.

"I ought not to have listened either to Greece or to the Metropolitan," he brooded. "Captain Michales, that wild boar, has done the right thing! I too ought to have stayed up there, to get killed. What good is life to me now? I'd like to join him again."

He coiled the mouthpiece round the neck of the *nargile* and went, sighing, over the threshold. At that moment Manóles the pope passed by. His grease-spotted cassock was bellying in the wind. He had not stirred out of Megalokastro. He had buried, baptised, censed people's houses, filled his pockets and added yet more fat to his neck. Now he was bearing the sacred chalice and patten, while before him, sombre and pale, Múrzuflos paced, carrying a lit lantern in the brightness of noon. Captain Polyxigis crossed himself. He had heard the sad news: the pope was on his way with the last sacrament for Captain Stefanés. On the return journey a shell fired by a Turkish patrol-boat into his smuggler ship had torn off both his feet.

"God bless his soul," he muttered. "He's borne himself like a man."

He was about to withdraw again into the half-darkness of his shop when he caught sight of Vendúsos. He was coming past, wrapped in a rug and shivering with cold. He kept waving his hands and talking to himself as he went. For two days he had been running through the streets as though haunted by some curse, and could not come to a decision: Should he open his tavern and bring back his wife and daughters and engage once more in his old trade? Or should he throw everything to the winds and return to Captain Michales, to show him that he too was a man who would not let himself be knocked about and trampled on? "Good-bye, Vendúsos," the other had said to him the day before yesterday as he sent him with his message to the Metropolitan, "you won't come back. You're Vendúsos, I don't ask anything of you, behave like a Vendúsos if you wish!"

Vendúsos kept thinking angrily of those words. A thousand demons surrounded him. Now the sense of honour seized hold of him, and he decided to return to the mountain, to show Captain Michales; and now he remembered his wife, his two daughters and the tavern, and this sent him running down the mountainside again.

When he caught sight of Captain Polyxigis on the threshold of the shop, he stood still. Halt! That was a mighty captain, and yet he's put his tail between his legs and keeps his mouth shut. Why? Because it was in the interest of Crete. And would you, you lousy Vendúsos, think things out and act on your own? Come on, you idiot, don't be ashamed. Leading in battle is heavy work, work for a palikare. But the leaders show themselves even more like palikares when they order the laying-down of arms! Law them down, then! Let's have a talk with Polyxigis, to give ourselves courage. I've got children. Poor me, I must keep alive.

"Good-day, captain," he said, walking in. "I've come from the mountain. I have many greetings for you——"

"Leave me in peace, the Devil take you!" roared Captain Polyxigis, and raised his hand. The sight of Vendúsos moved him to wrath, because he was ashamed. But this made Vendúsos in his turn wild. Indeed! This great lord thought he was to be knocked about and trampled on, did he? He would show him!

"I'm going back to the mountain. I'm not leaving my post. And if you've any message . . ."

He said it without having really decided—simply to sting the other man.

"You're going back to the mountain? You, Vendúsos?" cried the captain with a disdainful laugh. "It's madness to do that!"

"Yes, it's madness, captain. I know. But there's no life without honour! Good-day!"

He said it, and before Captain Polyxigis could find time to answer, he was gone. The decision had really come to him now: he was not going to flinch, he was going to put Mylords Captains Michales and Polyxigis to shame! And, if God granted, he would then look after his house and marry off his two daughters.

He stepped out quickly and came to the church of Saint Menas. He paid him a farewell visit and lit a candle. The church was empty and warm and full of the scent of incense. Saint Menas, sunburned, clad in silver from head to foot and mounted on his horse, smiled at him as though giving him his blessing. "A good journey to you, Vendúsos," he said to him, "you are on the right track. Don't worry. I will look after your wife and children. And I will find two good palikares as husbands for them. Goodbye, Captain Vendúsos!"

Delighted, he crossed himself and left the church. Then he heard people talking and caught sight, through the window of the Bishop's Palace, of the fat, hairy face of the dwarf, Charílaos. What the Devil was that receiver of stolen goods, that plunderer, doing in the Bishop's Palace?

Vendúsos could not know, naturally, what the sly Metropolitan was up to with him. The gnome was at the Residence by invitation. They were now drinking their coffee together, and this is what the Metropolitan had on his mind: The Christians who had fled to Athens and to the Piraeus were now returning, to find their

P*

houses devastated. The Turks had smashed chests, cupboards and chairs to firewood, and had even taken down the doors and burned them. Only the disfigured walls stared at the homecomers. And this was why the Metropolitan had invited Charílaos, the banker, to come and see him: he wanted to get hold of him by his sense of honour and to persuade him to lend them money for the rebuilding at favourable rates. Charílaos had made thousands of pounds out of this rising, by keeping on the right side of the Pacha. Also, in exchange for a bit of bread, he was raking in ear-rings, rings, necklaces of precious stones and ducats from the starving Christians. His coffers were brimming over with gold and jewels.

Now, over the coffee, the Metropolitan skilfully and with great urbanity brought the conversation round to God. What profit was it if a man should gain the whole world and lose his soul? Then he adroitly guided it further—to the Fatherland. How many patriots were undying, because they had sacrificed themselves for the Fatherland! And such a sacrifice—it must not be forgotten—need not consist only in giving one's life. It could also be a sacrifice of money. Whoever gave his money would likewise be undying and would earn the title of "patriot". God then opens His records and inscribes in them the names of the patriots in golden letters; and, over against them, how many pounds each one of them has given for the Christian cause.

The wily gnome drank his coffee sip by sip, smoked his cigarette and looked out through the window at the ruined houses and, above them and beyond, at the white-foaming sea. The Metropolitan's words went in at one ear and out at the other. "The cleric's trying hard to get round me," he thought, blowing the smoke out through his nose: "he wants to goad my sense of honour, in order to plunder my coffers. Ah, I'm sorry for him! I'm more than a match for his tricks!"

Considering that the Metropolitan had come to the end of his beguiling arguments, he stubbed out his cigarette in the bronze cup and turned to him most respectfully. His voice sounded subdued and sad:

"Your words are saintly, Mylord. How many times have I not accused myself: ah, if only I were a proper man and could take a

gun and offer my life for the Fatherland! Or, since God has
cursed me and made me a weakling, if at least I were rich enough
to give my mite to the widows and help the Christian cause a
little! God might then have mercy on me at the Last Judgement!
But I'm ruined, Mylord, I'm lost. My businesses aren't going well,
believe me, Mylord, however much the people insult me as an
exploiter of the poor. A widow comes, or an orphan, and brings
me a little ring. I know perfectly well it's worth sixpence, not
more. And yet I give twice that for it, because my heart burns
when I see misfortune. I'm ruining myself and I know it. But
I'm human and I'm sorry for them! I've sold a vineyard, an olive
plantation as well, and they've gone on this. I've even had to
mortgage the house I live in, Mylord, God is my witness! What's
going to become of me? My kindness has devoured me, and when
you invited me to the Bishop's Palace my heart leapt with joy.
'God is merciful, then.' I said to myself. 'He is just, and rewards
fair dealing. The Bishop is summoning me, he has heard of
my good deeds—but also of my suffering. God has enlightened
him, and he will grant me support out of the diocesan money-
bags, to keep me from going to the bottom.' I hear the communal
fund is nice and full, thank God!"

The Metropolitan swallowed drily. "That God-damned, avaricious monster!" he thought. The sight of the dwarf became in-
tolerable to him. He drank up his coffee with one gulp and fingered
his rosary nervously. Charílaos had been sitting crosslegged on
the sofa: he now stood up on those small legs of his and rubbed
his hands. "It's cold," he said, "What's going to become of us
without fuel, without warm clothing, without enough to eat,
Bishop? I've been forced to sell all my hens. But for that, I'd have
been able to eat an egg every morning. That's over, too. God
have pity on us!"

Kissing the Metropolitan's hand, he took his leave.

"Pray for us too, Mylord. With your leave, I'll go now. I don't
feel well—I must lie down."

Out of the school streamed the schoolchildren, bumping into
each other, yelling and whistling. Tityros had kept them late
to-day, because tomorrow the Christmas holidays were beginning,

and so he had to give them a last-day-of-term address. He was now a Tityros grown strong, filled out and sunburned. The peasant girl whom he had married was expecting a child, and the schoolmaster was beside himself with joy over this. Before, everyone had shoved him on one side. Now he had won the upper hand. Woe to the schoolchildren who now tried to make fun of him!

Vendúsos let the schoolchildren run past. After them he saw Tityros come out, and in the first moment did not recognise him.

"Schoolmaster!" he called out to him, "you've been eating dragon's-wort and have turned into a dragon! I'm going back to the mountain," he went on, proudly. "What message have you got for your brother, Captain Michales?"

Moved, Tityros pressed his hand.

"Vendúsos, you're a palikare. Forgive me, I never noticed it, all the time I've known you."

"I wasn't a palikare, ever, schoolmaster. But how can I help it? I've become one. Who sits with a blind man soon squints. Captain Michales is the cause."

"I too am doing my duty. Tell him that. This is my way. Whole chains of Cretan children are hanging round my neck. I'm awakening Crete in them, to the best of my power. I only left the mountain to be useful to Crete. And that's why he ought to come down. Tell him that."

"Don't worry, I'll tell him. But we shan't come down. You mark my words! Goodbye, schoolmaster!"

"Good old Vendúsos," Tityros answered, and watched him with admiration as he went out, nimbly and bravely, through the Hospital Gate.

The Metropolitan, who had stood up as soon as Charílaos had gone out, called his deacon:

"I'm very tired, deacon. All the same, I must go to Archondula's—the Pacha will be there. We are going to meet again, for the first time for months. He would not come to the Bishop's Palace, I would not go to his *konak*, so we've agreed on Archondula's house."

"Shouldn't I saddle the ass, since you're tired, Mylord?" asked the deacon, a stately, dark-haired peasant's son whose voice rang like a bell. He was reputed to be formidably strong, and when the Metropolitan made him sit beside him it was as if a lion escorted him. A pillow could have been stuffed with the hair from his head and beard.

"You're right, bless you. Get the ass. That horrible miser has made me weak."

The deacon laid a rug over the eel-smooth, lusty ass, spread on top of that a cloth with a border woven in a design of cypresses and crosses, placed the beast close to a step and heaved the Bishop's heavy body on to it.

The Pacha, meanwhile, had been having a good meal—gnawed every bone of a chicken clean and drunk a jugful of Malvasia wine. Now he too called his Suleiman:

"Suleiman, you blockhead, I've got to go now and see the fat *giaour* parson, to show the Christians and Turks that the fighting's over. Wolf and lamb have forgiven each other. Bring me my horse. It is not seemly that I should go on foot. And come with me. I've eaten too much ánd I'm sleepy. Hold me as we go through the streets, so that I don't fall off!"

But when he had descended the stairs and was about to mount the horse in the yard, there appeared before him, locked in a close embrace, the two seers of spirits, the two choice fools of Megalo-kastro, Barba Jannis and Efendína. The two were well away in the seventh heaven, hooting and swaying and urging each other on.

Barba Jannis was celebrating to-day as a festival. One of his grand-daughters had borne a son, so now he was able to hold in his arms his first great-grandchild. A sufficient ground for getting drunk. In his tipsiness he had remembered Efendína. He had summoned him. "Sit down, Efendína," he had told him, "eat and drink."

"Swear to me you won't defile my faith," said Efendína, sniffing uneasily and greedily at the food on the table.

"I swear, Efendína. Have no fear. No pig's flesh and no wine, I'll drink that all myself."

"Wine wouldn't be so bad," said Efendína. "I can drink that. Everybody drinks it."

"I don't want to have your reproaches hanging round my neck later on," Barba Jannis persisted. "I'll give you some salepi to drink."

"No, no, salepi doesn't agree with me, Barba Jannis. I'll drink wine. It does no harm. Only pig's flesh does any harm."

They therefore emptied a bottle between them and became happy.

"What do you think, Efendína?" said Barba Jannis all of a sudden. "Shall we do something?"

"Whatever you like, Barba Jannis. As long as I don't have to cross any streets."

"I'll carry you over on my back. Don't worry. Well then, listen: you're a Turk, I'm a Christian. D'you want to kill me? There, take the knife, slaughter me!"

"No, by my faith," shouted Efendína. "Put that knife away, Barba Jannis! You're giving me a heart attack!"

"There! I don't want to slaughter you either. Shouldn't all Turks and Christians be like us two? Live like brothers? Haven't you seen how sometimes a bitch will give suck to a kitten among her puppies? Well, that's how it is with Crete. What am I driving at? That the two of us should now go arm-in-arm to the Pacha and say to him: 'Here, look, Pacha Effendi, how Turks and Christians have made it up. Efendína is Turkey and I am Christendom, We've become brothers. Give us something to drink!' And the Pacha, who's a good man, Devil take him, will burst out laughing and call that Suleiman of his. 'Serve them!' he'll say, 'they have my blessing!' And out of his cupboard he'll take a decoration for each of us. Then we'll bow to him and go off arm-in-arm—you, Turkey, and I, Christendom—across Broad Street to the church to pray. And afterwards to the mosque to pray. And finally to Hussein Aga's coffee-house, where the Turkish youths sing and the spirit of Man languishes happily. Understand, Efendína? Will you?"

"What about the gutters?" asked Efendína, as a cold sweat broke out on him.

"No fear, I tell you. I'll carry you across on my back. I've learnt to swim. Just wait while I arm myself—I mean, take my scimitar and pin on my decoration."

He took the scimitar from the wall, and fetched the tin decoration out of a kitchen drawer. It was a simple piece of tin, such as they hang on trees to keep off the evil eye.

"Forward!" he said, "in the name of Christ and Mohammed! Say the same, Efendína, you idiot, and then you'll be all right."

"But I must put Mohammed's name first. Let's be fair!"

"What's it matter? Well then?"

"In the name of Mohammed and Christ," said Efendína, and the two stepped over the threshold with the right foot.

In the street Efendína turned and said to Barba Jannis:

"What do you think, Barba Jannis? Shall we go by Ali Aga's and take the poor man with us too? He's neither Turk nor Greek. He's Turk and Greek, the one just as much as the other. So let's take him with us, to be able to show the Pacha all the nations."

"Why not?" shouted Barba Jannis, who in his joy would have liked to give the whole world a kiss.

They reached Captain Michales's quarter and knocked at Ali Aga's low door. Wooden clogs rattled in the yard.

"Who's there?" said a high little voice.

"Two friends, Ali Aga. Open!" shouted Barba Jannis. "We've come to bring you luck."

"I'm afraid, children. Go about your business. . . . What friends?"

"It's me, Ali Aga," Efendína announced himself. "Efendína Horsedung."

The little door opened. The poor old man was all creased and shrivelled. Since the flight of his Christian neighbours he had ventured nowhere. Christians mistrusted him, and Turks would have none of him. Every morning he went into the fields and gathered a few weeds, which he ate with oil. He knitted stockings and hawked them about, limping. And waited for men to acquire reason and for the neighbours to come home. Then there would once more be evening visits, with tit-bits to eat.

Barba Jannis saw how badly Ali Aga had fallen in the world, and suddenly he felt very fond of this Turk. His misery frightened him.

"What's the matter with you, Ali Aga?" he asked, and fell into his arms.

"I'm old, Barba Jannis. I can't bend down any longer. . . . I can't shake it off."

"Are you coming with us to the Pacha?" asked Efendína.

"To the Pacha?" cried the old man, terrified. "What should I do there? I don't go anywhere."

"It's in your interest, Ali Aga," Barba Jannis explained. "You'll get a decoration."

"For the love of God, go about your business and leave me alone!" screamed the old man, slamming the door.

"Leave him, Efendína," said Barba Jannis. "He's only a bit of dead meat. Let's get on!"

They reached the main square and went in through the Pacha's gate. And so the two choice fools presented themselves at the moment when the Pacha was descending the stairs.

"Pacha Effendi," they cried, as they saw him. "Stand and admire us!"

"What do you chicken brains want?" asked the Pacha, laughing. "What sort of a masquerade is that?"

Efendína hitched up his sackcloth breeches, for the string had broken again, and Barba Jannis's scimitar got between his legs so that he was riding astride it. The two advanced, and the representative of Christendom spoke first, solemnly:

"Pacha Effendi, think not that I am Barba Jannis the salepi-vendor! I am Christendom. And that man there is not Efendína Horsedung, as he has been named, but Turkey. We ate the weed of dissension and became enemies. Afterwards we ate honey and were reconciled. Now we are brothers. Pacha Effendi. Do you see? Crete is like a bitch that can give suck to puppies and kittens at the same time. Milk for all is there in plenty, do you see? Then concord, love, well-being and happiness! To-day I've become a great-grandfather, up with reconciliation!"

"Suleiman," the Pacha ordered, when he had had his fill of

laughing, "that man's no fool! Who would believe it? The two of them have more sense, by my faith, than the Metropolitan and me. Give them a raki and something nice to eat as well."

"And a decoration?" asked Barba Jannis, disappointed. "Isn't there a decoration, Pacha Effendi?"

"Hey, you've got one. That's enough."

"But what about Efendína?" said Barba Jannis, pointing to his friend, whose breeches were sliding.

"Give him a bit of string, Suleiman, for him to make his breeches fast with," the Pacha ordered. "That's enough. That's all the decoration there is for you. Out with you, I'm busy."

As the Pacha arrived at Archondula's, he saw to his satisfaction the Metropolitan's ass tied up to the door-ring.

"There, the priest's arrived before me," he said. "That means he recognises my seniority."

Suleiman lifted him down from the horse. He walked across the big, paved yard with its pots of flowers. The old maid who was mistress of it all came out to greet him. She was laced up in stays and as thin as a bean-pole, and out of her powdered face there stuck a spiteful nose.

The Metropolitan had already risen, and the Pacha bowed as he came into the room. He sat down in a chair opposite him and took out his rosary. The old maid withdrew, leaving the two high authorities alone to discuss the great questions concerning the country.

For a while they made no sound. The Metropolitan warmed his hands over the bronze brazier in front of him. He was frozen. The Pacha yawned sleepily. When the Metropolitan saw him yawn, he also yawned.

"It's cold to-day, Pacha Effendi," said the Metropolitan at last, to open the conversation.

"Yes, winter's come, Metropolitan Effendi," replied the Pacha, yawning again. He bent over the brazier and opened his mouth again, but with great difficulty:

"The fumes of charcoal, so I've heard, cause dizziness. I feel dizzy."

"If the charcoal isn't red-hot all through, so I've heard," said the Metropolitan, and yawned.

They fell silent again. The Pacha grew tired of holding his hands over the brazier and placed them on his knees. He looked about him. He glanced at the big clock on the wall. On top of a carved chest there stood a green vase filled with red velvet roses, and near it a plaster Moor with a hollow head full of matches. And above the door there was his own portrait, resplendent with reds, golds and blacks. He was staring out of it with great vigour, and not a hair was missing. As he admired his own handsomeness, the Pacha suddenly gave a start. It seemed as if the tassel on his fez had moved.

He shuddered: "Metropolitan Effendi," he asked uneasily, "the tassel on my fez in the picture has just moved. Is that possible? What do you say?"

The Metropolitan was tired and depressed, for he missed his usual afternoon sleep. But he gathered all his strength together, to examine the painting.

"Is it possible, Metropolitan Effendi?" asked the Pacha again.

"What, Pacha Effendi?"

"There! For the tassel in the picture to move."

"No, it's impossible, Pacha Effendi," the Metropolitan asserted, and leaned his heavy head against the back of the chair. The Pacha did the same and closed his eyes. When the Metropolitan saw this, he closed his.

The cuckoo came out of the clock and called out the hour. The North wind outside blew the shrivelled leaves violently across the yard. A sparrow hungrily pecked the pane with his beak. Hearing a terrible snore, it flew away in alarm. The gigantic cat belonging to the house glided in and jumped on to the Metropolitan's lap. Curling up, it warmed itself at his belly and slept contentedly, purring. . . . And then the cuckoo came out afresh and again announced the hour.

Archondula anxiously put her ear to the door and heard no speech. Only long-drawn-out, comfortable sounds of snoring, the one heavy, as from a drum, the other blaring cheerfully, as from a trumpet.

"I'll make them some coffee to rouse them," she said to herself. She went into the kitchen and put the pot on the fire.

Soon afterwards the Pacha heard the door creak, opened his eyes, and saw the old maid with the round salver.

"Sleep has overcome him," he said mockingly, and pointed at the slumbering Metropolitan. "The poor man's no longer up to it. He's grown old."

As the scent of the coffee entered his nose, the Metropolitan too opened his eyes.

"Hearty thanks, Archondula," he said, reaching out for the cup. "I was longing for that. A hair's breadth and I'd have fallen asleep."

Both of them sipped loudly and happily. The Metropolitan turned to the Pacha: "The wheat promises well this year, Pacha Effendi."

"The barley too, Metropolitan Effendi," answered the Pacha in faulty Greek, and stood up. "We have spent our time well to-day. Let's meet another day and negotiate further."

"With pleasure, Pacha Effendi," said the Metropolitan, gripping the chair and standing up likewise.

A crowd had collected outside. It had become known that the two leaders had met in that grand house, for the first time for so many months, to negotiate and to restore concord in the land. And so the people were waiting in the cold, to gape at them as they came hand-in-hand out of the door.

Kasapákis, the doctor, came by and stopped. He saw Aristoteles, the chemist, standing there waiting.

"What's up, Mr. Aristoteles?" he asked. "Somebody died?"

"Bite off your tongue, doctor," answered Mr. Aristoteles. "The Pacha and the Metropolitan are in there, holding council how to bring back concord to the land. Someone caught sight of them through the window. He saw them in the room, with papers spread out before them. The Metropolitan was writing and the Pacha was speaking, making gestures with his hands. Now they're putting their seals to it. How's Madame Marcelle?"

The doctor shurgged his shoulders.

"Always the same. To give her a change of air, I've sent her to my brother's Katsabas's country place."

He spoke with contentment, for he had succeeded in throwing her out and staying on alone with the servant-girl.

While they were still chatting, there came hobbling up from the end of the street Mr. Demetrós Leanbottom. For the first time in seven months he had come home from the villages, where he had been wandering about with his umbrella, in order, so he said, to get rid of his congestion of the heart. He had seldom opened his mouth to speak. The peasants said that the fairies had robbed him of his speech, and they honoured him as one smitten by demons. They would offer him a piece of bread, and he would take it and push on, chewing, to another village. Sometimes he held the umbrella gripped tightly under his arm, sometimes he opened it, according to sunshine and rain.

As long as Crete was struggling with Charos, Mr. Demetrós had wandered about, full of anxiety. Now that Crete had reached peace, he too found peace and returned to his wife, Penelope. His boots were worn out, his clothes torn, he had lost his hat. His breeches, too wide now for his thin thighs, flapped in the wind like a woman's skirts. Leaning on his umbrella he hobbled up.

"How thin the sad fellow's got," said the fat doctor with a laugh, "his breeches are empty."

"Don't worry, he'll fill them again," replied Mr. Aristoteles, shaking his cucumber head, as though to say: "Ah, that's nothing by the side of my misfortune!" He thought of his grocery in Broad Street, and of how he had no son to inherit it. And he thought of his three shrivelled sisters and the three peep-holes in the door, through which—their only pleasure—they observed the world.

"Welcome, Mr. Demetrós," said the doctor to the newcomer. "How are things going with you?"

"Glory to God, I've broken my foot," replied Mr. Demetrós, and passed on.

"Only the weak in the head enjoy the world," muttered the chemist, gazing after him. "Woe—three times woe—to people of sense!"

"O, I'd quite forgotten," cried the doctor, "I must go."

"Whom have you forgotten? A patient?"

"Yes. It's the Jewess whom Captain Michales's nephew has brought us. She's had a miscarriage. Pretty fair-haired girl—have you seen her?"

"So that's his game now," said the chemist with malicious pleasure, and raised himself on tip-toe to see what was going on in Archondula's yard, so to be able to tell his sisters. The excited crowd now saw the stately, white-bearded Metropolitan stepping solemnly across the yard between the pots of flowers to the door, arm in arm with the plump, bristle-bearded Pacha. Christians and Turks made room for them, to let them through. The Pacha, now wide awake once more, gave smiling greetings to right and left. But the Metropolitan was frowning, and leaned heavily on his crozier. He was impatient to be rid of the Turk. The deacon untied the ass from the ring; Suleiman brought the fox-red horse.

Meanwhile a weight of suffering had broken over Noëmi in the house of her parents-in-law. Last night she had not closed an eye. She kept thinking of her husband, of what mountain he would now be climbing, and thinking of her son, who was growing in her and pressing her hard. A strange dread kept her awake, a dark menace lay in the air. An invisible body, a soundless voice, a ghost. . . . Was it the dead man? As this thought came upon her, cold sweat flowed from her pores. She sprang up, in order not to stifle, and opened the window. Cutting morning air came in. Day was breaking. Noëmi went downstairs and found the old mother bent over the hearth, lighting the fire.

"Mother," she said, "I don't feel well. I'm going out to get some air."

When the mother saw her, she shrank back. The young woman seemed devoured by fear, her bones stuck out. Great dark rings lay round her eyes.

"Where are you going so early in the morning, in this cold, my child?" she asked, full of pity. "You'll overstrain yourself."

Noëmi hesitated. She was ashamed to betray what dread had fallen upon her at dawn, and where she now planned to go.

"Don't you know where you're going?" the old woman asked afresh.

"I know, Mother. To church. To light a candle."

The mother gave a cry: "Have you seen him in a dream, my child?"

"Yes."

The mother stared into the air. Her chin was trembling. The young woman was right. He was not dead yet. He came through the air. He passed through doors. He still had some evil design. "Child," she said at last, in a muffled voice as if she was afraid the dead man might hear her, "go, light a candle for him. Pray to him, to have pity on you. But in God's name don't tell him that his grandson—that you——"

"No, Mother, I won't tell him."

"Take my shawl as well. And wrap yourself up properly. Otherwise you'll catch cold."

The church was empty. Sparse light made its way through the coloured windows and awoke the Saints in the ikons, the candelabra, the bronze candle-sticks and, on the right above the shrine with the prayer-books, Saint Menas on horseback. Noëmi picked up a candle from the bench and went over to the big ikon of the Virgin, which hung on the ikonostasis beside the Beautiful Gate. She dared not speak immediately to the dead man, she wanted to call upon the Virgin, the Mother, as mediatress between the two of them.

The silver lamp burning before the Virgin lit up softly her stubborn chin, her two sad almond eyes, and the cherry-red band embroidered with gold stars around her head. Noëmi knelt down and looked up at her speechlessly for a long time. The longer she looked, the lighter and milder her heart became. The young woman was holding her Son tightly in her arms, as though she were afraid she would be robbed of Him: she leaned her cheek tenderly against His cheek and held a small wooden cross before Him as a toy. . . .

Noëmi stood up, lit the candle in the candlestick, put her mouth close to the Virgin, and spoke to her. She did not yet know the prayers: she spoke to her as to a good neighbour at whose door you knock in heavy trouble.

"Mother," she said to her, "I am the Jewess Noëmi, I've come from the other end of the world. I've left my father's faith and become a Christian. I am in great trouble, Mother, help me! Tell him he's not to come at night to torment me, tell him he's not to do me any harm. I wish nothing but good for his house, I love his son, I have no other pleasure. Mother, I will tell you this too, but don't tell him: in three months I too will be a mother. I'm afraid of his doing my son some harm. Don't let him! I fall at your feet, Mother of all the mothers in the world. Have mercy on me!"

She raised her eyes, she saw the Virgin looking down sadly and hopelessly. Her eyes seemed suddenly to be full of tears. Noëmi shuddered. She took from her ear the golden ring, a present from Kosmas, and hung it on the ikon shrine. "It's all I have, Holy Virgin," she whispered. "This ring is for you. Think of me!"

When she came home, Maria saw her and turned her face violently away. The old mother went to meet her and asked:

"Did you light a candle to him, my child? Did you hear a voice? Did he say anything?"

"Mother, I'll go and lie down. I'm tired," she answered, and slowly and breathing heavily went upstairs, stretched herself on the wide iron bed on which, while he was alive, the dead man had embraced his wife.

The air was heavy. Noëmi breathed hard and kept her eyes open. She was afraid the dead man might enter in the darkness, if she closed her eyes. The clock downstairs struck and struck and from the minarets there rang out, passionately and harmoniously, the voice of the muezzin: Noon! She had a bitter taste in her mouth, she did not go down to eat, she fixed her eyes on the tall date-palm which rose above the roofs from Archondula's courtyard. A violent wind was blowing, the shutters clattered, and the scimitar-like leaves of the palm clashed against each other. Opposite her, on the ikon shrine, the little lamp flickered—the tiny flame

seemed to want to fly away from the wick. But Noëmi had not
the strength to get up and fill with oil the lamp battling with
Charos.

Gazing exhausted her, and she closed her eyes. Did sleep overcome her, or did it not? She did not know. But when she had
closed her eyes, she felt, with horrible certainty, that someone,
without opening the door, had come into the room. Noëmi
cowered to the furthest edge of the bed and, with all her strength,
opened her eyes. No one! And yet she felt, someone was standing
in front of her, between the bedposts.

"It's him," Noëmi whispered, full of dread, staring into the air.
The little lamp had gone out. The ikon was sunk in shadow.

The longer she stared, the more strongly she felt the air in
front of the bed thicken and take on a shape. At first two silver
pistols gleamed in the air, and then a powerful neck and a black,
waxed moustache and two eyes, lowering from behind thick,
bristling brows. . . . Between the two bedposts there became
visible a man.

"Holy Virgin!" Noëmi screamed. "Help! Drive him away!"

But he at once raised his hand, seized the coverlet and wrenched
it aside. Then he struck at Noëmi's body with his fist.

The poor girl gave a shrill shriek and rolled from the bed on to
the floor. The mother heard her, ran upstairs, and found the young
woman in a pool of blood.

"Maria," she cried, "the doctor! Quick!"

She removed the still-born child, rubbed Noëmi's temples with
perfume, lit the extinguished lamp and waited for the doctor. As
she waited she made secret lament for her still-born grandson. And
now her daughter-in-law, pale as wax, opened her eyes and cast
bewildered glances about her. Where was she? What was this
blood. Who had struck her? Whence came this unbearable pain
inside her? She pressed her lips together, not to cry out. She saw
the old mother bending over her and stretched out her hands
towards her:

"Mother," she whispered, "it hurts," and closed her eyes again.

The mother sat down beside her, moistened her temples with
perfume, and thought of her son. When would her dear one learn

of this misfortune? Where might he be at this moment? In the grandfather's courtyard?

But Kosmas was already a long way away from the grandfather's courtyard. Through night and rain he had climbed the steep slope of the mountain.

He had been followed in silence by the bowed body of old Charidemos, while the picture of the grandfather, dying as the lyre gave him the answer to his question, soared before his soul in overwhelming beauty.

Suddenly Charidemos stopped dead. He could bear the silence no longer. To go on a journey meant for him conversation and jesting, but this man in the Frankish clothes did not talk and did not laugh.

"Why are you in such a hurry, master? To see Captain Michales? Damn him! The best thing would be for you not to see him. But if your destiny demands you should see him, then as late as possible. And as shortly as possible. I was sent the day before yesterday by the grandfather, to tell him that he lay dying and expected him to come and say good-bye. When he turned and looked at me so savagely, it gave me a turn."

"Don't worry, Charidemos. He's my uncle. His blood is mine. I'm not afraid of him," answered Kosmas, without stopping.

"Are you strong enough to oppose him? Bet you you won't be strong enough!"

"I shall be strong enough. But don't talk now! Hey!"

Kosmas was determined not to profane by talking this hour of silent gathering. For he was brooding not only over his grandfather, that mighty root of the stock, but over that hard, knotty bough on this tree, Captain Michales, who perhaps held in his hands the fate of Crete. How was he to speak with him. Where could he lay hold of him? What was he to say to him? What demon was riding him?

"It was his fault that the 'Christ The Lord' monastery was lost," the Metropolitan had told him. "And now he wants to wash away the dishonour. That's why he won't give in. Perhaps he wants to be killed, to pay in full."

"But if the well-being of Crete requires otherwise?" Kosmas
had asked.

The Metropolitan had remained silent for a while. He seemed
to be weighing his words, he hesitated.

"God forgive me," he had murmured at last, "but I believe
your uncle has inside him a demon, whose name is not
Crete."

"There's a dark moment in his life," his other uncle, Tityros,
had confided to him. "A mystery about Captain Polyxigis and a
Turkish woman. There's a lot of talk about it. His heart was wild,
it no longer follows his brain."

"He was jealous about Arkadi," the gnome Charilíos had told
him mockingly. "So the rascal took it into his head that he too
would blow something sky-high. So that people should sing a
song about him!"

Perhaps they were all right, thought Kosmas, as he climbed
upwards through the rain, often sliding on the slippery stones.
How could he move him to make use of the Pacha's promise,
to retire intact with weapons and banners to wherever he
wanted. Should he stress that the Metropolitan desired it? That
the King of Greece demanded it? Would he not shrug his
shoulders with contempt? Was he not devoid of all trust in
human beings?

Kosmas kept thinking out fresh ways of speaking to the wild
beast, so as to guide him into this course. At the same time he was
inwardly torn by his own grave anxieties. What sort of son would
the sickly body of Noëmi, to which he had entrusted the terrible
seed of his race, bear him? He trembled when he thought of it.
Then again his thoughts would rush back to the land of the Franks,
to the injustice, shamelessness and poverty he had seen there. . . .
And finally, what about his own course? In what place was he to
situate his life's battle? His grandfather had had his place, so had
his father, and this uncle still had his. But he? Where was he to
take up his position and say: "Here I fight, no one's going to
drive me out." For the first time he felt that he was hanging in the
air.

The rain was at last exhausted, Heaven had shaken out all its water over the mountains. A sharp frost-wind blew, chasing the clouds. Constellations appeared, and Charidemos stopped and looked searchingly at the sky.

"It's after midnight. We've made good going," he said. "If you believe in God, master, let's stop a while under this cliff. It's out of the wind here, and we can light a cigarette."

"Are you tired, Charidemos?"

"Yes, I'm tired. You must realise, I'm old. My bones are getting heavy."

The sly head was not tired at all. But he was dying for a talk. They took up position under the cliff. Kosmas gave him a cigarette. And now, how was Charidemos to begin the conversation? He looked first at the sky. What could one say about that? He let it be and considered, one after another, as possible themes his village, Megalokastro, Crete. But what there was to say about them, this Frank certainly had at his fingertips. So that was no good. Suddenly his mind stood still before an uncle of his, a little fellow called Andrulios. What was this lean-bottom's uncle compared to him? What was Captain Michales compared to Andrulios? A midge. Now I'll show him.

He pulled eagerly at his cigarette. He had crumbled it all up and it burned his fingers. But he did not let it go. He turned to Kosmas:

"Do you know, master, what's the biggest wild beast in the world? The lion, you'll say. Not a bit of it! Man! You ask: why? Because he fights and kills Turks like your uncle? Or because he invents weapons with the Devil's cunning and kills the lions? Not a bit of it! I'll tell you. I had an uncle. They called him, God forgive him, Andrulios. He was only a half-helping. So they gave him the nickname 'Brownie', because he was no bigger than a pea, poor man. God's refuse, not worth spitting out. He ran here and there—no, he didn't run, he hopped like a grasshopper, and moaned because his kidneys hurt him. The doctors said he had a stone and was sure to die. And he, my child—yes, what a thing a man is!—he took his axe and went out, and knelt down on the mountain outside his village—Venerato. Ping! Ping! Ping! He began breaking up the mountain with the axe. One year, two

years, three. The peasants used to come by, see him and shake
with laughter. 'Pitting yourself against the mountain, Andrulios?'
—'Yes, against the mountain! I'm going to eat it up!' he answered,
without taking his eyes off his axe. In the third year he began
building a house at the bottom of the mountain. 'Don't build a
house, Andrulios, just take our advice. Whoever builds a house
gets married.'—'I shall do that too, you sausages,' Andrulios
answered those who made fun of him. 'I mean to marry and beget
children, so that they can help me beat the mountain.'—The
peasants laughed: 'What woman will take you, Brownie?'—'In
butchers' shops when there's a crowd nothing gets left over,' he
answered. 'There'll be a wife even for me.' He built the house, and
one day a peasant's widow, short and fat and ugly, came by. But
she was young. She had a good look at the yard, the cellar, the
kitchen, the bedroom. She liked the house. 'Andrulios,' she said,
'what do you think?' And winked at him. My uncle understood.
To cut a long story short, they got married. He slept with her and
made the best use of the night. But next morning, first thing,
when he was still sleepy, he looked out at the mountain, took his
axe and began hacking at it again: ping, ping, ping. Every day he
bit off a piece of it. When enough fresh stone had been hewed out,
he built a house next door, with another bedroom. He enlarged
the yard and built a stable as well. 'Andrulios,' said the peasants,
making fun of him again, 'do you mean to build a town?'—'Yes, a
town,' he answered. 'My wife's with child, where am I to put my
children?'—'And you haven't any pains in your kidneys any more?'
—'What's that about pains, you idle carcasses? I haven't the time.'
Years passed. The women bore children, always two at a time.
He went on with the axe. There were caves and pits in the mountain—Andrulios was eating it up. He could no longer be parted
from it. My uncle's hair had grown grey meanwhile, and his body
even more like a hobgoblin's, but his arms had now a mighty
strength, and his paws got broader and longer—they reached down
to his knees. Soon he had such a stoop that his paws touched the
stones. Whoever saw him burst out laughing. He looked like an
ape the Pacha once brought to Megalokastro. Whoever saw Andrulios laughed, certainly, but he trembled too. The peasants kept

their distance. For one day he had stretched out his paw and caught one of the laughing louts by the knee-joint and squashed his bones, so that he limped ever afterwards. His children grew up, they too threw themselves upon the mountain with the axe, ate it up bit by bit, and built. They married and begot children. My uncle Andrulios was now old and weak, the axe grew too heavy for him. And one evening, as he came home from the mountain, he felt his end drawing near. He lay down on his bed and called his children and grandchildren to him. He ordered them to bury him in the mountain, and to lay his axe by his side. Then he folded his arms and departed. If you happen to pass by Venerato one day, master, have them point out to you Andrulios' Village too. My uncle's buildings are now a model place."

He stopped. He was pleased with himself for having impressed the Frank properly. His eyes shone with satisfaction and excitement through the darkness.

"Charidemos, I know another wild beast, bigger than the lion and than your uncle Andrulios."

"Which one?"

"The corpse-worm."

"Heaven preserve us! In God's name, don't think of that! Bad cess to it!" muttered Charidemos, and crossed himself.

He spat, and grabbed hold of his stick.

"Forward, master," he said, impatiently.

By grey of dawn Kosmas reached the peak of Selena. Charidemos hung back:

"Go ahead, master," he said, "and when you've done what has to be done, call me, so that we can go back together. I'd rather not see your uncle. Forgive me!"

Standing upright at his look-out post, Captain Michales had not slept all night. At the first glimmer of light he picked up his field-glasses and spied out one Turkish post after another down below. They were dug in a little higher each day. The Turks were not hurrying. From the few salvos the Christians now sent them, they concluded that their supply of powder and shot must be meagre. They knew, too, that the people up there had only a little barley

bread left to put between their teeth. The siege was perfect and
let neither man nor beast through. There was now only one concealed goat-path by which a native could reach the eagle's nest
by night.

The Pacha had kept on sending messages to Captain Michales,
to persuade this last of the leaders to obedience. It would be more
useful to Turkey, he had been informed from Constantinople,
if the rebels humbled themselves than if they were killed. For
then Crete would have gone back under the yoke of her own free
will, and the claim of the Franks would fall to the ground.
Yesterday evening the Pacha had once more sent a messenger
to Captain Michales: "I grant you a last respite. Surrender
tomorrow morning, and retire with all military honours. I shall
not touch you. Otherwise I shall pound you all to pieces. By
Mohammed!"

All night Captain Michales had weighed which course he should
choose—not for himself, for he had already chosen, but for his
companions. There was no hope of winning, and he did not want
to burden his conscience with their fate. So let each of them be
free to go his way. Already that evening he had told them of the
Pacha's message. They were to let it work through their heads
and at break of day bring him their answer.

None of them had closed an eye. And as the sun touched the
mountain, each man separately had glided up to the captain. Unwashed, uncombed, in torn clothes spotted with blood, they now
squatted round him and waited for him to open his mouth
first. But he stared at the rocks and held himself in, until that
wrathful heart of his should become calm. When he did open his
mouth, a serene voice must ring out, and not a roar. Thought
after thought shot through him like a flash: Thrasáki, the Circassian woman, the monastery of 'Christ The Lord'. . . . He let out a
curse, picked up a stone and clasped it till the blood dripped
from his hand.

His lips and his brows contracted. He looked about him at the
comrades, down at the Turks far below, up at the uninhabited
sky high above. "Freedom or death," he muttered, shaking his
head fiercely. "Freedom or death! O poor Cretans! Freedom *and*

death—that's what I should have written on my banner. That's
the true banner of every fighter: Freedom *and* death! Freedom *and*
death!"

As he said this, he grew easier. After so many years he at last
had clarity. His heart strengthened. He now turned calmly to the
comrades:

"You know what that dog announces to us. You're men, we're
struggling for freedom, speak out freely! We've no more powder
and shot, no bread, no hope. The Turks are an army, we a
handful. Whoever of you wants to leave, let him go: by my sabre,
which I shall give up only to God, it's no dishonour! I'm not
going. That's what I have to say to you."

For a while nobody raised his head to speak. The sun already
stood a hand's breadth high in the heaven, and the drums began
beating—the Turkish soldiers were mustering.

"Speak out freely!" Captain Michales repeated. "And be quick
about it!"

A dark-haired, haggard man, whose ancient gun was tied together with string, opened his mouth:

"That I'm a man, you all know. That I never gave way before
anyone, you also know. I'm not afraid of being called unmanly,
and I mean to give my opinion frankly. Captain, we're foundering
uselessly. It brings no profit to us, or to Christendon. Soon there
will be another rising in Crete, and we shan't be there to strike
our blow too. Our life is now much more important for Crete
than our death. Honour or dishonour, I don't care. Advantage
or damage to Crete—that's what is on my mind."

Captain Michales listened with bent head. When the voice
fell silent, he asked:

"Have you done, Janaros?"

"I have spoken."

Captain Michales turned to those squatting beside him:

"One after another," he ordered. "Your turn, Furógatos."

Furógatos stroked his moustache, turned his face away, and
said:

"All night two devils have been struggling inside me. One of
them said: 'Leave, there's no hope of winning.' The other said:

'Stay, because there's no hope of winning.' When dawn came, one of the two devils won."

"And which?" asked Captain Michales, now boring with his eyes into those of his companion.

"As for you, Captain Michales—damn the hour in which I got to know you!"

"Well?"

"I'm not going!"

Captain Michales went on round the circle:

"And what about you, Kajabés?"

"I," he answered with a sigh, "am newly married; I've a wife and haven't had a chance to enjoy our happiness! That's burning inside me!"

"Well," insisted the captain. "Leave the woman aside. What's the man say? We're asking him."

"Curse the hour in which I met you, Captain Michales. I too say that. I'd like to leave, but I'm ashamed in front of you. I'm not going."

"And you, Thodóres?" said the captain, turning now to his nephew who, while his companions had been speaking, had cleaned and loaded his gun. "What do you say, beardless one?"

Thodóres scowled. He stared, full of anger, admiration and envy, at his uncle:

"Do you think because you've got a beard, you're the only one with courage? I'm not leaving."

"Nor I!"

"Nor I," two others, with greying temples, exclaimed.

The others, some twenty or so, remained dumb and bent their heads.

"We've no time, the sun's already two hand's breadths high," cried Captain Michales. "Speak! Do you want to go? You're free. Good-bye!"

Krasojórgis whispered with his neighbour. Then he stood up and laid his hand on his breast.

"Forgive me, brothers," he said in a strangled voice. "We have sisters unmarried, sons unemployed, wives and children. And our death does nobody any good. We are leaving."

"Forgive us, brothers," said Mastrapas too, "we're going."

"Bless you! Bless you. brothers!" cried Captain Michales, and stood up. "God is my witness, I have no complaint against you. Greet the people down there. But go quickly, each man for himself, in turn, and don't let 'em see you. Quick, before the sun gets higher still."

"Forgive us, and may God forgive you!" said the twenty as with one mouth.

"You are forgiven," answered Captain Michales. "Damn the man who says anything against you! Good homecoming!"

Five remained, Captain Michales looked at them, one after another, and said:

"There are six of us. It's enough. It's more than enough. The brain says: 'we want to leave!' But the heart—God help him!— won't allow it. We are not leaving. Here we shall die as a sacrifice for Crete. Let her speak. We, who are dying, are doing better than they, who will live. For Crete doesn't need householders, she needs madmen like us. These madmen make Crete immortal."

He looked up at the sky. The sun was climbing into the height with powerful strides.

"Pick up your guns. Keep changing loop-holes, so they don't notice there are fewer of us. In God's name!"

But at the moment when the palikares were dispersing and Captain Michales was kneeling down at his loop-hole, pebbles clashed behind him and Kosmas arrived. Captain Michales turned round and stared at him.

"Well, who are you?" he asked. "Keep your head down, if you don't want a bullet through you. Who are you? Keep your head down, I tell you."

"Your nephew, Captain Michales. Kosmas."

The captain frowned. He understood what wind brought this one here. He said, roughly:

"A most welcome visit. Why have you come all the way up here? What does the fox want in the bazaar?"

Kosmas bit his lips, to prevent any angry word from escaping him:

Ϙ

"I'm no fox," he said with a dry laugh, "and this is no bazaar. I too am a man, Captain Michales. Your nephew."

"Only someone who fights is a man. Lie down beside me and tell me why you've come. But in a few words, I'm busy."

He glanced again at the sky. The sun was moving on towards the midday height. He shouted to his companions:

"Get ready, children! Load! But wait for my signal before you fire!"

Wild shouts came from down below. Kosmas peered through a gap in the rock and saw thick masses of Turkish soldier's climbing upwards.

"Speak! Who's sent you?" said Captain Michales again, without looking at his nephew, for he was keeping his eyes sharply focussed on the Turks

"Crete," Kosmas replied At this word Captain Michales caught fire and bellowed:

"None of your big words, schoolmaster! Talk like a man And don't tell me Crete sends you! D'you hear? I am Crete!"

Kosmas felt at once that he had before him an unyielding man. Why should be demean himself by begging? Even God could not change the mind of this man—he had made his decision unshakeably. Why then grovel before him? The proud Cretan heart in Kosmas rose up. He was ashamed of clever tricks of speech.

"Well, what do you want?" roared Captain Michales, without looking round.

"I want nothing," answered Kosmas defiantly. He chased away, out of his mind, all the words he had prepared.

"So you've come to pay a visit to your uncle?" scoffed the other. "Greetings!"

"I did come to tell you, my grandfather's dead."

Captain Michales laid down his gun, to cross himself.

"God be gracious to him," he said. "He was an honourable man indeed. His dealings were good, his life was full. Now he departs, to sleep. . . . And as for you: good-bye. Here we're at war."

"Have you no message?"

"Go."

"For your wife? For your son, Thrasáki?"

Captain Michales's veins stood out, his look grew troubled. He raised his hand, smeared with powder and blood, put it to his mouth and yelled. "In God's name, brothers, freedom or death!"

He took aim and fired. The mountains echoed. And at once Turkish bullets whistled upwards and a small cannon on the slope thundered. The shell landed behind Captain Michales and set the stones whirling.

"Oh," rang out an agonised cry. The comrades looked round. Kajabés rolled off the rock on to which he had climbed, and crumpled up at Captain Michales's feet. He opened his mouth and tried to speak. But the stream of blood which flowed out stifled his voice.

Down below, the trumpets brayed, the soldiers and, at the head, the dervishes with the green flag of the Prophet, bawled.

"Let 'em have it, children!" yelled Thodóres. "Let fly at the dogs!"

The scraping of those feet came nearer and nearer.

Captain Michales threw himself upon Kajabés, to take him in his arms. In doing so, he fell over Kosmas, who was lying by his side.

"Are you still here, schoolmaster?" he shouted at him. "Run away, don't get mixed up with men!"

But Kosmas did not rise. Smeared with powder and blood, he was listening now to his heart, which had gone wild. In his breast his father, the terrible leader in battle, had awakened, and his grandfather, and Crete. This was not his first battle: for a thousand years already he had been fighting, a thousand times he had been killed and had risen again. His blood stormed.

Captain Michales hastily felt the body of Kajabés over to find his wound. For a second the man's eyes still flashed, one last time, then they glazed. The captain laid the corpse back on the ground.

"Remember Arkadi, brothers!" he cried. "Let's all die like men!"

The gasping breathing of the Turks could now be heard.

"We're lost," yelled Furógatos, and felt a quivering in his chest and belly.

"Shut up!" cried Thodóres, from whose forehead the blood

was flowing over his eyes and blinding him. He wiped it off
with his arm, saw the Turks in front and threw his gun away.

"Children," he cried, "guns are no use now. Draw your
knives!"

He pulled out his father's black-hilted dagger and fell upon a
dervish, who had rushed ahead and was frantically waving his
flag in the air. But he had hardly reached the dervish when a bullet
pierced his heart and he fell backwards.

"Health and joy to you, palikares!" a high voice was heard all
of a sudden crying behind them. "I've got you to just in time,
Captain Michales!"

"What, are you Vendúsos?" cried the captain, with his eyes
gleaming. "Have you come back?"

"I'm Vendúsos, and I behave like a Vendúsos. Take back what
you said, Captain!"

"I take back what I said. Forgive me, brother. Come here, to
me!"

Vendúsos took a step, but a bullet hit him in the forehead and
he fell to the ground.

Captain Michales's eyes were wet. He grasped the dead man and
kissed him on the forehead. Then he turned round and caught
sight of Kosmas. He raised his fist:

"Be off!" he cried. "You've still got time. Clear out!"

"I'm not going!" With one bound he seized Kajabés's gun, slung
his cartridges round him and tore the dagger out of the dead man's
belt. Captain Michales looked at him in amazement: "You're not
going?"

"I'm not going."

Suddenly Captain Michales understood. His face beamed. He
took Kosmas's head in both hands.

"Hail to you, nephew," he cried. "So you too mean to sacrifice
yourself? Immortal Crete!"

A storm was rising. The sky, which had clouded over, glowed
a buff red. From afar the cawing of hungry birds could be heard.

Furógatos now sprang up. He was ashamed of having been, for
a moment, a coward. Death seemed to him the great Merciful
One, who washed away all dishonour. He crossed himself and

drew his short knife. "Freedom or death!" he shouted, and rushed out from his cover, bareheaded and unprotected, against the Turks. Five or six fellows surrounded him; he fell upon them savagely, but they threw him to the ground. A dervish knelt on his chest and slaughtered him like a ram.

When Captain Michales saw this he gave the order:

"No one else to leave cover!"

But of his companions only the two grey-haired ones were still left. Sheltered behind boulders they took aim imperturbably, and not one of their bullets went wide.

Captain Michales, too, aimed serenly at the forehead of each soldier who emerged. A bullet had scored his cheek, another had hit his right thigh. Blood was streaming from him, but he felt no pain. From time to time he cast a glance at his nephew, who was beside him, shooting away imperturbably. "Hail to you, nephew," he shouted to him. "Your father has risen again. Brother Kostaros, you've done a good job!"

"Well met, uncle," the other answered, as though drunk with joy. He was transformed. A dark, unfathomable ecstasy possessed him. He felt light, and released, as if at this precise moment he had at last come home to his own country. He thought of nothing any more. All Frankish, intellectual ideas had vanished, together with mother, wife and son. Nothing remained standing, except this single, ancient duty.

"Freedom or death," he also roared, as he looked at the Turks.

A sudden darkness fell. Snow came down in thick, noiseless flakes. Behind the cherry-red clouds the course of the sinking sun could be divined.

"A happy meeting, Captain Michales!" a voice made itself heard, and the old muezzin of Megalokastro, with his green turban on his head, emerged suddenly over a boulder.

"My greetings, *hodza*!" Captain Michales answered, and sent a bullet exactly through his Adam's apple.

A fountain of blood spurted out, and the muezzin caved in.

"Kill them off!" cried a Turkish lad with flowing golden hair. He let fly with a long whip at the back of the soldiers. Bellowing, they rushed forward.

"Don't flinch, nephew," said Captain Michales to Kosmas. "There's no hope. Long live Crete!"

"You're right. There's no hope, uncle. Long live Crete!"

They drew their daggers and rushed forward. The snow was already beginning to veil the outstretched dead. Every red fez grew white. Two vultures swooped down towards the men busy killing one another. They described their circles and craned their necks.

In the tumult of the hand-to-hand fighting, uncle and nephew were parted. The Turks surrounded Kosmas. Captain Michales saw it from a distance, broke through the chain of soldiers with which he himself was surrounded, and rushed forwards to free him.

"Wait a moment, nephew," he called out to him, "I'm coming!"

But it was too late.

"He's coming himself, Captain Michales," screamed one of the native Turks, mockingly, and threw Kosmas's head at his face.

Captain Michales stretched out his hand and raised the severed head by the hair like a banner. A wild light haloed his face, which was filled with an inhuman joy. Was it pride, god-like defiance, or contempt of death? Or limitless love for Crete? Captain Michales roared:

"Freedom or . . ."

. . . and did not finish. A bullet went through his mouth. Another pierced his temples. His brains spattered the stones.